Praise for

Laura Resnick

"Celebrate! Laura Resnick's *Disappearing Nightly* is not only a delight, but the start of a new urban fantasy series that is smart, cool and wicked funny. Swift, fresh and inventive, *Disappearing Nightly* is Laura Resnick at her witty best. Not to be missed!"
—*New York Times* bestselling author Mary Jo Putney

"With a wry, tongue-in-cheek style reminiscent of Janet Evanovich, this entertaining tale pokes fun at the deadly serious urban fantasy subgenre...while scenes of slapstick comedy will have the reader laughing out loud and eager for further tales of Esther's adventures."
—*Romantic Times BOOKclub* on *Disappearing Nightly*

"Fast-paced, witty and full of action, the book is a marvel of storytelling, but it's the credible, complex relationships among the characters that elevates this far above the usual fantasy standard."
—*Publishers Weekly* [starred review] on *The Destroyer Goddess*

"This stunning novel tantalizes right up to the last cliffhanger page."
—*Publishers Weekly* [starred review] on *The White Dragon*

"Resnick writes with the shining wonder of truly great fantasy."
—*Romantic Times BOOKclub* on *In Legend Born*

"A smoothly narrated, intricate tale of revolution and the human heart."
—*Library Journal* on *In Legend Born*

Laura Resnick

DISAPPEARING NIGHTLY

LUNA™

www.LUNA-Books.com

LUNA™

DISAPPEARING NIGHTLY

ISBN-13: 978-0-373-80259-3
ISBN-10:   0-373-80259-5

Copyright © 2005 by Laura Resnick

First mass market printing: November 2006

First trade printing: December 2005

Author Photo by Lee Ann Thomas

This edition published by arrangement with Harlequin Books S.A.

® and TM are trademarks of Harlequin Books S.A., used under license. Trademarks indicated with ® are registered in the United States Patent and Trademark Office, the Canadian Trade Marks Office and in other countries.

www.LUNA-Books.com

Printed in U.S.A.

Horatio: O day and night, but this is wondrous strange!

Hamlet: And therefore as a stranger give it welcome.

There are more things in heaven and earth, Horatio,

Than are dreamt of in your philosophy.

—William Shakespeare, *Hamlet*

In memory of Fabian—
I finally kept my promise.

PROLOGUE

I'm not a heroine, I just play heroines. Also psychotics, vamps, orphans, hookers, housewives, and—on one memorable occasion—a singing rutabaga. It was never my ambition to utilize my extensive dramatic training by playing a musical vegetable. However, as my agent is so fond of pointing out, there are more actors in New York than there are *people* in most other cities. Translation: Beggars can't be choosers.

This same sentiment explains how I wound up painting my body green and prancing around stage half-naked the night Golly Gee disappeared.

For those of you fortunate enough to be unfamiliar with the world of rock idols, Golly Gee was the wet-lipped, surgically improved, B-list pop star who had been chosen to play Virtue, the female lead in *Sorcerer!*

I, who had studied my craft at Northwestern University and the Actors Studio, was cast as her understudy. Such is the life of an actor.

However, *Sorcerer!* was a respectable off-Broadway musical, and I had been "resting" (i.e., waiting tables fifty hours a week) for four months. Although I was only a chorus nymph in *Sorcerer!,* at least I was working again. Besides, with any luck, Golly Gee would have an accident—not a fatal accident, mind you, just a disabling one—and I'd step into the lead role.

Sorcerer! had no plot, and Virtue had the only good songs. The Sorcerer, played by magician Joe Herlihy, was the centerpiece of the show, which had been conceived and designed around his magic act. Joe was a highly strung guy whose wife's production company had financed *Sorcerer!* He was a competent magician, but he couldn't sing or act, and he was too inexperienced to carry an entire production comfortably on his shoulders. Although his magic act had improved considerably in recent weeks, his performance still varied unpredictably. He was losing weight, and he lived in terror of Golly Gee, who bullied him during rehearsals and upstaged him in performance.

The really worrying thing about working with Joe, though, was that he panicked whenever anything went wrong, and with all of the changes that are made during the development of a new musical, *lots* of things go wrong. Anytime someone missed a cue or bumped into a misplaced piece of scenery, Joe lost his concentration. So, although I wanted Golly's part, there were days when I was glad that I wasn't the girl Joe sawed in half eight shows per week.

We were still ironing out the kinks at the end of our first week of public performances the night that Joe went to pieces. Golly Gee's nasal singing had already inspired a series of tepid-to-scathing reviews, so she was feeling nasty that night—and Golly wasn't the sort of person who kept it all bottled up inside. During intermission she accused Joe of nearly immolating her during the flame-throwing routine. Personally, I wouldn't have blamed him.

However, despite Golly's histrionics, we were getting through the show smoothly for once, and I grew optimistic as I frolicked around the set dressed as an oversexed wood nymph who never felt the cold. Joe's concentration was better tonight than it usually was, so this was our best performance to date. Waiting in the wings during the final scene now, I heard my cue and gamboled onto the stage.

Amid a bucolic forest setting, I capered and cavorted with elves, hobgoblins and faeries. I wriggled delightedly when a satyr caressed me, biting back a scream at the touch of his ice-cold hands on my skin as we performed a lift. The satyr grunted as he heaved me overhead. His arms trembled under the strain, and he glared up at me. I had promised to give up Ben & Jerry's ice cream for the duration of the run; I had lied.

My long green hair fluttered around us as we twirled around and then subsided onto the floor to gaze at the Sorcerer with rapturous fascination. This was the point in the story when the Sorcerer, feeling kind of bitter about things, threatened to make Virtue vanish forever, which would be a pretty sad thing for the Kingdom (indeed, as one reviewer pointed out, it would then be just like New York City).

All the scantily clad woodland creatures watched while the Sorcerer demonstrated that he was putting Virtue into a perfectly ordinary crystal cage—the sort of thing you might find in any enchanted forest. I had spent enough rehearsal time in that cage to feel a little sorry for Golly Gee, who would pass the next few minutes squeezed into the false bottom like a jellied eel.

My sympathy was limited, though. I was a broke, half-naked understudy in the chorus, and that overpaid, egotistical slice of cheesecake was going to reappear in a puff of smoke—while the Sorcerer was busy fighting the handsome Prince—and give a nasal rendition of the best song in the show while I discreetly exited stage left.

The Sorcerer covered the crystal cage with a shimmering gold cloth. I and another nymph spun the covered cage around on its wheels three times while the Sorcerer muttered spells and incantations beneath the swelling music.

I heard a faint noise come from beneath the gold

cloth as we brought the spinning cage to a stop. It was a brief, shrill squeal, muted by the orchestra. I entertained my favorite fantasy, the one in which Golly's expensively augmented breasts could no longer fit inside the false floor of the cage and she had to leave the show. I would take over her role, and my agent would get every reviewer, producer and director on the East Coast to come see the show. I might even let my parents come to New York to see *Sorcerer!* once I was playing someone who wore clothes.

Lost in this pleasant fantasy, I was almost disappointed when the Sorcerer lifted the golden curtain to reveal that Virtue had disappeared. Golly was safely hidden, and I was still an obscure dryad. Someone wheeled the empty cage offstage. The rest of the scene passed quickly, and soon it was time for Virtue to reappear in a glorious cloud of smoke and sing the ballad that would make the Sorcerer and the Prince both see the error of their ways and be nice to each other.

There was a small explosion. Smoke billowed. The music throbbed.

And Golly missed her cue.

For once, I was glad to be nothing more than a chorus nymph. The most dramatic moment in the show had just bombed, the audience stopped suspending their disbelief, and Joe was staring blankly into the smoke, wondering what to do.

Luckily the conductor was on his toes. He had the orchestra repeat the last eight bars before the smoke cleared completely. The cue echoed, faded and died—and still no Golly.

We all looked at one another. This was one of those moments that all actors enjoy telling war stories about but which none of us actually wants to experience. This was considerably worse than losing a prop or flubbing a line. What the hell should we do now?

Joe looked around the stage with glazed eyes. His face shone with sweat. He appeared to be hyperventilating. He was obviously done for the night. In fact, somebody had better get him offstage right away.

Then I remembered that squeal. I'd been so busy wishing evil things upon Golly, it hadn't even occurred to me she might be in trouble. Injured, stuck, unconscious... She was still in the crystal cage, of course, trapped beneath the false bottom. We had to get her out of there. Then we could figure out how to finish the show.

In sheer desperation, I hopped up and down, pointed into the wings, and cried, "Look! There goes my lady! She has escaped the Sorcerer's spell! Let us go...you know...hear what she has to say!" I cheered wildly.

The other actors looked at me as if I'd gone mad.

I elbowed the satyr and whispered, "Come on, cheer! And help Joe offstage before he passes out."

"Huh? Oh, right."

The other actors followed suit, cheering and waving as they hustled Joe offstage while the orchestra tried to cover the moment with some transition music.

I ran over to the crystal cage and started trying to tear it apart with my bare hands. Everyone stared at me. "Help me get her out of here!" I urged my fellow forest creatures. "She's still inside. She must be stuck."

"You don't get it, do you? You don't get it!" Joe cried, still hyperventilating. He started to laugh hysterically.

"Pull yourself together," I told him. "Has anybody got a hammer back here?"

"No!" cried Joe's wife Matilda, rushing into the fray. "You can't destroy that cage. Not on our budget!"

"Who's the Equity deputy on this set?" one of the nymphs demanded. "There must be a rule about this kind of thing."

"Man, you just don't get it!" Joe shrieked.

"Darling, say your mantra," Matilda instructed him soothingly, patting his sweaty face.

"I can't remember my mantra! Ohmigod, ohmigod, ohmigod!"

I got a hammer from one of the techies. "Stand back," I ordered the milling cast and crew.

"No!" cried Matilda, abandoning Joe. "I'm warning you—this will come out of your paycheck!"

"I wouldn't say that to her while she's got a hammer in her hand," advised a satyr.

I panted as I smashed the glass and pried open the

bottom of the cage. "You want to leave a union member in here to suffocate? I'm sure Equity will be—"

"She's not *in* there. Don't you get it?" Joe said, his voice raspy.

I gave a mighty heave and fell back a few steps as the secret compartment was revealed. There was a moment of astonished silence as we all stared at its vacant interior.

"Joe's right," I said at last. "Golly's vanished."

CHAPTER 1

I despise movies where the heroine is threatened and simply ignores it, acting as if there's nothing to worry about. I mean, if you got a mysterious note telling you not to go into the attic, and you knew that the last person who'd gone into the attic had gotten into a whole lot of trouble—well, would you really just shrug, toss the note aside, and head for the attic without another thought?

If you would, then frankly, you're the kind of person who *deserves* what's going to happen to you up there.

So naturally, when I received my mysterious threatening note, I gave it my full attention.

It arrived a few days after Golly Gee disappeared.

The night of the performance the stage manager had brought the curtain down in front of a surprised audience, the hapless house manager had announced that there'd been an accident backstage and the show was over, and we had spent the rest of the evening giving our statements to the police—who were less interested in the case than you might suppose.

Golly wasn't all that stable to begin with, and her recent discovery, during hypnotherapy, that she had been Marilyn Monroe in a previous incarnation had resulted in some very strange behavior, including a marked obsession with the Kennedy family.

The police seemed to think Golly had walked out in the middle of the performance and gone off on some bizarre quest. Since there was no sign of violence or foul play, the good-looking detective who interviewed Joe and me evidently didn't plan to do much more than file a missing persons report if Golly didn't reappear (so to speak) in a couple of days.

I didn't necessarily agree with Detective Lopez's view of the matter, but I hardly knew Golly and certainly couldn't claim to miss her. Besides, with the leading lady missing (and in breach of contract), I finally had that big break I'd been fantasizing about since the beginning of rehearsals: I'd be playing Virtue from now on. If, that is, we could get Joe back onstage.

The night Golly vanished, Joe had been too hysterical to give a coherent statement to Detective Lopez—who had, in any case, not seemed to expect much coherence from any of the actors. (I sensed that our being painted green and covered in glitter affected the detective's impression of us.) Joe seemed to blame himself for Golly's disappearance, and he refused to do the show again. Consequently, Matilda was forced to cancel our next few performances while she tried to talk some sense into him. We didn't have an understudy for Joe. He *was* the show.

We couldn't even get him into the theater for the rehearsal I had requested. I didn't want to go on as Virtue without a complete run-through. For one thing, there had been several changes in the show since my last rehearsal in the role. More importantly, I wanted to make sure I could trust Joe to pull himself together before I let him saw me in half, balance my body on the point of a sword or do the flame-throwing routine with me. Things can go terribly wrong onstage when people lose their concentration. Actors have been stabbed to death while playing Richard III. They've been shot to death with misloaded prop guns, as well as strangled to death in malfunctioning harnesses. It's a much riskier profession than you might suppose, and I was determined not to be among the ranks of thespians whose reviews read "R.I.P."

It was in this frame of mind that I read the messages handed to me by the assistant stage manager as I arrived at the theater on Tuesday. The first note informed me that Joe would not be at rehearsal today. The second note advised me that there would be an

Equity meeting that afternoon to discuss our circumstances; in other words, the actors would all get together to fret about whether we were going to lose our jobs, as well as to make empty threats about what we'd do to management if they folded the show on us just because a pop singer had gone AWOL and a magician was having a nervous breakdown.

The third note was handwritten on expensive monogrammed paper, initials *M.Z.* It was written with a black fountain pen in elegant, archaic-looking script. It read:

As you value your life, do not go into the crystal cage. There is Evil among us.

"I'm looking for Detective Lopez," I told the uniformed sergeant at the muster desk. The precinct house was chaotic and noisy, just like in the movies. I had practically sprinted here from the theater on Christopher Street. The desk sergeant sent me upstairs to the squad room, a large, cluttered, overcrowded area painted a vile green.

I spotted Lopez right away. He was sitting at his desk, apparently begging a chubby white man with a loud tie not to force a large, overflowing box of file folders on him. The man, whose expression was irritable, dropped the box on Lopez's desk and walked away. Lopez, looking like he wanted to weep, lowered his head and banged it against his desk a few times.

Perhaps I had come at a bad time.

However, the mysterious note was burning a hole in my pocket, and there was no way I was going to turn around and leave without reporting it to the police.

I took a breath and squared my shoulders as Lopez lifted his head and reached for his ringing phone. After a moment, he cradled the phone between his ear and his shoulder and, still talking, started unpacking the overflowing box. It appeared to contain a lifetime supply of old paperwork—dog-eared, a little dusty and flaking. Frowning, Lopez brushed something away from his face and kept unpacking the box while he continued his phone conversation.

I crossed the room, nearly bumping into someone whose hooker costume looked really authentic, right down to the runny mascara and handcuffs. Lopez, whose gaze was fixed on his mountain of paperwork, didn't see me. His jacket was slung over the back of his chair. He wore a holster over his shirt; the gun inside it looked really authentic, too. I stared at it while he kept talking on the phone.

He had the body of an athlete—soccer or tennis, perhaps, a sport that required lithe muscles and physical grace. He was around thirty years old, and he had a dark, strong, slightly exotic face framed by thick, straight, jet-black hair. His eyes were blue, and just as I was wondering where that trait had come from, I read the nameplate on his desk: Detective Connor Lopez.

"Connor?" I said in surprise. He didn't look like a Connor.

He glanced up and saw me. There was no look of recognition, but my use of his name must have made him realize I was there to see him. He gestured to a utilitarian chair next to his desk, and I sat down.

"Uh-huh," he said into the phone. "Yes. No. What time?... Can't you get it to me any sooner? I need it before I can apply for a warrant."

Someone called across the squad room, "Lopez, line four!"

He raised a hand in acknowledgment, then closed his eyes and rubbed his forehead as if it ached. Well, he *had* banged it rather hard against the desk. "One hour," he said firmly. "No, one hour. *Please*." He grinned after a moment and said, "I almost love you right now." Then he hung up and said to me, "I'm sorry, miss, I'll be with you in a minute." He hit another phone line and said, "Detective Lopez."

It was clear from his expression a moment later that the call was personal. "Hi. Uh-huh... What?" His expression darkened. Turning away from me, he said, "No, I can't."

Though I could tell he didn't remember me, he had certainly made a memorable impression on the cast of *Sorcerer!* the night he'd questioned us.

"Okay, you're right," Lopez said to his caller, "I don't *want* to. Now I have to go. I've got—"

He was interrupted by a voice on the other end of

the line, loud enough that even I could hear it. The caller sounded like a woman.

Some of the show's nymphs had been openly interested in him, and although his behavior couldn't be called unprofessional, he'd obviously enjoyed their flirting. He'd been caught off guard by the same sort of interest coming from a couple of the satyrs, but he'd nonetheless been courteous about it.

"No. *No*. No!" Lopez sounded exasperated. "Look, what part of 'no' didn't you—" He sighed and closed his eyes, listening again. After a moment, he said, "Why do you persecute me like this? Why, *why?*" A pause. "Besides that."

Two cops hauled someone past me who looked like a rapper. A very annoyed rapper.

"Look, this isn't a good time," Lopez said into the phone. "Can we—" He winced.

Even I winced. His caller's voice was getting shrill.

Lopez took a deep breath and said, in a voice filled with dark despair, "Mom, I can't talk now. Goodbye... *Bye*." He scowled and said, "I'm hanging up now. *Right* now."

The voice was still squawking as Lopez gently placed the receiver in its cradle. Looking a little paler than when I'd arrived, he turned to me and said, "Now, what can I do for you, Miss..."

"Diamond. Esther Diamond. You took my statement Saturday night at the New View Venue on Christopher Street."

"Oh, yeah! Miss Diamond." His gaze traveled over me slowly, then he grinned. "You look different without all that green body makeup."

"I'm also wearing a lot more clothes today," I said, noticing where his eyes lingered.

He raised them to my face. "And much less glitter."

"Have you made any progress on the case, Detective?"

"That singer who disappeared—Gosh Darn?"

"Golly Gee."

He smiled at me, and I realized he'd been kidding. "She's still missing," he said.

"I know."

"No ransom demands?" he asked.

"No."

"Have you heard from her family? I've tried to get a hold of her mother, but—"

"Oh, I doubt that Golly was of woman born," I said.

"Excuse me?"

"Um, her mother's in Europe just now. Golly's manager got a hold of her yesterday. She hasn't heard from her, either." I shrugged. "She's really missing, Detective."

He nodded. "I've filed a missing persons report."

"That's all?"

"It'll be compared to any likely Jane Doe that turns up."

"You mean, like…a body?"

"Yes."

"Oh."

He said, "Her family—or her manager—might consider hiring a private investigator."

"I see."

"Anything else?" he asked.

"Yes. This is a little strange...."

He raised one black brow. "Last week you told me that a woman had vanished into thin air in front of hundreds of people—"

"Not hundreds. Our house wasn't that good."

"But you're afraid that what you're going to tell me *now* is a little strange? I can hardly wait."

I pulled out the note and handed it to him. He read it over briefly and then frowned at me.

"This came in the mail?"

"No. Someone left it at the theater for me."

"Did you get a description?" he asked.

"The assistant stage manager, who accepted the envelope from him, says he was a short, slightly chubby, white man, at least seventy years old. Lots of white hair and a beard. He wore a fedora and a duster."

"A what?"

"You know. One of those long coats they wear in cowboy movies."

"Oh. Anything else?"

"I don't think so."

"'As you value your life, do not go into the crystal cage,'" Lopez read aloud. "'There is Evil among us.' It has a certain ring to it. But why does this guy think you intend to go into the cage?"

I explained. When I was done, Lopez studied me speculatively. His silence got on my nerves, so I asked, "Do you think it's important?"

"What?"

"The note," I snapped.

"Well, it provides a new theory."

"So you no longer think Golly walked off on her own?"

"Actually, that's exactly what I think happened. According to the statements I took, Miss Gee is a temperamental twenty-three-year-old who's got less fame than she wants and less sense than she needs."

"That hardly—"

"She's got cash flow problems, and she's deep in debt—mostly to plastic surgeons and diet clinics. She's also got a police record—mostly minor drug busts. Two of the Kennedys have had to slap restraining orders on her, and—"

"You've checked up on her!" I shouldn't have sounded so surprised. He looked insulted.

"Yes, Miss Diamond, I did. But now I find myself obliged to concentrate on more mundane matters—assault, murder, armed robbery, extortion and so on." As he gestured to the mountain of paperwork on his desk, a clerk dropped another armload of files onto it. Lopez stared after her with a tragic expression.

"But what about the note?" I said. "Do you think—?"

"I think it's a hell of a promotional opportunity for an off-Broadway show with overextended producers and an ambitious understudy."

"You think *I* had something to do with this?"

"I have to consider all possibilities."

Okay, I had seen enough cop shows on TV to know that. So I tried not to take offense. "Look, I'm not reaping any benefits from this fiasco. Joe Herlihy is refusing to perform the show again."

"He didn't get along with Golly Gee, did he? She insulted him, humiliated him, upstaged him and accused him of attempting to set her on fire that very night."

"Surely you don't think Joe is behind this?"

"I'm still not even sure what 'this' is," he said.

"But—"

"Look, we know the girl was in the cage before it was rolled offstage. A dozen witnesses backstage saw no strangers, no violence, nothing unusual. The only people who touched that cage were you, Herlihy and the other nymph." He paused before saying, "As it happens, Herlihy hates her, and you wanted her job."

"Joe and I were onstage the whole time!" I said.

"And besides Miss Gee, does anyone in the cast know that prop as well as the two of you do?"

"I'm the one receiving threats!" I waved my note in his face.

"I'll keep that in mind," he said courteously.

Getting exasperated, I said, "Look, just tell me if you think it's safe for me to get in the cage."

"I thought you destroyed that thing? It was all your producer could talk about."

I grunted. "It's being repaired."

"I see."

"Listen," I prodded, "can't you at least turn this note over to the lab and see what they can find out?"

He looked at it for a moment, then shook his head. "We have no proof that a crime has been committed, Miss Diamond. Unless further evidence comes to light, I can't submit this for forensic examination. Besides, it's not a threat, it's a warning."

"Should that comfort me?"

"It's probably from a superstitious fan or a religious fanatic—someone who believes that Golly Gee really did vanish into thin air and that anyone else who does that trick will follow her into oblivion."

"You've been a real help, Detective." I stuffed the note into my purse and turned to go.

"Uh, Miss Diamond?"

"What?" I said over my shoulder.

"If the show does reopen…"

"Yes?"

He hesitated, then lowered coal-black lashes over those deep blue eyes as he said, "I'd like to come see you in it."

"Book your seat," I said. "The show must go on."

* * *

I returned to the theater for a musical run-through with the cast and orchestra. Without Joe, there wasn't much else we could do. Then, ignoring the dirty looks I received, I slipped out of the Equity meeting early and went to Joe's place. He and Matilda had the entire second floor of a brownstone all to themselves on the Upper West Side. Everyone knew it was her money, not his, that paid for this luxury. He wasn't a successful magician, and I suspected that only his recent second marriage to an ambitious producer had provided him with an opportunity like *Sorcerer!* He was in his late thirties, an age at which many performers feel time is running out for them to achieve success in our youth-oriented society. I knew Joe craved name recognition, national tours and television specials. Just like me, he was hoping that *Sorcerer!*'s initial run would be successful enough for us to move the show to a major Broadway theater where we'd enjoy a higher profile.

His behavior baffled me. Joe was neurotic, sure, but I knew how much the show meant to him. If he blew this chance—and cost our backers a bundle in the process—he could probably count on playing nothing but birthday parties and Renaissance fairs for the next thirty years. If I let him live, that was. With Golly gone, this was my big chance, and no high-strung, rabbit-in-the-hat asthmatic was going to ruin it for me. That's why I had to talk to him. We both wanted the same thing. I was sure I could get through to him, reason with him, convince him to go on with the show. And if reason didn't work, then I'd make sure he understood that whatever he feared might happen onstage was nothing compared to what *I* would do to him if he closed down the show.

It was obvious upon arriving at Joe's place that I was desperately needed there. No wonder Matilda wasn't making any progress. Why do married people behave in ways specifically designed to drive each other crazy?

"Darling, Esther's here," Matilda crooned loudly as she let me into the foyer. She turned to me and added in a stage whisper that they could probably hear as far away as Cleveland, "Try not to upset him. He's very sensitive about the whole subject right now."

"Tough," I said.

"What subject?" Joe demanded, shouting at us from three rooms away.

"Why don't you come here and greet Esther, darling?"

"No! *What* subject?"

"He's been like this since Saturday night," she mega-whispered at me again.

"Like what?" Joe shouted. "*What* have I been like?"

Luckily, the phone rang. The combatants went to their separate corners, so to speak, while Matilda answered it. Unfortunately, she came out swinging only a moment later, and this time she was aiming for both of us.

"Darling, it's Magic Magnus's shop calling," she bellowed down the hallway. "The crystal cage—you know, the one Esther smashed to bits and pried apart? It's ready to be picked up. Isn't that wonderful, darling? You can rehearse with it tomorrow!"

While Joe screamed an emphatic negative, she turned to me and added, "It was horribly expensive to repair, Esther."

"Uh-huh."

"Considerably more than your salary."

"That's easy to believe."

She frowned at me, then bellowed, "Shall I tell them you're coming, dear?"

I don't think Joe heard her. He was still shouting. So I said, "Tell them someone will come for it. If he won't go, I will."

"Well, yes, I suppose it's the least you can do."

"Look, Matilda, someone had to get Golly out of—"

"She wasn't *in* there, if you recall," Matilda said through clenched teeth.

Joe heard that. "Go on, remind me, remind me, just keep *reminding* me." He hurled the words at her, coming down the hallway toward us. "Just keep rubbing it in that I made a woman vanish!"

Matilda glared at him and went back to her telephone conversation. I stared at Joe, thunderstruck.

"Wait a minute! Wait just a minute!" I realized I was shouting, too, and lowered my voice. "What's going on here, Joe? Are you having delusions of god-hood? Do you honestly believe—do you even enter-tain the possibility—that Golly really vanished? Abracadabra, a puff of smoke and oblivion? Do you believe all your own hocus-pocus publicity?"

He had the good grace to look sheepish. "You don't understand, Esther. She… I felt… There was…"

I took him by the shoulders and shook him hard. "Joe! Pull yourself together! Let's have a reality check here!"

Matilda put down the phone. "The shop closes at six o'clock. You'll have to hurry."

"But she *did* vanish," Joe insisted.

"She didn't vanish!" I snapped. "She…wandered away. Maybe she felt an urgent need to speak to Robert Kennedy Junior. Maybe she thought she saw Elvis. Maybe she was abducted by one of those plas-tic surgeons she owes so much money to."

"Huh?" Joe said.

"Or maybe she's just trying to get a raise," Matilda said.

I stared at her. "Good God, there *is* evil among us."

"Excuse me?"

"Forget it. Give me the keys to your truck. I'm going to go get the crystal cage," I said. "It, and I, will be at the theater tomorrow morning at ten o'clock sharp for a full dress rehearsal. And so will you, Joe, or I will come here and get you—and this time the beautiful assistant will saw the *magician* in half!"

* * *

"Beautiful assistant" is an exaggeration in my case. Indeed, being fitted into Golly's wardrobe that morning had driven that point home like a wooden stake: her costumes were all a little too large in the chest and extremely tight everywhere else. I figured the girl must never eat. The wardrobe mistress advised me to suck in my stomach—and give up the Ben & Jerry's.

At five foot six, I was also shorter than Golly, so all the costumes had to be hemmed. Some of the colors would never look quite right on me, since I'm fair-skinned and brown-haired. I wondered if I'd be given a wig to play Virtue, since my simple shoulder-length hairstyle didn't resemble Golly's waist-length blond ringlets (which, in my darker moments, I had described as "hooker hair").

I inherited my father's brown eyes and my mother's good cheekbones. The result is a face which, as one of my acting teachers put it, is more versatile than beautiful. Still, I was rather flattered when Golly asked if I'd had cheek implants. (The feeling wore off when she told me she knew a doctor who could fix my nose.)

As I drove downtown, I wondered how a young woman Golly's age knew so much about fake body parts. She must have had a pretty dreadful life. Now that she wasn't around to irritate me, I felt kind of sorry for her.

I guess I felt kind of guilty, too. Except for a few

stunned moments Saturday night, I hadn't worried about Golly at all since her disappearance. Mostly I'd gloated over getting her job.

Now I tried to imagine what could have happened to her. How had she disappeared like that? And why? And where was she now?

And what about that note? Lopez was unmoved by it; but then Lopez was an overworked cop with other cases on his mind. Besides, he half suspected *me* of perpetrating Golly's disappearance. And his smile wasn't charming enough to make up for that insinuation, I thought grumpily. Anyhow, easy for him to make reckless accusations—he wasn't the one being threatened. Or warned. Or whatever.

He was right about one thing, though. The notion of "Evil among us" did suggest an unbalanced person. But was I right, too—did it suggest a *dangerous* person? Anyhow, just because someone's unbalanced doesn't mean they don't know what they're talking about.

Do not go into the crystal cage.

Why the cage? I wondered. Did the author of the note mean that the prop itself was dangerous? Did he think that Golly's disappearance was due to its faulty mechanism rather than to a mental breakdown or foul play?

I shook my head to clear it as I double-parked the truck outside Magic Magnus's shop on Worth Street, in Tribeca. I felt a headache coming on and decided to forget the whole mess for a while. If I kept up this merry-go-round of speculation, I'd wind up beating my head against hard objects before long, just like Lopez. And that habit didn't seem to be doing him any good.

I had assumed Magic Magnus's shop would be a dusty little storefront selling tricks and supplies. I was surprised to discover that the magic business filled an entire five-story building. The structure was one of those nineteenth-century relics of cast-iron architecture, when they found that buildings could be built more quickly and cheaply by using iron beams rather than heavy walls to hold the weight of the floors. This left more space for windows, not to mention fabulously decorative facades. Inside even the grubbiest and most run-down buildings in this area, you can find Renaissance columns, baroque balustrades and Second Empire ornamentation. I know all this because I once went on a blind date with one of the Friends of Cast-Iron Architecture.

Tribeca isn't quite as gentrified as Soho, but many of the buildings down here have been renovated. Magic Magnus's place wasn't one of them. In fact, as I pushed open the door and entered the vast ground-floor showroom, I thought even the dust looked nineteenth century. I assumed that Magnus must be doing good business if he could afford to operate in this part of town, but I doubted he did much trade with walk-in customers. A couple of dusty display cases held old-fashioned props: wands, hats, cards, false-bottom cups, that sort of thing. One wall was lined with a long row of costumes of astonishing vulgarity. The rest of the showroom was filled with a bewildering variety of poorly displayed props and many boxes, crates and cartons. Judging by the markings on these containers, Magnus got shipments from all over the world.

I looked around for a shopkeeper or clerk but saw no one. Walking toward the main counter, I tripped over something on the floor and nearly flew headfirst into an Iron Maiden. A little stunned, I examined the thing and realized it was just a grisly version of something Joe used in *Sorcerer!* You stick a girl inside and run swords through her. I shook my head in disgust. This whole business of magic tricks always seemed to involve mutilating a half-naked woman.

There was a wall behind the counter. A doorway at its center was covered by a red velvet curtain.

"Hello?" I called.

No response.

I noticed a small bell sitting on the counter. A sign propped up next to it said Ring For Assistance. I did. A moment later there was a small *pop!,* a puff of smoke and the smell of sulfur.

I found myself facing one of the biggest men I'd ever seen. Easily six and a half feet tall, broad and beefy without being fat, he displayed a remarkable set of tattoos on both bare arms. He had wild red hair and a well-trimmed beard. He grinned at me. His teeth were very long. One of them was gold.

I took a step back. He gave a full-throated laugh, booming and lusty.

I said, "Magic Magnus, I presume?"

"The one and only!" He reached across the counter, seized one of my hands and brought it to his lips. "And who might you be, fair wench?"

"I'm Esther Diamond. I came to get Joe Herlihy's prop. The crystal cage that—"

"Ah, yes. You're the actress who tore the thing apart with her bare hands."

"He told you about me?"

"His wife did."

"Oh."

"I like a woman with spirit. Are you free Friday evening?"

"I hope not. I mean—I should be performing then."

"And afterward?"

"Magnus, you overwhelm me."

"I have that effect on women." He smoldered at me.

"Or it may be the dust." I sneezed.

"Sorry about that."

"Don't you ever clean in here?"

"I had a cleaning woman, but she vanished."

"That's not funny," I said. "You heard about Golly Gee?"

He nodded. "Joe swore me to secrecy."

"Yeah, we're trying to keep it out of the papers."

"So the official story is that she just ran off?"

I shrugged. "Or ran amuck." I leaned forward. "What do you think happened?"

Magnus shrugged, too, making his tattoos dance. "Who knows? We're dealing with other realms when we venture into the magical arts. If Friday's bad for you, how about Sunday?"

"Magical arts, my foot. It's mechanics, timing and performance skill. I'm Golly's understudy. I know how to do every trick she's involved in."

"Trick?" He looked outraged. "Please, love, at least say *illusion*."

Joe always said that to me, too. I found it pretentious. "Trick, illusion, what's the difference?"

"The difference is in perception." Magnus waved a hand and a little bird appeared, nestled in his palm. It looked ruffled and surprised. "After all, what is a trick, fair one?"

"I'm a brunette."

"It is deceit. It is a fake, a fraud, a hoax." He folded his fist gently over the little bird and covered the fist with a handkerchief drawn from his pocket. "But an illusion—ah, that is a fantasy, a mirage, a flight of fancy. An illusion is the edge of a dream we cannot enter. It is the essence of imagination, that very quality which makes men different from animals." He drew away the handkerchief and opened his fist. The bird was gone. In its place was a lovely crystal wrapped in a fine thread of silver and dangling from a silver chain. "Illusion is the shadow of the world as it might be, if you only believe in it."

My mouth was dry. He was much better than Joe. "Why aren't you performing?" I asked.

"I used to. Too much traveling." He hung the chain around my neck. The crystal rested between my breasts.

"Oh, I can't accept this. I—"

"I insist. Wear it and think of Magnus and magic."

"But—"

"At least think about it. If you don't feel right about keeping it, you can return it. Sunday at dinner, perhaps?"

I heard footsteps overhead and remembered why I had come here. "I, uh, think I'd better get Joe's cage."

"You'll want to take a look at it. It's upstairs. I'll just—" The phone rang. He smiled apologetically. "This will only take a minute. Excuse me."

He exited conventionally, lifting aside the heavy red curtain for a moment and then letting it fall into place behind him.

The call took more than a minute. After five minutes, I got bored and called, "Magnus? Is it all right if I go upstairs?"

There was no answer. After calling to him once more without results, I headed for the stairwell at the back of the building. I didn't need his help to exam-

ine the cage, after all. I knew how the thing was supposed to work. I'd give the cage a quick once-over
while he was on the phone, then sign any paperwork
while it was being carried out to the truck.

The second floor was even dustier, darker and
more chaotic than the showroom. Why did Magnus
keep the windows covered? Was the work he did so
secret? After fumbling in the dismal shadows, I
found a yank-cord for an overhead light and turned
it on. I surveyed the vast tumble of boxes and cartons and equipment, and wondered how I'd find the
crystal cage.

Where was Magnus's staff? I'd heard footsteps earlier.
Surely a place this size needed a few people, especially
with all the equipment they appeared to be building or
repairing. I glanced at my watch: it was after six o'clock
already. Magnus's staff must have quit for the day.

I was shoving past a wooden crate when I heard footsteps again. They were directly above me, on the third
floor. Maybe whoever was up there could help me find
my cage. I went back to the stairs and called, "Hello? Is
someone up there? Hello? Can you help me?"

Footsteps approached the stairs. I ascended a few
steps. An anxious-looking, slightly exotic woman appeared above me. She was petite, Asian, and wearing a
tight animal-print outfit. "Um, hi," I said. "I'm a customer. Magnus is on the phone, and I—"

"Esther?" Magnus's voice boomed from below. "Esther, are you up there?"

"Yes!"

He seemed to come up the steps in a single bound. "What are you doing?" He sounded a bit breathless.

"I thought I'd look at the cage while you were busy. I was asking one of your employees to help me." I gestured over my shoulder and then looked toward the woman. "Oh. She's gone."

He put a large hand on my shoulder and turned me away from the stairs, guiding me back into the maze of cartons and equipment. "You should never come up here alone," he said. "It can be very confusing."

"Yes, that's why I asked that woman—"

"But I'm here now. And here's the cage, good as new."

It was indeed as good as new—although it damn well should be, I thought minutes later when I saw Magnus's bill. "Wow. No wonder Matilda is pissed off at me for tearing it apart."

"You did quite a thorough job."

"How was I to know Golly wasn't inside?" I looked at him curiously, remembering the note I had received. "Do you think this thing is safe for me to get into?"

"Absolutely!" he boomed. "You have my personal guarantee. Besides, this crystal I gave you—" he seized the excuse to touch my chest "—will protect you from all evil."

"Evil?" I pounced. "Why did you say that?"

He blinked. "Figure of speech."

"Magnus, do you think...?"

"What, love?"

"Oh, never mind. Just load it into the truck, please."

Considering how bulky and unwieldy the cage was, I had expected him to need help getting it out to the truck. Silly me. He wasn't even breathing hard by the time he was done loading it on board. On the contrary, he still had enough wind left in him to ask me out to dinner again.

Joe was at the theater when I arrived for rehearsal the next day. I was already in full costume and makeup when one of the nymphs came up to me and said, "I slept in the dressing room last night." She made a vague gesture. "Big fight with my now-ex."

"Oh. Sorry."

"Anyhow, someone slid this under the door in the middle of the night."

"In the middle of the night? But the whole place is supposed to be locked up."

"I know. It scared the hell out of me. I didn't have the guts to get up and see what it was until the sun came up." She handed me an envelope. "Anyhow, it's for you."

To say my blood ran cold would not be overstating things. My hand trembled as I took the envelope. My name was written on it in an elegant, archaic-looking hand that I recognized with a sinking heart.

Beneath my name was a single sentence:

Do not risk it.

Feeling sick, I opened the envelope. There was nothing inside except a newspaper clipping.

It was enough.

CHAPTER

2

Detective Lopez looked like he'd had a rough night on the tiles. I had a feeling I looked worse. In any event, there was no doubt that I looked ridiculous. Virtue's flowing yellow and gold robes, elaborate headdress and sparkling makeup looked distinctly out of place in the squad room. If we had been anyplace other than New York City, I would be attracting attention. As it was, Lopez stared at me as if he dearly hoped I was a figment of his imagination.

"Someone left this clipping at the theater last night," I said, handing him the envelope. "I think it must have been the same person."

"The man wearing a duster who thinks Evil is among us?"

Surprised he remembered yesterday's conversation

so well, I blinked. Glitter fell from my lashes to my cheeks. I brushed it away. "Yes."

"I don't think your hair goes with that outfit," he said, studying me with bloodshot eyes.

"Just read it," I snapped.

"No, I mean, I *like* your hair," he said. "I just don't think... Um, never mind. Sorry. Late-night bust. I'm a little..." Lopez shook himself, then opened the envelope, took out the enclosed clipping and read aloud, "'Woman Vanishes into Thin Air.'" He gave me an enigmatic glance and continued. "'The Great Hidalgo's Marvelous Carnival of Magic and Illusion brought Catherine Harrington Lowell's eighth birthday party to a crashing halt in her parents' Upper East Side home two days ago. Having caused his beautiful assistant to disappear, the Great Hidalgo was unsuccessful in any of his attempts to make the woman materialize again.'" He stared at me. "Oh, Christ. You can't be serious."

"Come on, Detective. Don't you find this too improbable for coincidence? Two women disappear during vanishing acts, and now *I'm* being warned not to do the vanishing trick? Don't you think something strange is going on?"

He was rubbing his forehead again. "I think it's a hell of a tabloid story."

"They don't mention Golly. No one knows about that yet."

He closed his eyes. "Are you actually suggesting—?"

"Don't you think we should talk to this Hidalgo guy?"

His eyes snapped open. "We?"

"Yes. After all, I'm the one at risk here, and y—"

"So don't do the trick, Esther."

"It's my job!"

He shook his head. "This is crazy! This is *really*…" He paused, took a long breath and seemed to count silently to ten or perhaps recite The Serenity Prayer. Then he said more calmly, "Look, if you're really worried about vanishing into thin air, shouldn't you be talking to Herlihy? He's the one who made Golly Gee disappear, after all."

"That's exactly what he thinks."

"Is it really?"

"He's irrational on the subject. I don't dare tell him about this."

"But you felt obliged to tell *me*," he said wearily.

"You're the investigating officer."

"Miss Diamond—"

"You called me Esther a minute ago," I said inanely.

"And I'm already regretting the impulse," he replied. "Look, aside from the fact that I am an extremely busy, overworked, underpaid—"

"But this is what you're underpaid to do!"

"There still isn't anything for an investigating officer to investigate."

"But—"

"Show me a corpse!" He made a sharp gesture of exasperation. "Show me evidence of blackmail, extortion, kidnapping. Show me a woman who was acting strangely—"

"Golly always acted strangely."

"I mean, a woman who had changed her habits lately," he said, "who seemed to be afraid of something. Give me one witness who saw a stranger backstage. Show me signs of a struggle. I'm a dedicated cop, Esther. Make me believe a crime has been committed and I'll be johnny-on-the-spot."

I indicated the newspaper clipping. "But what about—?"

"No. Don't." He shook his head and put his hand over mine. "Don't show me cryptic notes from a prankster or tell me that women are vanishing into thin air as part of some mysterious scheme perpetrated by the forces of Evil."

I looked down at his hand covering mine. He did, too, for a moment; then he took a quick breath and drew away.

I gave myself a mental shake and said, "But how do you explain—?"

"How do *you* explain it? Tell me what you believe."

It was a little hard to admit fears to him that I wasn't even really admitting to myself. "Um…"

"Esther, come on. The night I questioned you at the

theater, you seemed like the most sensible person there."

"You remember me?"

His expression changed again. "I remember who had the tightest costume."

"That's not nice."

He grinned. "On the contrary, I thought it was *very* nice."

"You're not supposed to talk to me this way," I said. "You're the investigating officer."

"Good point." He banished his smile, and I was sorry. "Please just tell me you don't really believe you'll blink out of existence if you do the vanishing trick."

"No. Of course not," I said. "Don't be silly. No."

He folded his arms. "Well, then?"

I felt kind of deflated. In the cold fluorescent light of the squad room, full of telephones, cops, coffee cups and criminals, I also felt pretty foolish. "So, I, uh, I guess I shouldn't bother you if I receive any more of these—"

"Oh, no. Please stop by." He grinned at me again. "These encounters are becoming the highlight of my dreary days."

I sighed and rose from my chair. "I'm late for rehearsal. I should go."

"Esther." His voice stopped me as I turned to leave. "I'm serious. Let me know if you get any more warnings."

I met his gaze. "I will. But you don't think there's anything to worry about."

"I don't. And I don't want *you* to worry." When I didn't respond, he prodded, "Okay?"

I wasn't as sure as he was, so I just repeated, "I'm late for rehearsal." And I left.

The music cued me in to the final scene, the one where the Sorcerer tries to make Virtue vanish forever. Forever and ever and ever... Where *was* Golly?

I pushed the thought out of my mind. Lopez was right. And I wasn't going to let a couple of silly notes and a mysterious disappearance destroy the show and ruin my career.

Besides, I'd done the vanishing trick many times during previous rehearsals. I knew exactly how it worked. There was nothing to be afraid of. Absolutely nothing.

Joe gave his speech, stumbling over his lines. His hands were shaking as he grabbed me and dragged me toward the crystal cage. His palms were so slick with sweat that he lost his grip on my arm and I went crashing to my knees, missing my song cue.

The director stopped the scene. We went back to the beginning of Joe's speech. The next attempt was worse than the one before. He grabbed my arm again, and this time he hauled me off in the wrong direction. We went back and tried it again. Joe's face was dripping with sweat.

Christ, he was more terrified than I was. He *believed* it, he really did. When he dragged me toward the cage this time, my resistance was real. How had Magnus defined an illusion? *The shadow of the world as it might be, if you only believed.* Now on the brink of following in Golly's wake, I suddenly believed with a vengeance. I believed so hard that my stomach churned and my eyes watered. I was shaking like a leaf as I sang a few lines begging the Sorcerer not to send me into oblivion.

Joe's fear-glazed eyes looked half mad. He opened the glass door and ordered me inside. I stared at the gaping void and realized I didn't want to find out what had happened to Golly Gee. I never, ever wanted to know.

"No!" I screamed. I jumped away from the cage and threw my golden handcuffs onto the stage. "No, no, no, no!"

"What?"

"What's she doing?"

"Esther!"

"What's going on?"

"Oh God!" Joe cried.

The music stopped as chaos erupted onstage. Joe and I both kept screaming. The chorus ran around wildly. The Prince came onstage waving his sword. The director started shouting.

"What the hell do you think you're doing?" Matilda screamed right into my face.

I turned around and raced straight for the bathroom. I was panting like a long-distance runner by the time I reached it. Matilda was hot on my heels. I tried to close the door on her, but the scrawny little witch was a lot stronger than she looked.

Nausea overcame me a moment later and I abandoned the struggle in favor of reaching the toilet in time. She was something, that woman. She never lost a beat, not even as I knelt down and retched pathetically again and again.

"And if there is a repetition of that appalling scene," Matilda shrieked, "you can forget about working in this show, or even in this town ever again! Do I make myself clear? Don't think it's too late for us to rehearse someone else into that part!"

"It *is* too late," I mumbled, my voice echoing in the cubicle. "If you want to reopen tonight, it's too late."

"And another thing!" she cried.

I winced. Those were my mother's favorite words.

Matilda plowed on. "If you upset Joe like this again—"

"Me?" I blurted. "*He* was the one who—"

"He has a very sensitive, artistic nature, and this ridiculous stunt that Golly pulled has ruined his nerves. He has given *everything* to this show, Esther."

"Uh-huh." I flushed the toilet and rose wearily.

"He has sacrificed his own career opportunities as a solo act for the good of the show."

"Oh, come on." I threw her an openly skeptical look before lurching toward the sink.

"He's acquired all-new equipment, studied new techniques, worked with a coach, developed new standards, trained day and night, refined his abilities. And in return, you completely disrupt a dress rehearsal and throw a hysterical fit at the climax of the play!"

"He was the one who wouldn't perform, wouldn't even rehearse after Golly—"

"Don't mention her name!" Matilda screamed. "I never want to hear her name again!"

I splashed cold water on my face and rinsed out my mouth. Feeling a little more rational, I said, "I'm sorry about what happened today. If I told you why I got so scared...well, it would only make things worse, especially for Joe."

She glared at me. "I need to know what you intend to do about tonight."

"I intend to go on," I said with determination.

"Fine. Can we try that last scene again, then?"

"No."

"Why the hell not?"

"There's something I have to do before tonight."

"What? In God's name, *what?*"

I looked at my dripping image in the mirror. "I have to talk to the Great Hidalgo."

It took all afternoon to hunt him up via various booking agencies (all of whom seemed stunned that anyone was interested in the Great Hidalgo). I finally got him on the phone, and he agreed to meet me at Fraunces Tavern, a renovated eighteenth-century establishment down in the Financial District. A nostalgic reminder of what Old New York must have been like two centuries and umpteen million people ago, the tavern's location (and prices) virtually guarantee that you never bump into starving actors there. The Great Hidalgo, it turned out, was only a part-time magician; his real name was Barclay Preston-Cole III, and he worked for his father's finance company.

"Miss Diamond?" A mousy young man approached my table in the corner.

"Barclay?" I didn't even consider calling him Mr. Preston-Cole. He looked about sixteen, despite his twelve-hundred-dollar suit and his Rolex watch. He was a little taller than me, with wavy brown hair, fair skin, pink lips and big, brown, cow-like eyes. Kind of cute in a sensitive way. "Have a seat," I said. I waved to the waiter and asked Barclay, "Are you old enough to drink?"

He flushed. "I'm twenty-two."

He ordered a white wine spritzer, then insisted on picking up the tab for both our drinks. I let him. Mom had told me that the man always paid, and common sense told me that Wall Street bankers always paid.

"So, Barclay," I said after he had relaxed a bit, "tell me about that society kid's birthday party."

He turned red again. "Oh God. Ohgod, ohgod, ohgod." He looked around as if afraid we were being spied on, then leaned forward and whispered, "I swear to you, I'll never do it again. Just don't tell my father."

I tried to look as if I was considering his request. "Well, I'll have to know all the details before I make any promises."

He swallowed and asked, "Who are you, anyhow? CIA? FBI? National Security Agency? NASA?"

The lad's imagination was spinning out of control. "I'm with Equity," I said.

"The actors' union?" His voice broke. *Everyone's* afraid of Equity.

"Special Investigative Branch." Okay, I exaggerated a little. So sue me.

"Oh my God! I'm never going to work again, am I?" Barclay wailed.

"What do you care? You've got a good job on Wall Street. Nice office, your own secretary, expense account—"

"How do you know all of this?" he cried.

It had been a safe guess, but I said, "We have our ways."

"I swear to you, I don't know what happened! It's not my fault!"

"Tell me about it," I urged.

"I was really starting to get somewhere," he said mournfully. "The act was getting better. All my hard work was beginning to pay off. I just got my first ever real booking!"

"Real booking?"

"You know, from strangers instead of society girls and old school chums."

"Oh."

"I'm supposed to perform at the Magic Cabaret on Saturday. It's my big break! What am I going to do?"

"Can you work alone?"

"Not really. Besides, the disappearing act was my big finish, my best illusion! How can I face an audience without it?"

Seeing he was close to tears, I said, "This means a lot to you."

He nodded. "I *hate* being a Preston-Cole. I hate banking and finance! All I've ever wanted to be is a conjurer. I've given everything to my art, and now it's destroyed me!" He flung himself across the table and grabbed my hand. "What's going to happen to me?"

"What happened to your assistant?" I countered, squeezing his hand as hard as I could. He winced.

"She vanished, I tell you! I use a simple, old-fashioned prop box for the disappearing act. I put Clarisse inside, and she never came out. The box never left my sight, and there was nowhere for her to go." He downed half his spritzer in a single gulp. "I tore the thing apart, but she wasn't inside. Then things got really grim. Little Betsy Broadmore started wailing like the damned, the Biddle-Bond twins physically attacked me, and the nanny kept screaming that I should be sued for reckless endangerment."

"I see."

"I just don't understand what could have happened. Clarisse and I rehearsed that illusion dozens of times!" He downed the rest of his spritzer and reached for *my* drink.

"Could Clarisse be playing some sort of malicious joke on you?"

"She's not that clever. Anyhow, Adelaide Mercer's bridal shower was yesterday, and Clarisse never would have willingly missed that. They're bitter enemies."

Overlooking the baffling mores of the upper classes, I asked, "Was she nervous about your first real booking—performing at the Magic Cabaret?"

"No, she was looking forward to it. Planning what to do with her hair and makeup, that sort of thing."

Still searching for a clue, I said, "You said your father doesn't know about what's happened?"

Barclay finished my wine. "He doesn't even know I still perform. I promised to give it up after I graduated from Yale."

"What about Clarisse's family? Surely they're worried about her?"

"The Stauntons? They're still in Europe." He started turning red again. "It's a big apartment, but they're bound to notice she's missing when they get back, don't you think? What am I going to tell them?"

"That's a tough question." I frowned at the table and wondered what logical conclusions could be drawn from any of this.

"Miss Diamond, why is Equity investigating this? I mean, Clarisse Staunton and I aren't even members."

I decided to tell him. He could obviously keep a secret, and perhaps his magician's mind would recognize some common clue in the two cases that had eluded me. He ordered another drink (a Scotch and soda this time) when I told him about Golly, and he looked positively ill by the time I told him about the second message I had received before this morning's rehearsal.

"What are you going to do?" he asked.

"I'm going to get into the cage tonight. What choice do I have?"

"You mustn't! You'll go wherever the other two went!"

"It could be a coincidence," I said.

"You don't believe that."

"I find it a lot harder to believe that the laws of physics have changed since last week."

"Can't you talk to Herlihy about this?"

"He's hysterical," I said.

"I don't blame him. You have no idea what it feels like."

"I can imagine how you feel."

"No, I mean, what it feels like to make a woman disappear. What it felt like the moment she vanished. Because, you see, I *knew*. Before she failed to reappear, before I tore apart the box looking for her, I knew she had vanished for real. I felt it somehow." He buried his head in his hands and mumbled, "I don't know. There must be some kind of atmospheric disturbance or molecular dissolution when they dematerialize."

"You have been watching *way* too much of the Sci-Fi Channel," I said, not liking how believable he was making this lunacy sound to me.

"Then how do you explain it?" he shot back.

"I don't know, but if I work on it long enough, I'll think of something."

"How long is 'long enough'?" He looked at his watch. "You've got two hours till show time."

Dressed in Virtue's Act One finery, I stared at myself in the dressing room mirror and listened to the intercom as Joe and the chorus performed the opening number. I had about ten minutes, and I was so nervous I couldn't remember a single line, lyric or piece of blocking.

"Calm down," I ordered my reflection in a dry, husky voice that would never carry past the first three rows. Nothing eased my tension, not breathing exercises, vocalization, meditation or stretching. Not herbal tea, nor even the feel of Magic Magnus's protective crystal resting against my skin.

I tried to look at the positive side of things. The vanishing act was almost two hours away. Anything could happen between now and then. Why, Joe was so nervous, he'd probably stab me or set me on fire before I had a chance to get into the crystal cage....

"Oh, that makes me feel so much better," I told my hollow-eyed, red-cheeked, perspiring reflection. I was afraid I was going to toss my cookies again.

I turned away from the mirror just as a breeze ruffled my hair and made my wispy costume flutter. I looked up at the room's single window. It was closed, as always. Judging by the intensity of the odors in the women's dressing room, we figured that the window had been painted shut in Fiorello LaGuardia's time. I looked over my shoulder. No, the door was closed, too.

"Pssst!"

"Yah!" I nearly jumped out of my skin.

"Pssst! Over here!"

I looked around the room but saw no one. It was a man's voice, though. I picked up a blow-dryer and waved it like a weapon. "Where are you?"

"I'm sorry. I'm having trouble materializing."

"What?"

"If you'll just be patient…"

"Patient?" I bleated. "Who *is* this? What's going on?"

A voice behind me said, "Ahhh. There we go."

I whirled and faced him, my heart pounding so hard it hurt. He had come out of nowhere! "Who are you?" I snarled with false bravado. "How did you get in here?"

"I'm terribly sorry. I didn't intend to intrude this way," he said. "I meant to wait for you outside earlier, but I'm running late today." His voice was soft and scholarly, and he spoke with a slight foreign accent.

"Wait for me? Why do you—?" I stopped and

stared. He was an absurd-looking figure. A small, slightly chubby white man, at least seventy years old, with unkempt white hair and a beard, he wore a fedora and a duster. "It's you!" I screeched.

"We must talk. You can't—"

"You!" I shrieked again, beside myself. Finally, here was someone upon whom I could vent my wrath. Surely this was all *his* fault. "Who are you? Why are you after me?"

"After you?" Great, furry, white brows swooped down when he frowned. "I assure you—"

"Writing mysterious notes! Sending me newspaper clippings! Lurking around the theater!"

"Lurking? I never—"

"I'll have you arrested, you pervert!"

His eyes widened. They were sky blue, as clear and round as a child's. "Pervert? I think you misunderstand—"

"How did you get in here?" I demanded, pointing the hair dryer at him.

"Now, let's stay calm," he urged, backing up.

"Freeze!" My hand tightened on the blow-dryer's grip. I must have pressed the "on" switch, because it roared and started shooting hot air at the stranger.

"Arrrgh!" He dropped to the floor.

I squealed in surprise and hit him with the thing. His fedora flew off, and he crouched there, clutching his forehead while his long white hair blew around him in a wild torrent.

"Wait!" he cried. "I'm trying to help you!"

"By turning me into a nervous wreck? If I wanted that kind of help, I'd call my mother!"

"Excuse me?" He looked up, squinting against the blast of hot air. "Could you possibly turn that thing off?"

"Huh? Oh. All right," I said, "but make one false move and you're dead, pal. I'm obliged to warn you that I've got a black belt in kung fu." I turned off the machine.

"So have I," he said absently, hauling himself to his feet.

"Oh." This worried me, since I had been lying.

"Now can we please talk? We have very little time."

"How did you get past the guard at the stage door?"

"I transmuted and slipped through the wall. Now you must listen——"

"This wall?" I pointed to the foot-thick brick wall.

"Yes. I'm here to tell you that you mustn't partici-pate——"

"Wait just a goddamn minute. You're trying to tell me you simply walked through *this* wall?" I thumped it with my fist.

"'Walk' would be a misstatement."

"Oh, God forbid we should have a misstatement here. How would *you* put it?"

He stroked his beard. "Well, in classical terms, it's generally referred to as transference, although the de-velopment of modern psychology has made that phrase a trifle——"

"Okay, buddy, that's it. I'm calling Lopez."

"Lopez?"

"The cop investigating—if you can call it that—Golly Gee's disappearance."

"No! You mustn't!"

"Don't touch me!"

"No police!" he cried, lunging for me.

I screamed and clobbered him with the hair dryer again.

"Ow! God's teeth, that hurts!"

"God's teeth?" I blurted. "No one has talked like that since the Restoration dramatists."

"I'm a very busy man," he explained. "I find it difficult to keep up with trends."

"Never mind that. What about Golly? Are you responsible for what happened to her?"

"No, of course not." He winced and rubbed his forehead. "I'm going to have a considerable lump, you know."

"Serves you right."

Over the intercom, the voices of the chorus swelled with the final notes of the opening number. The faint applause sounded like static. Just a couple of minutes left before my entrance.

I knew I should call our sole security guard and have the old man arrested, or at least thrown out of the building. But I had a feeling that this strange person could answer the question that was plaguing me. "What happened to Golly?"

"She vanished, of course."

The brief silence on the intercom echoed through the room.

"What do you mean, 'of course'? People don't just vanish," I snapped.

"Do you mind if I sit down, Miss Diamond? I'm somewhat fatigued. I find transmutation rather difficult." He slumped into a chair in front of the mirrors.

"Who are you?" I asked again.

"My name is Maximillian Zadok."

"M.Z."

"Yes."

"What are you doing here?"

He blinked. "Surely that's obvious. I've come to stop you from going onstage tonight."

I backed away from him. "Did you try to stop Golly, too?"

He shook his head and frowned. "No. I didn't know she was in any danger. It was her disappearance that alerted me to the Evil among us."

"There you go again." I was annoyed. "Evil?"

"Yes!"

I studied him closely. "Look, are you on some kind of medication? Did you maybe forget to take your Thorazine or something?"

"No, no, no! I assure you, I'm quite sane. And frankly, considering the life I've led, that's saying a great deal." He shot to his feet with surprising speed and seized me by the shoulders. "Please, listen to me,

Miss Diamond. I became alarmed as soon as I realized you intended to go onstage in Miss Gee's place. You must believe me when I say that if you do that, you risk meeting the same fate that she did."

"What was her fate? Where *is* she?"

He looked a little embarrassed. "I'm afraid I don't know. Yet."

My heart was thundering inside Virtue's dress. My voice was barely a whisper. "Is she dead?"

"Not necessarily." He was apparently trying to be comforting.

The Prince's voice crackled over the intercom. "I'm looking for a woman of virtue," he proclaimed.

My vision swam. "That's my warning cue. I'm on in a minute. I have to go."

"No! Please! You must believe me! She really did vanish! And so did the Great Hidalgo's assistant!"

"I've got to go on. I have no choice," I hissed, trying to get away from him.

He threw his arms around me. I struggled. He tripped me and bore me down to the floor. "Of course you have a choice! Especially considering what they're paying you!"

I gasped and tried to roll away. "How do you know what they pay me?" I stuck an elbow in his eye.

"Please, we must stop this," he said frantically. "I deplore violence!" Then he pulled my hair and got me in a half nelson.

"Ow! Stop it! They're in the middle of a performance. If I don't go on now, my career will be over! I'll be lucky to play a cavity in a toothpaste commercial!"

"No! The performance must be stopped. There is great danger here. *Oof,*" he added as I kneed him in the stomach.

"If you don't let me go, you lunatic, I will prosecute you to the fullest extent—"

"You won't be in any condition to prosecute! Don't you understand? Golly Gee and Clarisse Staunton weren't the end! They're just the beginning!"

"How do—*oy!* Get off me!"

"No." He sat on my chest. "Not until you listen to reason."

"Reason? First you tell me those women really vanished, and now you're trying to tell me there will be more," I panted, shoving at him.

"Exactly."

"Oh, and what makes you think that?" I snarled.

"Because there's been another."

I stopped breathing. "What?" I croaked.

He nodded. "Last night. On the Upper West Side."

"No." I shook my head. "No, that's not possible."

"At the annual gala dinner of the Urban Cowboys Club of Greater New York."

I felt ill. "Who?"

"Duke Dempsey the Conjuring Cowboy. For the big finale to his act, he put Dolly the Dancing Cowgirl inside a large, wooden, rhinestone-studded horse for a disappearing illusion."

"Don't tell me any more," I begged.

"And she vanished."

CHAPTER

3

"What are you doing?" Maximillian Zadok demanded as I lunged for the sink.

"One of the faeries has a bad ankle. She brought this bag of ice to put on it during intermission, in case it starts acting up tonight." I hauled the ice out of the sink.

"So?"

"So I'm not just going to walk out of the theater in perfect health and destroy my career."

"Stop that! You'll make yourself sick," he exclaimed as I opened the silk bodice of my costume and hugged the ice to my linen-clad chest.

I sat down in a chair and curled my body around the freezing cold bag. "I read that Meryl Streep did this once before shooting a death scene."

"Zounds!"

"Zounds?" I shook my head. "Anyhow, it worked so well that when they finished shooting the scene, they thought she really was ill."

"I don't understand. Why do you—?"

"When I miss my cue, which will be any second now, they'll come looking for me. If I simply walk out of the theater, Matilda will fire me and turn my name to mud. But if I appear to be sick, she'll have to let me come back to the show."

I heard my cue over the intercom and suddenly *did* feel sick. What the hell was I doing?

"This is crazy," I muttered, starting to shiver. "Keep a lookout for me. Tell me when someone's coming."

"How is my presence to be explained?" he asked nervously.

"You're the doctor I called when I started feeling ill." That was the part of the performance that worried me. I knew I could play near-dead, but could Zadok fool anyone into believing he wasn't hopelessly insane?

"But shouldn't there be an ambulatory vehicle?"

"What?"

"You know. With the red lights and the wailing."

"An ambulance? No. I'll regain consciousness slowly and ask you to take me home. You tell them all how dangerously sick I am, and then we'll leave the theater together. Got that?"

He looked anxious. "But—" Then he flinched. "Someone's coming!"

"Quick! Put the ice back in the sink."

I sank to the floor and sprawled across it in a shivering heap. Zadok had just deposited the ice bag in the sink when I heard Matilda's strident voice in the hallway.

"Where is she? I'll *kill* her for this. I'll make her rue the day she applied to drama school! Of all the irresponsible, witless, unprofessional…" Her voice trailed off as she entered the dressing room. Then she must have spotted me. She also spotted Zadok bending over me, about to check my pulse. "Help! Help! Someone's attacking Esther! Help! *Get him!*"

Things went awry then. Joe, the Prince and the stage manager all came rushing in behind Matilda. The intercom blared with the noise of the chorus singing my introduction over and over, waiting in vain for me to appear. Two of the men jumped on top of Zadok and started beating him to a pulp while he cried, "I'm a doctor! Really! Oxford University! Class of 1678! You may verify it if you don't believe me!"

"Esther. Esther, are you all right?" Joe cried, shaking me like I was a rag doll.

Matilda slapped me sharply across the face. I'd have paid real money for the chance to hit her back. Instead, I moaned feebly and muttered feverish nonsense.

"My God, she's freezing!" Joe said. "And wet."

"She's also supposed to be onstage right now," Matilda snapped. She hit me again.

"Darling, stop! She's unconscious. And very ill. She can't go on like this." Joe sounded relieved.

"Doctor," I moaned.

Zadok pounced. "You see? She's asking for me."

"What were you doing to her, you fiend?" The Prince brandished his sword.

"Matilda, I think we should let the doctor have a look at her," Joe urged.

"Oxford University, did you say?" Matilda asked.

"Yes. Dr. Zadok." Panting from his fight, Zadok added bashfully, "I distinguished myself in science and theology."

"Can you get her up and on her feet, Dr. Zadok?"

He knelt beside me. Through my lashes, I could see that he had a split lip. "I doubt it. All her symptoms indicate cryogenic fever."

"Come again?"

"She's got to be put in a warm bath right away. I'm prescribing a strong dose of *aqua vitae,* to be followed by a course of *pollo brodo*—I'd say four times a day for a week."

"A *week?*" Matilda said. "Now wait a minute. She's got to perform—"

"And I'd advise you all to stand back," Zadok added. "Her condition is highly contagious."

Well, it's amazing how fast that room emptied out. Dismissed from work, I leaned feebly on Zadok as he escorted me through the stage door. I knew there was no such thing as cryogenic fever, but I was curious about his prescription. As soon as we were outside, I asked him what *aqua vitae* and *pollo brodo* were.

"Brandy and chicken soup." He dabbed at his lip and winced. "What a week I'm having."

"You did well, Mr. Zadok."

"It really is Dr. Zadok, you know."

"Oxford University?"

"Yes, among others. Shall I escort you home?"

"I'm not going home. I'm going with you, to talk to Cowboy Dan."

"Duke."

"Whatever. I want to know what's happening to these women. The sooner we wrap this up, the sooner I can go back to work."

"But—"

"And if we can resolve this…this thing before another actress has time to learn Virtue's part—"

"Miss Diamond, you—"

"Call me Esther."

"Max. How do you do?"

"Max, no one has a greater stake in this mess than I do. I can't go onstage now, and I very much *want* to go onstage."

He wrung his hands. "There may be great danger."

"I live in New York City—don't tell *me* about danger."

"I have to do this, but you—"

"Why do you 'have' to do this?" I asked.

"Well, it's my job."

"I see," I said, not seeing at all. "Well, if I'm ever going to do *my* job again, it seems that I must help you with yours. After all, three women have already disappeared, Max. Isn't that indication enough that you need a little help?"

"Oh dear. Perhaps you're right."

"Thank you." It was so nice to be told, for the first time in this whole affair, that I was right. "Shall we go?"

We took a cab up to the Waldorf-Astoria on Park Avenue. I figured Max must be from out of town—*way* out of town. Aside from his general strangeness, he had to be physically forced into the taxi; then he sat with his eyes closed and a fine sheen of sweat covering his face while he muttered incantations nonstop until we arrived safely at our destination. He was shaking when I paid the driver and helped him out of the cab.

"I could feel the forces of chaos encroaching on my cosmic destiny," he said in a shaken voice.

"New York cabs take some people that way."

I saw the doorman give us a doubtful glance as we entered the hotel's elegant lobby. Max looked peculiar enough, but I was still wearing Virtue's costume. I might have gotten away with the gaudy, low-cut, fluttering gown and ballet slippers, but the gold stars and fake bird nestled in my hair, not to mention the glitter dusted onto my cheeks, shoulders and chest, probably dented my credibility.

"Do you know what room the Cowboy is in?" I asked Max. I had a shrewd suspicion the desk clerk might not want to tell us.

"Yes. I wrote it down somewhere." Max started searching through the pockets of his voluminous duster.

"Nice coat," I said. "Looks genuine."

"Oh, it is. It was bequeathed to me by a gunfighter."

"A gunfighter?"

"The bullet hole left by his final encounter wasn't that difficult to repair, but I did have some trouble getting the blood out of... Ah, here it is!" He waved a piece of paper at me.

"This looks like a shopping list."

"Oops! So it is."

While he continued rummaging through his pockets, I looked over the list he had absently handed me. "Licorice, deodorant, honey, oil of roses..." I frowned. "Dare I ask why you need cobalt and zinc?"

"New experiment. Now, where did I put it?" He plucked an assortment of dried leaves and roots out of his breast pocket.

I continued reading. One item stopped me cold. "Dragon's blood?"

"I've been looking for months. I don't suppose you know a good source?"

"Not offhand. Uh, Max..."

"Oh! Here's that formula! I thought I'd lost it." He dropped a sheet of that familiar M.Z. letterhead onto the pile of stuff accumulating at his feet. It was covered with scribbling, strange charts and symbols. The lettering looked vaguely familiar.

"Is that Hebrew?"

"Aramaic."

"Why do—?"

"Aha! Cowboy Duke's room number." He showed it to me.

"It's on the ninth floor."

"Nine. That's a very good number," he murmured, shoving things back into his pockets. "A trilogy of threes."

We crossed the lobby and got into an elevator. "I prefer stairs," Max said uneasily.

"Not nine floors of them."

A respectable-looking middle-aged couple got into the elevator with us. "Twelve, please," the man said. I pressed the button.

"Costume party?" the woman asked me.

"Funeral," I said.

We rode to the ninth floor in silence.

Cowboy Duke Dempsey welcomed us personally into an enormous, plush suite overlooking Park Avenue. East Texas fairly dripped from his tongue. "Well, howdy! Come on in, come right on in, young lady!" If his handshake got any more enthusiastic, my arm would fall off.

"I'm real pleased to meet you!" the Cowboy assured me. "And it sure is a relief to see you again, Maximillian. Come on in, come in and make yourselves at home. That sure is a pretty outfit you're wearing, young lady. Now just set yourselves down, and Dixie here will get you whatever you need. Dixie, honey?"

"I thought Dixie disappeared," I said.

"That was Dolly," Duke explained.

"Oh."

"This here's my little girl."

"How do you do?" I said to Duke's "little" girl. She was about eighteen years old, tall, buxom and wasp-waisted, with miles of flaxen blond hair, cornflower-blue eyes and sun-kissed skin that fairly glowed with good health.

"Ain't she pretty?"

"Oh, Daddy!" Dixie blushed becomingly.

"Are you in the act, too?" I asked.

"She sure is," Duke said. "And she ain't doing that disappearing act until we find out what happened to Dolly."

"Oh, Daddy!" Dixie said again.

"You *want* to do it?" I asked.

"She's got show business in her veins," the Cowboy said proudly. Clearly a love of spectacle ran in Duke's veins; the sheer drama of his fringe-edged and rhine-stone-studded clothes made it clear why my own cos-tume didn't give him cause to pause.

I looked around the suite. "I can see that show business has been good to you, Duke."

"Oh, I don't earn nothing for the act. Magic is my hobby. Clubs, charity events, family gatherings. No, all this—" he gestured carelessly at our palatial sur-roundings "—is paid for by my business interests."

"Oil?"

"Condoms."

"Good investment."

He grinned. "I got in on the ground floor. Now what'll you have to drink, young lady?"

Max and I both declined food and drink before settling into comfy chairs and getting down to business. Cowboy Duke and Dixie, it turned out, lived on a vast ranch in Texas but had been staying in New York for the past six weeks. Dixie had finished high school one semester early, and with honors. Since she wouldn't start college until the fall, she had asked her father if she could come to New York this spring to participate in a prestigious (and expensive) eight-week drama program at one of the leading institutions.

"Of course I agreed," the Cowboy said. "I can't refuse her nothing, not since her mama died."

"Oh, I'm sorry. When was that?"

"Fifteen years ago." He smiled at Dixie. "Anyhow, there was no way I was gonna let my little girl live all alone in New York City. No, indeedy. I can operate my business interests from here, at least for a couple of months, so I came along with her."

"How nice." I suspected that half of Dixie's motivation for coming to New York had been an understandable desire to escape her father's watchful eye.

I said to Duke, "So tell me what happened last night." There had been no point in trying to get a coherent explanation out of Max during the cab ride.

Although the Cowboy was too much of a gentleman

to say so, especially in front of his daughter, it became pretty clear that Dolly the Dancing Cowgirl was his mistress. She and Dixie had been performing with him for several years, ever since a chance meeting with David Copperfield had gotten him interested in magic. Apparently, Copperfield had managed to make the Cowboy's whole house disappear on one occasion.

A relative newcomer to the art of magic and illusion, Duke (like Barclay Preston-Cole III) had the drive, money and time to acquire knowledge and props faster than he acquired skill.

"But it's just a hobby, after all. I'm really a businessman and a rancher," he said somewhat wistfully.

"Oh, but you've been doing real well, Daddy," Dixie said encouragingly. She seemed like a sweet girl. "You should see how much the act has improved, Miss Diamond. I'll bet Daddy could give up condoms and be a professional."

Duke blushed. "Oh, pshaw!"

I'd never actually heard anyone say that before. "So the Urban Cowboys Club invited you to perform at their annual gala?" I prodded.

"That's right. I flew Dolly up from Texas for the occasion." He shook his head sadly. "I sure do blame myself for what's happened."

"Oh, Daddy!" Dixie took his hand.

Like Joe and Barclay, he had put his assistant into a vanishing box (in this case, a large, complex and extremely expensive hollow horse decorated with—

what else?—fringe and rhinestones) that they had used many times in the past. Dolly had disappeared right on cue. And Duke, somehow sensing that she had *really* disappeared, tore that horse apart backstage, looking for her.

"But she wasn't there," he concluded.

Hearing nothing new or useful, I looked at Max. "How did you find out about this?"

"I felt the disturbance in the fabric of this dimension," he mumbled without looking up, "so I cast runes in search of its source."

"Uh, Max—"

"However he found out, we were sure glad to see Maximillian," the Cowboy said. "No one else seems able to help us."

"Certainly not the cops," I grumbled, thinking of Lopez.

"This is a realm in which the forces of law and order are helpless," Max said.

"What do you make of all this, Dr. Zadok?" Dixie asked.

Max looked around at all of us. "The question is, why?"

I shook my head. "No, surely the question is, *how?*"

"Some form of black magic, I suspect," Max replied.

"Black magic?" I repeated.

"Hmm. Teleportation. Or transmutation? Clearly an unorthodox method, in any event."

"Max," I said.

He stroked his beard. "Apparently the props—the boxes and cages—are necessary. Are they cursed?"

"Cursed?" the Cowboy repeated.

"Max," I said, getting to my feet.

"Are they specially designed to be windows to the other side? And how are the victims selected? How many are needed? How many more will there be?"

Dixie gasped. Duke went pale. I decided we'd made enough of an impression on our hosts for one evening.

"Thanks so much for your time," I said, yanking Max to his feet. "We'll be in touch. And don't worry. We'll find out what happened to Dolly if it's the last thing I do. Coming Max?"

"What is this mumbo jumbo about black magic and the other side?" I demanded as we walked down the street.

"I'm just speculating, I'm afraid. None of the usual signs of demonic possession, shapeshifting or infernal evocation seem to apply. Of course, I suppose time travel is a theoretical possibility, but it would seem to be involuntary and highly problematic in this case. No, for the time being, my theory—"

"Is crazy!"

"Hmm. Do you have a theory?"

"Not on the tip of my tongue," I said. "But I'll think of one."

"Very well. In the meantime, there are two things we must accomplish tonight."

"What?"

"If Mr. Herlihy's crystal cage is cursed—"

"Oh, for—"

"Then we must destroy it."

I stopped, surprised. "Destroy it?"

"We can't risk another woman getting into it. Surely you can see that?"

I didn't know what to make of all this, but Max was right. We couldn't let someone who didn't know the truth—whatever it was—risk getting into that cage.

"Okay, agreed," I said. "And the other thing?"

"We must determine the source of the latest disappearance."

"The latest?" I felt cold seep through me. "But I thought Dolly the Dancing Cowgirl was the latest—"

"That was *last* night," he said. "I didn't want to alarm Dixie and Cowboy Duke, but while we were in consultation with them this evening, I sensed it again. Unmistakable by now." He nodded. "A localized dimensional disturbance. Someone else has disappeared."

Max refused to get into a taxi again. Instead, we walked to the Plaza Hotel at the edge of the park and hired a horse and carriage. I'd never been in one of those things because they're outrageously expensive.

To my surprise, all the carriage drivers lined up across the street from the Plaza seemed to know Max.

"Yo! Doc Zadok! Whaddaya say?"

"Hey, Doc! What do you hear from the spirit world?"

"Good evening," Max said, taking off his fedora and shaking hands.

"Can I give you a lift, Dr. Zadok?"

"Hey, you boys get back in line! I'm first. Right over here, Dr. Zadok. Let me help you into my carriage, miss."

"Thank you," I said, taking the beefy hand offered to me. Now *this* guy could lift ice cream-loving nymphs overhead all night long and not feel the strain.

"Thank you, Ralph." Max clambered in beside me.

Ralph climbed up to the driver's seat. "You want I should take you home, Dr. Zadok?"

"No, we're going to the theater actually. The New—*oof!*"

"Just drop us off at Greenwich and Sixth," I said.

"Okay." Ralph flicked the reins and we were off.

"You idiot," I whispered to Max. "If we're going to break into the building and sabotage valuable equipment, the last thing we need to do is announce our presence to half of Christopher Street by pulling up at the front door in a horse-drawn carriage."

"I'm sorry, I didn't think. It's so seldom that I break the law."

"Oh, really? How about the night you broke into the theater to slip that newspaper clipping under my dressing room door?"

"That was an emergency," he pointed out. "Anyhow, I didn't damage anything."

"How did you get in, anyway? 'Transmutation' again, I suppose?"

"No. I only transmute in dire circumstances. It's much harder than it looks, you know."

"I believe that. I've seen Joe and Magic Magnus do it, and even Golly and I do a version of it when Virtue appears at the end of Act Two, but you did it in my dressing room. How?"

"Well, the principles of thaumaturgy rely largely upon the powers of the mind. Naturally, some technical ability is called for."

I sighed. He sounded like Joe. "Never mind. How are we going to get in tonight? I'm no lock-picker."

He frowned. "It shouldn't present too much of a problem."

Since he apparently wasn't going to elaborate, I said, "I gather you travel this way—horse and carriage—fairly often?"

"It's the only civilized way to get around town."

"You don't like elevators, you don't like cabs." He had also refused to take a bus or subway train when I suggested it. "Do you have some kind of phobia?"

"I just can't get used to modern transportation," he said. "Speed kills."

We rode the rest of the way in silence. I wrestled with the Mystery of the Vanishing Ladies, unwilling to succumb to Max's mutterings about curses and black magic. Could Golly, Dolly and Clarisse have vanished voluntarily? Since coincidence seemed astronomically unlikely, that would mean they had planned this together. That seemed equally far-fetched. How would they have met in the first place? A magicians' convention?

No, I decided. Even if Dolly, the Texan mistress of a multimillionaire condom cowboy, had met an uptown society girl like Clarisse at such a function, I doubted Golly Gee had ever attended anything like that. Before meeting Joe a couple of months ago, she couldn't even *spell* the word *magician*. (And wherever she was now, she probably still couldn't). Besides, Dolly had only arrived in New York yesterday, and according to Duke, it was her first time here.

And what about the magicians? Duke reported experiencing a strange sensation during the vanishing; like Joe and Barclay, he knew Dolly was gone before it became apparent to anyone else. There had been no press coverage of the Urban Cowboys affair. Clarisse's disappearance was so far the only one that had appeared in the news—and, as far as I knew, even that had received only the brief paragraph Max had sent me. If the magicians were somehow responsible, they weren't doing it for publicity. Quite the opposite, in fact; Joe couldn't bear the merest mention of Golly's disappearance, Barclay was terrified his father would find out, and Duke just wanted Dolly back.

Of course, that could be mere pretense. Perhaps

the magicians had found a brilliant way to murder their assistants? No, that didn't make sense. There was no need to go through elaborate rituals in front of an audience just to kill someone.

Did the three women have any enemies? Hard to say. I gathered Lopez thought *I* might be Golly's enemy. Barclay had mentioned Clarisse had a bitter enemy, some society girl. And Dolly? Who knew? Maybe Dixie knew Dolly was sleeping with Duke and hated her for it.

Did the magicians have enemies? Aha! Now, that was a good question. Certainly their lives were being disrupted by these strange events. Indeed, if we couldn't find out what happened to the women, the men's lives might even be ruined.

The carriage finally pulled to a stop outside a coffee shop on Sixth Avenue. I was relieved to get out; I didn't think we'd made many new friends by taking up a whole lane at our speed. My eyes bulged when Max paid the driver. Like I said, horse-drawn carriages aren't cheap. Whoever Maximillian Zadok was, he evidently had plenty of money.

I was still wearing Virtue's costume, which was gaudy enough to draw a few curious glances even here in the West Village. I brushed some flaking glitter off my flowing skirts and sighed, wishing I had thought to grab my clothes before fleeing the theater. The last thing I wanted right now was to attract attention or be memorable.

At my insistence, Max and I approached the New View Venue indirectly, by walking down West Tenth Street and creeping up behind it. Along the way, I suggested, "Perhaps we should sit down with the magicians involved. All together, I mean."

"Good idea," Max agreed.

"They may have a common enemy."

"That would make things considerably easier." He frowned. "On the other hand, they may simply have different enemies who are all clients of the same sorcerer."

"Uh-huh." I had no idea how to respond to such bizarre comments. Nonetheless, I couldn't deny that Max was the only person in New York who had discovered and made the connection among all three disappearances. Undecided about how to handle him, I followed him to the stage door of the New View Venue.

Luckily for us, the theater didn't employ an all-night security guard, and Matilda was too cheap to hire one to guard Joe's equipment. But that didn't mean that breaking in would be easy. Not only were the double doors locked, they were bound together by a heavy chain with a sturdy padlock.

"All right, Dr. Zadok," I said as I examined the lock, "I'm stumped. Any suggestions?"

"Stand back."

"What are you going to do?"

"Open it."

Wondering what he intended, I backed away. "Can you pick locks?"

"Not exactly."

He took several deep breaths with his eyes closed, as if preparing for meditation, then assumed a prayerful posture with his head bowed, palms pressed together and fingertips brushing his lips. He muttered something I couldn't understand, then opened his eyes and stared fiercely at the lock. Moving his hands, he made a sharp turning motion with his wrists.

The padlock snapped open as if someone had inserted a key and turned it. I stopped breathing.

Max spread his arms in a graceful waving motion. The chain slithered like a snake, unraveling itself to fall away from the doors and lie on the ground. Max pulled his arms toward himself, and the doors opened outward, welcoming us.

My blood chilled and my eyes watered. Max took my arm.

"You're shaking," he said in surprise.

"Wh-wh-wh-"

"Where do they keep the crystal cage?"

"Prop room." My legs wobbled as I led the way.

The door was locked, of course. Max opened it with a wave of his hand. I thought I was going to be sick. Blank-minded with shock, I followed him into the room.

"This is it?" he asked, examining the cage.

I nodded mutely, staring at him.

"There doesn't seem to be anything unusual about it. Still, there could be a protective anti-divinative shield around it. I have heard of such things."

I sat down quite suddenly. The floor was cold.

Max breathed, muttered and gestured some more. Nothing happened. He looked embarrassed. "Fire is my weakest element," he confessed. "I'll try again."

He did. This time, the glass sides of the cage seemed to melt and curl in on themselves. By the time he was done, the prop was a charred tragedy of twisted glass and metal.

"Oh, that was rather good." He sounded pleased. "Shall we go?"

"Wait." My voice was weak. "Max, who *are* you?"

CHAPTER

4

There are more things in heaven and earth than are dreamed of in our philosophy, Shakespeare tells us...and I know better than to argue with a playwright.

This observation about the strangeness of the cosmos is offered by Hamlet to his friend Horatio, who has trouble believing that the ghost of Hamlet's father is haunting Elsinore. Now I understood exactly how Horatio must have felt upon seeing the specter with his own eyes.

I gibbered incoherently as we walked to Max's place, which he decided should be our next stop. To say I was shocked by what I had seen would be rather like saying that World War Two was violent. I was incoherent (but highly verbal) with stunned disbelief. I kept blinking my eyes as hard as possible, then looking at Max to see if he was still there, strolling beside me. Several times, I stopped on the sidewalk and vigorously shook my head at odd angles, as if this would clear it—or else cause evidence of sudden madness to fall out of my ears.

Max murmured something about people staring, then added, "Of course, they may just be staring because you've got those glittery birds on your head."

Apart from that comment, he was silent while we walked and I mumbled. So I finally said to him, with a sense of outrage I couldn't explain, "Why don't you *say* something?"

"I've learned through experience that it's best to let this period of unpleasant surprise pass into acceptance before trying to converse rationally."

"You've learned? Through experience? Unpleasant surprise?" My tone was shrill, but I was in no condition to control it. "This happens *often*?"

"In fact, no. I try not to involve mundanes in my work—"

"Mundanes? *Mundanes?*"

"—for this very reason."

"*What* reason? What? What!"

"A certain agitation overwhelms most people upon being exposed to the multidimensional truths of a complex cosmos."

I seized his throat and throttled him.

"Esther, please! No violence!" he wheezed.

I realized what I was doing. "Oh! Sorry!" I backed off, hands raised in apology. "Sorry, sorry. I didn't mean to… What are…?" I felt dizzy and staggered a little.

"Breathe," he instructed, "breathe."

"Huh? Oh, right." I inhaled and exhaled a few times. "Max, I don't understand—"

"I think it would be best to provide you with a chair and a soothing beverage before we chat about this."

"Chat," I repeated.

"While I don't mean this as a criticism, your agitation is attracting some attention to us—even in this neighborhood, where flamboyant behavior is not unknown. And given that we're dealing with a treacherous problem—"

"What…what treacherous—?"

"The disappearing women," he reminded me gently.

"Oh, right!" Another wave of dizziness.

"Keep breathing."

"The disappearing…yes." I'd forgotten about them.

"So far, widespread panic has been avoided," Max said, "and it would certainly be best to keep it that way. So we should be discreet in public."

"Uh-huh." I looked around in bewilderment. We were on a street that was quiet by Manhattan standards. It was lined by elegant town houses, most of them from the nineteenth century. "There are trees here," I said, my shocked mind focusing on something manageable. Ahead of us I saw a church with gardens that looked vaguely familiar. "Is that…um?"

"St. Luke's in the Fields," Max said.

"St. Luke's..." I glanced around me, concentrating on facts I could actually assimilate. "We're still in the West Village."

"Yes!" He sounded pleased, as if I were a bright pupil correctly answering a difficult question.

We had, in fact, come very little distance from the New View Venue, which was barely two blocks away. "This is close to the theater," I said vaguely.

"Yes. That's why I was alerted to, uh...these events by Miss Gee's, um...unfortunate experience." He kept looking around warily, as if expecting the street's few other pedestrians to eavesdrop on us.

"Huh?"

"I mean to say..." We overtook two well-dressed men holding hands while walking a bull terrier. They were engaged in an animated debate about invest-ment strategies and they didn't pay any attention to us. Max lowered his voice. "I live just around this cor-ner. So it was due to the proximity of your musical play that I first noticed the phenomenon that con-cerns us." He steered me past the gay couple and into a mews that, even in the dark, looked charming and prosperous.

"You mean, because Golly's, er, unfortunate expe-rience occurred so close to you? To your home?"

"Yes." Seeing there were no people in this little court, he continued. "An expenditure of power great enough to make someone disappear involuntarily could not help but attract my attention when it occurred that close to me. Especially since there is, as near as I can ascertain, no attempt to disguise these disturbances with wards or cloaks."

"Why not?" I asked, though I didn't really understand what he was saying.

He shrugged. "Arrogance? A need for haste? Ignorance of my presence here? Insufficient power or skill?"

"Speaking of your presence here—"

"So I immediately hastened out in search of the source of the disturbance."

"And you found us?"

"Actually," he admitted, "I saw the police cars parked outside the New View Venue and realized that this was unlikely to be mere coincidence."

"So you lurked?"

"I made discreet inquiries," he said with dignity. "Avoiding unnecessary contact with the police, of course."

"That was wise." If Lopez had heard Max talking, he might have felt obliged to take him to a psychiatric hospital.

Max continued. "A young lady with a great deal of facial piercing who was loitering outside to enjoy some tobacco told me what had happened."

Recognizing our assistant stage manager from this description, I said, "And the game was afoot."

"Oh!" Max smiled in pleased surprise. "Are you a fan of Sir Arthur Conan Doyle's work?"

"Not particularly."

"I am. Though it cannot be denied that some of the ideas he adopted in his personal life were most peculiar." Max shook his head. "Séances, spirit guides, channeling… Really, the nonsense that some people are gullible enough to believe!"

My head was whirling. "Max…"

"Here we are."

We stopped in front of an old, ivy-covered town house. A big window on the ground floor displayed many books. The lettering across the window read "Zadok's Rare and Used Books."

"You're a bookseller?" I said in confusion.

"It's a sideline. Mostly to avoid unconscionable persecution by the Internal Revenue Service."

"Visible means of support?" I guessed.

"It seemed best to assume a profession they could easily categorize. My predecessor lacked such a ruse, and they hounded him until he was obliged to abandon his duty here and flee the country."

"There's Evil, and then there's *Evil*."

"Indeed." He put his hand on the door, pushed it open and gestured for me to enter.

"Don't you lock your door?" The shop was obviously not open for business this late.

"It is locked," he said, as I brushed past him. "But since I kept losing my keys, it seemed sensible to cast a spell so that it's always open to me."

I turned around as the door closed behind him.

"Okay, that's it! That's *it*. Who *are* you? Casting spells, melting the crystal cage, sensing Golly's disappearance from two blocks away, breaking into the theater tonight without even touching anything, dragon's blood, curses, black magic—"

"Some *aqua vitae*, perhaps?" Max suggested with a concerned frown as my voice grew shrill again.

I took a breath. "Yes." Another breath. "Yes. That's a good idea." If ever there was a night when strong drink seemed advisable, surely this was it.

Max turned on the overhead lights, then started rummaging around in a massive, dark, very old-looking, wooden cupboard. It was about six feet tall and at least that wide, and had a profusion of drawers and doors. Not finding what he wanted in the first two cabinet doors he opened, he tried another, higher up. A bunch of papers, a box of candles and some feathers fell on his head.

"Oh dear," he said, "I really should tidy up one of these days." He closed that cabinet and tried another. Flames burst forth from this one, and a roar that sounded like the wailing of the damned emerged from its interior. Max slammed the door shut and muttered, "God's teeth, not *again*."

I had meanwhile retreated halfway across the shop. "Max, what *is* the—"

"No, no, don't despair," he said cheerfully. "I know I've got some brandy here somewhere. I just can't quite remember where... Aha!" He triumphantly held up a crystal decanter containing glowing amber liquid. Literally glowing.

I said, "Um, I don't think—"

"I'll just find some glasses, and then we can…"

"Should you really keep a thing like that right here in the shop?" I asked warily. "Where, you know, unsuspecting customers might fiddle with it?"

Apparently not understanding what I meant, he glanced over his shoulder at me. I gestured to the cupboard and its contents. "Oh, no need to worry," Max said. "It's enchanted. Only I can open it. Well, Hieronymus will be able to open it, too, if he ever manages to say the incantation right. Poor boy. It's not his fault, of course…"

"Hieronymus?"

"My assistant."

As Max continued rifling through the cupboard, I backed a little farther away from it, feeling I'd had enough shocks for one night. I looked around, shivering with reaction, and noticed despite my jangled nerves that the bookshop was, in fact, quite charming. It had well-worn hardwood floors and a broad-beamed ceiling. The walls were painted dusty rose and lined with bookcases. Indeed, row after row of bookcases filled most of the shop, their symmetrical lines broken up by a comfortable-looking seating area, as well as a small refreshments stand where (I gathered from the sign written in Max's by-now familiar hand) customers could help themselves to coffee, tea, cookies…and snuff. I wondered if there was much demand for the snuff. There was also a large, somewhat careworn walnut table with books, papers, an abacus, writing implements and other paraphernalia on it.

While Max muttered, rummaged around, and then broke something that sounded like one of the glasses he'd been searching for, I browsed a little. I don't know much about collectibles, but some of these books looked valuable to me. A number of them were bound in leather and seemed extremely old, and many of the titles were in Latin. Other bookcases were filled with mass-produced contemporary books.

"Come, Esther, let's sit," Max said, now carrying a slightly tarnished silver tray that bore the brandy decanter and a couple of mismatched glasses.

I followed him over to two prettily-upholstered easy chairs next to a fireplace, sat down and accepted the glass of glowing spirits he handed to me. I sniffed my *aqua vitae,* studied its fluctuating light and asked, "Are you sure this is safe to drink?"

"Perfectly safe. Oh! Unless you're Lithuanian? You don't *look* Lithuanian, but I would be the first to admit—"

"No, I'm not Lithuanian."

"In that case, it's perfectly safe." He paused before taking a sip. "I'm not Lithuanian, either."

I couldn't place his faint accent, so I asked, "Where

are you from?" I set down my brandy and started un-tangling my hair from Virtue's headdress so I could finally take it off.

"I'm originally from a village near Prague," Max said. "But that was long ago. After my father died, having left me a small inheritance, I went to Vienna to pursue my education."

"Did you ever go back home?" I removed the head-dress with a relieved sigh, set it down on the side table and combed my fingers through my hair.

"No, I never did. My father was my only family. After Vienna, I went to England, and, well, one gets so busy..." After a moment, he said, "Do try the brandy, Esther. You still look pale."

I closed my eyes, took a gulp, and felt the brandy burn its way down to my stomach, spreading a fiery sensation that, after about half a minute, turned into a soothing glow.

Then I heard a muffled explosion, felt heat and sensed light dancing against my closed lids. My eyes flew open and I jumped a little when I saw a fire burning merrily in the fireplace while Max, still seated comfortably, sipped his brandy.

I swallowed, glancing nervously between him and the fire. "Did you...did you...is that magic?"

He seemed faintly puzzled as he waved a hand holding a remote. "No, I've switched it on."

I looked at the fire again and realized how regu-larly and quietly the flames danced between the artistically shaped pieces of fake firewood. "Oh." I swallowed some more brandy. "A gas fireplace."

"Yes. It's so convenient! None of the tedium of trying to get a fire built, none of the mess to clean up. I had it installed this winter and am so pleased I went to the expense!"

"But…you can…" I gestured feebly. "You don't need…"

Max shook his head, looking modest. "Oh, as I think I already mentioned, fire is my weakest element. Besides, any unnecessary expenditure of my power is to be avoided."

"It is? Are there…moral consequences? Philosophical objections? Rules?"

"No." He seemed surprised at these suggestions. "It's just very tiring."

"Oh."

I sought a coherent way to pose the questions tumbling through my head. "But how do you…*do* that sort of thing? Unlocking the doors of the theater, destroying the crystal cage… That's, um, magic?"

"Yes." He nodded.

"So how do you do it?"

"A lot of study, training and practice." Max smiled bashfully and added, "And, of course, one must have an inherent gift."

"So it's a special talent? It isn't something that just anyone can learn to do?"

"Goodness, no!" He looked a little shocked at the

suggestion. "Few people are born with the necessary gifts. And even fewer feel a call to rigorously pursue their gifts in service of a sacred duty."

"How about pursuing Evil and power?"

He sighed. "Well, yes, that's also an option."

"And...no one notices?"

"Notices what?"

"Notices people like you. And the things you do."

"Well, sometimes, of course. But we do try to be discreet. For most of my life, after all, mundanes have been tormented by dark superstitions that make many of them somewhat intolerant of the esoteric arts."

"Intolerant as in, oh, torture, imprisonment and execution?" I guessed.

"Yes. Times have changed, of course, but not necessarily for the better. In recent years, some of my colleagues have been committed to psychiatric wards, and several others have been hounded by tabloid writers."

"What about something like these disappearances? Don't such events raise speculation?"

"Until I intervened to protect you, you had no suspicion of the true nature of Golly Gee's disappearance, did you?"

"No." And I initially thought the truth sounded crazy and impossible.

Max said, "People explain events through reasoning which is already familiar to them. And they have a strong tendency to shrug off that which they *cannot* explain via a well-worn path of reasoning."

"So what are the limits of this…this power?" I asked.

"That depends on the individual."

"But there are limits?"

"Oh, of course! For one thing, as I mentioned, the work is tiring, and one can easily run out of power. Just as an athlete, no matter how fit, eventually runs out of energy. Or just as a singer, no matter how well trained, grows hoarse if she over-uses her voice."

"I see."

"And there's no denying that I'm not as young as I used to be."

"Not as young…" Realizing that, like it or not, more shocks were in store for me tonight, I asked, "What did you mean, back in my dressing room this evening, when you said you graduated from Oxford University in…in…" It was so absurd I couldn't say it.

"Yes, in 1678," Max said. "I don't normally brag about my education, of course, but the circumstances tonight seemed to call for some assurance of credentials."

"Uh, Max, if you were a university student in the seventeenth century, that would make you more than three hundred years old now."

"Nearly three hundred and fifty, in fact. I seldom tell mundanes, of course. But it seems there should be total frankness between the two of us, don't you think?"

"Uh-huh." I couldn't seem to close my gaping mouth all the way.

"In that spirit, may I ask you something?"

"Uh-huh."

He said seriously, "Does my age show?"

"Not really." My head was throbbing. "But it does happen to be impossible."

"Oh, no. Only very unusual."

I started to point out that this was ridiculous, there was no such thing as a three-hundred-and-fifty-year-old human being; it defied all laws of nature. Until I realized that the very thing I now believed in with all my heart—women magically disappearing nightly onstage—was also ridiculous, impossible, in defiance of everything I knew to be true and real and...

"I think I'm going to be sick," I muttered, suddenly feeling nauseated.

"You should drink that brandy more slowly," Max advised. "It's very powerful."

I laid my head on the backrest of my comfortable chair and gazed at a fixed point on the ceiling—which was now the only fixed point in my entire universe, it seemed. The heat from the fire was soothing. It was late April and the weather was mild tonight. But I felt cold in my bones right now.

After a moment, I said, "Okay, Max, let's say it's not impossible to be over three hundred years old. Let's say it's merely unusual."

"Well, *very* unusual."

"How is it possible?"

"That's a fair question."

"So glad you think so," I said, keeping my gaze locked on my treasured fixed point on the ceiling.

"While I was at Oxford—"

"You distinguished yourself in science and theology. Yes, I know."

"No, I mean to say, while at Oxford, I became interested in alchemy."

"Alchemy is in the syllabus at Oxford University?"

"Well, things have changed a great deal at my alma mater," he said sadly. "And not always for the better. Still, a dangerous art like alchemy, such a volatile science... Perhaps it's for the best."

"Which is it? Art or science?"

"Both. And certainly my theology studies were very helpful, too."

"Certainly." I stared hard at that ceiling, wondering if I'd wake up in a hospital soon and be told I'd been unconscious for days after an explosion in the dry-cleaning shop beneath my apartment.

"So, naturally, I was apprenticed to a learned alchemist after completing my university studies."

"Naturally." Or perhaps my last date, a musician whose conversation was, alas, no match for his Byronic looks, had slipped some weird psychedelic drug into my wine, and I would wake up from this bizarre dream with a terrible hangover and wearing clothing that wasn't mine.

"I learned a great deal from my master," Max said, "it cannot be denied. However, he continued his researches and experiments past the point in life when he was in full control of his faculties."

"Indeed?" I didn't think I was insane. I did have a great-aunt on my father's side who claimed she'd been abducted by aliens, but she was the only person in the family whose mental health was in serious doubt; and, besides, she was only related to me by marriage.

"I fell ill during my fifth year of study with him," Max said. "The ailment probably wasn't life-threatening, but the fever did weaken me too much for me to attend closely the nature of the medicaments he was giving me."

The other possibility, of course, was that this was really happening.

"And, as I've hinted," Max said, "he was no longer the best judge of his own actions."

And if this was really happening…

"There have been times when I have regarded what happened next as a misfortune," he continued, "and others when I have felt it a great gift. Mostly, however, I believe it is simply my destiny. At least, believing so is how I have maintained such a clear mind all these years."

If this was really happening, I needed to pull myself together and assist Max. If for no other reason, I realized, than the fact that he had quite possibly saved my life by preventing me from getting into the crystal cage. And he was trying to save other lives, too: the next potential victim…and the women who'd already vanished.

"What did happen next, Max?" I asked, feeling the brandy taking effect as I accepted that this was indeed really happening.

"Instead of a potion to ease my fever, he fed me the Elixir of Life."

Abandoning my fixed point at last, I lifted my head and looked at him. "What's that?"

"Well, it wasn't *the* Elixir of Life, it was *an* elixir of life," he amended. "But the effects have been pronounced."

"Go on."

"The elixir did not confer immortality on me—"

"Immortality?" I blurted.

"—but it did substantially slow down the aging process."

"How? How is that possible?"

"Unfortunately, I don't know."

"Why not?"

"I recovered from my illness shortly thereafter, but it was quite some time before I realized what must have happened."

"How long a time?"

"About thirty years."

"Oh. That long a time?"

"My master was long dead by then. To this day, I don't know if he never drank of the elixir, or if, for unknown reasons, it just didn't affect him as it did me."

"So he was dead, and thirty years later…"

"I noticed that I had changed very little, while my contemporaries were clearly in their declining years, if not already dead."

"I guess nothing slips by *you.*"

He looked embarrassed. "Well, to say that *I* noticed it is perhaps an exaggeration. I suspected something, but it was my wife who actually brought the matter to light."

"She was aging normally?"

"Yes. And once she raised the subject with me, it was some time before I could convince her that I did not know why I wasn't aging and that I was certainly *not* withholding the relevant potion or spell from her. Time and time again I explained that, now that it had come to my attention, I was as bewildered by my slow aging process as she was! But would she listen? No, of course not!" He was off and rolling now. "I lost count of how many nights I was forced to sleep in my laboratory because my wife had barred the bedroom door against me! I tried reasoning with her, but to no avail. I swore on every book that a person could deem holy that I was not lying to her or hiding anything from her, but the woman was simply *irrational,* I tell you! Do you know, she even—"

"Max!" I said. *"Max."*

"What?"

"I'm not good at math, but I gather this all occurred well before the American Revolution?"

"Well…" He blinked. "Yes."

"Perhaps it's time to let it go."

"Hmm." He sighed. "Perhaps you're right." Then he added, "After her death, it took me a century to contemplate marriage again." The expression on his face indicated that grief over his loss wasn't why he'd remained single for the next hundred years.

"So how did you figure out what had happened?" I asked.

"Well, once I realized that there was something distinctly unusual about my aging process, I reported it to the Magnum Collegium."

"The Great College?" I guessed. "What was that?"

"It is…" He shrugged. "A varied group of individuals united by a common interest."

"So it still exists?"

"Oh, indeed! And over the centuries it's grown to several thousand members worldwide."

"But what is it? What is the group's common interest?"

"We confront Evil."

"Well," I said. "Hmm. Uh-huh. I see." If someone ever tells you he's a member of a worldwide club whose mission is to confront Evil, I defy you to come up with a pithy reply on the spot.

"I know what you're thinking," Max said.

"I sincerely doubt that," I said.

"You're wondering why, if we've been confronting Evil for centuries, there's still so much of it in the world."

"I definitely would have thought of that," I said.

"If you hadn't, you know, brought it up before I had a chance to."

"It's a very big job," Max said sadly.

"What is?"

"Fighting Evil."

"Oh. Of course. Yes, I can see that it would be."

"And there aren't that many of us," he added. "Not when you consider the scope of the challenge."

"Indeed. The Internal Revenue Service alone…"

"You see my point."

"Uh, Max, when you say Evil…"

"The great, dark, spiritual Evil which is forever in opposition to all that is compassionate and virtuous."

"Well. Okay, then. I can see how that would be a bad thing." Returning to the original point, I said, "So you reported your strangely slow aging process to the Collegium…"

"And they investigated. When physical tests, many of which were unpleasant…" He grimaced and gave a brief shudder. "When they produced no answers, I was sent to a sorceress in China—"

"You went all the way to China? In, what, the eighteenth century?"

"The whole process consumed some decades of my life," he admitted, "but those years were not without educational value."

"And the Chinese sorceress figured out that your master had slipped you a Mickey Finn, so to speak?"

"She had special powers of insight that enabled her

to traverse the pathways of my memory." He frowned. "Sadly, she was never the same again."

"I totally believe that, Max."

"That I had swallowed an elixir during my illness was a logical answer to the question plaguing me, since my master had devoted years of study and experimentation to the problem of immortality. And also since, when *not* feverish, I touched his cooking as little as possible."

"But he had not, I gather, shared the winning recipe for slow aging with you?"

"No. Indeed, I think it entirely possible he never even knew he had succeeded to such an extent. As I've mentioned, his mind was a bit foggy with advanced age when I fell ill."

"So you're walking around very, very long-lived," I said, "but with no idea what was in the potion that made you this way?"

"No idea," he agreed wearily. "I experimented for years. And every few decades, I submit to more tests on my person performed by members of the Collegium in search of an answer." He rubbed his head as if it was starting to ache, and repeated, "No idea. No idea. I don't even recall what the elixir tasted like. I was very disoriented for more than a week in my illness, and my master and his servant fed me a variety of brews. It could have been any one of them."

"Or a combination?"

"Yes." He nodded.

"A combination," I repeated. "That would certainly explain why he never drank the elixir himself, nor even knew he'd invented it."

"Having thought of this, for years I experimented with countless combinations of potions, some of them quite unpleasant, before realizing that it made no sense to keep wasting, in this fruitless fashion, the long life with which I'd been gifted."

"So then you turned to fighting Evil?"

"I made it my priority," he replied.

"And now…" I said. "Now there's Evil here."

"Esther, this is New York. There's *always* Evil here. It just happens to be focused in this puzzling manner at the moment."

"Is this why you've come here? The disappearing— Oh, no, it can't be them. You were already living here when Golly disappeared on Saturday, right?"

"I was indeed. But this *is*, in the larger sense, why I've come. A year ago, I was sent here as a representative of the Collegium, entrusted with the sacred mission of confronting Evil in New York City."

"How many representatives of the Collegium do we have in New York?"

"Including all five boroughs?"

"Yes," I said.

"Just me, really."

"I see."

"And it turns out that it's a very big job."

"No doubt," I said.

"Much bigger than I anticipated."

"Indeed."

"That's why, last year, I requested an assistant," Max said.

"Horatio?"

"Hieronymus."

"Right. Where is he?"

"He may be upstairs asleep. We both keep rooms above the shop, mine on the second floor, his on the third. But he's a very dedicated, serious young man, deeply devoted to his duty," Max said. "So it's possible he's out patrolling the city, even this late at night."

"In search of Evil?"

"Yes, he often does that." Max added, "And sometimes he goes sightseeing."

"What," I asked, "does Hieronymus think about our problem?"

"He's most intrigued. He's researching vanishings of a similar nature."

That caught my attention. "*Are* there vanishings of a similar nature?"

"None whatsoever, so far as he can ascertain."

"Oh." I let my shoulders slump.

Seeing this, he added, "But our researches only began a few days ago, Esther. After Miss Gee disappeared. We'll no doubt find a precedent soon, and that will lead us to a culprit, I promise you! Perhaps even a whole army of culprits!"

"Just one will do for me, Max."

"Meanwhile, we can rest assured that Cowboy Duke will not perform his disappearing act again while this Evil lurks among us."

"Barclay Preston-Cole III won't perform it again, either," I said. "At least, not until he's sure it's safe." Poor Barclay. I wondered if he'd have to forgo his big break and cancel his appearance at the Magic Cabaret.

"Barclay Preston-Cole III?"

"The Great Hidalgo. I met with him after you left me that clipping."

"Ah! And, of course, upon learning from the young lady with many facial piercings that you were Miss Gee's understudy and destined to perform the act in her place, I took steps to discourage you—"

"You *terrified* me."

"—from entering the crystal cage. And now that we have disabled it, we will not need to, er, terrorize whoever might have tried to go on in *your* place."

Despite the mild night and the warm fire, I felt a chill come over me again. "But you said there's been another disappearance tonight? You felt it, sensed it?" When he nodded, I asked, "Was it near us, then? Somewhere near the Waldorf?"

"I don't think so. I think the effect of these disturbances is becoming more noticeable to me as the fabric of this dimension becomes increasingly unstable with each new disappearance that is orchestrated."

"How do we pinpoint the latest one? I mean, how

do we find tonight's victims so we can help them?" And how would we explain the situation to them without sounding like dangerous crackpots?

He started to rise. "We'll need to—*yah!*" Max jumped when the phone rang. He closed his eyes and said, "I believe I shall never get used to that."

"The phone ringing?"

He nodded, walked over to where it sat on the desk on the other side of the shop and answered it.

I didn't really hear the conversation, which was brief. After hanging up, he called to me from behind the bookcases separating us.

"Esther?"

"Yes?"

"I know who tonight's victims are."

"Dr. Zadok, thank you *so* much for coming," said Darling Delilah. "It means so much to me that a busy man like you just dropped everything and came straight to my aid as soon as I called. Of course, I became *hysterical* as soon as it happened tonight. There was no *dealing* with me at first. So I can't tell you what a comfort it is to have you here now. I telephoned you because Satsy said that if anyone can help me, surely it's you."

Max nodded and smiled graciously at this effusive speech. Then he turned and asked Satsy, whose bulk required her to sit a little away from the table, "How did you know of me?"

"Well, I come to the bookshop all the time," Satsy said with a smile, "don't I? You have the best supply of occult books in the whole city! That's why I knew we should consult you."

I was surprised Max could forget someone of Satsy's remarkable appearance. He said, "I'm sorry, I know most of my regular customers, but I can't quite place—"

"Oops!" A sheepish chuckle. "I guess I've never gone into the shop dressed for work, have I?"

Max beamed at the drag queen. "Ah! That explains it."

Following Satsy's advice, Darling Delilah, a performer who'd had the shock of her life earlier tonight, had summoned us here to the Pony Expressive, a nightclub on West Fourth Street. The joint was jumping at the moment, the customers enjoying themselves, the musical act onstage holding their cheerful attention.

I asked Delilah, "I take it no one else here knows what really happened?"

"Nope, just the two boys—and us," she said, gesturing at the little group seated around our corner table. "The two boys" were part of her act, but they weren't sitting with us.

In addition to me, Max and Delilah, our table included Khyber Pass, who looked barely twenty and was dressed like a harem boy, if there was such a thing; Whoopsy Daisy, blond, leanly muscled and wearing daisies over his crotch and nothing else; and Saturated Fats—Satsy—who weighed over three hundred pounds and was dressed in a long purple caftan, a long purple wig and long purple eyelashes. All were performers at the club—the exact nature of which I wasn't sure Max entirely understood. Though I was still wearing Virtue's costume, even some of the club's clientele were dressed more colorfully than me, never mind the entertainers.

"And if it wasn't for all of you," Delilah said, glancing around gratefully at the five of us, "I don't know how I'd bear this."

Darling Delilah's drag was darn convincing. A lot of women don't ever look that good—me included. She was about five foot ten, with a slim elegant figure and smooth café-au-lait skin. Her dark hair tumbled around her shoulders in lush curls, and her coquettishly feminine gestures were charming rather than absurd. She was a sloe-eyed vamp with a sensuous mouth and a stylish evening dress that suited her figure.

Max was quite taken with her. When she patted his hand while expressing more gratitude to him, he forgot his next question and fell into bashful incoherence. He and I were going to have to have a talk later.

"So, Delilah," I said, "can you walk us through what happened?" Though she'd obviously made an effort to repair her makeup before our arrival, I could see that tears had been part of the hysteria she'd experienced earlier.

"Well, the act started out perfectly normal," she said. "Exactly the way we've been rehearsing it. It's a new act. Tonight was the debut. We were so… Sorry. Sorry. I won't…" She blinked away some gathering tears, cleared her throat, and then began describing the act. "The lights come up, the music swells. Sexy Samson is dragging me onstage." She cast Max a sultry smile and said, "Wearing almost nothing."

"You or Sexy Samson?" Max asked, taking notes.

"Max," I said, "how is that relevant?"

"Any detail, however minor it seems, might be relevant," he said.

Delilah leaned toward him and breathed, "Me."

He swallowed. "I see."

"He ties me to the Twin Pillars of Hercules—the two boys, both painted gold. They're in a number of the acts." She pointed toward the stage, where they were right now. Sparkly gold all over and, by remarkable coincidence, also wearing almost nothing.

Max watched their antics for a moment, then said, "Doesn't that hurt?"

"Mmm," said Whoopsy Daisy.

"Please continue," I said to Delilah.

"Then Sexy Samson whips me."

"Doesn't that hurt?" Max repeated.

"I struggle, escape my bonds and start running around the stage while he keeps whipping me, and the two boys move around some of our props," Delilah said. "We do a levitation routine, some sleight-of-hand, a few rope tricks."

"Are the two boys involved?" I asked.

"No, they're basically pretty grips."

Max said, "I beg your pardon?"

I explained, "Grips are stagehands. They move furniture and props, keep the show flowing."

Delilah continued. "In the last of the rope tricks, I turn the tables on Samson, and now *he* winds up tied to the Pillars of Hercules and I whip *him*. But with each lash of the whip, a piece of his clothing disappears. Vanishes! Until there's nothing left but his G-string."

I thought I'd kind of like to come see this act one night, if we ever managed to reunite Darling Delilah with Sexy Samson. For some reason, I wondered how Detective Lopez would react to the Pony Expressive if I brought him with me.

Blandly, I decided. He was a cop, he'd probably seen it all before.

"Then," said Delilah, "with the final flick of the whip, Samson's hair disappears."

"He goes bald?" Max asked.

"No, I cause his long hair to be shorn, thus depriving him of his strength."

"I see." Max kept scribbling.

"So I can have my way with him."

"Of course," Max said.

"And what is your way?" I asked.

"I put him in the prop box and make him disappear."

"It's a *gorgeous* box," said Satsy.

"Looks like a tiny Philistine temple," said Khyber.

"We'll need to examine it," said Max. "But please, do continue."

The rest of her story was quite familiar by now. She somehow knew Samson had disappeared. She felt it when it happened. Opening the tiny temple and searching for him merely confirmed what she already knew.

"*Knew*," Delilah repeated. "Then I screamed and became hysterical."

After a brief period of confusion, she was hauled offstage, and the master of ceremonies told the audience there'd been a little accident during the act, but no serious injuries. The rest of the show continued.

"But I didn't perform during the second set tonight, of course," Delilah added, her eyes tearing up again.

After a moment of contemplative silence, Satsy asked, "So what do we do?"

"I'd recommend panicking," said Whoopsy Daisy, "but we've already tried that."

"Which is why we've called you, Dr. Zadok."

Delilah put her hand over Max's. "Please, tell me the truth. Do you think Samson is..." Her voice failed her.

"No," I said firmly. "Definitely not. It's our theory that the, er, disappearees are just being moved between dimensions, not being hurt." I had no idea what I was saying, but Delilah looked close to a meltdown now, and I saw no reason to be negative just because we knew nothing.

"Disappearees?" Khyber repeated.

"Do you mean..." said Satsy.

"Are there others?" asked Whoopsy.

I glanced at Max. He looked lost in thought. I glanced around—the club was noisy and no one was paying any attention to us. I gestured for my companions to lean forward so I could lower my voice a bit, then I took a deep breath and explained everything. After their initial exclamations of shock upon learning that Sexy Samson was the fourth victim, they listened to me in taut, stunned silence. When I finished my account of the scant and bizarre facts, everyone remained quiet for a moment.

Then Whoopsy zeroed in on what he found to be the most startling fact of all: "So Golly Gee is really a woman? I would have *sworn* that was just bad drag!"

"Girlfriend, *tragic* drag," said Satsy.

The phone rang, waking me up. Without opening my eyes, I fumbled for it on the nightstand beside my bed. "Hullo," I mumbled.

"You're through in this business! Do you hear me? Through! *Through! THROUGH!*"

Needless to say, I was by now holding the phone well away from my ear. When gurgling sounds followed these threats, as if my caller was strangling on her own rage, I brought the receiver within speaking distance and said, "Thank you for your concern, Matilda. Yes, I'm still feeling quite weak."

"I'm at the theater, Esther! I've seen the crystal cage!" Gaining volume again, she screamed, *"What the hell do you think you're up to?"*

I was so tired that, for a moment, I had no idea what she was talking about. Then I remembered the night's events, including watching Max turn the expensive prop into a twisted, charred vestige of its former self. I sat up in bed, rubbed a hand over my face and tried to think while my producer kept abusing her vocal cords.

When there was a break in the regularly scheduled programming, I said, not even needing to disguise my voice to sound frail and shaky, "What are you talking about, Matilda?"

It took a little time to convince her of my ignorance; but, hey, I'm an actress, I'm good at this. She may not have abandoned her suspicions, but she did at least abandon her accusations.

In a tone that was only middling hostile now, she informed me the crystal cage was on its way back to Magic Magnus's shop for repairs. "*Again,* Esther."

"Maybe it would be a good idea to have two of them," I said.

"We can't afford two of them!"

"Does Magnus think he can fix it?" *But preferably not very soon?* I thought, biting my lip.

"He thinks so. For a sum equivalent to the national debt of Thailand."

"When will it be ready?" My stomach churned.

"I don't know. Magnus says he's giving it top priority. But it would be too much trouble for him to give *me* an ETA, of course."

Top priority. I might not have as much time as I'd hoped.

Matilda said, "But I want to make one thing very clear to you, Esther."

"Yes?"

"I don't care if you've got the *plague*. When that prop box is returned to us, you'd better be here, waiting for it, in costume and ready for a complete run-through of the show."

"I will be." I crossed my fingers.

"Because if you're not—"

"I will be," I repeated, hoping it was true.

"I swear on my husband's grave—"

I frowned. "Uh, did Joe die since last night?"

"—I will not only fire you—"

"I'll be there," I said.

"—I will not only ruin your name and make sure no respectable producer ever gives you another job—" she continued, gathering steam.

"Matilda…"

"—I will not just destroy your career to such an extent that you'll feel lucky to play a condom in a porn film—"

"Do they use condoms in porn films?"

"I will sue you, Esther. For every penny you've got—"

"I don't have many pennies, I work for *you*," I muttered.

"—and for every penny you may ever earn. I will

sue you all the way through the end of this lifetime and into the next one. My lawyer will pursue you through eternity, be it through heaven or through hell!"

I'd had no idea she was so religious.

"Do you hear me?" she shrieked.

"If I don't show up for work when the crystal cage is ready, you'll sue me," I said.

"*And* fire you!" she shouted.

"Yes, I hear you. Everyone south of Forty-second Street can probably hear you," I said. "I understand the terms. And now, Matilda, I am extremely ill and in no condition to continue this chat, so I'm hanging up. Goodbye."

She shrieked at me while I disconnected the call. I lay back in my rumpled pillows and cradled the phone against my chest, seeking comfort from its solid, prosaic familiarity. I felt a sudden fondness for it because it was one of the few things in my world that hadn't changed unrecognizably since, oh, yesterday.

Two days ago, I'd arrived at the theater eager to step into the lead role of an off-Broadway musical. Now, instead, I was alienating my producer, letting down the cast, and afraid Evil would get me if I went on with the show.

I groaned and hugged the phone. Could things possibly get any worse?

The phone rang, startling me. I answered it reflexively. The new caller was my mother.

"Of course," I muttered. "Things can *always* get worse."

"What?"

"Hi, Mom."

"Esther, your Uncle Ben and Aunt Rachel are visiting New York next month. I told them you'd get them tickets for your new show."

"Oh, Mom," I groaned. "No. *Please,* no…"

"They'll take you to dinner," she said coaxingly. "Some place you can't afford."

I sighed. "I can't talk about this right now."

"Why not now?" My mother's voice is well-educated and vivacious. And sometimes it's shadowed by her lifelong suspicion that the hospital switched babies on her when I was born. "I'm giving you plenty of notice."

"This isn't a good time to talk about the show."

"Why?" she said. "What did you do?"

This is my mother's gift: an uncanny ability to make me feel even worse than I already do.

"It's a long story," I said. "And I don't have time for a long call this morning."

"Morning? It's after eleven." After a pause, she said, "Esther, are you still in bed?"

How does she always know? I sat up quickly, as if she could see me all the way from our family home in Madison, Wisconsin. "I was up very late," I said defensively.

"Oh, were you on a date? Someone nice, maybe?"

"No."

"Hmm. So you're still not seeing anyone?"

"No, Mom."

"Maybe you shouldn't be so picky. Do you want to wind up old and alone?"

"I'm only twenty-seven," I said wearily. "But I'll be old *real* soon if you nag."

"I'm just saying…"

"Mom, I have to be somewhere soon. I don't have time to talk right now."

"Well, if you'd get *up* earlier—"

"Agggh!" I said.

"What?"

"We'll talk next week. About the tickets. I have to go now."

"All right," she said with exaggerated patience. "Oh, and sweetheart? Your father says to send him any reviews of the show. Especially if they mention you."

"Reviewers don't single out chorus nymphs, Mom."

"Well, your father would still like to see the reviews."

"He can't just look online?"

"It would be nice if *you* would send them, dear." Her tone reminded me not to be a bad daughter.

"Okay, fine," I said. "I'll send some reviews."

My father and I mostly communicate via my mother. He likes me fine, he just has no idea what to say to me. He's a history professor. My mother manages a youth employment center. Neither of them is sure how they managed to raise an actress. But to give them credit, they love me, so they try to be supportive of my choices without understanding them at all.

"I have to go, Mom," I said again.

"By the way, have you heard from your sister?"

"No." Ending a conversation with my mother is a multi-phase process.

"Neither have I," she said gloomily.

As family tradition demanded, I briefly reminded my mother that my older sister was always very busy and pressed for time. Ruth was a hospital administrator and the mother of two. She lived in Chicago, and most of her conversation (on the rare occasions when we talked) was about how overwhelmed and exhausted she was. Talking to Ruthie always made me incredibly glad I was a struggling actress instead of a respectable professional and family woman.

"I really have to go, Mom."

"I meant to ask—"

"We'll talk next week. Bye, Mom."

I hung up and got out of bed, intent on leaving the apartment before anyone *else* could phone me.

As I thought over Max's life story, it occurred to me that accepting liquid refreshment from an alchemist was not without risks. So I brought my own coffee to the bookshop that day. Due to our very late night, followed by a restless post-dawn sleep that left me looking more like a troll than a nymph from *Sorcerer!*, it was after noon by the time I arrived.

Max and I had stayed late at the Pony Expressive, examining Darling Delilah's tiny Philistine temple and further discussing the disappearances. After that, I shared a cab with Khyber Pass and Whoopsy Daisy, who didn't think a lady should risk going home unescorted at that time of night—and who insisted on paying the cab fare, even though my place in the West Thirties was out of their way. (Not for the first time, I wished that straight men could all be as gentlemanly as my gay friends.) They insisted that paying for the taxi was the least they could do in exchange for all my help. I didn't really see how I was helping them so far, but I hoped that I would be able to. Although Delilah was the most upset of the bunch, they were obviously a close-knit group of friends, all deeply worried about Sexy Samson's fate.

And it was clear by now that my help was indeed needed. Although I had no doubt after last night that Max, with his special knowledge and abilities, was essential to solving our strange problem, I'd already noticed that organization wasn't his strong suit.

"We need to approach this methodically," I said to him when I arrived at the bookshop. I walked over to the large walnut table, set down a box containing half a dozen cups of carry-out coffee and dropped my daypack on the floor.

"Methodically?" Max repeated.

I nodded a greeting at Saturated Fats, Khyber Pass and Whoopsy Daisy, who had agreed to join us here for further consultation. Darling Delilah was in New Jersey today, explaining things as best she could to Sexy Samson's mother. "Help yourselves to the coffee," I said.

"I would have made coffee," Max said, looking hurt that I might have entertained doubts about his hospitality.

"It's better if I bring it."

"But—"

"Let's focus, Max. Sit." We all took our seats around the table, whose surface was overflowing with books, notes, bills, receipts, maps, writing tools, the abacus, and… "Feathers?"

"It's a long story," Max said wearily.

"We don't have time for it, then," I said.

"Let's get down, girlfriend," said Satsy.

"Right." Khyber, dressed in jeans and a peach shirt with an embroidered collar, made a gesture like a boxer ready to fight. "What's the plan?"

I pulled out a list, having penned some thoughts while hunched groggily over my first cup of coffee after my mother's phone call this morning. "First item—Hieronymus is researching disappearances."

"Who's Hieronymus?" Whoopsy asked.

"My assistant," said Max.

"We need to help him," I said. "Several of us researching similar phenomena and coordinating our efforts are a lot more likely to find an answer than one person working alone."

"Check," said Whoopsy. "If Hieronymus hasn't gone to the New York Public Library yet, I'll do that. There's some whacky stuff down in the research stacks that most people don't know about." When we looked at him, he added, "I worked there for two years, before I became a performance artiste."

"Right, then," I said, "Whoopsy's got the public library covered."

"I'll get Delilah to help me after she gets back from Jersey," Whoopsy added. "There's a lot of legwork involved at the main branch, so it'll go faster if there are two of us on the job. Plus, one of us may need to detour to a collection at another library."

"Good thinking," I said.

"And naturally," said Max, "the bookshop is at our disposal, as is my private collection, which I keep downstairs in the laboratory."

"Check," I said. "We should also look online."

"Online?" Max repeated.

"Yes."

"With a computer?" he asked.

"That is the usual way."

"I don't have a computer anymore. It blew up months ago."

"Blew up?" I repeated.

"A victim of Evil. Or possibly faulty wiring," he added. "To be honest, I never liked it."

Khyber said, "No problem. I do some part-time bookkeeping, so I've got a good setup at home. I'll work from there and stay in touch by phone."

"And I'll work here in the shop with Esther," said Satsy.

"Right," I said. "I made some calls before I came. Dixie Dempsey says that finding Dolly and the other victims is more important than her acting and dance classes. So she's on her way over here to help out. And Barclay Preston-Cole will be here as soon as he can get away from the office." I consulted my list. "Next item—Max, you need to examine Barclay's prop box."

"Yes, of course," he said. "Um, right. Er, check."

"And you should interview him when he comes here later."

"Oh, yes! Er, right. I think I should also interview Mr. Herlihy," he said.

"The magician who made Golly Gee disappear, right?" Satsy asked.

"Right," Max said, clipped and confident with the vernacular this time. "Check."

Satsy asked, "So Herlihy's coming here, too?"

"Negative," I said. "I haven't spoken to him. He and I need to be kept apart."

"Why?" Satsy perked up. "Is there a cosmic wobble in the dimensional fabric when you two meet?"

I recalled that Satsy was a regular customer here. Dressed in a flowing white smock shirt and trousers today, without wig or makeup, he looked so different

from last night's purple diva that I was no longer surprised Max hadn't recognized him—as a "her"—at
the Pony Expressive.

"No," I said. "But his wife is my producer, and I'm
supposedly too ill to work. Joe was so scared of performing the act last night that I doubt he'll intention-
ally expose my good health to Matilda if he finds out
about it. But he's so nervous, I think the truth could
easily slip out by accident, and I'm already having
more problems with his wife than I want."

"Check," said Max.

"So you'll need to interview Joe without involving
me," I said to Max.

"Right."

"But he's so high-strung, I think there's a good
chance you'll scare him out of his wits if you meet
with him alone." Max would prattle about Evil among
us, Joe would gibber with fear and guilt, and nothing
would be accomplished. "Besides, Matilda is protective of him. So a certain boldness may be needed just
to get in the door of their apartment. That's why you're
taking Cowboy Duke with you." I counted on Duke's
charm, common sense and brashness to conquer the
obstacles I foresaw.

Max made the boxer-ready-to-fight gesture. "Check."

"Next item—compare and contrast. I've ordered a
display board to be delivered here from an office supply shop. We've got to start assembling all the facts
we can gather together about the disappearees and the

magicians. What's the unifying factor here? What do they have in common aside from, well, doing disappearing acts? And what about the prop boxes—what, if anything, do *they* have in common?"

"Check!" they all said in unison, their simultaneous boxing gesture making them look a little like a cheerleading squad.

I went into the home stretch of my presentation. "Make no mistake about this, my friends. Our goal is not to learn enough to help the next victim."

"It's not?" Max asked.

"No. We've got to do better than that. Our goal is to learn enough to *prevent* the next disappearance."

"Oh, of course! Right. Check!"

"So come on, troops!" I said. "Let's get out there and kick Evil's butt!"

"Yes!" Whoopsy jumped up to punch the air. "Go, go, *go!*"

"Team Pony Expressive is on the job, girlfriend!" Satsy pounded on the table.

Khyber leaped to his feet. "Let's do it!"

"No prisoners!" cried Max.

We looked at him.

"You're sure I can't make you some coffee?" he said.

"So here's a question, Max," I said.

"Hmm?"

"Where *is* Hieronymus?"

"Oh!" He blinked. "Downstairs, probably."

"In your laboratory?"

"Yes."

"We should have asked him to sit in on the meeting. Let's go talk to him now."

Whoopsy and Khyber had left the shop, bound for their respective duties. Satsy was browsing the store in search of books that might prove useful in our research. I had accepted delivery of a huge display board and had neatly written on its surface, in various colors of Magic Marker, the few facts I knew about the victims. Now I followed Max to the back of his shop in search of Hieronymus. A little cul-de-sac there contained some storage shelves, a utilities closet, a bathroom and a door marked "PRIVATE." Max opened that door onto a narrow, creaky stairway that led both up and down from where we stood. There was an overhead light bulb, but Max didn't bother to switch it on; the stairway was illuminated by a burning torch stuck in a wall sconce.

"I thought fire was your weakest element," I said.

"It is. That was left there by my predecessor and I can't figure out how to put it out."

"Your predecessor? The one who had to flee the IRS?"

"Yes."

"He inhabited this building, too?"

"It belongs to the Collegium." He led the way down the narrow staircase. "Be sure to hold on to the railing, Esther. These stairs are a little uneven."

"You don't say?" Descending carefully, I asked, "So what was on the main floor before it was a bookshop?"

"His laboratory. That enormous cupboard, which houses some of his, er, leftovers, is still up there because it contains elements that do not respond well to involuntary relocation."

"I see." No, I didn't, but I suspected that asking for details would lead us well off track, and we had work to do.

Max continued. "I gather that having the laboratory at street level caused some problems with the neighbors."

Upon hearing a muffled explosion below us, I said, "Go figure."

"I thought it best to be more discreet, so I installed my laboratory in the basement. Unfortunately, I didn't realize that this would occasionally lead to widespread plumbing mishaps, so there is still some discord with the neigh— Ah, here's Hieronymus."

We entered the laboratory, which was cavernous, windowless and shadowy. The walls were decorated with charts covered in strange symbols and maps of places I didn't recognize. Bottles of powders and potions, dried plants and what appeared to be dried animal parts jostled for space. Beakers, implements and tools lay tumbled and jumbled on the heavy, dark furniture.

Dusty shelves and cabinets were densely packed with jars of herbs, spices, minerals, amulets and neatly sorted claws and teeth. There were a few pieces of medieval-looking weaponry, some urns and boxes and vases, a tarot deck spread across a table in mid-reading, a pile of runes lying next to it, two gargoyles squatting in a corner, icons and idols, and a scattering of old bones. An enormous bookcase was packed to overflowing with many leather-bound volumes, as well as unbound manuscripts, scrolls and even a few clay tablets.

All over the lab, there were also little piles of...

"Feathers?" I said.

Max shook his head. "It's so discouraging."

A young man stood at the massive workbench. He had a rather slight build, fair skin, innocent features and cropped, mousy brown hair. The source of the explosion I'd heard was presumably the experiment he'd been working on. A charred beaker sat cracked and smoking atop a little flame, looking like a high school chemistry assignment gone wrong. The young man—Hieronymus—was wiping orange liquid off his face, his clothes and the workbench.

He glanced up at Max, then noticed me. He looked momentarily startled, then wiped off something in his hand—his glasses, I realized, as he put them on. His brown eyes, which gazed directly at me, were magnified by the thick lenses. He wore black trousers, a shirt that had obviously been white before the explosion and a blank facial expression.

"Difficulties?" Max asked with concern.

The young man shrugged, looking a tad sullen.

"Well, then… Hieronymus," Max said, "please allow me to introduce my new friend, Miss Esther Diamond. This is the brave young lady I mentioned to you this morning. She'll be helping us from now on, and she's doing a wonderful job of organizing the rest of our new acquaintances into productive tasks, too."

Feeling moved by this little speech, I smiled warmly at Hieronymus. "How do you do? I gather you're Max's apprentice?"

A frown of irritation transformed his blank expression. "Athithtant," he said.

"Pardon?" I said.

"Not appwentith. Athithtant."

"What?" I said, thinking his accent was much stronger than Max's.

"I'm hith *athithtant.*"

Max said, "He was promoted before coming to New York. Assistant is one level above apprentice."

"Oh!" That was no accent, I realized, mortified at my clumsiness. It was a speech impediment. A pronounced one. "Assistant! Of course! My mistake!" I heard the exaggerated cheeriness in my voice and tried to modify it. "Assistant. Yes, that was what Max told me, I just got confused. How are you? I mean, it's a pleasure to meet you." I was conscious of every *S* and *R* in my jabbered comments.

Hieronymus gave me a curt nod.

"Well…" I looked at Max, who made encouraging gestures. "I and the others are going to help you research disappearances."

"*Mythtical* dithappeawantheth," he said tersely.

"Right. Mystical disappearances," I said. "I mean, sure, New York City is full of ordinary disappearances. Uh, people who go missing. We're looking for the supernatural kind. People who go *poof!*"

His eyes rolled. "Evewything ith natuwal."

Not quite sure what Hieronymus had said, I looked at Max, who explained, "The notion of supernatural phenomena is a false construct."

"It is?"

He nodded. "Everything in the cosmos is essentially natural—except for certain forms of fast food, of course, and possibly some aspects of Los Angeles."

"I see."

"And some natural things are mystical," Max said. "Such as these disappearances."

"Gotcha. Whatever." I turned back to Hieronymus and started explaining the plans we'd formed and how we were dividing up our tasks. I concluded by saying, "But, of course, you're point man on the research, so we should start by reviewing what you've learned or ruled out, as well as what specific areas, if any, you want the rest of us to start exploring."

This friendly speech produced another sullen shrug. I smiled and exercised my patience. Obviously, his speech impediment made him self-conscious and shy. His sullen demeanor was probably a defensive posture, a way of coping with his frustration and embarrassment.

"I will make a litht of what I've done," he said, his tone still unfriendly.

"Good!" I said with exaggerated enthusiasm. "If you want to bring it upstairs when it's ready…"

"You can come get it."

On the other hand, while I felt sympathy for him, I didn't think a speech impediment entitled him to bad manners. I didn't care for the way his dark expression and brusque tone persisted despite my best efforts to be cordial.

Still trying to overcome his defenses, I moved a little closer to him and said, "Is there anything I can help you with?" When he raised his brows in silent query, I added, "Some specific research you'd like me to start going through?"

"Ah." He turned his back on me, walked over to a desk piled high with books, and brought back three massive, leather-bound volumes. He dropped them into my outstretched arms heavily enough to make me grunt.

"Okay," I said, taking a dislike to Hieronymus despite my sympathy. I looked down at the books in my arms. "I'll just get started…uh…well, actually…"

"Pwoblem?"

"Yeah." And I could tell from the slight smirk on

his face that he'd already guessed the nature of the problem. I gestured with my chin to the top book on my stack and read aloud, "Er, *Tomus Secundus De Praeternaturali*...um...*Microcosmi*..." I shook my head. "I don't read Latin." I struggled with my arm-load so I could glance at the title of the second book in the pile. "Or Greek. *Is* that Greek?"

"Modern education is sadly lacking," Max said. "Never fear, Esther, we understand that you are to be pitied rather than blamed."

Hieronymus's expression conveyed his unmitigated contempt for my weak intellect as he removed the books from my arms. Then he pointed straight up, indicating the shop overhead. "Bookth in English."

"Thanks," I said. But he had already turned his back on me.

As Max and I went back upstairs, he confided, "The poor boy's personality is not, it must be admitted, particularly amiable. But one can imagine how difficult his childhood must have been."

"Didn't his parents ever consult a good speech therapist?"

"Yes, but they knew there was little hope, and events proved they were right."

"Why? With good training, people often overcome speech impediments."

"The problem is mystical, Esther, and, alas, seems to be irrevocable." As we reached the top of the stairs and reentered the shop, Max explained, "His mother was a member of the Collegium. While she was pregnant, her womb was cursed by a particularly vicious djinn she was trying to destroy. Despite the unfortunate result, one is relieved the poor lad didn't suffer something even worse."

"Such as a sour disposition?" I said. "Oh, well, never mind. In any case, it seems that he will be happier working alone in the basement."

"He is a rather solitary person," Max agreed, as we reached the main floor and reentered the bookshop.

"But free-flowing communication is important, Max, if we're to solve this problem and prevent another disappearance." Or get back the people who'd already vanished.

Max sighed. "You're right, of course. I'll have a word with him about trying to be a bit more civil."

"Good." I wondered if it would have any effect. With the Collegium for an opponent, no wonder Evil was making such a good living in this dimension! Some assistant those masterminds had assigned to Max to help him protect the greatest city in the world: sullen, solitary and making things explode.

I found Satsy seated at the table again, this time with a large pile of books.

"Esther," he said, "I think we may solve this case even sooner than we'd hoped!"

I stared at the book in his hands, which he waved in my face with excitement: *Supernatural Disappearances*.

"Ah, but that's a false construct, Satsy."

"Excuse me?"

I made a gesture to brush aside my comment. "Sorry. I mean, yes, I hope there's something very useful in there."

A little bell rang, heralding the arrival of a customer.

"Well, howdy, folks!" cried Duke Dempsey, ushering his daughter into the shop. "Why, this certainly is a lovely place you got here, Maximillian. Looks just like an old bookshop."

"It *is* an old bookshop," I said. Being from Texas, maybe he'd never seen one before. "Thanks for coming."

"Pshaw! You're helping us, so we're helping you. No thanks needed, young lady."

"Duke, Dixie, this is Satsy," I said, "who's also got a stake in trying to solve this case."

Seated at the table, Satsy gave a friendly wave from behind his stack of books. He eyed Duke's fringe-and-rhinestone cowboy outfit with obvious delight and asked, "Darlin', do you mind if I ask where you got those *wonderful* clothes?"

Looking pleased, the Cowboy offered to give Satsy the name of his tailor.

CHAPTER 6

"Transportation…translocation…teleportation…transmutation…lateral levitation…dematerialization…dissolution…" I put down the book in my hands and gently rubbed my throbbing temples.

"Okay, Esther, according to this book, apparently the last two books I was reading were just *swamped* in Christian propaganda," Satsy said slowly, turning the pages of the volume he held. "So ignore what I was saying before." He glanced up and, seeing my puzzled expression, added, "The Church."

"Huh?" I said.

"Well, the stuff I was reading about mystical disappearances being the work of witchcraft and devil worship was apparently a post-antiquity, pre-modern notion developed by the Catholic Church in an attempt to establish and maintain its power. And the

Church's propaganda on this score was so influential that this stuff was considered 'true' even by Protestants—once, you know, there *were* Protestants."

"Huh?" I said again.

"The point, girlfriend, is that the idea that mystical disappearances are the work of devil-worshipping witches—"

"An idea you were propounding so emphatically an hour ago," I said, "that my whole skull started propounding."

"—was basically just the Church messing with people's heads."

"I thought so," said Dixie. "Everybody knows that witches aren't really like that. I have Wiccan friends."

"I dated a Wiccan," said Barclay, who had joined us about an hour earlier. "She was a perfectly nice girl, but a vegan. I don't have anything against vegans per se, but have you ever tried to plan dinner dates with one?" He shook his head. "It couldn't last, of course."

"So," I said to Satsy, "we've gone from narrowing it down to witchcraft and devil worship to opening the field back up to any and all possibilities?"

"Uh-huh."

Dixie frowned doubtfully at the book in her own hands. "I don't think the Bermuda Triangle's going to give us any answers. I think I should start on something else."

Barclay, perusing another of the books, said, "Hey, here's one from Europe, during the Napoleonic wars.

A guy vanishes right in front of his cell mates. Disappears into thin air before their very eyes. Six witnesses swore to this!"

"His cell mates?" I repeated.

"French prisoners of war. Being held by the Prussians."

"Of course," I said, "the missing prisoner's comrades-in-arms could have had no possible motive for making up such a story when asked by the enemy army where he was."

"But their jailer supported their story when he was questioned by his superiors!"

"And it's not remotely possible that the jailer was trying to avoid blame for having let a prisoner escape?"

"Oh. Hmm. Good point."

Feeling a bit desperate, I asked, "Does it say anything about how the prisoner disappeared? I mean, how it was done?"

"No." Barclay went back to reading.

After a few minutes, Satsy said, "Here's another one from Europe, also during the Napoleonic wars."

"It's a pattern!" said Dixie.

I rested my forehead on the table. "Well?"

"He was a Pisces, which is…'the most psychologically unstable zodiac group.' I don't agree with that," Satsy added.

"Neither do I," said Barclay. "*I'm* a Pisces."

"You are?" said Dixie. "I'm a Leo. What sign are you, Esther?"

"Tell us about the disappearance, Satsy," I said without lifting my head.

"His name was Benjamin Bathurst, and he was in Europe on a secret diplomatic mission for the British government in 1809. He broke his journey at a place called Perleberg, where he asked the Prussian army for an escort because he feared for his safety."

"Prussians again!" said Dixie. "There *is* a pattern."

"He rested at an inn called the White Swan by day, thinking he'd be safer traveling by night. After dark, he watched his coach being loaded. As he prepared to board it, suddenly...he was gone."

I waited, but Satsy said nothing more. So I said, "A guy on a secret diplomatic mission during wartime, who has stated to the local military that he's in danger, goes missing after dark. So why does the author think the disappearance was mystical?"

"As Bathurst prepared to leave, he walked around to the other side of the coach, out of sight, and...was never seen again!"

"It was dark," I said. "And he stepped out of sight."

"What could have happened to him?" Dixie asked.

"Did you ever lose a nephew at the department store?" I finally lifted my head. "You look away for a *second,* or he steps behind a toy display for a *second*...and the next thing you know, he's gone, nowhere to be found, and you're wondering whether even to try explaining this to his parents before you hang yourself. And then! *Then* the brat turns up twenty minutes later at the customer service desk, eating candy and claiming *you* disappeared!" Seeing they were all staring at me with puzzled expressions, I said, "Never mind. I mean to say, a couple of skilled, armed assailants, operating after dark, probably only needed that brief opportunity, when Bathurst stepped behind the coach for a minute or so, to capture a frightened diplomat."

"Frightened! Exactly," Satsy said. "The author says that supernatural disappearances can sometimes be a protective mechanism, something that happens to some people when they're terrified or facing death!"

Dixie said, "Hey, maybe that's what been happening here!"

I asked her, "Was Dolly the Dancing Cowgirl scared?"

"Huh? Oh... No." Dixie looked deflated. "She and Daddy have done that act lots of times, and she was real excited about going shopping on Fifth Avenue next day."

I asked Barclay, "What about Clarisse? Did she seem scared?"

"No." He shrugged. "Before we started the performance, she was just complaining that her manicurist hadn't done a very good job that morning."

"What about Samson?"

Satsy shook his head.

"And Golly Gee," I said, "didn't seem to be scared

of anything the night she vanished. Not even bad reviews." She'd fought with Joe about endangering her during the show, but she was obviously annoyed, not frightened. "Are we done with Benjamin Bathurst, Satsy?"

"No. Three weeks after he disappeared—"

"Went missing."

"—they found a pair of his trousers in a grove."

"How did they know the trousers were his?"

"A letter from him to his wife was in the pocket."

"What did the letter say?" I asked.

"It said he was in danger and feared he'd never reach England alive," Satsy replied.

"Indeed," I said.

"It also asked her not to marry again if he died."

"Jeez," said Dixie. "Some guys are so selfish."

"But here's the interesting thing, Esther," Satsy continued. "The letter was intact, even though the weather had been mostly wet since his disappearance. So it should have disintegrated if the trousers had been lying outside for three weeks."

"So Bathurst was held captive for a while," I surmised. "That makes sense. A diplomat with secrets would have been interrogated by his enemies rather than immediately killed. Maybe they even toyed with trying to ransom him. Anyhow, he somehow got separated from his trousers after three weeks. Maybe when he was executed, or maybe when he was recaptured during an escape attempt."

"Actually," said Satsy, "the author believes Benjamin Bathurst was transported to another dimension."

"But his trousers stayed here?" Dixie asked with a frown.

"No, according to the author," Satsy explained, "the trousers were 'suspended between two dimensions' during those three weeks, then recrossed the divide between the two worlds, propelled by the force of Bathurst's love for his wife!"

Barclay had brought us coffee, so Satsy, who'd already drunk three of the cups I'd brought, had had two more cups in the past hour. I made a mental note to bring decaf only from now on.

"The other theory," he said, "is that the trousers may have spent those three weeks in a dimension where time passes much more slowly than it does here. So even if the weather was bad there, too, the letter wouldn't have had time to disintegrate."

"Does anyone have an aspirin?" I asked.

Hoping it would help relieve my headache, I went back down to the laboratory and nagged Hieronymus for a report of his findings. Still sullen and brusque, he provided a list of the tomes he'd been through—all of them in Latin—and a few bullet points in English summarizing what he'd learned.

"Well," I said, perusing his notes in disappointment. "This doesn't tell us much, does it."

"I have another theowy," Hieronymus replied. "One I didn't put on that litht."

"Oh?"

"Youw people did it."

"*My* people?" I blinked. "Jews?"

He snorted. "No. The mundane people."

"Oh. Mundanes." He was a jerk, but apparently not an anti-Semite. "I'm still willing to consider that, though I may be the only one by now. Do you have any idea how mundanes *could* manage these disappearances?"

He shrugged and said he was still thinking about it.

"Well, I'll leave you to it, then."

Happy to abandon Hieronymus alone in the cellar, I thought over his suggestion as I went back upstairs.

I wasn't particularly surprised by how many people (many, it turned out) had disappeared mysteriously over the course of history; but I was stunned by how many people, past and present, believed that the causes of such disappearances were necessarily supernatural (false construct or not). Most of the cases we'd come across so far could be explained by any number of mundane possibilities, but emphatic assertions that they *must* be mystical events had persisted for centuries, right up to the present day.

I wondered if I was an unusually skeptical person. So far, everyone involved in this case seemed to have accepted the mystical nature of our problem (Hieronymus's suggestion notwithstanding) much more easily than I did.

Of course, the magicians had all actually *felt* something extraordinary occur when the victims disappeared, something that even today, in a calmer frame of mind, Barclay still couldn't really articulate. Having talked to him, Duke and Delilah, and recalling Joe's guilt and fear after Golly's disappearance, I supposed that whatever they had experienced had made them believers on the spot. But Whoopsy, Khyber and Satsy had already believed in Samson's magical disappearance by the time Max and I arrived at the Pony Expressive a few hours later; and Dixie didn't seem to have wrestled much with skepticism before accepting that Dolly had genuinely vanished.

I, on the other hand, had strenuously resisted the whole idea of mystical disappearance until there was simply no escaping it. Maybe I was too secular, too unimaginative, too wedded to the earthly dimension?

Or maybe they all were just weird.

My cell phone, clipped to my waistband, jingled a happy tune. I held it to my ear while reading over Hieronymus's notes as if something useful might suddenly leap out at me. "Hello?"

"This is Khyber, checking in. Did any of the disappearing acts involve lightning?"

I frowned. "Um, no. Why?"

"I've found a Web site. There've been a number of disappearances, going all the way back to Roman times, involving people being struck by lightning. I mean, you're hit, and—*poof!*"

"Really?"

"Sometimes you reappear elsewhere, sometimes you disappear forever."

I wasn't particularly hopeful, but nonetheless I said, "Put together a summary and bring it to the shop tomorrow."

"Check."

"Good work."

"Over and out."

The phone rang again only a minute later. I took a seat near the fireplace, out of earshot of Barclay, Satsy and Dixie, who were discussing how someone (or his trousers) might move across dimensions. My caller was Cowboy Duke.

As predicted, Joe Herlihy was a seething mass of nerves and Matilda was shrill. Max felt they had learned nothing new, but the interview had not been thorough enough to satisfy him. Joe was so highly strung that it took considerable patience to get useful answers from him, and Matilda kept disrupting the proceedings.

"Maximillian eventually brought the conversation around to the other disappearances," Duke said. "You know, looking for a common factor."

"Uh-huh."

"And the interview ended on the spot."

"Why?" I asked.

"Matilda started screaming, fit to be tied."

"Oh?"

"I'm not sure if she thought we were threatening her with blackmail, or accusing her husband of masterminding a deadly conspiracy, or if she just thought we were nutcases."

"I gather her screams conveyed all of these possibilities?"

"Yes, indeedy. Anyhow, she threw us out of the apartment."

"That was going to be my next guess."

"She also made a number of unladylike comments about you, since Max met her and Joe through you."

"Yeah, they were all sort of introduced in my dressing room last night," I said wanly.

"Esther, I don't want you goin' near that woman anytime soon, you hear me?" he said. "She is the meanest person I've met in this whole city, and that's saying something."

"No argument, Duke, I'm steering clear of her."

"Good."

I had a feeling my answering machine at home had already been incinerated by a message of blistering fury. I hoped Matilda didn't think to ask the stage manager for my cell-phone number.

Duke told me that he and Max had just finished an uneventful inspection of the rhinestone-studded hollow horse from which Dolly had disappeared two nights ago. Now they were headed back here to interview Barclay. After that, they'd go with him to his apartment to examine the prop box in which Clarisse Staunton had vanished.

"How's the research going?" the Cowboy asked.

"Not well. I blame my parents for forcing me to study Hebrew instead of Latin," I said. "I'll see you later, Duke."

After hanging up, I found Barclay proposing a new theory to our companions: "What if some focus or effort of the mind, or some technical means we don't know about, can reduce the physical body to sub-microscopic particles of vibrating energy?"

Dixie frowned. "So the victims are still here, but we can't see them?"

"Exactly!" Barclay said. "*Or,* maybe they aren't still here. Maybe that same force can propel them through great distance, so they reappear somewhere else."

"Like on *Star Trek?*"

"Yes!"

"I just love *Star Trek,*" Dixie said.

"You do?" said Barclay. "Me, too!"

"Really? What's your favorite *Star Trek* show?" Dixie asked, eyes shining.

"I like the classic series best," he said promptly. "Captain Kirk, Mr. Spock, Dr. McCoy."

"Me, too!"

"You're kidding!"

Dixie said, "I thought I was, like, the only one. I thought *everyone* else was more into the newer series."

"I had the biggest crush on Lieutenant Uhura," Barclay said.

"I was in love with Mr. Chekov."

They smiled and their eyes met in warm understanding.

Satsy destroyed the moment by saying, "Back up a step. If our victims have reappeared elsewhere, then why haven't any of them phoned home?"

"Hmm," Dixie said. "That's a good point. Dolly would've phoned."

"Samson, too."

"Maybe they're somewhere without phones?" Barclay guessed.

"Some of them have been gone for days now," Satsy said. "Where could they be, that they're that far from a phone?"

Barclay slowly looked heavenward.

"Outer space?" Satsy cried in despair.

Dixie gasped. "But that means they're all…"

"Uh, okay, bad theory," Barclay said quickly. "Maybe they've been propelled through time, instead of space."

"Well, that would explain why they haven't gotten in touch," Satsy admitted.

"*Time,*" I said, glancing at the clock. Although these had felt like some of the longest hours of my life, it was now later than I'd realized. "I'm going to have to leave for a while," I said. "I'll be back."

"We're thinking about Chinese," Barclay said.

I blinked. "You think Chinese people are causing the disappearances?"

"No, we were thinking of ordering Chinese food," he said. "Should we get enough for you, too?"

"Oh! Yes, thanks." I told him to include Duke and Max, too, who'd be back soon. Then I picked up my heavy daypack, particularly glad after that phone call with Duke that I'd planned ahead before leaving my apartment today. I took the pack into the bathroom at the back of the shop and assumed my disguise: boots with three-inch heels; a blond wig; heavy makeup that exaggerated the fullness of my mouth; very dark sunglasses; and a high-collared raincoat in a leopard-skin print that belted tightly at the waist.

When I came out, Satsy asked, "Why are you in drag?"

"I'm not in drag," I said, "I'm incognito."

"Wow!" Dixie's eyes widened. "Are you, like, famous?"

"I have to go to check on Herlihy's crystal cage, and I can't risk being seen by anyone else who might be checking on it. Such as my producer." I spun around once, then struck a pose. "If you walked past me in the street, would you recognize me?"

"No," Dixie said, sounding like she hoped this was the right answer.

"No way," Satsy said. "I *never* would have figured you for an animal-print person."

"Barclay?" I asked.

"No, you look sexy!"

Trying to view this deflating comment in a positive light—I was evidently as unrecognizable as I wanted to be—I told them I'd be back in about an hour. Then I went outside, cut over to Hudson and hailed a cab. No way was I *walking* to Magic Magnus's shop in three-inch heels.

If Magnus was giving priority to repairing the crystal cage, as Matilda had told me, then he could put me in an impossible position if he worked fast enough. So I was hoping to convince him not to tell Matilda the cage was repaired until I gave him the heads-up. He'd get paid for his work, either way; but I'd only be able to keep my job in the show if the cage wasn't ready to go back onstage until *I* was.

On my previous visit to the shop, Magic Magnus had given me the impression that he liked me. And I thought it unlikely that anyone but Joe liked Matilda. So there was a reasonable chance I could get Magnus to cooperate. Especially if, as Barclay thought, I looked sexy in my disguise.

More anxious than ever to avoid Matilda now that she was undoubtedly in a vindictive mood, I got out of the cab half a block away and approached Magnus's shop with stealth. I paused casually in front of the window to make sure there was no one I recognized in the shop, and—

I gasped and shrank away from the window.

Good God! Lopez. Inside the magic store.

The very last person I expected to bump into! What was *he* doing here?

Realizing that I wasn't doing a good job of looking casual, I stepped closer to the window and pretended to browse as I spied on the detective. He was talking to Magnus, and neither of them noticed me. Lopez was taking notes. Magnus was nodding and gesturing.

So Lopez was still investigating the case! I reached for my cell phone, planning to notify Max. He might be back at the bookstore by now.

Then I hesitated. What I would tell him? All I knew right now was that, contrary to what we'd thought last night, the police were interested in this matter. All I would accomplish by giving Max this news would be to make him anxious. He'd already said he didn't want them involved, and now I agreed with him; it would only complicate an already perplexing situation. Whatever was going to stop the disappearances, it wasn't going to be a pair of handcuffs, that much seemed certain.

All right, simply alarming Max was pointless. I needed more information. *Why* was Lopez back on the case—or still on the case? The last time we met, I thought he had dismissed it altogether unless further evidence came to light.

"Further evidence…" I murmured.

Is that why he was here now? Did he know something new? Something we didn't?

I had to find out.

Counting on my costume and a little acting to protect my identity, I entered the store. Both men looked at me. Magnus's eyes lingered with interest. Lopez dismissed me with a glance and returned to questioning Magnus.

"I'll be with you in a few minutes, miss," Magnus said to me.

"Take your time," I said in a Queens accent.

I browsed while listening to their conversation. Within moments, I realized that Matilda had reported the destruction of the crystal cage to Lopez. I wanted to slap myself on the forehead. Of course! She couldn't let vandalism like that go unreported, and it made sense that she'd call the cop who'd given her his card after interviewing her about Golly's disappearance just a few days ago. Lopez was following up on her complaint.

Damn.

Destroying the cage last night had been necessary; I didn't question the decision in hindsight. But in doing it, we'd inadvertently wound up drawing Lopez's attention to the prop. His presence in Magnus's shop now and the detailed nature of the questions he was asking made me uneasy. I could tell we had stirred some instinct in him. Even if he still believed Golly had simply walked off when no one was looking, two incidents involving the crystal cage, just a few days apart, bothered him. He smelled something now. He didn't know what it was, but he was following his nose to see where it led.

I wondered how to get him off the scent. Should I even try? The truth of this case was something beyond his earthbound cop's imagination. Maybe he'd just chase his tail a bit, then give up. So maybe doing nothing was the best way for me to ensure he never got any closer to connecting the vandalism to me and the three-hundred-and-fifty-year-old wizard who'd used his magical powers to disable the locks of the theater and melted the crystal cage with pyromancy.

In response to Lopez's questions, Magnus was talking about a marginally similar repair job he'd done two years ago. When Lopez asked for the customer's name and address, Magnus said it was in the office and gestured to the red curtain behind him, adding, "But it would take me a while to find it."

"It's important," Lopez said.

Magnus shrugged. "Okay, but I need to help this customer first."

"I'll wait," said Lopez.

Since I couldn't talk to Magnus about stalling Matilda with Lopez standing right there, I said, "Oh, I just *love* these clothes!" I gestured to the vulgar costumes on the clothing racks. "Would it be okay if I tried on a few things?"

Magnus smiled, oozing sultry delight. "It would be my pleasure to indulge you."

It apparently didn't occur to him to wonder why I was wearing my sunglasses indoors. But I suspected Lopez was starting to wonder. He wasn't ogling me, the way Magnus was, but he was paying attention to me now, and something bothered him. Maybe it was my sunglasses, or maybe it was unconscious recognition of something familiar. He'd seen me in costume twice before now, so there might be things about me ringing a bell even in this disguise.

I turned my back and started choosing outfits. "Where's the dressing room?" I asked, keeping my accent firmly in place.

"Back there." Magnus pointed. "Take your time, love. I'll be only too happy to give you my *full* attention as soon as my business with this gentleman is finished."

"Thanks." I gave *my* full attention to a lime-green lace-and-sequined confection, hoping they'd both ignore me now.

"Detective?" Magnus said.

"Hmm?" I sensed from Lopez's distracted reply that he was still looking at me.

"Right this way, Detective."

"Oh, right."

I heard footsteps moving away from me, and then the rustle of the red curtain that hung in the doorway to Magnus's office. I looked over my shoulder and saw, with relief, that I was alone. I wondered if I should just leave now, before Lopez came back out of that room and got another look at me.

Then I thought of the crystal cage. It was probably upstairs, right where I'd seen it last time. I could go have a look, see if Magnus had done any work on it yet. See exactly how damaged it was. I'd been so shocked last night after watching Max destroy it with his strange power, my memory of its condition was rather vague. And I could hover up there, out of sight, until I was sure Lopez had gone. I checked my watch. It was closing time for Magnus, so no one else (no one named Matilda, for example) was likely to come into the shop and disturb my conversation with the red-haired magic maven once Lopez left.

I put a slinky, hot-pink gown back on the rack and, moving on tiptoe, crossed the shop and went upstairs in search of the crystal cage.

At the top of the stairs, I took off my sunglasses so I could see, took off my raincoat so I wouldn't be hot, and removed my boots so Magnus and Lopez wouldn't hear my footsteps over their heads. The second floor of the building was just as chaotic as I remembered, a maze of jumbled cartons, boxes, crates and equipment. It was dark, due to covered windows, and very dusty, due to Magnus's lack of a cleaning service. The crystal cage was not where I had expected to find it. Nor did it seem to be anywhere on the second floor, which took me some time to search in silence.

This was turning into more of a quest than I had anticipated, and I was getting exasperated. But since I hadn't heard Lopez leave the shop, I couldn't go back downstairs. So I ascended to the third floor, figuring

I might as well use my time productively instead of just squatting at the top of the stairs and cursing Lopez. I found a yank cord, turned on the light over the stairwell and stealthily climbed the stairs to the third floor in my stocking feet. At the top of the stairs, there was a big rack of sequin-and-lace-and-Lycra outfits in colors so bright they made me blink.

I rounded the rack—and walked straight into a small Asian woman with a huge snake wrapped around her. I squealed and jumped. She screamed and flinched.

"Urk!"

"Argh!"

The snake moved its head, and I realized it was real. I started screaming in earnest. I'm scared of snakes.

"Yaaaagh!"

I stumbled backward into the rack of clothing. It fell over with a deafening *smash-bang-clatter-clang!* I fell on top of it. Two more people started screaming— which was when I noticed there were two more people here. I was lying on my back atop the fallen garments, my arms and legs flailing. The snake-wrapped lady leaned over and extended a hand to help me, but the sight of the snake's face approaching mine only made me scream louder. Then the other two people were tugging at her arms, trying to haul her away from me. After a moment's hesitation, she went with them.

Magnus was shouting somewhere below, then I heard footsteps thundering up the stairs behind me. A moment later, two stunned men were looking down on my prone, flailing body with identical expressions of astonishment.

Magnus stood there holding a spear (a *spear?* I thought), gaping at me in stupefaction. His red-bearded jaw worked a few times, but no words came out. Then he looked around quickly, as if searching for the other people. But he still said nothing.

Lopez sighed, holstered his gun and squatted down beside me to remove my blonde wig. "Hello, Esther." He looked me over for a moment. "I assume there's a perfectly reasonable explanation for all this?"

CHAPTER

7

I've studied improvisation, which teaches you to think on your feet. So I was ready for Lopez's interrogation by the time he seated me in a straight-backed chair downstairs in Magnus's office and asked how I happened to wind up sneaking around the magic warehouse in disguise.

"I was looking for the crystal cage." Spy novels had taught me to stick as close to the truth as possible.

"Why didn't you just ask Magic Magnus where it is?"

"Yeah!" Magnus piped up, sitting at his desk.

"Where is it?" I asked.

"Before now," said Lopez.

"In my truck," Magnus said. "I picked it up from the theater today. Planned to unload it tonight or tomorrow."

"I thought you were giving it priority!" I said in vexation.

"I am."

"By leaving it in the truck all day?"

"I'm a busy man."

"Not too busy to flirt with customers!" I shot back.

"I— You— Well, I... Oh, never mind." He made an exasperated gesture and gave Lopez a look that indicated how unreasonable I was being.

Wearing his cop face, Lopez was watching us lose our tempers with each other, clearly waiting to see if any interesting comments would slip out in the heat of the moment.

I met Magnus's eyes and wondered why there was a big snake on the third floor. As if reading my mind, he suddenly flushed.

Evidently recognizing that we were done snapping at each other, Lopez said to me, "I see you've made a remarkable recovery."

"Recovery..." I suddenly realized that Matilda had talked about me. That should have occurred to me before now. "Yes, I became ill during the performance last night."

"All better now?"

"No," I said. "I'm feeling quite weak. May I go?"

"Not yet."

"I may vomit," I threatened.

"We'll get a bucket," Lopez said.

"I think I should go home." I stood up.

"Sit down." His voice was clipped and hard.

"But—"

"*Sit.*"

I sat.

He propped himself on Magnus's desk, folded his arms over his chest and stared at me. I stared back. It would never do to tell him so, of course, but the stern, don't-mess-with-me attitude was kind of sexy on him.

"What happened last night?" he asked.

Still sticking close to the truth, I said, "My whole worldview changed."

He frowned. "Go on."

I said, "Look, I *told* you I thought something was wrong. I *told* you I was anxious about getting into the cage without knowing what happened to Golly."

Magnus muttered, "Women are always saying 'I told you so.'"

"So you ran out on a performance?" Lopez asked, looking like he might be willing to believe me.

"I can't answer that in front of *him*." I pointed at Magnus. "He knows Matilda."

Lopez glanced at Magnus. Magnus blinked and said to me, "I won't tell Matilda what you say now if you don't tell her the crystal cage has been sitting in my truck all day."

Lopez looked back at me, a faint sparkle entering his long-lashed blue eyes. "Deal?"

I sighed. "Okay."

"Well?"

I explained that Joe had been such a wreck during rehearsal, as had I, that I wound up preparing to go onstage last night, in Golly's place, without having done a complete run-through of the show. And without having practiced the vanishing act since her disappearance. I just couldn't do it, I told Lopez. I was too scared of what might happen in the crystal cage. "I wasn't entirely faking, I did feel ready to toss my cookies. *Again*. And, well…" I shrugged. "I freaked out and, yes, ran out on the performance. Which," I added defensively, "is the only time in my life I've ever done that. *Ever.* I even went on as Little Red Riding Hood in the third grade when I had stomach flu and kept throwing up backstage."

Lopez startled me by asking, "Who was the doctor?"

"The doctor?"

"You know," he prodded. "The doctor who made a house call to your dressing room last night? The one who told your producer you were too ill to go on? That your condition was highly contagious?"

"It is?" Magnus blurted.

We both looked at him.

"Never mind," Magnus said.

"Well, Esther?"

"Just a performer," I said.

"Where'd he come from?"

"The street," I said. "He was a street act. I offered him twenty bucks to help me."

"His name?"

I wondered if Matilda had told Lopez the name. I wondered if she had reported or would report Max's visit to her today, now that she and Lopez were on such chatty terms. Could I risk pretending I didn't know Max's name, or would Lopez just catch me in the lie?

I said, "I told him to call himself Dr. Zadok."

"Why?"

"Just came into my head." I couldn't tell if Lopez believed me.

He switched the subject on me again. "How'd the crystal cage get destroyed?"

"Is it really destroyed?" I asked, feigning dismay rather well. "Matilda wasn't exaggerating?"

Lopez unfolded his arms and lowered his hands to his sides, bracing them against the desk. He had nice hands. Nice wrists, too, smooth and golden-skinned. Not hairy like some guys.

"Why were you looking for the cage here?" He couldn't stop his lips from twitching when he added, "In disguise."

"Matilda called me this morning making all sorts of threats and accusations. I don't know what happened to the crystal cage, but I know she's blaming me for it."

Lopez seemed to be trying to keep a straight face as he said, "And the obvious solution to the problem was to behave as suspiciously as possible?"

"I wanted to find out what happened to the cage. I couldn't call Matilda back and ask her, she was so vicious to me. I had to see Magnus. But I couldn't risk bumping into Matilda if she happened to come here this afternoon to nag Magnus."

"Which would be just like her," Magnus said wearily.

"So I had to make sure Matilda wouldn't recognize me."

"I didn't recognize you," Magnus admitted.

"But you did?" I asked Lopez curiously.

He smiled a little. "No. The high heels, the makeup, the wig, the sunglasses, the voice, the accent, the posture... It was all good. Very good."

I beamed. "Thanks!"

"But I wondered why you were still wearing sunglasses while you were looking at clothes."

"Ah." I'd thought so.

His gaze lingered on my face. "And even skilful makeup and a wig can't hide those cheekbones."

Our eyes locked, and I suddenly felt warm.

"I didn't know it was you, but I'd have figured it out if I'd had another couple of minutes. Something clicked."

"That's why I turned my back."

"Of course." He lowered his gaze. "But even from the back..."

"Yes?"

"Well, there's something about you in tight clothes that sticks in my mind," he admitted. "So you still looked familiar. I just didn't know why."

"Tight?" I said indignantly.

"That raincoat's tight, Esther." He glanced up and added, his eyes glinting, "In a good way."

"Well… I guess it is a bit tight," I said, flustered. "I get stuff like this at church sales and thrift stores to wear as rehearsal costumes. It's a lot easier to start getting into a role if you dress for it."

"That makes sense."

"Anyhow, yeah, I guess that coat is a little small for me." I was babbling. "But it only cost me seven dollars, and—"

"It looks good on you."

I blinked. "Really?"

"*Excuse* me," said Magnus. "Are we done here?"

Lopez cleared his throat and resumed questioning me. "So you come into the shop, and Matilda's not here. Why not take off the dark glasses and be straight with us?"

Thinking it best to avoid explaining that I was spying on him so I could report back to the Magnum Collegium's local representative, I said, "Because it was obvious Matilda had reported the attack on the crystal cage to you."

He pounced. "Attack? What makes you think it wasn't an accident?"

"Because she'd reported it to a cop. And since I knew she was blaming me, I thought you were probably blaming me, too. Which," I added sourly, "seems to be the case."

"Finding you sneaking around here in disguise has contributed a lot to my blaming you," he shot back.

"I was just trying to avoid exactly what we're doing right now!"

"What *are* we doing right now?" Magnus asked plaintively.

"I was going to come downstairs and talk to Magnus as soon as you'd left," I told Lopez. Looking at Magnus, I added, "I was going to ask you what had happened to the crystal cage and how long it would take to repair it."

Lopez said, "So now you're suddenly eager to do the act?"

"Not really," I said. "But with Golly missing, whatever happens with the cage affects my career. So I am interested."

"What made you start screaming?" Lopez asked, in yet another deliberately sudden change of topic.

"Up on the third floor?" Out of the corner of my eye, I saw Magnus suddenly shaking his head at me, behind Lopez's back. I said, "It's dark upstairs. There are shadows, weird magic props, creepy replicas. Something up there moved…."

Magnus shook his head a little more frantically.

Still looking at me, Lopez said, "What moved?"

"I didn't know at first, so I screamed. I was startled. Then I realized it was a mouse. And I fell over at the same time. Then I screamed because I didn't like being on the floor with a mouse running around."

Both men looked like they weren't sure whether I was telling the truth.

I added with a shudder, "I *hate* mice."

That helped. They both seemed to relax a little.

I didn't know why Magnus didn't want me mentioning the three staff members I'd seen upstairs, but he evidently didn't. Now he looked as if he hoped I hadn't seen them and really was as scared of mice as I claimed. Or maybe he was worried about the snake? Was there some reason he couldn't risk a cop hearing about it? I wondered if permits were needed to keep a reptile that big in the city. Maybe it wasn't properly licensed or something?

So apparently I now knew a secret that Magnus wanted kept. That might come in handy, if I needed any leverage to convince him to stall Matilda about the crystal cage until Max and I had solved the problem of the mystical disappearances. But talking to Magnus about that was not something I could do with Lopez present. So I decided to try to get rid of the detective, who was running a hand over his ruffled black hair as if his head was starting to ache.

"Are we done now?" I asked him.

"For the time being," he said.

"I can go?" I'd lurk outside, wait until he left, too, then double back here to confront Magnus.

"I'll take you home," Lopez said.

"What?" I blurted.

"Or wherever you're headed next."

I was headed to Zadok's Rare and Used Books next. But not with Lopez as my escort.

"Not necessary, Detective," I said firmly, rising to my feet.

"Oh, I insist."

"But I—"

"Let's go."

He took my arm. We both paused and looked at each other. It was nice to be touched. By him. He blinked, then dropped my arm and stepped away. He thanked Magnus for his time, then held aside the red curtain and made a gesture for me to precede him.

"After you, Miss Diamond."

Lopez had a nondescript car parked illegally near the magic shop. A handy official notice propped in the window warned other cops not to make the mistake of assuming that parking statutes applied to this vehicle the way they did to others.

He opened the passenger door for me, then got into the driver's seat while I buckled up.

"Where to?" he asked. He kept his gaze forward and was frowning slightly.

"I haven't had dinner yet," I heard myself say.

He let out his breath and leaned his forehead against the steering wheel. "Esther…"

We were silent for a moment, not looking at each other.

"We can't have dinner together," he said at last.

"I wasn't asking—"

"Yes, you were." He lifted his head and sat back.

In for a penny, in for a pound, so I said, "Okay, why can't we have dinner together?"

"I can't date someone who's part of a current investigation."

"It wouldn't be a date."

"Yes, it would," he said, "and you know it would. You know it's been on my mind ever since I saw you without glitter and green body paint all over everything but your teeth."

"It has?" I asked, pleased.

He gave me an exasperated look. "No, I always make inappropriate comments when I'm interviewing women, Esther. It's my ambition to get suspended for sexual harassment."

"I think your comments to me are nice." But only because *he* was the one making those comments. I liked Lopez saying things to me that, in fact, we both knew he shouldn't be saying, given the nature of our acquaintance.

"Well, they're meant to be nice." He smiled as his gaze traveled over my face. "But the point is…" Our eyes locked and we found ourselves in a staring contest. "The point is…"

"Yes?"

"Huh?"

"The point is?" I prodded, unable to look away.

"Um… I think I've forgotten the point."

"I think it was that we can't go on a date?" I said.

"Oh! Yes!" He blinked. "Yes, that's the point."

"But I don't see why—"

"Just how much are you not telling me about what's going on?"

That caught me off guard. As it was meant to do. The cop's tactic of changing the subject abruptly with a new question. "Uh… I don't know what—"

"I should press you harder," he said, looking down. "I should take you down to the station, get in your face, scare you."

"We could still do that," I said. "The night is young."

He laughed. Then he sighed and shook his head. "The problem is, I can't do that to you."

"A cop who can't pressure and scare people? Maybe you're in the wrong line of—"

"I can't do that to *you*."

"Oh." I got a little warm again.

"But I'm not an idiot, Esther."

"I know." I'd never thought he was.

"How much of what you told me in Magnus's shop was true?"

My heart thudded. "Um, quite a lot of it, actually."

"What part wasn't true?"

I looked out my window, feeling both anxious and disappointed. My previous instinct to get away from him as soon as possible had been the smart choice, I realized. So I said, "I live on West Thirty-third Street, between Tenth and Eleventh."

"What did you leave out of your story?"

"You can just take me home. Forget about dinner. It was a silly idea."

He put his hand on my arm. I closed my eyes, and my heart pounded even harder.

"You're a suspect," he said.

"Suspected of?" My voice was a little breathy.

"Vandalism, at the very least." He squeezed my arm gently. "What's going on?"

I was trying to think about something aside from the way his skin felt on my skin, his palm on my bare forearm, the subtle pressure of his fingers.

I swallowed and gave myself a mental shake. I couldn't be sure how sincere that gentle touch was. Even if he felt something, he certainly knew by now that *I* felt something, and he wanted answers from me. And I doubted anyone could be an effective cop without being a little ruthless. Even with himself. Even with a woman he...

"What's going on?" I repeated. I gave my confused feelings a solid shove in the direction of anger. "I came to you with two threatening notes. I told you I was scared. Golly Gee is *missing*. You didn't take any of that seriously!"

He frowned and took his hand away. "Yes, I—"

"But Matilda calls you about vandalism—of a fragile prop in an unguarded theater—and suddenly you're all over the case!"

"Yes, I am," he snapped, sounding angry, too. "For

one thing, there actually *is* a case this time. Breaking and entering, and vandalism."

"Why am I a suspect?"

"Apart from your bizarre behavior today?"

"I explained—"

"Come off it, Esther. If you knew I was in the shop to question Magnus about the vandalism that Matilda was blaming on you, why'd you come inside? Why'd you stay?"

"I—I—" Improv lessons suddenly weren't helping so much.

"You're not an idiot, either." He didn't make it sound like a compliment. "You took that risk for a reason. You were there for something else."

I hoped that a little more truth might help the situation. "Okay, I went to ask Magnus not to return the crystal cage to *Sorcerer!* until someone finds out what happened to Golly. And I went upstairs looking for it to see if it was as damaged as I hoped." While he studied me in silence, I added, "Anyhow, I thought I *was* avoiding you. I didn't expect you to find out I was prowling around upstairs." I shrugged and glared at him. "And I sure didn't expect you to recognize me."

"Well, now you know better."

"I certainly do. I guess I'll wear a gunny sack the next time we meet, if I don't want you ogling me!"

"I did *not* og— Well, okay, maybe a little."

"You did?"

Our eyes met again. "Yeah," he said. "Very subtly, mind you."

We both laughed a little in mingled pleasure and embarrassment. Then he looked away.

"Look, Esther," he said, sounding tired, "if you're that afraid to get into the prop box, why not just quit the show?"

"I can't do that! Do you have any idea how hard it is to get a job? I mean, a *real* job—an acting job? I was waiting tables for months before this! And do you know how much harder it would be for me to get another job once word got out that I'd abandoned this show as soon as I stepped into the lead role? Besides, even if quitting would solve *my* problem, it wouldn't solve *the* problem."

"It wouldn't?"

"What if the show doesn't fold even after losing the female lead and her understudy? What if someone else takes over playing Virtue?" I exclaimed. "What'll happen to *her* when she performs the act?"

"Oh my God," he said slowly, looking at me with a dawning expression of amazement. "You did vandalize the cage, didn't you?"

I blinked, thinking maybe I'd been a tad too truthful. "No."

He nodded. "You destroyed it thinking you were in danger. Thinking anyone who gets into it is in danger."

"No!"

"Esther, why destroy the thing? Why not get an expert to examine it? Why not ask Magnus to go through it piece by piece with you to make sure it was safe?"

"I didn't vandalize it!"

And I hadn't. I was just an accomplice. One who was currently digging a hole for herself, like a perfect idiot, because I'd briefly wallowed in my attraction to the investigating officer.

"Look, if you vandalized the cage," Lopez said, "it would be a first offense. You've got no priors."

"How do you know that?"

"Uh, well—"

I gasped. "You've been checking up on me!"

He looked exasperated again. "Of course I have! You're a suspect, Esther."

"I can't believe this! You had the nerve to ask me out to dinner while you're *investigating* me?"

"*You* asked *me.*"

Since he had a point, I changed the subject. "I want to go home now."

"Listen to me. It's a first offense, there were no drugs involved… Er, there *were* no drugs involved?"

"Oh, right, I'm an actress, so naturally I must be a drug user!"

"That's not what I—"

"Also promiscuous, right?"

"Okay, let's calm down."

"After all, everybody knows that 'actress' is practically synonymous with 'prostitute'!"

"What?"

"In some languages, it's even the exact same *word!*"

"A first offense, no drugs, no one got hurt," he said doggedly, refusing to be distracted (as I'd hoped) by my tirade, "and there were extenuating circumstances. The DA will be lenient. You can plead it out without serving any time."

"What extenuating circumstances?" I snapped, spooked by the mention of serving time.

"Golly Gee went missing in the middle of the act, Herlihy couldn't explain what had happened to her, and you were receiving mysterious notes warning you of the same fate if you got into the crystal cage. You're an artiste, you're sensitive... It's going to be fine," he said soothingly. "I'll give you the name of a good defense lawyer who'll make sure you don't get slapped with anything worse than a little community service."

"I thought cops hated defense lawyers," I muttered.

"I do. But they have their uses."

"Are you charging me?" I demanded.

"Did you save the notes you received? I'll tell the DA that I saw them, of course. But it would help if..." He frowned. "The notes..."

"What about the notes?" I asked uneasily.

"They were signed M.Z."

I didn't like his expression. He seemed to be looking inside himself, suddenly connecting random facts scattered in his head. I decided to try distracting him again.

"You can't pin this bum rap on me," I insisted.

For a moment, my attempt seemed to work. "Where do you *get* that kind of dialogue?"

"I'm not guilty, and I'm not confessing to anything."

But then he said, "M.Z."

"And you can either cease these insulting accusations right now—"

"What made you think of that name for your 'doctor'?"

I tried not to drop my lines. "Right—right now, or else you can charge me. But since I didn't *do* anything—"

"Dr. Zadok," Lopez said. "M.Z."

"I'm going home." I unbuckled my seat belt and reached for the door handle.

"What's going on, Esther?" He stopped me when I tried to exit the car.

"Let me go!"

"Half of this is an act, isn't it? You're not silly or skittish. A little eccentric, maybe…"

"I'm leaving now." I pushed at his restraining arm.

"But not a hysteric," he said with certainty. "So what aren't you telling me?"

"Let go."

"Is someone threatening you? Scaring you?"

"Stop it!"

He put his hand on the back of my neck and pulled my head close to his. "Just tell me that much," he breathed into my ear, making my hair flutter. "Just tell me if you're afraid of someone."

I closed my eyes, breathing hard, my chest pounding.

"Esther." His breath fanned my neck and my cheek. His dark hair brushed against my temple. "Talk to me."

"You're the one I'm afraid of." I choked out the words, pulling away from him.

I turned the door handle and jumped out of the car. He didn't stop me this time.

"The only thing we've done that's illegal," I reiterated to Max, "is breaking and entering, and vandalism."

Yes, indeed, after careful examination of the facts, I was positive those were our "only" prosecutable crimes.

"And given the way we did what we did," I continued, "it'll be hard to prove."

"That's a relief. I think." Max tugged a little at his white beard. "I do feel bad about breaking the law. It's just sometimes unavoidable in the struggle against Evil."

"Right now, I'm the only one suspected of destroying the crystal cage. I think." By the time I'd fled Lopez's car yesterday evening, he'd been highly suspicious of the mysterious Dr. Zadok a.k.a. M.Z., but I didn't know if he suspected him of *this*. "We want to keep it that way. We want to keep suspicion off you," I reminded Max. "Right?"

"Oh, Esther, I still don't feel right about this!"

I had come straight to the shop after leaving Lopez yesterday, and I'd waited impatiently for Max to return with Barclay and Duke. Examination of the Great Hidalgo's prop box had revealed nothing new to Max, who returned to the bookshop frustrated and puzzled. The Pony Expressive performers all had to abandon their various research posts when it was time to go perform their first show of the night at the club. Barclay and Dixie kept at it for another hour, then called it quits and went out for a nightcap after I told them Max and I had to consult in private. Duke, a little teary eyed with worry about Dolly, went back to his hotel after being assured that Barclay would not buy alcohol for Dixie and would escort her back to the Waldorf-Astoria before her midnight curfew.

I hadn't wanted to alarm the others by talking about the police before I had settled on a plan with Max. Now, after a restless night, I was back in the shop the following morning, reviewing what we'd decided. Or, rather, what *I* had decided and had told him was the plan.

"Max, this is damage control," I said now. "Yes, it's extremely inconvenient that Lopez suspects me of vandalizing the cage—but I'm safe." I hoped I was right about that. "I don't have keys for those locks you opened, I don't know how to pick locks, and I don't have any experience with a blow torch—or whatever it would have taken to melt the cage if a mundane had destroyed it. And no one can prove otherwise. So Lopez can make me uncomfortable, but he can't charge me. Because he's got no real evidence against me."

I hoped I was right about that, too. Lopez had tried to make the consequences of getting caught sound minor, but I had no intention of going through the rest of my life with a criminal record. I didn't want to check the box marked "Yes," on every employment and rental application I filled out, asking if I'd ever been convicted of a crime. And it seemed particularly unfair that I might get stuck with a burden like that as a direct result of, you know, fighting Evil.

Max protested, "But it seems wrong for me to cower behind you—"

"The struggle against Evil will not be served in any way by you also coming under suspicion for what happened that night."

"That's true, but—"

"So it will be much better for the disappearees if you just *don't* come under suspicion," I said. "Agreed?"

"Um—"

"Good." If Max got locked up, our problem would seem hopeless instead of just dire.

"But I—"

"Now let's review, Max. What's our story about that night?"

He nodded and concentrated. "We left the theater, pretending you were ill so you wouldn't have to perform the disappearing act. We went to the Waldorf. Then we came here. Later, we went to the Pony Expressive."

Unfortunately, he was a terrible liar. And he wasn't improving with practice. He sounded stilted and awkward.

But I said, "Okay. Good." I looked him over. "Are you all right?"

"I feel a bit light-headed."

Max was very anxious about the prospect of being questioned by the police. I was anxious about it, too. After yesterday, I was sure that Lopez would soon track him down. So I was trying to prepare him.

Based on the assumption that Lopez would dismiss almost everything Max said as sheer nonsense, I had decided it was best to fabricate nothing, and omit only one fact from any account we gave of our activities—the fact that we had gone back to the theater that night and actually committed the crime in question. I'd rather not have to explain our presence at the Waldorf and the Pony Expressive to Lopez, but I didn't want Max to get caught in a muddle of lies, which I knew could happen pretty easily. Besides, so many people had seen us at both places that, if this case got any more complicated, it was possible Lopez would learn we'd lied. And that would be a problem. So I figured that the fewer lies we told, the fewer lies we'd have to worry about keeping straight.

The rest of the group started arriving at the shop shortly after noon. (You keep late hours when your research team consists largely of nightclub performers.) By one o'clock, we were ready to convene a meeting to share our findings to date, in what Whoopsy was calling "Project Bookworm."

"The good news, my friends," Max announced, "is that I do not believe another disappearance occurred last night!"

Everyone else cheered.

I spoiled things by asking, "Can you be positive?"

"Er, no. But the localized dimensional disturbance, which has by now become both pronounced and familiar, does not seem to have occurred since Sexy Samson disappeared."

"Do we have any idea why not?" I asked.

"No."

"Maybe this means there'll be no more disappearances?" Satsy suggested hopefully.

I wasn't optimistic. "There were a couple of days of inactivity after Clarisse disappeared and before Dolly vanished."

"Hmm," Max said. "Yes, this may just be another lull."

I grumbled, "Where's His Royal Highness Hieronymus, Prince of the Cellar? Too busy manufacturing explosions to join the meeting?"

"He went out early this morning," Max said. "He thinks he may have a lead."

"What kind of a lead?"

"He didn't tell me."

Unfortunately, the rest of Max's news was negative. Having talked to all of the magicians and examined all the prop boxes by now, he couldn't spot a common thread.

"We'll need to do a second interview," I said. "We need to go into more detail than we have so far. We should gather all four magicians here together."

"Me, Barclay and Miss Delilah are willing and eager," said Duke, with a gracious nod of his head to the dusky drag queen. She was wearing a tight red dress and gold hoop earrings, and her makeup was flawless, though her eyes were red. "But how are we going to get Herlihy to sit through another interview, let alone join us here?"

After a brief silence, everyone looked at me. "*I* don't know," I said crankily.

"You know him better than anyone else here," Satsy pointed out.

"But I don't know him *well,* and I don't like him." In fact, my whole mode was cranky today.

"Maybe if I asked him?" Delilah suggested.

I thought it over. I resisted the urge to dwell bitterly on how unfair it was that a drag queen had more power to move straight men than I did, and I acknowledged that, of all of us, Delilah was probably the most likely to sway Joe. Men can rarely resist a sultry beauty with tears in her eyes. Especially if they haven't yet realized she's got a penis under that tight red skirt. There was a certain talk I still hadn't had with Max. Thinking about it made me even crankier.

"Well?" Delilah prodded gently.

I shook my head. "How would you get past his wife? No way will she let a stranger into the apartment to talk to him now."

"Then let's figure out a way to separate them," said Duke.

"Let's nab him!" said Barclay. "Or her!"

"Good idea!" said Whoopsy.

"I'll help," said Khyber.

"Whoa! Hang on," I said. "Let's see if we can think of a less felonious way of getting Joe here for an interview." No need for *all* of us to wind up under criminal investigation.

"Speaking of interviews…" said Whoopsy. He held up *The Exposé,* a tabloid newspaper that made other tabloids look like serious journalistic endeavors.

I read the front-page headline. "'Zombies in Manhattan'?" I shrugged. "So what?"

He handed the tabloid to me. "Page three."

I opened it and read the headline there. "Oh. That's not good."

"Well?" Barclay prodded.

"'Golly, Golly's Gone!'" I read.

"The press has got a hold of this?" said Max. "Oh dear."

"How?" Dixie wondered.

"Not just the press, I'm afraid," said Khyber. "That's part of my report. Golly Gee's name is showing up on some conspiracy-theory BBs."

"BBs?" Max repeated.

"Electronic bulletin boards. Internet gossip."

"Oh dear," Max said again.

"So far," Khyber said, "Golly's the only one of the victims being mentioned."

"Makes sense. She's the most famous one," I said, skimming the *Exposé* article. "Max, remember the assistant stage manager who talked to you? She talked to these guys, too."

"So that's how the story broke!" said Dixie.

I finished skimming the article. "Ironically, they got some of the facts right. I think that may be a first for *The Exposé*. But it sounds so absurd, especially in their prose style, I wouldn't expect this to get much attention."

"Even though Golly Gee really is missing?" Satsy said.

"And, her being so famous, that's bound to be noticed," Whoopsy added.

"Probably by now," Barclay said.

"Oh. Good point." I folded the paper. My hands were dirty now from its cheap ink. "I suppose I might as well take this opportunity to mention that we're expecting a visit from the police at some point."

"Fuzz?" Whoopsy leaped to his feet.

"Calm down," I said. "I'm under suspicion. Max

may be under suspicion, too, though we hope to avoid that."

Max protested, "But Esther—"

"But no one else here has done anything wrong or has any reason to be concerned."

"I'll call my lawyers, tell them we may need help," said Barclay, pulling out his cell phone.

"Good man," said Duke.

Dixie beamed at Barclay as he stepped away from the table to make his call.

We proceeded with reports. Khyber summarized the history of supposedly mystical disappearances (and re-appearances) caused by lightning strikes, violent thunderstorms, thick fog and eclipses. Most of these seemed (to me, at least) to be clear cases of frightened, disoriented people seizing upon a supernatural explanation after a confusing experience. Khyber also summarized a slew of other supposedly mystical disappearances he'd found online that did not involve bad weather. Mostly, I was amazed at how many men turned up naked after a bender and claimed they were the victims of supernatural events about which they could give no details.

My own team reported that faeries sometimes made people disappear. In fact, Dixie informed the group, there were said to be whole islands in the United Kingdom that faeries had caused to vanish.

Max resisted blaming faeries for our problems, though. "They're relatively scarce in the New World, and rarely this energetic."

Satsy asked if there'd been a shower of toads accompanying any of the disappearances. Upon being told that there had not, he said, "Okay, that rules out one theory, so never mind."

"It's funny that no horses or cattle have been involved yet," Dixie said. According to her reading, the mystical movement of livestock was a common phenomenon.

"Otherwise known as rustling," I muttered.

"It's possible the disappearees are being transported to a duplicate dimension," Barclay reported. "In fact, they may not even realize they've disappeared."

Even I found this theory interesting, but discussion of it didn't get us any closer to solving our problem.

In Hieronymus's absence, I reported that he had found nothing in the Latin and Greek texts yet, and he thought it was possible that mundanes were responsible for the disappearances. This provoked considerable controversy in the group, and I eventually said, "Look, take it up with him, if you're that offended. When he gets back from following his lead." I wondered if it was a mundane lead, and I decided to try to like him a little if he came back today with something more useful than theories about faeries, falling toads and duplicate dimensions.

Whoopsy's research had produced a list of the most common types of supernatural disappearances. I cut

Max short when he tried to explain why *supernatural* was the wrong word, and Whoopsy said, "About twenty percent of mystical disappearances are classified as 'spontaneous total disappearances,' which means that someone or something vanishes without warning and is never seen again."

Dixie gasped. Duke looked upset. Barclay made a little noise and checked his watch—perhaps wondering how soon Clarisse Staunton's parents would be back from Europe. Delilah bit her lip and tears started flowing.

So I said, "Only twenty percent? That's excellent news! Did you hear that, guys? There's at least an eighty-percent chance we're going to get the disappearees back!"

"Well, not really," said Whoopsy, glancing at his notes.

So much for trying to maintain group morale, I thought.

"For example," Whoopsy said, "several kinds of disappearances involve corpses."

"Ah," said Khyber, nodding. "Since our disappearees were all alive when they vanished, that skews our stats."

"Why would a corpse go missing?" Dixie wondered.

"What are some of the other kinds of disappearances?" I asked quickly.

"Well, there are disappearances that are followed

almost instantaneously by reappearance at a distant location."

"Aha!" said Barclay.

"*Star Trek,*" said Dixie.

"These disappearances can be willed, or they can be spontaneous. They account for somewhere between thirty and forty-five percent of cases."

"Why is the margin for error so wide?" Khyber asked, bookkeeper-like.

"There's a stats-skewy thing whereby some people appear out of nowhere who have not, as far as anyone knows, *dis*appeared from somewhere else."

"Ah." Khyber nodded again.

"Some disappearees vanish on the basis of a strong desire to be elsewhere," Whoopsy continued.

In which case, I should have vanished twenty minutes ago.

"And some disappear involuntarily due to an overpowering emotional state, such as frustrated love, anxiety, concern for the well-being of a loved one, fear of moral compromise…" Whoopsy had a good snicker over that last one.

"Or just plain fear?" Satsy suggested.

"Yes."

"You know…" I began.

"What?"

"Maybe we know more pertinent facts about the victims than I realized," I said slowly. I rose from my seat and went to the display board.

"What do you mean?" Delilah asked.

I erased the notes that I'd made yesterday and started over. I wrote the names of the four disappearees across the top of the board. Then, using a blue marker, under the name of each one, I wrote: *Not afraid.*

"We've talked about their mental states. Whatever happened once they were alone inside the vanishing boxes, the one thing we all seem sure of is that each victim was in a normal frame of mind upon entering the prop."

"That's right," said Duke.

I picked up a pink marker and wrote: *Wanted to stay.*

"We know they each had plans in this dimension. Dolly wanted to go shopping. Golly wanted to win a Tony Award. Clarisse wanted to attend a bridal shower and to perform with Barclay at the Magic Cabaret on Saturday."

"And Samson was really looking forward to taking his mother to Atlantic City next week." When we looked at her, Delilah added, "They do it twice a year. They're very close."

I picked up a green marker and wrote: *Spontaneous???*

"We can assume the victims didn't plan this. We know the magicians didn't plan this. But does that mean it wasn't planned? We don't know yet."

"That's right!" Satsy said.

"Are these spontaneous events brought about by common circumstances we haven't yet identified? Or are they planned events brought about by an entity we haven't yet detected?"

"Priority research question," Khyber said, taking notes.

"We can say confidently that the victims didn't want to vanish," I said. "Which means we know one more thing."

"What's that?" Delilah asked.

I took a red marker and wrote the answer on the board in big red letters. Four times. Once under each name.

MADE TO DISAPPEAR.

They all nodded.

"The two questions we must address," I said, "are *how* and *why* were they made to disappear?" When they all nodded again, I added, "Figuring out one may lead us to answering the other."

It was perhaps unfortunate that Detective Lopez chose that moment to enter the bookshop.

I froze when I saw him. He looked around, then froze when he saw me. Next to me, Whoopsy gasped and rose to his feet. Lopez's glance flickered to Whoopsy, then rested there. He frowned, as if trying to remember where he'd seen him before.

"Hello!" Max stepped forward to greet Lopez. Mistaking him for a customer, he asked, "Can I help you find something in particular, or are you just browsing? Do be sure to check out our section on ritual sacrifice and prophecy, we're having a sale this week."

I covered my eyes with my hand, unable to bear the moment.

"Dr. Zadok, I presume?" Lopez said.

"Yes!" Max replied with friendly cheer. "Were you referred by one of our regulars?"

I looked up and said, "Max." But my well-trained voice was dry and faint at the moment, and he didn't hear me.

Lopez pulled out his gold shield. "Detective Lopez, NYPD."

"Ah, you're looking for books on reincarnation and reanimation," Max guessed. "A wise investment. The mortality statistics for members of your profession are not encouraging."

Lopez looked amused and a little puzzled. "Are you trying to threaten me?"

"Dr. Zadok," Whoopsy said. *"Fuzz."* He nudged me.

"Max," I said, my voice carrying this time.

Suddenly realizing whom he was facing, Max gasped and fell back a step. "Detective Lopez!"

"Apparently I was expected." He looked around the room, taking in the interesting assortment of people gathered there. When his eyes rested on Whoopsy again, he said, "How are you, Seymour?"

"Uh. Um." Whoopsy looked anxious.

"Seymour?" I said blankly.

Lopez glanced at me. "Seymour Barinsky."

"My real name," Whoopsy said faintly.

"You two know each other?" I asked in confusion.

Whoopsy sighed. "He busted me."

"Back when I was in uniform," Lopez said.

"You've got a good memory, Detective," Whoopsy said.

"You made quite an impression."

"What did you do?" Dixie asked.

Whoopsy replied with an air of defiance, "Indecent exposure, obscenity and disturbing the peace."

"Several times, in fact." Lopez said to me, "I had no idea you consorted with such persons."

"He's a librarian," I said. "Or was."

"I'm an artiste!" Whoopsy cried. "You were stifling my First Amendment rights!"

"So you remember me, too," Lopez said. "I'm flattered."

"Honey, who *wouldn't* remember someone as cute as you?" said Delilah.

"Why, thank you." Lopez smiled politely at her. I got the impression that Delilah's feminine grace and clothing didn't mislead him about her true gender. His gaze moved around the group again. This time it stopped on Barclay. "The Great Hidalgo?"

Barclay gasped. So did I. Lopez had covered more ground than I'd suspected.

"Um, yes," Barclay said. "How did you... I mean, *I've* never been arrested."

"I stopped by your office a little while ago. They said you'd be here."

Well. That had certainly taken the challenge out of finding Dr. Zadok.

Rising to the occasion, Duke said, "Well, howdy, Detective. Very pleased to meet one of New York's finest. I'm Duke Dempsey the Conjuring Cowboy, and this beautiful young lady here is my daughter, Dixie."

"Oh, Daddy!"

Duke made the other introductions, which gave me time to collect my wits. That was when I realized my hands were liberally stained with the various colors of markers with which I had written, under the names of the victims, in letters that looked awfully big and bright to me now, phrases that might appear rather incriminating if viewed in the wrong context.

I was wondering if I could casually erase the whole board without being noticed when Lopez caught my eye. He glanced at the display board, then at my hands.

"Hello, Esther," he said. "I assume there's a perfectly reasonable explanation for all this?"

"What are you doing?" I demanded, trying to stop Lopez. "You can't take him to the precinct house!"

Lopez replied, with patience that seemed to be fraying, "I have to question him."

"We have rights," I said. "You can't make him go with you!"

"Esther," Max pleaded, "calm down, I'm sure everything will be fine."

I was far from sure of that. "No, Max, he can't force you!"

"Not this very minute," Lopez agreed. "If you'll just give me a little time, though, I'll come back with a warrant."

"A *warrant?*" I blurted.

"If he won't come voluntarily with me now for questioning, Esther, that's the way it'll have to be," Lopez warned.

The bastard! "I can't believe I almost went out to dinner with you!"

"You *did?*" Whoopsy said, horrified.

Khyber said to Whoopsy, "You have to admit he's hot."

Max said to me, "So you've met a young man you like? How nice!"

"I don't like him that much," I said, glaring at Lopez.

"You were going to *date* him?" Dixie asked.

"Honey, *I'd* date him," said Delilah. "If he weren't, you know, trying to arrest Dr. Zadok." She leaned closer to Dixie and added, "Don't you just *love* his eyes?"

"I don't think he's very nice," Dixie said, shaking her head.

"Now, Dixie. Manners," Duke admonished. "The man's got a job to do, same as you and me."

"But his job is interfering with *our* job," Satsy said. "Detective, we need Dr. Zadok to help us find the disappearees!"

I said to Lopez, "Max hasn't done anything wrong!"

"Then he's got nothing to worry about," Lopez replied. "Shall we go, Dr. Zadok?"

"All right," Max said, trying to be a good citizen.

"No, Max!" I grabbed his arm and pulled him away from Lopez.

"You're not helping him this way," Lopez warned me.

"Why can't you question him here?" I demanded.

"How will we know if there's another localized dimensional disturbance if Max isn't here to sense it?" Satsy cried.

"How will we get Dolly the Dancing Cowgirl and Sexy Samson back from the other side?" Delilah asked, getting teary again.

"Or possibly from another time-space reality?" Barclay added.

Lopez looked at me. "*This* is why I can't question him here."

I rubbed my forehead, then stopped when I realized I was getting tabloid ink on it. I had to admit Lopez's position was not entirely devoid of reason. And there seemed to be no realistic way of preventing him from doing what he wanted, anyhow.

"All right," I said. "But I'm coming with you."

"Actually," said Lopez, "I would prefer that Mr. Preston-Cole come with us. I have some questions for him, too."

Dixie seized Barclay's hand. "He can't go with you! We have to rehearse!"

"Rehearse?" Duke repeated.

"Barclay's not going to miss his big break at the Magic Cabaret tomorrow," Dixie announced.

"That's not tomorrow," I said, "it's Saturday."

"Tomorrow *is* Saturday, Esther," Lopez said.

"Oh!" I'd lost track. "How time flies when you're fighting Evil."

"Indeed," Max said.

"What?" Lopez said.

"Never mind," I said.

"We talked about it last night," Dixie told us all, "and I'm going to perform with Barclay tomorrow."

"What?" cried Satsy.

"Honey, no!" Delilah protested.

"You can't do that!" Max cried. "It's not safe!"

"It's sure not!" Duke agreed.

"Dr. Zadok, Mr. Preston-Cole," Lopez said, "let's go."

No one paid any attention to him.

"I'll be perfectly safe," Dixie said firmly. "We won't do the disappearing act."

"Well, that might be all right," Khyber said judiciously.

"Can we be sure?" Satsy asked.

"Yes," Dixie insisted. "The disappearing act is the only thing we have to fear. "

I saw Lopez's expression as he looked at me. "Don't look at me like that."

"As long as we leave that out of the show," Dixie continued, "there's no reason to worry about us performing tomorrow."

"Boy, I don't know, Dixie," Duke said, shaking his head.

"Daddy, I promised Barclay, and I won't let down a friend."

"What do you think, Dr. Zadok?" Barclay asked. "I'll cancel the show if you don't think it's safe."

Lopez scowled and folded his arms, looking at me as if this delay was *my* fault. I scowled back.

While we glared at each other, Max stroked his beard and said, "Well, as long as you don't attempt the disappearing act until we've solved this case…"

"Speaking of solving—" Lopez blinked when Delilah shushed him.

Max nodded. "Yes, all right. I believe Dixie and Barclay can safely perform at the cabaret."

Dixie squealed with delight and gave Barclay a hug. Barclay blushed and said to Duke, "That is, if it's okay with you, sir?"

"As long as you make sure I get a good seat for the show!" Duke replied. "I can't miss seeing my little girl onstage in New York City, now can I?"

"Oh, Daddy!"

Barclay and Duke shook hands.

"Esther," Barclay asked, "is it okay if we miss some research duty today so we can go rehearse?"

"Of course," I replied. "The show must go on."

Lopez said to Barclay, in a cop tone that made further protest seem unwise, "First, we have some business to take care of down at the station. Let's go."

Looking pale and wide-eyed at this reminder, Barclay said, "I think I should call my lawyer."

"You're not under arrest," Lopez said, "I'm just asking you to answer some questions, as a law-abiding citizen, about Clarisse Staunton."

"Oh, God!" Barclay looked panicky. Dixie murmured encouraging words to him.

"I'm coming with you," I said firmly to Lopez.

"Suit yourself," he replied.

"No, Esther." Max squared his chubby shoulders. "I need you to stay here and mind the store for me. Please?"

"Max…"

"I was once questioned by the Inquisition," he said, trying to reassure me. "I feel sure this won't be that bad."

I didn't like letting him go without me, but I doubted I could help him much at the police station anyhow, and I hated to refuse a request he was making with such a heartfelt expression.

"All right," I said. "I'll wait here for you."

"Let's go, gentlemen." As they left, Lopez looked over his shoulder at me. "You and I will talk later."

It sounded much more like a threat than a promise.

W hoopsy checked in by phone later that day. "Any news from the prisoners yet?"

"They're not prisoners, they're just being questioned in connection with the case," I replied.

"Sweetie, you are so naive. A good-looking cop turns on the charm, and—"

"I haven't noticed him making much effort to be charming to me," I said grumpily.

"He's had them in custody—"

"They're not in custody," I insisted.

"—for *hours*."

I glanced at the clock. It was late afternoon by now, and I was more worried than I was letting on to anyone. "Don't worry. Barclay's got lawyers."

"Speaking from experience," Whoopsy said, "a fat lot of good *that'll* be in dealing with police persecution."

"How about you?" I decided to change the subject. "Any luck in the stacks today?"

"Yeah! Delilah and I found something interesting. An account of a magician who vanished onstage."

"One that Max doesn't know about?"

"It's not part of our case. This was yonks ago."

"How many yonks?"

"Many. This was back in the days of vaudeville. I looked the guy up, just in case, but no luck. He's been dead for years. Natural causes."

"But he vanished onstage?" This was the first case we'd come across that sounded at all similar to ours.

"Well, he didn't exactly vanish. He was onstage one Saturday afternoon, doing his regular act, and he gradually got sort of…transparent for a while."

"Huh?"

"Kind of see-through. Not invisible, but an eyewitness claimed he could see through him."

"It was part of the act?"

"No, apparently the magician didn't realize what was happening. Just kept on delivering his patter, as if nothing odd was going on. And then, slowly, the effect reversed and he looked normal again."

"Did anyone ask him how he'd done it?"

"Yes. But he had no idea. It just happened."

"Hmm."

"We found this account under a whole category of similar cases we're reading about, all spontaneous and involuntary. So far, no real disappearees, they're all just people who got a little transparent for a while. This one rang a bell with me, though, because he was doing a magic act onstage at the time."

"Good work, Whoopsy. Let me know if you turn up anything else."

"Roger. I'll check in later to see if the prisoners have been freed."

"They're not—" But he'd already hung up.

I walked over to the table where Duke, Dixie and Satsy sat with piles of books. They all wore identical expressions of anxiety.

"Was that news about Max and Barclay?" Duke asked.

"I'm afraid not." I was about to relate Whoopsy's anecdote when the bell chimed, heralding a new arrival. I peeked eagerly around a bookcase to see who it was. "Oh. Hieronymus." I couldn't keep the disappointment out of my voice. I glanced behind me and saw three pairs of shoulders sag after hearing me greet him. I relieved a little of my nervous tension by saying snappishly, "Where have you been all day?"

Hieronymus glared at me, then walked to the back of the shop with his head down, looking sullen.

"That boy is useless," I muttered.

"Someone ought to tell him that Max is being questioned by the police," said Satsy.

"If 'someone' means me," I said, "then it can wait. I'm in no mood for his sulks."

"I'll do it." Dixie patted my hand. "You shouldn't have to do everything, Esther."

She was a sweet girl. "Thanks, Dixie. He's probably gone down to the lab. It's—"

"Back of the shop, down the stairs?"

"Right. Uh, the lab is a little weird. So is Hieronymus."

She made a pretty little gesture indicating she didn't mind, then went off to inform Hieronymus that his master had been taken down to the station house by Detective Lopez.

I stared at the display board, wondering if there was any relevance to the story Whoopsy had just told me.

I read what I'd already written under the names of each victim: *Not afraid. Wanted to stay. Spontaneous??? MADE TO DISAPPEAR.*

Why would someone or something make four magicians' assistants disappear?

This one rang a bell with me, though, Whoopsy had said, *because he was doing a magic act onstage at the time.*

But that incident wasn't really similar to our cases. The guy hadn't vanished, he'd just gone a bit transparent. And it had happened to him, not to an assistant.

Why make a magician's assistant disappear?

Or maybe...maybe that wasn't the most obvious question, I realized slowly. Maybe the question I'd been overlooking was...

I slapped my forehead. "Of course!"

Duke jumped. "What?"

"There's something else we know about the victims," I said. "Something so obvious, I can't believe I didn't think of it before!"

"That's how it is with obvious things," Satsy said. "But, darlin', *what's* obvious?"

I wrote it under Golly's name, then wrote the same word under the name of each of the other victims:

Onstage.

"Every one of them disappeared onstage," I said. "While in performance."

"Well…yes. So?" Satsy shrugged. Then his eyes widened. "Oh. Oooh."

"Great balls of fire!" said Duke.

"As far as we know, these are the only disappearees so far. Since they were all onstage at the time…"

"Then that can't be coincidence!"

"At least, coincidence seems unlikely. That means that either an entity causing these disappearances specifically *wants* the victims to disappear during performance, or else the right conditions for disappearance only occur during performance."

"Hot damn, I think you're onto something, Esther!" cried Duke. "Pardon my language."

"So why would someone or something *want* the disappearances to occur during a performance?" I asked.

"Publicity?" Satsy guessed. "To spread panic? To demonstrate power? To prove something to the public?"

"Hmm. Public attention," I mused. "That might explain why there've been multiple disappearances. Maybe the, er, perpetrator never realized that the Her-lihys would keep the disappearance of someone as al-most-famous as Golly Gee so quiet after it happened."

"Right," Duke said. "Maybe the son of a gun thought it'd be in all the morning papers or some-thing!"

"And when that didn't happen," Satsy said, "he… she…it…uh, the perpetrator caused another disap-pearance, hoping this one would draw attention! And when that didn't work, either—"

"Wait a minute," I said, spotting the flaws.

"What?"

"I don't think it makes sense." I shook my head. "If you wanted to be sure the disappearances would be noticed, would you really choose a B-list pop singer in an off-Broadway show with a scant audi-ence?"

"Well…"

"And when that didn't create public furor, would your next victim be Clarisse Staunton, an amateur performing in a private household for some chil-dren?"

"Hmm. I think I see your point," Duke said.

I nodded. "If public attention is the goal, why pick *these* victims? Why not choose a really famous act, such as David Copperfield? Why not arrange for a disappearance to happen on live television? Or in front of a packed house on Broadway? Why not choose someone whose disappearance would be difficult to keep quiet for days—or even hours?"

"Like the mayor!" said Satsy.

"Or Donald Trump!" said Duke.

"Oooh," said Satsy. "Wouldn't it be cool to make Donald Trump disappear?"

"Also," I said, "once you realized that Joe Herlihy wasn't eager to publicize what had happened, why go to the trouble of making more victims vanish? Why not just make sure that a bright spotlight got turned on Golly's disappearance, despite the magician's silence?"

"Good point," Duke said. "So far, there's just one inside-page tabloid story about Miss Golly Gee and one quick paragraph about the Great Hidalgo misplacing his assistant during his act. That seems like a pretty pitiful PR effort for something powerful enough to make four people disappear within a week."

"So, all things considered," I said, "I think we can say that the quest for public attention is *not* why the disappearances are occurring onstage."

"So what else could be the reason?" Duke wondered aloud.

"Someone is trying to destroy the acts?" Satsy suggested.

"An enemy of all four magicians?" I considered this. "Barclay's a banker and Joe's married to a pro-

ducer," I noted, "so I'm sure they've both got more enemies than we could count. It would probably be
more productive to figure out who Duke's and Delilah's enemies are and narrow it down from there."

"All my enemies are in the condom business,"
Duke said. "In magic, as far as I know, I've got only
friends."

That was one of the advantages of its being his
hobby rather than his profession, I supposed.

"I don't think Delilah has any enemies," Satsy said.
"Especially not in the condom business."

"Hmm." It seemed unlikely that the magicians or
the assistants, with their varied backgrounds, all
shared an enemy. Still, we couldn't rule out the possibility until we could get them all together for a detailed group interview.

I drummed my fingers on the table, thinking
aloud. "Why else might someone *want* the disappearances to occur during performance?"

"A joke?" Satsy suggested. "A particularly cruel
one."

"That's a possibility," I said. "Each time it happens,
the magician panics in front of a live audience."

Satsy said, "Some sick perpetrator might find that
hysterically funny."

"You mean, all of this might just be done for
kicks?" Duke said in outrage.

"Maybe," Satsy said.

I leaned back in my chair, contemplating another

argument. "On the other hand, maybe it's just that, for some reason, the conditions for disappearance only occur during performance."

"In which case," Duke said, "we're back to asking, why does someone *want* to make the victims disappear?"

"If their disappearance *is* something that someone wants," I said, starting to chase my tail. "Do you think it's at all possible that the disappearances are just…" I shrugged. "I don't know…an accident?"

"If they are," Satsy said, "then why is this happening all of a sudden?"

"I never made Dolly disappear before," Duke pointed out.

"And *four* disappearances? In one week? An accident?" Satsy shook his head. "You're getting tired, Esther."

"Yes, I am." It had been a while since I'd had a good night's sleep, and my brain was so stuffed with weird theories and demented speculation, I felt like it would start dribbling out my ears any moment. I put my head down on my arms and closed my eyes, trying to relax.

I heard footsteps, then Dixie's voice. "Well, now, that Hieronymus isn't so bad!"

I didn't even open my eyes. Just listened.

She pulled up a chair. "He's painfully shy, poor guy, and it sure is easy to understand why. But he's kind of sweet, if you just draw him out a little."

"Humph," I said.

"We got to chatting for a while."

"My Dixie can make friends with anyone," Duke said proudly.

"By the way, Esther?" Dixie said.

"Yes?" I yawned.

"Hieronymus says that he thinks we're on the wrong track."

"Of course he does," I grumbled. The cellar-dwelling creep.

"He's been out all day chasing down a lead. He says he thinks the culprit in the disappearances is a mundane. He says we should look for someone with access to the prop boxes."

"Well, that makes some sense," said Duke.

"He's really a very bright young man, Daddy. And a good listener, too."

"Don't tell Lopez about this," I muttered. "I had all kinds of access to the crystal cage. And he already suspects me...."

"Pardon, Esther?" Dixie said.

"She's awfully tired," Duke said. "Let her be, honey."

I felt someone pat my back, and Satsy said, "Why don't you take a little nap, Esther?"

"No," I said. "I'll, uh... I should, um..."

I fell asleep with my cheek pressed against *The Exposé*.

The sound of someone pounding on something woke me.

As I opened one eye I realized where I was, and

lifted my head. I looked around, disoriented and groggy. I was alone at the table. *The Exposé* was creased and smeared from my sleeping with my face pressed against it. It was dark outside the shop window. Someone had turned on a light nearby, not close enough to wake me but close enough to ensure I wouldn't wake up in the dark.

The pounding continued, and I realized someone was at the door. I rose to go see what the problem was, but then a note propped up near my arm caught my eye. I picked it up and read it, ignoring the pounding for a moment:

> *Esther,*
> *Barclay called Dixie's cell phone. He and Max are free! Details to follow.*
> *We're locking the front door and going to dinner. Then Duke and Dixie are coming with me to the Pony Expressive, to see the show and keep Delilah company. She needs moral support. Max and Barclay are coming back here to feed you and then bring you to the club, too. We all think you need a night off.*
> *Satsy*

Relieved that Max and Barclay weren't behind bars now, I figured I'd join them for a quick bite and then go home. Right now, my idea of a perfect night off was a hot bath followed by a quiet glass of wine and an early bedtime.

I looked up when I heard footsteps. Hieronymus came from the back of the shop, heading for the front door. He jumped nervously when he saw me, then gave me an exasperated glare.

"Didn't you notith the knocking?" he said.

"Um, yeah. I just woke up. Wait," I said, as he continued toward the door. "What time is it? Are we closed now?"

Hieronymus opened the door, brushed past the person standing on the doorstep and walked away. I stuck my head out the door and called after him, "Wait! Where are you going? What did you find out today?" He pretended not to hear me, and I didn't feel like running after him. "Oh, good riddance anyhow," I muttered.

"Excuse me?" said the man on the doorstep.

"Oh! I'm sorry. I think we're closed now."

"I'm looking for Dr. Zadok." He was tall, slim, dressed in a nice casual-wear suit without a tie. Clean-shaven, he appeared to be about fifty, looked East Indian and spoke with a Masterpiece Theater accent.

"He's not in just now. But if you'll come back during business hours tomorrow…"

"This isn't bookstore business. May I wait for him?"

The man seemed quite respectable, so I decided to let him in. Just to be on the safe side, though, I said,

"Actually, Max is on his way here now. Should be just a few minutes."

"He's all right, then?" the stranger asked eagerly.

I glanced at him in surprise as I turned on some lights. "Yes." I showed him toward the table and chairs. "Did you have reason to think he wasn't?"

"He hasn't answered any of my recent e-mails."

"He doesn't have a computer anymore," I said.

The stranger stared at me for a moment, then closed his eyes. His lips worked silently, and I had the impression he was trying to control his temper. "Ah," he said at last, opening his eyes. "Well, then. That explains it. And I seem to have wasted a trip."

"Why didn't you just phone?"

"I did. Several times. No answer."

"Oh." I had already noticed that Max had no answering machine. "Well, he's been out of the shop a lot lately, Mr...."

He exclaimed, "I'm so sorry! Do forgive my lapse of manners. Allow me to introduce myself. Lysander Singh."

"Esther Diamond." We shook hands, then took our seats. "Can I offer you something? Tea? Water? Um..." I wasn't sure what else we had on hand. I definitely didn't want to search that big cupboard for the *aqua vitae*.

"Nothing just now, thank you."

He studied my face, looking as if he was trying to decide whether to say something about my appearance. I scrubbed self-consciously at my cheeks, realizing they must be filthy with tabloid ink. "We've been working so hard lately," I said. "I, uh, fell asleep on the job."

His brows lifted. "You're an employee here?"

"No, I'm...a friend of Max's."

"One whom he trusts enough to leave in charge here, I see." His tone was courteous, but I sensed disapproval.

"Yes."

"May I ask where Max is?"

"Police station." I was still groggy. Otherwise I might not have answered so directly.

"Has there been a mishap?"

"You might say that."

"The shop's been burgled?"

"No... I... It's complicated."

"I see." After an awkward moment, he asked, "Is Max's assistant here? I think perhaps I should speak with him."

"That was him just now," I grumbled. "Leaving. Without warning, apology or explanation."

"*That* was Hieronymus?"

"You know Hieronymus?" I asked in surprise.

"Well, we've never met..." His gaze roamed over the books stacked all over the table, then moved to the display board, which was covered in my multicolored notes. After a moment, he said faintly, with a frown, "There've been four mystical disappearances here?"

I gasped and rose to my feet. "Who are you?"

"As I said, Lysan—"

"Where did you come from?" I demanded, backing away in dawning fear. Could *he* be our nemesis?

"Altoona," he said. "Young woman, there's no reason to—"

"Altoona?" The word sounded exotic and otherworldly. "Is that in another dimension?"

He blinked. "Er, no, it's in Pennsylvania."

"What? Oh!" I stopped backing away. "Oh. That Altoona." My family had once stopped there for lunch on a road trip to the East Coast, during my childhood. "You... Are you causing these disappearances?"

"So there *are* disappearances occurring?" Then realizing what I'd just asked, he added, "No, of course I'm not causing anything! And who, may I ask, are you?"

"I'll ask the questions, Singh," I said, imitating Lopez's cop tone. "What's your business here?"

"Now see here, young woman—"

"Sit down," I barked as he started to rise.

Startled, he sat.

"You're no friend of Max's," I said, attempting to bluff the truth out of him.

"I never claimed to be," he said tersely.

"Well?" I prodded in a menacing tone.

"I'm...a colleague of his."

I gasped. "You're with the Collegium!"

"He *told* you about the Collegium?" Singh sounded scandalized. His gaze flashed to the display

board and he added, his tone growing genuinely appalled, "He's *told* you about these disappearances!"

"So that's how you know Hieronymus's name," I said.
"You knew he'd been assigned to Max as an assistant."

"As the most longstanding representative of the
Magnum Collegium in the eastern half of the United
States at this time," Singh said, "I, in fact, authorized
the assignment."

I returned to my chair and sank into it. "Well, now
we know who to blame."

"For the disappearances?" he said in confusion.

"For burdening Max with that sulking, smirking,
uncommunicative cellar-dweller who's never around
when you need him."

"Am I to understand that you're criticizing a junior
member of the Collegium?" His tone could have
frosted glass.

"I'm also criticizing you, Lysander," I said, feeling
all the crankiness of the day return in full force.

His posture became even more rigid. "I realize,
from the reports of his apprenticeship, that the poor
boy's unfortunate affliction prevents him from utter-
ing certain incantations accurately, causing some unpredictable results. But I don't see how that is any of
your affair, young woman. Moreover, I would have
thought that compassion rather than contempt would
be the civilized response to his predicament, even in
a savage outpost like New York City."

"'Savage outpost'? Oh, for God's sake! This is the

greatest— Wait, no, never mind." I controlled myself and focused on the most relevant part of his comments. "Look, if Hieronymus's speech impediment makes him a danger—"

"I didn't say that. Besides there was only that one mishap."

"Only that *one?*" I repeated.

"I think only a petty personality would count the others," he said, eyeing me coldly.

I thought of the orange explosion in Max's cellar the other day. "How many have there been?"

"Ah. I begin to understand," Singh said in a snide tone. "You're hoping to replace Hieronymus. You have ambitions to follow in Max's footsteps."

"Of course not," I snapped. "I'm hoping to go back onstage as Virtue and move the show to Broadway."

"What?"

"I'm involved with these people because of the disappearances," I said, "and my objection to Hieronymus is that he's *rude,* and also the worst team player I've ever met."

"Fighting Evil is not a team sport, young woman!"

"My name is Esther!"

"And it's not entirely surprising that Hieronymus's manners might be a bit strained, considering that Max is evidently giving mundanes free access to his work, his lab and the secrets of the Collegium! This is *most* irregular!"

"Yeah, I guessed that," I said. "But we've got a huge

problem on our hands here, and Max can't handle it all alone! By now, half a dozen of us have been on the job for forty-eight hours—though, frankly, it feels like much, *much* longer than that—and we're *still* a long way from solving these disappearances or finding the victims. And I don't see that Max's 'assistant' is helping him much."

"You are no judge of his assistant's contributions. Or of the challenges facing us in our sacred work!"

Few things spark my temper more effectively than pomposity. "Well, at least the Collegium knew what it was doing when it sent Max here, where there's real work to be done," I said, "and sent *you* to Altoona, where you can enjoy your sacred status in peace and quiet."

He rose to his feet in offended fury, and I didn't tell him to sit back down. I was half hoping he'd just storm out the door. "I'll have you know, young woman, Altoona was a seething cauldron of riotous demonic Evil when I went there. Twenty years ago, if you wanted to frighten small children at bedtime—"

"What kind of twisted person would want to do that?"

"—or make experienced sorcerers shudder with dread, all you had to do was mention the doomed name of Altoona."

I blinked. "You're kidding me."

"It was thought to be a place beyond redemption, beyond retrieval, beyond all hope!"

"*Altoona?*"

"You have no *idea* of the challenges I faced there. All alone, a young mage with no help, against over-whelming odds."

"Altoona, PA?" I said.

"It was a horrific battle, and at times there seemed to be no end in sight. But with talent, grit and deter-mination..." He took a breath and nodded. "Yes, I succeeded in the end."

"The same Altoona where I had a grilled-cheese sandwich at some diner when I was eight? *That* Al-toona?"

"And so Altoona is the peaceful hamlet we know today. But make no mistake, young woman." He raised a warning finger. "Evil still lurks at the edges of Altoona, searching for a weakness, awaiting its op-portunity to regain a foothold there and once again grow in strength to dominate the entire town!"

"You're *sure* we're talking about the same Al-toona?"

"Positive. So I know whereof I speak when I say that Max should perform his duties here without in-volving or endangering mundanes. Ours is a solitary vocation of individuals specifically gifted and equipped to deal with the perils we face." He sat back down, apparently past his pique now.

"Not to minimize your achievements, Lysander," I said slowly, "but Altoona is not exactly the Big Apple, after all."

"Oh?" Lysander gave me a worldly wise smirk and gestured to the display board covered in my notes about the four mystical disappearances. "And when was the last time you heard of anything like *this* happening in Altoona?"

"You were questioned by the *police*?" was the first thing Lysander said when Max and Barclay entered the bookshop.

"Lysander?" Max made a vague gesture. "What a pleasant surprise! What brings you to Manhattan?"

"You were questioned by the *police*?" Lysander repeated.

"Since he's here," I said to Max, "I've explained our problem to him." I had just finished summarizing everything, including most of today's events, when Max and Barclay arrived.

"The *police* are involved in this matter?" Lysander said.

"Oh, are you a colleague of Dr. Zadok's?" Barclay extended his hand. "How do you do?"

Lysander ignored him. "These events are being re-

ported in the *press?*" He waved our smudged copy of
The Exposé at Max. "And *online?*"

"As you can see," I said to Max, "he's rather
alarmed."

"Max!" Lysander cried. "I demand an explanation.
How do the press and the police know of these affairs?"

"Skip that part," I advised Max. "I've already explained everything to him. This is just a touch of
hysterics."

"Are things very bad in Altoona these days?" Max
asked, studying Lysander with some concern.

"A murky quagmire of festering Evil," I said.

"Altoona?" Barclay said.

"A shocking place," Max told him.

"Altoona, PA?" Barclay said. "*That* Altoona?"

"Yes!" Lysander exclaimed. "That Altoona! But
things are fine there."

"And we're all relieved to hear that," I said.

"We brought food." Barclay set a big paper bag on
the table, then took another one from Max. While unpacking both bags, he said, "We're starved after that
interrogation! We figured you'd be hungry, too, Esther. And when we talked to Dixie, Duke and Satsy,
they said you were all smeared with tabloid ink and
probably wouldn't want to eat out when you woke up.
I hope Thai is okay?"

Opening a container of food that smelled delicious,
I said sincerely, "I think I love you both." I set out the

paper plates and plastic utensils Barclay handed to me. "There's enough for four, Lysander, so you must join us."

"Thank you, but I couldn't eat a thing," he said stiffly. "Max, I demand you explain what's going on here!"

"I'm setting a place for you, Lysander," I said. "Perhaps food will improve your mood. Here, start with a dumpling."

"I refuse to— Humph! *Urgh!*" His comments were interrupted by my forking a fried dumpling into his mouth.

Seeing Lysander trying not to choke on his dumpling, Max said, "I'll get some water."

He came back a few minutes later bearing a tray with four glasses and a pitcher of water, by which time I had introduced Barclay and Lysander.

While Max poured a glass of water and handed it to Lysander, I said, "So what happened with Lopez?"

"Ah! Yes." Max sat down and began selecting cartons of food and filling his plate. "I must say, Esther, interrogation by the authorities isn't nearly so unnerving in a society where one knows they are prohibited by both law and custom from using implements of torture."

"I can see how that would be so, Max." I scooped some chicken in red curry sauce onto my plate. "But I was still worried."

"Yes, well, one is sadly aware, of course, that the police do not *always* stay within the letter or the spirit of the law when interrogating suspects."

"Especially in this city," Lysander said disdainfully.

"Which is why I was glad," Max continued, "that we were protected by the appropriate incantations."

Lysander frowned. "What incantation is appropriate for police interrogation?"

Max replied, "It was Barclay, not I, who uttered the spell."

We looked at Barclay, who said, "I invoked the names of my family, my lawyers and my cousin the Congressman. Repeatedly."

"Ah. So Lopez was forced to tread lightly?" I guessed.

"Yes," Max said.

"Not really," Barclay said.

"I find the detective an admirable young man," Max said to me. "A bit impatient, perhaps, as so many young people are, but devoted to his duty and sincere in his convictions."

"He scares me," Barclay said.

"I'm sure he intended to." I asked Max the question that worried me most. "So does Lopez know now who vandalized the crystal cage?"

"No, of course not," Max said, surprised. "We had agreed it was necessary to lie about that, so I did. You and I never returned to the theater and have no idea what happened."

"Well done, Max!" I ignored Lysander, who was muttering and shaking his head. "Did Lopez believe you?"

"I'm not sure," Max admitted. "He adopted a manner of belligerent skepticism at the start of the interview, and he was slow to shed it."

"He shed it?" I asked, both surprised and suspicious. "When? What were you talking about?"

"About the disappearances, of course. And the theories we have so far explored and eliminated in our investigation of them."

I considered this. "You told him the truth?"

"Yes. Mind you, I avoided discussion of Sexy Samson and Dolly the Dancing Cowgirl, since he did not ask me about their disappearances."

"He didn't ask me about them either," said Barclay. "We just went over—and over and *over* and over— what happened when Clarisse disappeared. And how I met you, and then Dr. Zadok."

Max said, "In fact, I believe the police are still unaware of Samson's and Dolly's disappearances." When I glanced at the display board, where their names were clearly written, Max added, "Yes, Detective Lopez is a very observant young man. I, too, believe he saw their names written here—"

"And heard Delilah mention them," I said.

"But I think it possible he doesn't believe they're people."

"He thinks they're pets?" With names like theirs, I supposed it was possible.

"Perhaps. Or figments of our imagination," said Max.

"Ah." Yes, it was even more possible that he thought we were crazy.

"But only for the time being. He strikes me as an individual who does not long overlook details once he's interested in something. However, it's clear he does not believe that my interpretation of the situation is a reliable one."

"You told him your interpretation?" And Lopez hadn't made Max undergo psychiatric evaluation?

Max nodded. "As you and I had already discussed, I felt it imprudent to lie about anything besides the actual crime we were obliged to commit. So I was frank in my responses to all other questions posed to me."

"How did Lopez react?"

"Initially, he had many, many, many questions."

"I'll bet," I said.

Barclay added, "It was the same with me, too."

"Then…" Max paused and frowned at his noodles.

"Then?" I prodded.

"Poor fellow. The headache which had been troubling him for much of the interview became so pronounced that he asked me to leave."

"I see."

"He looked rather ill by then."

"Hmm." I knew exactly how Lopez must have felt.

"I offered to attempt treatment, but he became emphatic in his insistence that I absent myself."

"Uh-huh."

Barclay said, "And he was already done with me by then. So we were *finally* able to leave."

"After such lengthy and intense questioning, even without torture, I felt in need of a rejuvenating beverage," Max said.

"So we stopped for a couple of smoothies," Barclay said. "And phoned Dixie."

"Well." I thought it over. Lopez might not be eliminated as a problem, but it sounded as if he was temporarily neutralized. "You two did an excellent job. Good work." I dug into my dinner while Max and Barclay beamed at me.

"An excellent job?" Lysander repeated with appalled incredulity. "Are you mad, young woman?"

Barclay murmured helpfully, "Her name is Esther."

Lysander ignored him. "The mundane police are investigating a mystical matter and have interrogated a representative of the Collegium!"

"Without implements of torture," I pointed out.

"A representative who has *lied* to them about the *crime* he committed—"

"Surely you don't think he should have confessed?" I said.

"—and who shared esoteric knowledge with the interrogating officer! And also with, I gather," he added, with a dark look at Max, "a throng of mundanes whom he has invited to help him with his sacred duty!"

"Try the asparagus dish," Barclay said. "It's great!"

"And the press is reporting on this matter!" Lysander added. "Max, this situation is a disaster! A travesty! A catastrophe!"

"The chicken's really good, too," I said.

"Oh, I haven't tried the chicken yet," said Max, reaching for it.

"Max," Lysander said insistently, "what are you planning to do to rectify this mess?"

"Hmm…" Max frowned, thinking about it.

I said, "Well, *I*, for one, plan to…plan… Oh, no!" I slapped my forehead—again.

"What's wrong?" Barclay asked.

"My plan," I said in disgust. "I can't believe I fell asleep today! Look at the time now. It's much too late to go see Magnus about the crystal cage. Damn!"

"Magnus?" Barclay repeated. "Do you mean Magic Magnus, that huge weird guy with the gold tooth?"

"Yes. I wanted to ask him not to turn the repaired cage over to Matilda until I'm ready…" I looked at Barclay. "You…you know Magnus?"

"Yeah. I got my vanishing box from him." Barclay reached for more noodles.

My heart started thudding. "You did?"

"Uh-huh. That's who's repairing your cage? Figures."

I put down my fork. "Why does it figure?"

"More noodles, Esther?" he asked.

"No. Why does it figure, Barclay?"

"Hmm? Oh! Just that he does so much business. Seems like everyone…" He paused, seeing how intensely I was looking at him. His eyes widened as he realized why. "Oh my *God*." He nodded slowly, suddenly recognizing the importance of what he was saying. "Seems like everyone you meet in magic deals with the guy."

"Oh my God!" I echoed. Barclay and I rose to our feet at the same time. "That's it! That's the link! The common factor!"

"Magic Magnus?" Max said, rising, too.

I went to the display board, picked up a marker, and wrote under Golly's and Clarisse's names: *Access to prop—MAGIC MAGNUS.*

"We need to get hold of Duke and Delilah!" Barclay said. "We've got to find out if they were dealing with Magnus, too!"

"Yes, we do!" I agreed. "And Lysander, I withdraw my comments about Hieronymus, with apologies."

"You do?"

I nodded. "I should have taken him more seriously. He said today that the perpetrator was a mundane with access to the prop boxes. He said that's who we should be looking for." I forgot my apology as I added, "Damn him, anyhow! Where is he? Never around when you need him!"

"Zounds!" Max cried.

I glanced at him. He wasn't looking at the display board anymore. He was staggering toward the front of the shop, his arms outstretched, as if trying to touch something I couldn't see.

"Zounds?" Barclay repeated.

Lysander rose from his chair, looking around the room in sudden alarm. "What *is* that?"

"What is *what*?" Barclay asked.

"Max?" I said.

"Shh!" Max responded.

"Great Scott!" Lysander started to breathe hard. "Is that…is *that*… It's happening, isn't it?"

Barclay and I exchanged glances. My dinner started churning in my stomach.

After a moment, Max turned around to face us. Looking like he felt sick, he wiped his brow. Lysander, gasping for air, sank clumsily into his chair.

"Esther?" Barclay whispered.

"No." I shook my head and whispered back, "No, I didn't feel a thing."

"Me, neither."

Lysander said, "Max?"

Max drew in a long breath, then nodded. "Yes. It's just happened again." He met my eyes. "Somewhere in the city, another victim has disappeared."

"I would like to go on record, officially, as saying I consider this a *terrible* idea," Lysander muttered.

"Fine. You're on the official record," I said. "Now quit stalling, let's get busy with breaking and entering." I was fast becoming a hardened criminal.

After considerable debate, the four of us had decided to break into the magic shop sometime after midnight. Well, no, *three* of us had decided; the fourth, Lysander, was participating under protest. However, if we were invading the lair of a powerful and evil mage, as we suspected, it seemed best to include Lysander in our raid. In such circumstances, two sorcerers on our side were better than one.

We knew that Magnus had access to at least two of the prop boxes used in the disappearances. And, as I'd told my three companions tonight, I had twice seen mysterious people wandering around the upper floors of the magic shop. The first time, I had mistaken an elusive woman for a staff member. The second time, there were three people— one of them wrapped in a snake—and they hadn't acted like staff. They'd acted frightened. Of me? Or of something more sinister—such as the huge weird guy with the gold tooth who charged up those stairs with a spear only moments later?

Magnus had made it clear he didn't want me mentioning those frightened people to Lopez that day. And he'd looked as if he hoped I'd never seen them. Who were they? Victims of disappearances we didn't know about? Victims of another scheme he was perpetrating aside from the disappearances? Minions of Evil?

Hieronymus had said we should be looking for a mundane, but Max and Lysander were both positive that the disappearances were mystical. Magnus, they surmised, merely posed as a mundane, as someone who possessed well-rehearsed skills of misdirection and illusion. In reality, he was probably a true mage, like the two of them. It seemed likely now that the amazing magic trick he'd performed the day I'd met him, making a bird appear out of thin air and then turning the bird into the crystal pendant he'd given me, had been real magic, rather than stunning sleight-of-hand. It also seemed likely, Max said, that the crystal had been some sort of charm—perhaps an attempt to make me attracted to Magnus, perhaps something more dangerous. Magnus had, after all, assured me I could perform the vanishing act in perfect safety. Maybe he'd given me that pendant in an attempt to make sure I did the act, never suspecting that Max would show up in time to stop me.

"I still say we shouldn't do this without talking to the others first," Lysander said as we approached Magnus's building.

"We've been all through that," I said impatiently. "Now concentrate on the job."

We had tried Dixie's cell phone, as well as Satsy's and Whoopsy's, to no avail. The Pony Expressive was below street level and cave-like; cell phones evidently didn't get a good signal there. We could go there to ask in person about Magnus; but if we did that, our friends would insist on assisting in our raid on his shop. And what we were about to do was illegal.

Moreover, if we were right about Magnus, it was also dangerous. Barclay was emphatically opposed to letting Dixie risk her safety. None of us was very keen on risking anyone else's safety, either; four of us were risk enough, we figured, if someone had to come in harm's way tonight. Besides, breaking and entering without getting caught called for discretion, and I foresaw difficulties in that area if accompanied by Cowboy Duke and several drag queens.

Nor could we afford to postpone our plans. The perpetrator of these disappearances had to be stopped as soon as possible. We hoped to rescue all the disappearees; but even if the victims didn't survive for long after disappearing, there was still a chance we could rescue tonight's victim—*if* we acted fast.

So now Lysander and I, wearing dark clothing and low-brimmed hats from Max's personal collection, strolled arm in arm along Worth Street trying to look inconspicuous. I was glad Magnus's shop wasn't on one of the more fashionable streets in Tribeca. It would have been impossible to break into it unnoticed if it had been two doors down from Robert De Niro's restaurant on Greenwich Street or squatting amidst some of the hot spots on Hudson.

As it was, even after midnight, we had to stroll tensely up and down the street a few times before it was deserted enough for us to approach the magic shop without risk of exposure. I kept a lookout while Lysander, pretending to browse the dark window, muttered incantations to open the locked door. We'd decided he should do this instead of Max, in case we were seen—or in case there was a security camera somewhere—since Max was so distinctive-looking and was known to Detective Lopez. Lysander was bitter about this part of the plan. However, we kept our heads down and our fedoras pulled low, and I thought it unlikely that we could be identified.

After a moment, I heard the *clatter* and *click* of the door unlocking. I looked over my shoulder to see it swing open by itself. Though I'd been expecting it, the sight still made me feel disoriented and a little jumpy.

We entered the shop and closed the door behind us. I autodialed Barclay's number on my cell phone. He and Max were around the corner, awaiting our signal. When Barclay answered his phone, I said, "All clear. Meet us inside."

"Roger. Over and out."

"I can't see a thing," said Lysander.

"No light," I warned, putting my phone in my pocket. "Not until we get upstairs." The windows above the ground floor were all covered, but someone might see us if we used a flashlight down here.

"Are the stairs this way?" Lysander asked.

"Um…"

"And where are *you*?"

"Maybe you should hold still for now."

"If I could just orient my—*oof!*"

A split second after he bumped into something, a

huge, glowing monster face appeared out of the darkness. It laughed and waved hideous, hairy spider legs at us while bells clanged overhead.

"*Arrgghh!*" Lysander screamed.

"*Yaaagh!*" I screamed.

The door opened. Max and Barclay came racing into the shop. They saw the thing confronting us and both started screaming, too.

After a few seconds of mindless terror, I realized it was a stage prop. A pretty silly-looking one, in fact. But effective, appearing suddenly out of the dark as it had. *Very* effective, considering the way Lysander was still screaming.

In the glow it gave off, I oriented myself and saw the stairs leading up to the second floor. "Come on!" I shouted at my companions. "Up there!"

"That's just...*evil!*" Barclay said, trying to shake off his shock. He nervously adjusted the fedora he was wearing.

"Lysander," I said.

"I wonder if something like that would work in my store?" Max mused. "A most effective deterrent. Any sensible thief would leave immediately."

"Lysander!" I said.

Barclay asked, "Er, does that mean *we* should leave immediately?"

"No," Max said. "We could not hope that our presence here would go undetected for long. Not considering the strength and cunning of our adversary."

"Thanks to Stealthy Feet over here," I grumbled, taking Lysander's arm, "our secret infiltration lasted all of five seconds."

"Still, we must attempt to search the building before Magnus interferes," Max said. *"Excelsior!"*

I had to admire his courage as he charged up those stairs, the flaps of his duster flying, his hat set at a rakish angle. He was unarmed, half Magnus's size, and about three hundred and ten years his senior, but those disadvantages didn't even make him pause.

Barclay dashed after him. I dragged Lysander with me. "Come on," I urged, "keep up!"

When Max reached the top of the stairs, he shouted down to me, "You're right! I hear voices and footsteps overhead! I'm going up!"

"Be careful!" Using the railing to guide me, I hauled Lysander the rest of the way up the dark stairs.

When we reached the landing, I let go of Altoona's savior and fumbled around for the stairwell light, since our presence was no secret to anyone by now. I could hear scrambling and shrieking overhead, Max's thunderous progress up the stairs, and Barclay cursing as he stumbled.

I flicked the light on, started up the next flight of stairs, and looked up just in time to see Max reach the third floor. Then a large, dense, squirming mass of something fell down on him from overhead, hissing and writhing. Snakes! He screamed and fell backward, tumbling down the stairs and taking Barclay with him. I heard louder screaming overhead and many feet racing upstairs to the next floor, but I didn't really pay attention. Seeing Max and Barclay hurtling toward me in a rolling mass of writhing, hissing snakes terrified me into sheer horrified paralysis. I was standing rock still, open-mouthed and flat-footed when the whole messy heap smashed into me.

I fell backward down the stairs, then hit the floor with an agonizing crash that should have broken every bone in my body, especially with the weight of two grown men on top of me. After a moment of panicky revulsion, I realized that the "snake" on my face was plastic. As soon as the air puffing it up finished escaping, it stopped squirming and hissing. Now it lay over my nose and mouth like a plastic baggy, suffocating me. I started shoving clumsily at Barclay and Max, eager to free an arm and remove the plastic snake from my face before I passed out.

It took several long, painful, expletive-filled moments for the three of us to sort out our tangled limbs and get up off the floor. Then Barclay slipped on the slick bits of deflated plastic that were now everywhere and fell back down. He lay there for a minute, winded and disheartened.

"Come on, you three!" Lysander cried. "Don't just muddle around down here! I hear people in distress up there! Into the breach!" He charged up the stairs.

Max and I helped Barclay off the floor.

"Okay," Barclay said, looking like he might vomit. "I'm… I'm… I'm ready."

"Take a moment," Max panted. "Get your breath back."

"I think I have a concussion," I said.

"You know what's interesting about this?" Max said.

"There's something interesting about this?" I said.

"What's interesting is that Magnus has gone to a lot of trouble to discourage unauthorized visitors after hours, yet none of these elaborate wards is magical in nature."

"You mean," Barclay said, holding on to his ribs as if they hurt a lot, "these are the sort of booby-traps he'd install if he was exactly what he says he is—a magician who's retired from the stage?"

"Yes!"

"But these, er, wards *are* elaborate, Max, as you said." I rubbed my aching head. "What has he got here, or what is he doing here, that's so secret he's going to this much trouble to protect it?"

We heard more screaming overhead. Then Lysander shouted, "Max! Help! *Help!*"

"We're about to find out!" Max turned and headed up the stairs again.

We followed. We reached the top of the stairs, rounded the corner, and climbed the next flight, following the sounds of Lysander's shouts, some thuds and a number of other people shouting. When we reached the fourth floor, we were confronted by a confusing scene.

Lysander lay on the floor, unconscious. Eight people crowded around him. One was the snake-wrapped lady I had seen before. She and her snake looked much as they had the last time we'd met. She and five of the people were Asian. The other two people, a man and a woman, looked Middle Eastern. No one was speaking English. One of the Asian women was standing over Lysander with what appeared to be a long, thick, bamboo pole. She had apparently clubbed him. Now she was arguing with a man who was kneeling over him, examining his head injury. When the woman with the deadly pole saw us, she dropped it, raised her hands as if we were pointing guns at her, and spoke rapidly to us with obvious anxiety. I wasn't sure what the language was. She seemed to be disclaiming all knowledge of how Lysander had wound up unconscious at her feet while she held a heavy weapon over his head.

The other people in the group raised their hands, too, evidently thinking this a wise posture to assume in such awkward circumstances.

"They seem to be surrendering to us," Barclay said.

"They're under the impression that we're immigration authorities," Max said.

I looked at him. "How do you know that?"

My question was answered when he started conversing with the six Asians in their own language, which he later identified to me as a dialect of Chinese. The other two people spoke Farsi, which was not a language Max knew, but they had enough Arabic to communicate reasonably well with him.

"I always meant to learn another language," Barclay said wistfully.

After several minutes of discussion, Max said to Barclay and me, "I'm afraid we've been operating under a misapprehension. These people are neither Magnus's victims nor his partners in a scheme to inflict harm on anyone. They're performers—magicians and illusionists—who've been persecuted in their own countries. Magnus uses the cover of his worldwide business, which includes receiving shipments and supplies from many different countries, to smuggle them into the U.S., where they may pursue their profession without fear of oppression."

"He's...smuggling *magic acts* into the country?" I said.

"*Persecuted* magic acts," Max said. "From countries ruled by governments that do not protect the rights of all artistes to express themselves through their work. Once he gets them into the U.S., they hide here in the upper floors of the shop until he can place them discreetly in shows around the country. With, I assume, forged immigration papers."

"He's smuggling magic acts?" I repeated.

Noting my incredulity, the lady who had clubbed Lysander picked up her big bamboo pole again.

I fell back a step. "Now *wait* a minute!"

Her eyes widened and she spoke in a nervous tone and made a gesture indicating she intended no harm. Everyone else made similar gestures and comments. Then she balanced the pole on the floor and climbed up it. When she was about six feet off the ground, she turned upside down. Then she did a little flip and landed on the floor while holding the pole across her back. She said something and indicated that Max should translate.

"She says she can make the pole disappear." He added, "There is, I gather, a suggestive sexuality about that portion of the act which disturbed the authorities in her native land."

"I see."

"In any case, she says she can't demonstrate the disappearing illusion here, because she needs more props and the right set for it."

"Speaking of disappearing," I said, "we can't assume this means Magnus isn't guilty. We know he had access to at least two of the prop boxes involved in the disappearances."

"Hmm, yes, we need to question him."

Barclay's eyes widened as we heard a bellow from below and someone started charging noisily up the stairs. "I think now's our chance."

Magnus appeared at the top of the stairs moments later, his hair wild, his teeth bared, his eyes menacing. He was carrying a medieval-looking mace (a *mace?* I

thought) and making guttural noises. He stopped in
his tracks when he saw all of us.

"Dear me," said Max, "this is rather awkward."

When Magnus recognized me, his eyes bulged.
Then he dropped his mace on the floor. "I might
have guessed."

"You thought I did *what?*" Magnus said.

Max explained our concerns again.

"You thought I did *what?*" Magnus said again.

He, Max, Barclay, Lysander and I were sitting in his
office downstairs as Max attempted to make him understand why we had broken into the magic shop
after midnight and terrified his illegal aliens. Lysander was sitting morosely in the corner clutching his
aching head while Max walked Magnus through the
basic facts of our problem once more.

Then Magic Magnus said to me, "Exactly what
kind of lunatic fringe are you involved in? I mean,
sure, I thought you were a little weird, but I had no
idea…."

"He's telling you the truth," I said wearily.

Magnus asked me, "Tell me, that cop who's hot for
you—does *he* know you're this troubled?"

"It was my impression, too, that Detective Lopez
rather likes Esther," Max said chattily. "But apparently
this attraction comes into conflict with his duty, and
he seems to be, at heart, a serious young man devoted
to his profession."

"Look, I don't mean to be judgmental," Magnus said, "but I must ask—are you all insane?"

"You are the only person we've come across who had access to all the prop boxes," I said testily.

"All of them?" He frowned. "Are you sure?"

"Um…" I looked at Max. He looked at Barclay.

"No, I'm asking seriously," Magnus said. "If it's true, if you found an evidence trail leading to me, then I want to know about it. Because that cop—Lopez?— will find it, too. He seems like a thorough son of a bitch. And forewarned is forearmed. I don't want to get arrested for something I didn't do." He looked upward for a moment and added, "I also don't want to get arrested for what I *am* doing. Are we clear on that?"

"You mean…" I frowned. "You want to cooperate with our investigation?"

"'Want' would be a wild exaggeration," he said. "But I have decided to cooperate, in order to serve my own interests—i.e., avoiding nasty surprises from the cops. So, how many vanishing boxes are involved. Four, you said?"

"Five, as of tonight," Max replied. "But we don't yet know who the fifth victim is."

"Well, Joe and Barclay got their boxes from me, we all know that," Magnus said. "Give me the names of the other two magicians."

He'd never heard of Duke Dempsey or Darling Delilah. Duke's rhinestone-studded horse and Delilah's little Philistine temple sounded unfamiliar to him—though he'd like to see them sometime, he said with professional interest.

"You're bluffing," I said, trying to sound cop-like. "Hoping to get rid of us."

"Esther, I am decidedly *eager* to get rid of you. But what would be the point of my bluffing, when you're certainly going to ask your friends if they know me?"

"Oh. Right."

"And they're going to tell you they *don't* know me. I'm not the, er, evil perpetrator you're looking for, folks." Seeing our dejected postures, he sighed. "Look, if you can give me some more details about the disappearances, maybe I can figure out how it was done."

Max shook his head. "It wasn't done your way, young man. It was done my way."

"It looks like we've wasted an evening," I said morosely.

"And I'm going to waste tomorrow morning cleaning up the mess you've made of my place," Magnus grumbled.

"Serves you right," I said. "Those hokey booby-traps."

He grinned. "And you only had time to stumble into a couple of them."

My cell phone rang. I glanced at the time—nearly two o'clock in the morning—and realized who must be calling. "Hello?"

"Esther, it's Satsy. I've just come out onto the street for a few minutes to check my call log. You were trying to reach me a few hours ago?"

"Yeah." I sighed. "It's been a busy night. We'll swing by the club and make a report." So much for going straight home and to bed, I thought.

"We'll be here."

"Time to go," Max said. He settled his hat on his head. We all did the same, including Lysander.

Magnus looked at our hats and asked, "Is there some kind of dress code in your group?"

"I'll make a deal with you," I said to him.

"And why is your face all dirty, Esther?"

I brushed self-consciously at my cheek. Ink wasn't easy to wash off. "I won't tell anyone you're smuggling illegal aliens into the country—"

"Persecuted magic acts," he corrected me.

"—if you don't tell Matilda the crystal cage is ready until *I* tell you it's okay to do so. Agreed?"

"I can't stall her forever," he warned me.

"I know. But I need a little more time. And you don't want to *do* time. So do we have a deal?"

He sighed and nodded. "We have a deal."

So one problem was solved, at least. However, by now, it seemed like an awfully small problem.

CHAPTER 11

It seemed I had only just fallen asleep—in a post-dawn, headlong crash into my mattress—when my doorbell rang. The loud, bone-jarring buzz made my whole body do an improbable leap straight up into the air. I landed facedown on my bed and contemplated staying there. Forever.

Predictably, though, the buzzer disturbed me again a minute later. I groaned and heaved myself out of bed. As I headed for the bedroom door, staggering with exhaustion and pain—last night's adventures at the magic shop had taken their toll on my body—I caught a glimpse of myself in the dresser mirror and flinched.

I was a sight that would send small children fleeing in terror. My hair was matted. There was a red scrunchy so thoroughly woven into the tangles that I didn't even bother trying to get it out. I was still wearing yesterday's clothes, navy blue sweatpants and a gray T-shirt. The shirt was stained with the glass of red wine I'd spilled on myself during our war council at the Pony Expressive around three o'clock in the morning. There was a big, dark bruise on my arm, from last night's tumble down Magnus's stairs; I could feel other bruises elsewhere, hidden beneath my wrinkled, dirty clothing. My face was pale and still liberally smeared with tabloid ink. My eyes were bloodshot, puffy, and had dark circles under them. I looked like some hideous hag from the bizarre drawings reproduced in Max's occult books.

The buzzer made me jump again. I stumbled toward the intercom next to my front door and pressed the button to open the downstairs door for my visitor. Anything to make the infernal buzzing of my doorbell stop—*now*. Only as I staggered toward the coffeepot in the kitchen did it occur to me that I should have used the intercom to demand the identity of my visitor before letting him into the building.

"It would be just my luck to be the victim of a random homicide now," I muttered, searching vaguely for coffee.

There was a knock at the front door. I groaned again and stumbled back over to it, dazed and confused. I opened the front door without remembering to ask who was there.

Lopez took one long look at me, then said, "Yeah, I didn't really figure you for a morning person."

I stared at him in blank-minded stupefaction.

"Can I come in?" he asked.

There was a bag in his arms. I smelled something seductive. "Is that coffee?" I croaked.

He nodded. "And bagels. I brought breakfast."

"You can come in." Turning away from the door I shuffled over to my kitchen table, where I slumped into a chair and closed my eyes. I heard the front door close and footsteps approach me. Then there were rustling noises right next to me, and I realized Lopez was unpacking the coffee and food.

"Plates?" he said.

I opened my eyes and squinted up at him. "Huh?"

"Do you have plates?"

I stared at him. "Plates." I repeated the word slowly, waiting for it to register meaning in my brain.

His lips twitched. "Have some coffee, Esther."

I accepted the foam cup he pressed into my hand, closed my eyes again and took a grateful gulp of the hot liquid. Then I wrinkled my face in distaste and said, without opening my eyes, "I take it with milk."

"Okay."

I felt him remove the cup from my hands. The refrigerator clicked open softly, there was a little shuffling and a pouring sound, and then my cup was placed back in my hands. I raised it to my lips, gulped again, and said, "That's better."

After another gulp, I opened my eyes and saw Lopez

rummaging around in my kitchen cupboards. "What are you doing?"

"Looking for— Ah, here we go." He came back to the table with two plates, then went back to searching my kitchen. He returned to the table again a moment later with knives and napkins. He unpacked the bagels and some cream cheese.

"Okay," I mumbled, gazing at the offerings with my dry, aching eyes. "That's fine. You can go now."

"Actually, I was thinking of joining you."

"Huh?"

He sat down, put a bagel on his plate and picked up the other cup of coffee.

I said, "No, I need that." Before he could raise his coffee to his lips, I took it away from him and cradled it against the stained fabric covering my chest.

"No, no, please don't stand on ceremony," he said. "Help yourself."

"Why are you bothering me at the crack of dawn?" I demanded.

"It's after ten o'clock."

"I didn't get to bed until…" I shook my head. "I don't know. But it wasn't long ago, I know that much."

"What kept you up so late?"

Breaking and entering, followed by the discovery of illegal aliens whose presence here I have conspired to keep secret, followed by a long postmortem with two wizards, a cowboy and some drag queens.

"Uh…" I blinked, afraid for a moment I'd spoken

aloud. However, I could tell from Lopez's expression that I hadn't. Besides, my tongue wasn't yet working well enough to say that much.

Late last night—well, early this morning—Duke and Delilah had both confirmed, as Magnus predicted, that they'd never met or dealt with the red-haired illusions expert. By dawn, Max still had no idea who had disappeared last night, and we'd all agreed that none of us would be of any use unless we got a little rest. I was due back at the bookshop around noon today; I'd been planning to sleep until 11:45, then brush my teeth, run outside and catch a cab.

Now I glowered at Lopez, thinking I could have slept another ninety minutes if he hadn't come here and bothered me.

"You were saying?" he prodded.

"Huh?"

"What were you doing last night that kept you up so late?" Lopez was watching me intently.

"Um…"

"Fighting Evil, by any chance?"

My heart sank as I suddenly remembered everything *else* that had happened yesterday. "Oh."

"Esther…" He paused. "Uh, are you hungover?"

"No, just exhausted, demoralized and in more than a little pain."

"Pain?" He glanced at the big bruise on my arm. "Did someone hurt you?"

I tried to pull my sleeve over the bruise, then

stopped when I realized that just increased his interest in it. "It was an accident. Someone fell on me, then I fell and..." I shrugged. "Big accident. Clumsy."

"In the bookshop?"

My brain was still working slowly. I just stared at him, wondering what to say.

"Esther?"

"Thanks for the coffee," I mumbled, realizing I needed to pull myself together and make sure I edited my comments appropriately.

After a moment, he sat back, evidently deciding to let the subject drop. For the moment, anyhow. He nodded to the coffee and said, "You're welcome. It's the least I can do if I'm going to call on a woman unannounced in the morning."

"Do you do this for all the female suspects that you wake up from a sound sleep?" I grumbled.

There was a pause before he said, "Actually, I'm off duty right now."

"Oh, really?" I was skeptical that this was purely a social call.

"Just wanted to talk," he said, spreading cream cheese on his bagel. "You and me. Off the record."

"*That's* what looks different about you today," I said, as the caffeine infiltrated a few brain cells. So far, I'd seen him only in his detective clothes—neat, slightly conservative suits that looked budget-conscious but well-made. Today he wore jeans, a denim jacket and a nice T-shirt that nearly matched the blue,

blue color of his dark-lashed eyes. "You're not dressed for work."

"I don't go on duty until four o'clock."

"What do you want to talk about?"

"Have some food," he suggested. "You seem a little cranky."

"I've had three hours of sleep. I think."

"I'm relieved." He glanced at me. "That you're not *always* like this in the morning, I mean. Uh, you're not, are you?"

"Humph." I bit into my bagel.

He looked around. The kitchen had almost enough room for a sit-down table big enough for four people. The kitchen (and the table) flowed into the living room, the two rooms being partially separated by a counter. The bathroom was off the living room, which was moderate in size, and there was a door at the other end of the room leading onto a very small balcony. It overlooked a claustrophobic space between four close-together buildings and offered no privacy, but it was nonetheless a balcony.

"This is a good apartment," Lopez said, with a New York resident's standard interest in living spaces.

"Uh-huh."

He leaned way back in his chair so he could look down the hallway. "You have *two* bedrooms?" It was clear that this astonishing fact momentarily drove all other thoughts from his mind.

"Yes."

"No roommate?"

"No."

"*Two* bedrooms?"

"You cannot have one of them," I said firmly.

"How can you afford two bedrooms?" When I gave him a chilly look, he added, "I just mean, I don't know anyone living alone who can afford two bedrooms in Manhattan."

I sighed and loosened up a little. "Yeah, it's a great apartment. I'm really lucky." It was old and shabby, there was a mold problem in the bathroom, and it certainly wasn't the swankiest neighborhood in the city—though it was safer than most people supposed, and almost everyone who lived on my street was a longtime resident who knew most of the other neighbors by name. The landlord responded to repair requests in geological time, the window-unit air conditioners were unreliable in summer, and the heating system was unpredictable in winter. But by New York standards, this was a great apartment—especially at the rent I was paying. And it was a real luxury for a struggling actress to have this much space to herself.

I poured milk into Lopez's coffee and started drinking it. Then I said, "It's rent controlled. I moved in here with two other girls when I first came to New York—the back bedroom's tiny, barely big enough for just one person. Anyhow, there was a series of roommates over the next few years, and then finally, I was getting enough work that I decided to stop collecting new roommates when the last two left the city." I shrugged. "I figured I could cover rent by myself, and I was more than ready to live alone by then."

"If *Sorcerer!* doesn't reopen, can you still cover rent by yourself?"

"You're great company in the morning, too," I said sourly.

"When the crystal cage is repaired, will you go on with the show?"

"When did *that* become police business?"

Off the record or not, he was on the job again. "Esther, just tell me straight up. Do you really believe the stuff that Max Zadok was spouting in my house yesterday?"

"He went to your house?" I said, puzzled.

"My precinct house," Lopez amended.

"You tell *me* something straight up," I said. "Are you satisfied that he's no threat to—" I stopped when I heard an unfamiliar jingle. "What's that?"

"Excuse me." He reached into his pocket and withdrew his cell phone, then frowned when he read the caller ID. "I'd better answer it. She'll just keep calling every twenty minutes if I don't. I'm sorry, Esther. This won't take long."

He flipped open his phone and, with a look of long-suffering patience, said, "Hi, Mom."

I snorted into my coffee and smirked at his warning glare.

"Yeah. Uh-huh. No. No." After a moment, he said, "Let's try this again. *No.* I said no. Have you gone deaf? Mom…" He winced and pulled the phone away from his ear, then covered the receiver with his hand and said to me, "You would be amazed at the number of friends my mom has who have single daughters living in the city. All of them, it would seem, in such desperate need of a date that they have authorized our mothers to act as matchmakers."

"Surely not."

"Yeah, I don't really think so, either, but my mom keeps swearing it's so. I'm guessing her Confessor knows the truth, though. Lucky for her, lying's only a venial sin."

I guessed, "Your mom is where your blue eyes come from?"

He nodded. "Bridget Eileen Donovan."

"And your Dad?"

"From Cuba. Came over when he was young."

And was, no doubt, the source of Lopez's exotic good looks, I thought, aware of the crisp black hair brushing his collar and the smooth, dark skin of his throat.

He put the phone back to his ear. "Yes, Mom, I'm still here. No, I can't. No." He listened. "There *is* a good reason." In response to her next question, he said, "Because I've met someone I like."

Our eyes locked. I suddenly wished I didn't look like such a hag today.

"No," he said into the phone, "I'm not lying just to get rid of you. Uh-huh. Yes, she's female. No, not married. Yes, still in her childbearing years."

I choked on my coffee.

"Well, I haven't looked *everywhere* yet, but I haven't noticed any excessive piercing." He listened for a moment. "Pretty?" His gaze ran over me. "Well, sometimes."

I glared at him.

He grinned and added, "In her way."

I drank more coffee, pretending to ignore him.

"No, I think she's Jewish." When I continued ignoring him, he poked my calf with his foot. "Right?" I nodded and he said, "Yeah, Jewish. No, she won't convert. Yes, I'm sure. No, I don't want Father Devaney to give her a call." After another moment, he said, "No, we haven't talked about how we'll raise the children. Or the wedding... Actually, no. No. No, not that, either... Well, because we haven't been on a date yet. No, I'm not sure we will."

He held the phone away from his ear again while his mother squawked. Then he said to her, "Because I suspect she's crazy, and I'm a little afraid that she's committed a felony. And you can see how that would be a conflict of interest for me." In response to his loving mother's next question, he said, "No, no, nothing quite as bad as homicide or armed robbery." He glanced up and asked me, "Er, I'm right about that, aren't I?"

"I'd like you to go away now," I said sincerely.

"In fact, Mom, I'm trying to have breakfast with her right now, so if you'll just... No, I did not spend the night with her."

"Why are you talking about this with your *mother*?" I demanded.

He said to me, "Because it's so much less time-consuming than resisting. Believe me. I speak from experience." Into the phone, he said, "Huh? Okay, good. Say hi to Pop for me. And Mom? Try not to call me again for a while, okay? It's making a bad impression on this woman." He grinned. "Well, even felons have their standards, Mom. Bye."

I stared at him in mingled outrage and amazement after he hung up, too dumbfounded to come up with any of the scathing comments that he and his mother deserved.

"Don't look at me like that," he said, spreading cream cheese on the other half of his bagel. "You have no idea what a huge step it was for me to admit to my mom that, in a city of eleven million people, I've met a single, female person of childbearing age." He added with a frown, "It was getting a little difficult to keep convincing her that there were no such people in New York."

"If she's so determined to marry you off," I asked, "how have you stayed single this long?"

"Well, this is kind of a recent thing. She and my dad hit their sixties a few years ago and suddenly realized they didn't have any grandchildren. Then my older brothers—there are two, I'm the youngest in the family—well, they screwed me over."

"They did?"

"My eldest brother told Mom he's gay." Lopez scowled. "I could kill him."

I blinked. "Er, you didn't strike me as homophobic."

"I'm not. And he's not gay. He just said that to get her off his back about marrying and providing her with grandchildren. But it worked out so well, he intends to keep that story going unless he meets someone he wants to marry."

"Oh."

"And when my other brother saw how well that worked, he more or less did the same thing."

"Told your parents he's gay?" I said.

"No, that excuse was taken, and Tim—the eldest—wouldn't let us use it. Said it might look suspicious if we *all* suddenly became gay. So Michael—my middle brother—told Mom he's had a spiritual revelation and is planning to enter the priesthood."

"*These* days?"

"Hey, the Church needs all the help it can get. Mom's thrilled. Me, I think it was a tactical error. It'll be years before she wonders why Tim never brings a man home for Christmas, but she's bound to notice pretty soon that Mikey's not in seminary."

"I see," I said. "So your brothers abandoned you. No cover, no camouflage."

"It's been rough," Lopez said wearily. "The whole force of that woman's grandmotherly instincts concentrated on me, and me alone. I ask you, what's the point of putting up with siblings all through childhood if something like this is going to happen to you in adulthood?"

"You're in a tight spot," I observed.

"But not anymore." He smiled at me. "Now I've got *you*."

"Me?"

"A crazy felon who's not Catholic. And I didn't even tell her yet that you're an actress. I'm saving that for an emergency." He looked smug. "Could I have picked *anyone* better to turn my mother off the idea of my getting married?"

I propped my chin on my hand and stared into my coffee as the disappointment sank in. "Oh. So you don't like me that much, after all. I'm just a convenient foil."

"Actually, I like you a lot." He kept his eyes on his bagel as he added, "And I think you're pretty." After a moment, he admitted, "Well, not so much right now…"

"I'm having a very difficult week!" I said defensively.

He smiled and reached over to brush some of the tangles away from my sleep-deprived face. "But I have to admit, it's handy that you're tailor-made for my mom to hate."

"This is some sort of weird Catholic mother-son thing, isn't it," I said, pushing his hand away.

"Speaking of weird…"

"Here we go," I muttered.

Cop-like, he caught me off guard with his next question: "Why does Barclay Preston-Cole think you're with the Special Investigative Branch of Equity?"

"He thinks what?" My eyes widened. "Oh my God! That's what I… Er…"

"Yes?"

"I may have allowed him to believe something along those lines when I first contacted him." But it had never occurred to me that Barclay still believed it. Obviously, I needed to have a little talk with him.

Lopez looked amused. "Relax, Esther. It's not even a misdemeanor to pretend to be a member of a fictional investigative unit that no sensible adult believes in." After a moment, he added uneasily, "Um, as long as you didn't fake an ID to go with your story?"

"No, of course not," I said.

"Just checking." He added, "Barclay's not exactly the sharpest knife in the drawer, is he? Maybe too many generations of upper-crust intermarriage?"

Remembering the brave way Barclay had charged up those stairs last night, I said, "You leave him alone."

"Do I have a rival?"

"Barclay's a good boy."

"Damned with faint praise," Lopez said.

"It wasn't faint! It was... Never mind. You let Barclay and Max go," I noted. "Does that mean you're done with them? They're not under suspicion for anything?"

"No, it just means that there's no law against being nutty and naive."

"Are you still investigating them? Us? Me?" I asked.

He lowered his lashes over his eyes. "You left the New View Venue in costume the night you 'became ill' during the performance. And you were still dressed as Virtue hours later, when you turned up at the Pony Expressive."

"How do you know... Never mind." He'd followed up, of course.

"So tell me, Esther. If I canvassed the neighborhood, would I find out that someone saw a woman in a glittery costume and an old man in a fedora and a duster lurking around the theater after hours that night?"

"No," I said firmly, praying I was right. Then I realized what he'd said. "You haven't canvassed the neighborhood?"

"Luckily for you, I suspect, I don't have much time to devote to a vandalism case where no one got hurt and only one well-insured item got damaged."

"It's insured? All that bitching Matilda's been doing about the cost of repairs, and it's *insured?*"

"Since the crystal cage has been destroyed twice in one week, I'm guessing her premiums are about to skyrocket," he said dryly.

"But you questioned Barclay and Max for hours," I pointed out. "You *are* devoting a lot of time to this."

"I'm looking for Golly Gee and Clarisse Staunton."

"Oh. I see." Then I said, "But so are Barclay and Max! You must realize that, after talking to them for so long?"

He sat back, folded his arms and studied me. "You're in cahoots with them?"

"Yes. And they must have told you that. Though not in those exact words, I hope."

"Esther…" He looked at a loss for words.

"You think Max is crazy," I said.

"Don't *you?*"

"But do you think he's dangerous?" I prodded, worried about Lopez hounding Max.

"I don't know. He doesn't seem dangerous. Crazy, but not dangerous. But I'm no psychiatrist. And I can't request he be evaluated by a psychiatrist unless I find evidence that he's done something more than just talk a lot. And although his theories about Golly Gee and Clarisse Staunton make me want to stick my head in a bucket of cold water and keep it there until someone else solves this case—"

"I sometimes feel that way, too," I admitted.

"—bizarre talk about involuntary mystical translocation, combined with a fervently expressed desire to protect people from the mysterious forces of Evil doesn't qualify as evidence. Or even as probable cause."

"Exactly! So you'll leave him alone?"

"You know I can't promise you that."

"You have no right to harass him," I insisted.

"Why are you so protective of him? You don't— Oh my God." He rubbed his forehead. "You *do* believe it, don't you? All that bizarre crap he was spouting? He implied you believed it, but I hoped he was just deluding himself. I mean, sure, you're a little off the wall, but mostly you seem pretty sane to me."

"Go on," I said sourly, "lay on the flattery with a trowel."

"How can you possibly believe… Wait, no, never mind." He held up his hand and seemed to be gathering his patience. "Okay. Let's go back a step. The point I want to make—"

"Oh, there's a point to this?"

"The point," he said doggedly, "is that I'm not as convinced as you are, I gather, that Max Zadok isn't dangerous. At least, to you."

"To me?" I blurted, stunned.

"He convinced you to vandalize the crystal cage, didn't he?"

Lopez had caught me off guard again. "You need to go now," I said, my voice faint.

He pulled me back down into my chair when I tried to stand up. "Esther, what else has he got you involved in?"

"We had nothing to do with what happened to the crystal cage."

"I know you're lying," he said. "I'm a cop, Esther. I'm good at this. I *know*."

"I want you to go now."

"What if someone gets hurt the next time Max talks you into some crazy act?" Lopez persisted.

"You're way out of line, Detective!"

He took my hand between both of his. "Please, Esther, stay away from him. Please."

"Lopez... *Don't*." This was not how I had wanted things to be, the first time he held my hand.

"Promise me," he insisted.

"Okay!" I said. "I promise! I promise I'll stay away from Max! Now just *stop*, would you?"

He let go of my hand, sighed and looked away. "You're lying. You have no intention of staying away from him."

"Of course I'm lying! Four people are missing— no, five! And I want to get them back. So does Max!"

Lopez rested his forehead on the table and mumbled, "*God*, I wish my transfer would come through. I wish I could just leave today. Dump this case. Dump the whole thing. Dump *you*."

"Excuse me?"

"Just in a professional sense."

"Oh, right. In the *personal* sense, I'm the woman you're hoping to get your mother to hate."

"Yes," he agreed. "And that can't happen until you and I stop going round and round about this case."

"Or until you stop suspecting me of being a criminal?"

"That would help, too."

"Sit up." I shoved at his shoulder.

He slowly sat up. His face looked tired now, the freshness of the morning already worn off. He picked up his coffee cup and peered into it. "You drank it all."

"Sorry."

"You could offer to make some," he said hopefully.

"You won't be staying that long."

"Oh."

Studying the slump of his shoulders, I asked something that probably should have occurred to me before now. "Why don't you have a partner? Don't cops usually work in pairs?"

"He quit last month. Now he's making six figures a year in private security consulting and has weekends off. And I," Lopez said morosely, "I am interviewing dim-witted society boys and nutty bookshop owners, looking for girls who reputedly vanished during magic acts, and trying—with less and less success every day—not to flirt with a woman I may have to arrest. *And* I'm doing all this despite understandable pressure from my increasingly exasperated lieutenant," he added bitterly, "to devote all my attention to more concrete matters."

"Well," I said. "I guess that was some stuff you needed to get off your chest."

"Yes, it was."

He looked sulky. The same expression that usually made me want to wallop Hieronymus looked kind of cute on Lopez.

"It's not easy being you," I said.

"No, it's not," he agreed. "And, of course, you already know about my mother."

"We should just call you Job."

"Now you're ridiculing me."

"'Now'?" I said. He smiled. But I suddenly realized with a sinking heart what he'd said earlier. "You've applied for a transfer?"

"Yes."

"You're leaving New York?" I asked plaintively.

He squinted at me. "No, of course not."

"Oh!" I smiled with relief. I didn't want him investigating me—let alone arresting me—but I'd be upset if he just *left*.

"I've applied to join the Organized Crime Control Bureau." He sighed. "But with my partner having left suddenly, the squad's already short one guy, and I can't go while I'd be leaving them short by two. So I'm working my cases alone, and also working my way through a mountain of paperwork on some cold cases the boss has suddenly decided we should reopen."

"All that paperwork I saw on your desk, the first time I came to the squad room," I said, remembering.

"Uh-huh."

"When do you expect your transfer to come through?"

"Soon, I pray to God." His tone was heartfelt. "But not until they get one or two guys transferred into the squad and bring them up to speed." After a pause, he added, "But if you're hoping I'll leave and someone else will take over this case, Esther—"

"Wouldn't that be for the best? I mean—"

"I know what you mean. But no one else will cut you the slack that I have."

"But I haven't done anything—"

"Stop. If you're not going to tell me the truth, could you at least stop lying to me?" There was a long silence, since I didn't know what to say in response to that. Then he surprised me by asking, "What did you mean, five?"

"Huh?"

"*Five* people are missing?"

Another instance where I'd said a little too much to him in the heat of the moment. "Um…"

"Golly Gee, Clarisse Staunton…and those other two names that Max was so careful to avoid mentioning in the station house yesterday." He frowned. "The names are in my notes…they sounded like strippers, I remember that."

"They're not strippers!"

He lifted his brows.

I sighed. "Sexy Samson and Dolly the Dancing Cowgirl."

"Ah. Yeah. Those were the names."

"They vanished, too. Onstage. During their acts."

"Just to clarify... We're talking about real human beings now?"

"Yes! But, um, come to think of it, I don't know what their legal names are."

"I can find out."

"I'd rather you didn't. Max would rather you didn't. Even your lieutenant, I gather, would rather you didn't."

He ignored that. "Who's the fifth?"

"We don't know."

"Esther."

"No, we really don't know. We're just sure it's happened."

"What makes you sure?"

I sighed, knowing what he'd think. "There's been another localized disturbance in the fabric of this dimension."

"I see."

"Max can sense these things." It sounded silly when I said it to Lopez, even though I knew it was true.

"But you can't sense it?"

"No."

He thought it over. "Okay, let's focus on the part of the problem that matters. You really believe these people have vanished—in an unusual sense, shall we say?"

"Yes."

"You and Max really want to find them?"

"Yes."

"Then maybe my looking into it can help," he said reasonably.

"But you don't believe what we believe," I said.

"So what? Is that going to matter to the vanished ladies—?"

"They're not all ladies."

"Now is that nice?" he admonished.

"I mean, Samson's a man."

"And *I* mean, if they're really missing, will it matter to them what I believe, if I can find them? Or help you find them?"

"I don't think you *can* find them," I said honestly. "I think what you believe—or don't believe—will stop you."

"To be perfectly honest," he said, "I never believed in transubstantiation, but that didn't stop me from being a pretty good altar boy."

"*You* were an altar boy?"

"And I'm not positive that marijuana and prostitution should be illegal, but that's never stopped me from being a good cop."

"Speaking of being a cop..." I felt a little Evil stir in me as I smiled. "Whoopsy Daisy says—"

"Whoopsy Daisy?"

"Seymour Barinsky," I clarified. "He told me last night that you looked very sexy in uniform."

"How flattering."

"And Khyber Pass thinks you're hot. He has a thing for uniforms. He says if you'd wear yours, he'd do you in a New York minute."

"In his dreams." Our eyes held as we grinned at each other. After a moment, he said, "I don't mean this to sound critical—"

"*Now* what?"

"Why is your face all dirty?"

"Oh. *The Exposé*. You wouldn't believe how hard it is to wash off that damn ink."

"*You* read *The Exposé*?"

"Not habitually. There was a story about Golly's disappearance in it yesterday."

"Anything accurate?"

"More than you'd expect." I scrubbed at my face, then ran a hand over my tangled hair. "I really need a shower."

"I can't argue with that."

"You're getting better at the not-flirting thing."

He grinned. "I could join you."

"You haven't even taken me out for dinner yet. Showers are *way* out of your league." Getting more serious, I said, "Look, I know I can't stop you from pursuing this business—"

"That's right, you can't."

"Though I'm guessing your boss can stop you— and probably will, if you put much time into it."

"That's right, too," he admitted.

"But I wish you'd trust us."

"And I wish you'd stay away from Max."

We stared at each other, both realizing this was as far as negotiations were going to get today—or perhaps at all.

My cell phone rang. I excused myself and rose to answer it. A moment later, I said, "Hi, Mom. No. Yes. I know. Okay." I put my hand over the receiver. "This is going to be a long call."

He took the hint. "I should go." He rose to his feet. "I'll be seeing you."

"Okay." I watched him head for the door. "Thanks for breakfast."

"My pleasure. Next time, I'll bring more coffee."

I was letting a sexy, employed, straight, single man whom I really liked leave my apartment with a brief wave and no plans for a date. It was just barely possible, I mused, that I wasn't running my life as well as I might.

After I heard his footsteps going down the stairs in the hall, I said, "Okay, Khyber, he's gone."

Upon realizing I wasn't alone, when I'd said "Hi, Mom," Khyber had immediately guessed who my company was.

"Did he spend the night there?" Khyber asked with interest.

"No! Even *I* didn't spend the night here. He brought me breakfast, that's all."

"Did he grill you?"

"A little. But it's okay." I omitted mentioning that I'd told Lopez about Samson and Dolly. It wasn't as if he wouldn't have picked up that trail on his own, anyhow.

"He's hot," Khyber said with reluctant approval. "Have you seen him with his clothes off yet?"

"No!"

"Or in his uniform?"

"Why did you call?"

"I've found last night's victims."

"*You* found them?" I said in surprise.

"Yeah. Lots of online chatter. Are you decent? Dr. Zadok told me to stop by your place in a cab and bring you with me. He's already on his way there."

"Where?"

"To meet Garry Goudini. Last night, one of his assistants vanished during the act. So did his white Bengal tiger."

"Things have gone wrong before, of course," Garry Goudini admitted, gazing out over Times Square from the window of his hotel suite. "You've got to expect that in this business. For example, there was that time I was levitating a Toyota onstage. It was supposed to go up eight feet in the air. Well, it got to about four feet, then fell. With a big crash." He took a long drag on his cigarette. "If it had gotten up to eight feet, I'd have been standing under it when it fell. My God, man, I could have been *killed* that night!"

Khyber and I exchanged glances as Goudini took another gulp of his whiskey and soda. This was the magician's second drink since we'd arrived barely fifteen minutes ago.

Max said, "How dreadful for you, Mr. Goudini. Now, about last night—"

"Then there was the time I tried to make a girl disappear as she dived from a high platform down through a ball of fire," Goudini said. "Well, she simply hit the ground with a thud one night in Vegas. It was so embarrassing."

"Did she survive?" Khyber asked in appalled fascination.

"Hmm?" Goudini looked over his shoulder at us. "Oh, yes. The hospital bills nearly killed *me,* though." He took another sip of his drink, then drew some more smoke into his lungs.

Goudini's thick, wavy, black hair, with its faint streaks of gray at the temples, looked as if it was made of patent leather and wouldn't get ruffled by a stiff wind. His deep, even-all-over tan had the faintest orange tinge to it. His eyebrows were shaped into dramatic arches, and he wore a touch of eyeliner. He was clad in black leather pants, and a black silk shirt that he left unbuttoned halfway down his hairy, slightly orange chest.

According to Khyber, who'd done the research online and briefed me on the way here, Goudini had done very well in Vegas for a few years, about a decade ago, but gradually got squeezed out of the limelight by other acts. He hadn't given a performance anywhere in at least two years; last night's gig, the opening night of a pretour, one-week appearance in Manhattan, was intended to launch his comeback. He'd been rehearsing the new act for several months at his home outside the city.

Max tried again. "About last night, Mr. Goudini…"

But Goudini launched into a rambling reminiscence of yet another onstage mishap, this one involving a water tank in which he'd nearly drowned. I started feeling glad that the man I was interested in these days was in a nice, safe profession like police work.

"I nearly died that night," Goudini said, concluding his anecdote about being chained up underwater. "So it's not as if I'm not used to surprises onstage. It's not as if I lack experience in dealing with emergencies before a live audience."

"Of course not," Max said soothingly.

"But what happened last night… My *God*, man! I've never experienced anything like that!" Goudini finished his drink. "I panicked. I admit it. *Anyone* would have panicked, and no one can tell me differently." He went to the wet bar and started mixing yet another whiskey and soda. "You're sure no one else wants one?"

"No, thanks," we said, almost in unison.

According to Khyber, with the failure of the disappearing act, Goudini's performance had bombed so badly last night that magic buffs were talking about it on BBs all night and all morning. The chatter had been easy to trace when Khyber got up today and started checking the sites he'd been monitoring in recent days.

"It was a shattering experience," Goudini told us. I was so recently out of the shower that my hair was still damp, and my face was probably still pink from the determined scrubbing I'd given it. Max looked as weary as I felt, but his expression was intent as he extracted the details of last night's disappearance from Goudini.

The magician's account was similar to the others we'd heard, except that it was *bigger! better! bolder!* His prop box was an enormous tiger cage with shiny silver bars, and it levitated fifteen feet above the stage while music blared and lights danced. The cage filled with smoke, there was a momentary blackout of the whole theater, a few flashes of thunder and lightning—

"Lightning?" Khyber asked, recalling his research.

"Simulated," Goudini clarified.

—followed by some sinister twirling effects of the cage, and a sudden, heart-lurching drop as the apparatus fell to the stage with a crash as if to release the deadly tiger inside—

"Poor thing," Khyber murmured. "Was it scared?"

—to prey upon the magician and his audience.

"Then the lights come up, the smoke clears and the tiger has been replaced by a beautiful girl, who steps out of the cage and takes a bow with me." Goudini gave another shudder. "Except, of course, that things went wrong last night. Very wrong."

"We'll need to examine that cage," Max said.

Goudini gave a little cry of despair. "How can I go on with the show this afternoon?"

"This afternoon?" I repeated.

"Saturday matinee," Khyber said.

It was Saturday, I realized. Golly had vanished one week ago. I fought off a sudden, gloomy fear that our quest was hopeless and we'd never find the disappearees—whose numbers were certainly increasing faster than clues were accumulating.

Goudini was agitated enough to run his hands through his hair. I was right—it didn't move at all. "What am I going to do without her?" he wondered brokenly.

"Don't you worry, Mr. Goudini," said Khyber. "We'll find her."

"Yes," I agreed firmly, stiffening my resolve. "We're going to find… I'm sorry, what's her name?"

"Alice."

"Alice," I repeated. "Can we get a description?"

"Of Alice? Well, she's nine years old," Goudini said.

I blinked. "What?"

"A white Bengal tiger. Average size for an adult female. And she has a scar on her nose from getting caught in some brambles as a cub."

"Oh," I said. "Alice is the tiger. Right. Gotcha. What's the young lady's name?"

"Hmm?"

"The woman who disappeared?" I prodded.

"Oh. Sarah Campbell."

I started to inquire about Sarah's mood and attitude last night, but Goudini interrupted me. "You really think you can get my tiger back for me?"

"We certainly hope so," said Max.

"We also hope to find your beautiful assistant," I said tersely.

"Hmm? Oh! Right. Well, that's good," Goudini said. "But Alice is the irreplaceable part of the act. I'll do anything—I mean, *anything*—to get my tiger back!"

"I see."

"It isn't just that tigers are so expensive," Goudini explained, as if fearing I might think him mercenary. "They're also incredibly difficult to train."

"I totally believe that, Garry," I said.

"I've got two grown cubs of Alice's," he said, "but they're just set dressing. They sit in cages on either side of the stage, looking fierce and pretty. They've never taken after their mother, they're really of no use in the act."

"Uh-huh."

"I must get Alice back!"

"Roger that," I said, rising to my feet. "Max, shall we examine the cage?"

"Yes, but I think perhaps we should question Mr. Goudini a bit more."

That was no doubt a wise suggestion, but I thought there was a good chance I'd clobber Goudini if I spent much more time with him. I wondered if he'd even be talking to us about the disappearance at all if Alice was safe now and Sarah Campbell had vanished alone.

However, we needed Goudini's cooperation. So, in order to avoid alienating him (by, you know, clobbering him), I suggested that I interview members of his performance team while Max continued talking with the magician. Max approved of this time-saving plan, and so I spent the rest of the afternoon tracking them down and questioning them.

All of them wanted Alice back. And, oh, yeah, Sarah, too.

Back at the bookshop, I wrote the names of the two latest victims on the display board, *Alice the Tiger* and *Sarah Campbell*.

"The human body," Lysander was saying to Satsy, "like virtually everything else in the cosmos, consists of more empty space than it does of solid matter. Therefore, the puzzling thing is not really that something can be made to vanish, but rather that things don't vanish more often."

Satsy said, "That's such clever reasoning!"

"No, no, merely the result of years of arduous study."

I gave up staring at the display board and went to the refreshments stand in search of sustenance. There was a mini fridge there. Max kept little pints of milk in it, to go with the coffee and tea he provided for his customers. I'd stored last night's Thai leftovers in there. When I opened the door now in search of a meal, though, I discovered the food had disappeared.

"Of course," I muttered.

The Chinese leftovers from Thursday night had also disappeared. Our research team ate too much, I thought bitterly.

"Vultures," I muttered.

Preferring to starve in a sulky mood rather than go back out onto the streets in search of food when I was so tired, I sat down at the research table with a sigh. I picked up a copy of John Aubrey's *Miscellanies* and opened it to the chapter entitled "Transportation by an Invisible Power." Within minutes, my head hurt. Seventeenth-century English prose isn't exactly light reading.

Satsy was perusing Colin Parsons's *Encounters With the Unknown.* There was a stack of books at his feet, under the table, but he'd already declined my offer to help him go through those. Lysander was working his way through an ancient-looking grimoire in a language I didn't recognize. According to what Max had told me, a grimoire was sort of a manual on ritual magic, both "good" and "evil"—which were concepts, I gathered, grimoire authors cared about less than they cared about simply how to get the job done.

I looked up as Max and Khyber entered the shop. After a quick greeting, Khyber set up his laptop, using Max's telephone line to get online, while Max explained that they'd learned nothing particularly useful from interviewing Goudini or examining the magician's tiger cage.

"I gather Goudini didn't feel like coming back here with you and hitting the books?" I said cynically.

"He's busy finishing his matinee performance," Max said.

"Without his big finale of the tiger and the girl swapping places in the levitating cage?" I asked.

"The show must go on." Khyber noticed our scant numbers and asked, "Where is everyone?"

"Whoopsy and Delilah are at the public library again," I said. "Hieronymus is down in the cellar. Of course."

"I should check on him," said Max. "He was looking rather haggard when I left this morning. I think the poor boy's been working too hard."

"Yeah, *that* sounds likely," I grumbled.

Satsy said, "Barclay and Dixie are rehearsing."

"Oh, that's right—tonight's performance!" Max said.

"Barclay's big break," Satsy said. "And what with so much of yesterday being devoted to police interrogation, he had no time to rehearse, so they've got a lot of work to do today if they want to be ready by showtime."

"Is Duke with them?" Khyber asked.

Satsy nodded. "He ducked out a while ago with apologies. Dixie phoned in, said she and Barclay would need some help loading his props into his van and setting up at the cabaret."

"It must be a more elaborate act than I pictured." I set aside John Aubrey's book and the undisciplined spelling that always seems to characterize prose of that era.

"Well, Barclay's worked awfully hard lately, from the sound of it," Satsy said. "Devoted himself to study and practice. All to arrive at this big day!"

"Yes." I rubbed my tired eyes. "He told me. When we met." What had he said? The act was getting better, all his hard work was paying off.

"I'd really like to go to Barclay's show tonight," Khyber said.

"Me, too," said Satsy. "But we have to do our own show, girlfriend."

"But maybe Delilah should go," Khyber said. "It might cheer her up."

Delilah at the Pony Expressive was like a widow holding vigil. Maybe it *would* be good for her to go somewhere else tonight.

I said, "I could take her to the Magic Cabaret."

"Good idea," Khyber said. "We should suggest it to her."

"Where *is* the Magic Cabaret?" I asked.

We all looked at one another and realized none of us knew. Khyber tried looking it up online but didn't find it.

"We'll call Barclay and ask." I glanced at the clock and decided there was no rush.

"Maybe I'll come to the show, too," Max said.

Lysander said repressively, "Don't you think an early night might be wise, for a change?"

I made an involuntary sound of longing. "An early night does sound good."

But I supposed I couldn't just go home and go to bed, much as I'd have liked to. Barclay probably needed some moral support, and Delilah certainly needed a distraction. They were having a very difficult week, too, after all. Barclay almost had to cancel his longed-for debut at the Magic Cabaret, and Samson and Delilah's brand-new act had resulted in disaster.

I frowned.

Garry Goudini's comeback was in dire straits...

Something clicked in my head, like the numbers on the lock of a bicycle chain tumbling into place and giving that faint snap as the chain sags and slips away. Something had fallen into place, but I didn't know what. I was so tired, and so confused by now.

"So are you going to go, Esther?" Satsy asked me.

"Hmm?"

"Esther?"

"Shh, she's got that look on her face," Khyber said.

Barclay had been upset, like Goudini, about losing the disappearing act from his routine. It was his best illusion, his big achievement. Goudini's, too. Barclay and his big break, Goudini and his comeback... Joe Herlihy, hoping to propel *Sorcerer!* to Broadway...

Was ambition what united the magicians? Was *that* the common factor?

But Duke was an amateur who had denied any expectation of turning pro. Still, the night we met, Dixie said he'd been working on the act, trying to improve it....

Goudini and his comeback. Joe with his ambitions. Barclay and Cowboy Duke, amateurs striving for improvement. Delilah and Samson had a brand-new act, one they'd been rehearsing...

"Striving for improvement..." I murmured. I looked at the display board. Or was I reaching? Wasn't *I* always striving for improvement, too? Wasn't every performer?

"Esther?"

I felt like I couldn't see the forest for the trees.

How had five magic acts, all of them striving for improvement, become the fertile ground where something Evil had taken root?

"Five disappearances," I muttered. "What *is* it that we're missing?"

"I'm wondering the same thing." Max tugged at his beard in obvious frustration.

"Five disappearances in one week!" I slammed a book down on the table, making the others jump. "How can we not see the clues, the key, the answer? How many more people have to vanish before we can figure out why this is happening?"

"And how?" Lysander added.

Khyber said, "Dr. Zadok, do you think we should rule out translocation or teleportation as possibilities?"

"Why?" Max asked absently, still tugging his beard.

"Well, those are phenomena in which someone who vanishes reappears somewhere else, usually instantaneously." Khyber looked worried. "And I think we'd have heard from Samson or the others by now if they'd reappeared elsewhere."

Max shook his head. "No, we can't rule it out. There are too many reasons they might be unable to contact us. They might be in another dimension, or in another time period—"

"Or being held prisoner somewhere?" I guessed.

"Four women, a man and a tiger?" Khyber frowned. "Why would anyone hold them prisoner?"

Satsy said, "I don't want anyone to mention this to Delilah, but…" He pushed his bulk well away from the table, reached under it, and sat back up a moment later, holding the books that had been sitting at his feet. He set them on the table. "I've been reading some of the books on ritual sacrifice. You know, from this week's sale section?"

While Satsy gestured to that part of the store, I saw Max and Lysander exchange glances.

"And?" Khyber said.

"And, well, it looks to me like there are all sorts of reasons someone might summon that many people— including the tiger—for…for ritual sacrifice."

Lysander lowered his eyes. Max froze, didn't even blink.

"Oh. My. *God.*" I realized what that brief look between them had meant. "You knew all along that might be why this was happening!"

"Now, Esther," Max said anxiously, "it's just one possible theory."

"Among many possible theories," Lysander added.

Max said, "We can't be sure—"

"They're being *sacrificed?*" Horrified, I rose to my feet. Khyber gasped.

"Not necessarily," Lysander said.

Satsy's face crumpled. "Oh, no! I didn't want to be right!"

"You may not be," Max said, "and we ought to remain optimistic."

"We also ought to remain calm," Lysander added, eyeing me warily.

"Calm?" I repeated shrilly. "*Calm?* Are you nuts? If ever there was time to get hot under the collar, this is it!"

"No, Lysander's right," Max said. "We don't want to jump to conclusions."

"*Why* are they being sacrificed?" I asked.

"Oh, no!" Satsy said again.

Lysander shook his head. "Speculating about that won't help. There are too many possibilities."

"Such as?" I prodded.

Apparently forgetting I wasn't supposed to learn the secrets of the Collegium, Lysander replied, "Well, for example, sacrifices can be used to summon a demon, summon Satan, placate a demon or devil—"

"My *God*," Khyber said.

"—placate a god," Lysander said, nodding at Khyber as if he'd suggested this, "request help from any number of forces, imbue some spells with special potency, increase an individual's power, protect some locations or ward certain areas, open the gateway to prophecy or divination, grant specific powers such as flight or the ability to translocate—"

"It can't be that last one," I said, realizing that Lysander might go on forever now that I'd encouraged him to lecture me. "Whatever we're dealing with, it can make the victims translocate, so surely it has that ability itself?"

"That's if they *are* translocating," Lysander said. "It's possible that the disappearances are caused by dissolution, and that it might be occurring in a form that causes instantaneous death."

"*Samson,*" Satsy said broken-heartedly. "And poor Duke—how will he face Dolly's death?"

"But if they're being translocated," I said quickly, as if translocation for the purpose of being sacrificed was a good alternative to instantaneous death, "doesn't that narrow down the possibilities? I mean, what ritual would call for the sacrifice of five people?"

"And a tiger," Khyber added.

"That's what I can't understand," Lysander said. "For any ritual involving multiple human sacrifices, the individuals being sacrificed should be far more homogenous than our disappearees are."

Satsy gasped and his expression brightened with hope. "That makes sense!"

"It does?" I said.

"Yes, it fits with what I've been reading," Satsy said. "For example, if you wanted to make a bargain with the gods for victory in war, you'd sacrifice, say, thirty nubile young women."

"That's horrible," I said.

"Precisely," Lysander said to Satsy with approval, ignoring me. "And if you wanted to summon an army of demons to destroy a nation, you'd sacrifice four hundred white mares."

"You would?" I said.

"If you wanted to destroy just one enemy, you'd only sacrifice seventeen brown hares." Max frowned and added, "Or, in some places, twenty-one green parrots."

"And if you wanted to control the outcome of the World Series, you'd need to sacrifice more virgins than anyone is likely to find in New York City these days," Lysander said primly.

"Those damn Yankees," said Khyber, a dawning suspicion creeping across his face.

I realized our problem. "But our disappearees are three young women, a middle-aged woman, a man and a tiger."

Lysander nodded. "They do not seem to have any requisite qualities in common."

"They have one," I pointed out. "They were all performing disappearing acts."

"And I assure you," he replied, "there is no ritual for which *that* defines the requisite quality of a sacrifice."

"Then we're missing something," I said, "or on the wrong track."

"Yes," Max said. "What is it we're missing?"

I asked, "Was there any relevant way in which the magicians' acts were similar, Max? Any way at all?"

"None that I can ascertain. I've thought about this until my brain is a seething mass of confused despair—"

"I can believe that," I said.

"—but I cannot find a link, a common factor, in the disappearing acts. The magicians all used different incantations, different gestures, different props. And I can find nothing unusual or similar about any of their props—except perhaps that some of them are not in the best possible taste."

"I looked through the *Village Voice* on the subway ride here this afternoon," I said. "Other magic acts besides these have performed in the city this week. At least a few of them must have done disappearing acts. So why are *these* the only acts in which someone really vanished? What is it about them that's different from those others—and similar to one another?"

"What is it that we don't know?" Max mumbled. "What can't I see?"

"What's the 'it' factor?" Satsy said.

Lysander frowned. "Hmm."

292   *Laura Resnick*

We all fell into silent cogitation, pondering the problem. When the door chimes rang a few minutes later, I nearly jumped out of my skin. I gestured for Max to remain seated, and I went round the bookcase to see who the newcomer was.

Garry Goudini, wearing makeup and a tight, glittery costume (open halfway down his chest) stood just inside the door of the shop. "Where's Max?" he cried. "We have *got* to get Alice back!"

CHAPTER

13

Goudini's act had bombed that afternoon, even worse than it had the night before. His concentration had been shot by last night's events, and his act today fell far short of its well-publicized promises. Without his tiger and without his biggest set piece, the vanishing illusion, he was finished—*finished!* He had just cancelled the rest of his performances in New York, and now he was here in the shop to help with our research—thereby proving he really was willing to do anything to get Alice back.

Recognizing that our spirits had sunk to a new low, that Goudini was on the verge of hysterics, and that we needed emergency mojo to get us through the evening, I went out to a Korean deli on Bleecker Street and bought eight pints of Ben & Jerry's. Desperate times call for sensible measures.

Now, back at the bookstore, I let the spiritual nourishment of Vanilla Heath Bar Crunch soothe my troubled soul as we examined and discarded more theories.

"Should we go back to the idea that the evil perpetrator might be doing this to get attention or cause public panic?" Satsy asked me while filling his bowl with ice cream. "Now that this has happened to someone kind of famous?"

"*Kind* of famous?" Goudini repeated.

I shook my head. "No, I still think if that was the goal, then someone really famous would have been targeted."

"I *am* really famous!" Goudini insisted.

"You're keeping the disappearance a secret, right?" I asked him.

"Of course I am! My God, Ellen, don't you realize what it would *do* to me if word of this got out?"

"My name's Esther," I corrected.

Satsy said to me, "Yeah, you're right. If attention or panic was the goal, then why not pick on someone everyone's heard of?"

"Everyone *has* heard of me!"

"I never had," Khyber said, spooning ice cream into his bowl. "But I do like tigers. I like all cats, actually."

"I thought you seemed like a cat person," I said.

"I have two." Khyber pulled out his wallet to show me their photos. "I'd just die if they disappeared. But then, I'd never do anything so cruel as put them in a levitating, smoke-filled cage and then make it fall."

Luckily, Darling Delilah and Whoopsy Daisy arrived just then, forestalling Goudini's angry retort.

"Library closed at six. Our report can wait, we didn't find much today." Whoopsy plopped a large bag on the table and started unpacking it. "We brought sandwiches, chips and soda. Oh, and salads."

Delilah accepted one of the salads from Whoopsy and said to me, "Honey, I didn't know if you'd want a salad, too, or a sandwich like these men, so I got you both."

"Thanks, Delilah. But I'm having ice cream for dinner tonight." I glanced at the clock. "We should call Barclay as soon as we're done eating. To tell him we're coming to the show and ask him where it is."

Satsy said, "Delilah, we've decided you're going to Barclay's performance with Esther tonight."

"But—"

I said, "No buts."

"I don't believe we've been introduced," Goudini said, preening as he eyed Delilah with an expression that showed no lingering trace of grief over his tiger. (Or—oh, yeah—Sarah Campbell.)

I made brief introductions. Then Max offered ice cream to Delilah and Whoopsy.

"No, thank you, Dr. Zadok," said Delilah. "I've got to watch my figure."

"I think you have a lovely figure," Goudini said.

Ignoring him, Delilah picked up a napkin and gently wiped some ice cream off Max's beard.

"Oh, thank you!" Max blushed a little.

"Is that Chunky Monkey?" Delilah asked wistfully.

"It's not good for a woman to go too long without ice cream," I said. "It's a question of hormonal health, you know."

Delilah's beautiful face was marred by a little frown. "Really?"

"Trust me." I shoved the Chunky Monkey at her.

"Well, maybe just a little…" she said.

"Are you in show business?" Goudini asked Delilah. "It so happens, I may have an opening in my act for a woman just like you."

I said, "I thought you'd cancelled performances until further notice, Garry."

"One must shake off disappointment and look to the future, Ellen." He shot me a look before saying to Delilah, "Maybe we can talk about it later this evening?"

Delilah shook her head. "Thanks, but I have my own act. I'm just waiting for my partner to return."

"Oh? Well, depending on her qualifications, I might be able to find a place in the act for her, too. After all, I did lose *two* beautiful assistants last night, in a manner of speaking. What's she like?"

"He's six foot two and hung like a horse." Delilah spooned ice cream into her bowl without looking at Goudini. "I'm the drag queen who made Sexy Samson vanish. Any more questions, Garry?"

I enjoyed Goudini's awkward silence. Max's eyes widened, but he didn't look as shocked as I'd feared.

Either he'd realized Delilah wasn't quite what she seemed, or else three and a half centuries of living had taught him to respond to surprises with equanimity.

"Hey, is that Chubby Hubby?" Whoopsy reached for a bowl and a spoon. "Pass the carton!"

Lysander handed it to him, remarking, "It's my favorite."

"Chubby Hubby?" Delilah smiled. "But you're so slim, honey, and you've never been married."

I asked her, "How do you know that?"

"I can always tell the married ones." She gave Goudini a cool, pointed glance.

I said, "You couldn't ever find a woman to put up with you, Lysander?"

"On the contrary," he said. "There was once a young lady of good family and excellent education who pledged her heart to me."

"Oh, I love a love story!" Satsy said. "Did her parents disapprove of you?"

Lysander frowned. "Of course not! I am of excellent family and superior education."

"Of course," I said.

Licking chocolate ice cream off his spoon, Khyber asked, "So why didn't you marry the girl?"

"I felt I could better pursue my vocation through a life of celibacy," Lysander said.

Whoopsy choked on his ice cream. *"Celibacy?"*

"Why?" I asked curiously. "I gather Hieronymus's mother was a member of the Collegium."

"Who's Hieronymus?" Goudini asked.

I continued, "And Max was once married—"

"Twice, actually," Max said.

"—so obviously members of the Collegium do lead married lives. Why did you think you shouldn't?"

"What's the Collegium?" Goudini asked.

Lysander gave a smug little sigh. "I suppose I have always been more devoted to my duty than others. Some might say *too* devoted."

"Or not," I said.

"Preparation for so many of the rituals and feats involved in my vocation involves abstaining from relations, and often for such a prolonged period, that I realized it would be unfair to my dear Radha to marry her."

"I've often wished *I* could abstain from my relatives," Whoopsy said.

"Not relatives," Satsy said. "Relations."

Khyber added, "Sexual relations."

"My God, man!" Goudini said.

Whoopsy looked stunned. "No sex?"

Lysander said sternly, "Eat your ice cream, young man."

Whoopsy sought reassurance from Max. "But *you* still take the wheels out for a spin every so often, don't you, Dr. Zadok?"

"Um, er, no," Max said. "If, that is, you're asking what I think you're asking. I decided to give up the pleasures of a conjugal life after the death of my second wife. In devotion to my duty." After a pause, he added, "Also in consideration of my nerves."

"Oh, you're a widower?" Delilah said sympathetically. "I'm so sorry."

He patted her hand. "Thank you, my dear. But it was a long time ago."

"So neither of you has sex?" Whoopsy asked, clearly horrified. "*Ever?*"

"Spiritual and physical purity are essential companions on the path to true power," Lysander said.

"My *God*," Whoopsy said.

Goudini said, "I never want to get *that* obsessed with my work."

Ignoring Goudini, Delilah reminded Whoopsy, "We should be tolerant of every lifestyle that does not harm anyone else."

"I'm not intolerant," Whoopsy said. "I'm flooded with pity."

I finished my ice cream and picked up my cell phone while the rest of them continued talking. I autodialed Barclay's number. When I didn't get anything but silence, I tried again. Then a third time.

Seeing me frowning at my phone, Satsy asked me what was wrong.

"I'm not sure."

I tried Dixie's number and had the same problem. All I got was silence. I pulled my phone away from my ear and checked the signal and the battery power. It seemed to be in good working order. I was about to ask Satsy to try calling Barclay from his phone when Max startled me with a gasp.

"We forgot Hieronymus!"

"Huh?"

"He must be very hungry by now," Max said.

"Oh. Hieronymus." I shrugged. "I suppose someone should fetch him from the cellar before he starves."

"Girlfriend, that boy eats enough leftovers to feed a fraternity," said Satsy. "He won't starve."

"Ah, so that's where all the Thai and Chinese food went," I said.

"When I got here today, he was cleaning out the fridge," said Satsy.

"Youngsters do eat a lot," Max said cheerfully.

"He's awfully shy, isn't he?" Satsy said. "Took the whole armload downstairs to be by himself. Scarcely said a word to me."

I looked at Lysander. "I believe I mentioned a personality problem?"

He scowled. "I spoke with the lad earlier today. He was courteous to *me*, young lady. Perhaps because *I* was courteous to *him*."

"Or maybe he just knows where his bread gets buttered," I said. "You being such a big cheese in the Collegium, and all."

Max quickly said, "Esther, would you please go invite Hieronymus to join us? We should share this lovely ice cream with every member of the team."

"Team," Lysander repeated, scowling at Max now.

"Of course, Max." Picking an argument with Lysander might vent some of my tension, but it wouldn't bring us any closer to solving our problems. So I went downstairs in search of Max's assistant. However, I came back upstairs without him. "He's not there anymore."

"Not there?" Max repeated.

"No. And why is the lab full of feathers, Max?"

"Oh, dear. I suppose I should do some cleaning."

"Feathers?" Lysander said. "Still?"

"Well?" I said to Max.

"I've assigned Hieronymus the task of summoning a familiar," he said. "It hasn't been going well. His unfortunate disadvantage has been something of an obstacle. Plus, of course, familiars are notoriously recalcitrant."

"Dr. Zadok, I don't mean to be alarmist," Satsy said, "but is it possible that Hieronymus has…disappeared?"

"I haven't sensed another disappearance," Max said, shaking his head.

"Hieronymus hasn't vanished," I said firmly. "He wasn't onstage and he wasn't performing a disappearing act."

"Then where is he?" Satsy wondered.

"Is there another way out of the building besides the front door of the shop?" I asked Max.

"Yes. Particularly for someone with Hieronymus's skills."

I shrugged. "So I guess he went out. Without telling anyone or explaining himself. *Again.*"

"He is not required to explain his actions to mundanes," Lysander said tersely.

Venting some of my tension on Lysander might be very productive, after all, I decided. "Apparently he's not required to pull his weight around here, either! We've spent days interviewing victims, examining props, doing research, trying to find leads, breaking and entering! And what has *he* done?"

Goudini said, "Does anyone mind if I smoke?"

Our chorus of objections sent him outside with his nicotine.

Then Lysander turned angrily to me. "I'll have you know that earlier today, Hieronymus gave me a very thorough account of his research so far! And I can assure you it's been a good deal more productive than invading Magic Magnus's stronghold in the middle of the night!"

"Well, that's news!" I snapped. "Since Hieronymus can't be bothered to do it, why don't *you* tell us what his research has produced so far?"

By the time Goudini returned from his cigarette break, I was bitterly regretting the impulse that had led me to invite Lysander, a second time in one day, to lecture to me.

"These particles of energy," Lysander was now saying, "produce opposing forces, namely the weak force and the strong force, rather than being actual properties in and of themselves."

"Wait, how can particles *not* be properties in and of themselves?" Khyber asked.

I said to Khyber, "I *beg* you not to encourage him."

"Because they are only particles in *some* manifestations," Lysander told his attentive audience. "In others, they are waves, whose internal substructure is unstable due to the tension among gravity, electromagnetism and the vacua, or 'holes,' both shifting and semi-shifting, which I have already mentioned."

"My head hurts," I muttered.

"The question of translating matter into such particles and waves, that the matter may thus traverse these vacua, possibly into another dimension—"

"Please skip the technical details and just tell us: How does this get us any closer to figuring out how the disappearances are being orchestrated?" I said. "Or why? Or by whom or what?"

"As I've been explaining," Lysander said impatiently, "Hieronymus has been concentrating on the *how*."

"But these processes that you're postulating—that Hieronymus postulates—who would have such knowledge? And the ability to use it?" I asked. "A sorcerer? A mage? An alchemist?"

"Yes."

"Who else?"

"No one, I pray," said Lysander.

"So what happened to Hieronymus's theory that a mundane was responsible for the disappearances?"

Lysander shook his head. "I think he was mistaken

about that. Apparently he thinks so, too, since he didn't discuss it with me. Now, as I was saying, the nature of these shifting and semi-shifting holes may be—"

"Yes, that's very interesting," I said, "but how does the perpetrator arrange the cosmos so that an ordinary magician doing an ordinary disappearing act—"

"There is nothing ordinary about my act!" Goudini said.

"—becomes imbued with enough mystical power to make a person—or tiger—vanish? And how does the perpetrator get the magician to do this without conscious intent? Without even the suspicion that he holds such power?"

"If you'll stop *interrupting*…" Lysander said.

"Wait." Max looked dumbstruck. "What did you say, Esther?"

"Huh?"

"'Without conscious intent'?"

"Oh. Yeah. Without conscious intent, and without suspicion—"

"—that he holds the power," Max concluded. "Could *that* be it?"

"Max, if I may be allowed to continue," Lysander said impatiently, "I would just like to point out—"

"Wait a moment! I think Esther may be on to something." Max gazed thoughtfully at me. "That has been one of the most perplexing aspects of these disappearances."

"*What* has?"

"Well, I don't think such a disappearance *can* be managed without conscious intent," said Max.

Delilah said, "But I definitely didn't intend to make Samson vanish for real. I know that much."

"Exactly," Max said slowly. "So therefore… Yes, therefore it seems possible—no, I'd say it seems likely, in fact—that *you* did not hold the power!"

"I didn't?"

"No! You were a conduit for the entity that held the power!"

"Of course! A *conduit*," Lysander cried. "Why didn't I think of that?"

"I can't tell you, Lysander," I said. "Because I have no idea what you two are talking about."

"Conduit?" Delilah said. "Whoa! Whoa, wait a minute. Are you saying that someone—or something—was doing its nasty work through me? Are you saying I was possessed when I made Samson disappear?"

"In a sense," Max said.

"No, not at all," Lysander said. "Conduitism is completely different from possession."

"There are similarities," Max argued.

"According to the writings of Zosimus—"

"Who did not have access to the works of the great Chinese scholars on the subject—"

"Their conclusions are highly questionable, Max!"

"Cornelius Agrippa thought they had merit."

"Only if you completely misinterpret his writings on the Great Chain of Being!" Lysander said.

I felt like firing a gun in the air. "Stop! Guys! Guys, *stop*." When I had their attention, I said, "The rest of us would like to know what a conduit is."

"I'll field this one," Lysander said to Max. Then he explained conduitism to us. When he was done, we stared at him in silence for about fifteen seconds.

Then Khyber said, "Maybe we'd understand better if Dr. Zadok explained it."

Lysander frowned and sat down, muttering something bitter about mundanes.

"Well…" Max tugged at his beard. "Let's try this. Esther, would you go turn on the fire?"

Wondering why he'd requested it, I crossed the shop to the fireplace, picked up the remote and turned on the gas fire.

Max said to his audience, "Having seen that, who among you believes that Esther has the power to create fire at will?" No one did, of course. "Does anyone here believe that the remote in her hand is invested with independent power? That it could just as easily set this table alight, or start a fire in a garbage can?" When they all shook their heads, Max said, "But we have been seeing a remarkably similar set of events lately. And we have been making presumptions precisely like the ones we instantly realize are ridiculous when we try to apply them to Esther and the remote-control device she's holding."

"In other words," Khyber said, "the power originates somewhere other than the magicians or their props?"

"Exactly! I have turned my brain into porridge trying to figure out how the magicians were exercising such power without realizing it, or how someone was exercising such power through their props without the magicians' knowledge." He shook his head, making little *tsk-tsk* sounds. "Wasted time!"

"In all fairness, Max, you shouldn't blame yourself," Lysander said, exhibiting an unexpected side of his personality. "After all, conduitism is rare, arcane, obscure and so unpredictable that few adepts dabble in it."

"True."

"And that is, of course, why *I* didn't think of it," Lysander added, sounding more like his usual self. "A perfectly understandable oversight."

"In other words, there were other first-glance possibilities in the way," Whoopsy said.

"Yes." Max nodded. "After all, the first time Esther ever saw a fire in that fireplace, she mistakenly thought *I* was the source of the power that created those flames."

"Because I didn't know it was a gas fireplace," I said, thinking it over, "and I didn't see the remote in your hand."

"Right. Er, check. Now," Max said, "what if you picked up the remote and pressed the power button thinking it would turn on a TV set?"

"Then I'd be pretty startled when I started a fire, instead."

"Of course. Because you would have created fire without conscious intent. And if you had no prior knowledge of remote-control devices or of gas fires, you'd probably be frightened by the event—and perhaps even mystified by your sudden, strange power."

"But the power isn't hers," Whoopsy said, catching on, "and it doesn't come from her. It's invested in the remote."

"Correct! Yet the power doesn't *originate* in the remote," Max said.

"It originates with the manufacturer," Whoopsy said.

"Specifically, with the programmer," Khyber said. "The person who figured out how to get the remote to create fire when the right button is pressed."

"When it's pressed by *anyone*," I said.

"Anyone who happens to be holding the remote," Max agreed. "Whether such a person intends it or not, wants it or not, knows what's about to happen or not, he inevitably creates fire—as long as he is within range of the fireplace and presses the right button on the remote." Max beamed at us. "*That's* conduitism."

"Okay, now I get it," I said with relief. "But what's acting as the conduit in the disappearances?"

"Hmm." Max frowned. "This leads us right back to the same problem. We're still looking for a common factor among the magicians, the acts or the disappear-ees."

"There is a common factor," I insisted. "The dis-appearances all occurred while the victims and the magicians were onstage and in performance."

"Why then and there?" Max asked.

"Energy," Goudini said.

We all looked at him.

Seeing us suddenly pay serious attention to something he'd said, he looked a little startled. Then he shrugged. "Well, surely it's obvious? You can rehearse something a hundred times, imagine how the audience will respond, even practice the bows you'll take and the encores you'll give. But there is absolutely nothing like performing for real in front of a live audience. *Nothing.* No amount of rehearsal can simulate it or prepare you for what that'll be like."

"Of course," I said, too stunned at my own obtuse-ness to wallow in my astonishment that Goudini had contributed something useful to the discussion. It was yet another thing so obvious to me that I hadn't even seen it! "Getting in front of the audience brings everything—particularly the performer's energy—to a whole different level."

"It's why some people freeze up every single time they have to give a speech or accept a prize," Delilah said, nodding. "And why other people fall in love with performing by the time they're eight years old and know they've got to spend the rest of their lives working in front of an audience!"

"But what was different about *that* night?" I asked Delilah. "The night Samson disappeared? You'd been working together in front of audiences for a long time together."

"It was a new act," she said promptly. "We were so excited about it."

"Mine was a new act, too," Goudini said. "And last night was my first time before an audience in more than two years."

"And Duke and Dolly were incredibly excited about performing in New York the night she disappeared!" said Satsy.

"That's it!" cried Whoopsy. "We've found the common factor!"

"Not quite," I said. "We're still missing something."

"What do you mean?"

"Barclay and Clarisse weren't particularly excited about performing for a bunch of society children at a birthday party."

"But they *were* excited," Satsy said, "about the upcoming gig at the Magic Cabaret. Very excited."

"We *have* found the common factor!" Whoopsy said.

"No, not yet," I said.

"You're becoming a real wet blanket, Esther," he said.

"Why did Clarisse disappear at the birthday party?" I asked. "Why didn't she wait to disappear at the Magic Cabaret if that's the performance she was so excited about?"

"You're splitting hairs," Whoopsy complained.

"All right, how about this?" I replied. "Golly didn't disappear on our first night, she disappeared at the *end* of our first week of performances. And no one in the show was unusually excited that night. If anything, we were finding our stride, getting into a sustainable routine that night. Or so we thought, until Golly vanished. She claimed Joe Herlihy nearly set her on fire in Act One, but I don't think that was true, I think that was just Golly being a prima donna. Joe was getting through the show better that night than he had at any previous performance."

"Concentration," Goudini said suddenly.

"What?"

"That's the other thing performing for a live audience does for me," he said. "It totally focuses my concentration. I'm razor sharp, and nothing can distract me. Well...nothing apart from realizing how my show was flopping today without Alice and wondering how I'd made her vanish," he added wearily. "I was off today. So, so *off*. It's lucky I didn't decapitate one of the girls for real or accidentally immolate myself."

"Concentration. Yes!" I nodded. "That *is* what was different about Joe that night. He had it that night. For the first time since the show opened. I remember noticing it, and being relieved. It made me think we'd get through the whole performance smoothly for once."

"I had it the night Samson disappeared. I was totally in the zone!" Delilah's voice caught as she said, "The new act was going so well right up until he vanished."

"I had it, too, last night," Goudini said. "I was so on my game. So focused."

His face twisted and I could see he was mourning the loss of his tiger again.

"So…" Satsy thought it over for a few moments. "Our perpetrator looks for magic acts where the performers have good concentration or are developing it, and picks them as his targets?"

I shook my head. "I don't think anyone choosing his targets that way would pick Joe Herlihy. I'd say concentration is generally a weak spot for him."

"Pretty dangerous for a magician," Goudini commented.

"Pretty dangerous for those of us working with him," I said.

"So how did he manage to concentrate that night?" Goudini asked. "The night the girl disappeared?"

I shrugged. "I don't know. I gather he'd been working on the act, on his skills…."

Working on the act. Striving for improvement.

Something clicked again. What was it? Joe, Duke, Barclay…all trying to raise their standards and…

"Improve the act," I muttered.

"What?"

What had Matilda told me the day I'd fled the stage in panic during rehearsal and knelt heaving over a toilet while she screamed at me?

"Esther?"

She'd said...she'd said that Joe had studied new techniques, worked with a coach, developed new standards, refined his abilities.

"Developing...studying...striving for improvement..." I mumbled. Barclay, Duke, Joe...

"What did you say?"

"Esther's got that look again."

"Concentration," I said to Delilah and Goudini. "Pretty essential to a magician, would you say?"

"Definitely," Delilah said.

"Indispensable," Goudini said.

"Joe didn't have it. Not really. Not until that night."

"So he's learning," said Delilah.

"Yes." I nodded. "He's improving his concentration."

"Which is a good thing for any girls he saws in half," Goudini said dryly.

"How would you do that?" I asked him.

"Saw a girl in half? I can't give away trade secrets."

"No, how would you improve your concentration? Or, I guess, your act?"

"Well, *we* hired a coach," said Delilah.

The tumblers clicked into place and the chain fell away.

"You did *what?*" I snapped.

She blinked at my tone. "We hired a coach. I think Samson and I sensed we had hit a plateau, but we didn't really see it, hadn't defined it. Not until this guy came backstage one night after seeing our show and…" Her eyes opened wide. "Oh. My. *God.*"

"Joe hired a coach, too," I said. "His wife told me."

"God's teeth!" cried Max. "That's how the conduit was created! Someone gained intimate access to your practice of your art!"

"To your practice of a disappearing act!" Lysander added.

We all looked at Goudini.

"What?" he said.

"Did you hire a coach?" I said impatiently.

"*Me?*" He snorted. "No, of course not."

"So he wasn't the one?" Delilah asked Max. "Our coach, I mean?"

"I don't know," Max replied. "Tell us what happened."

"He came backstage and said…" Delilah started breathing faster. "He said we had talent, had spark, but we needed focus. Refinement. Said he could help us in just a few sessions. Offered the first session for free. We only had to pay him for it if we decided to hire him for the whole course."

"And then?"

She swallowed. "We felt like we learned something in the first session, and there were only three more to go, so we wrote the check. It wasn't expensive, it didn't take much time... Come to think of it, I haven't really thought about it since then, even though it inspired us to work up a whole new act."

"A blind?" Lysander suggested to Max.

"It sounds like it."

"What's a blind?" I asked.

"The perpetrator... This, uh, coach. He probably made sure Delilah *wouldn't* think about it much once the sessions were over. Made sure that he would seldom come to mind."

"How?"

"Any number of ways," Lysander said. "The easiest would be to use mystical influence in tandem with a hypnotic or hypnagogic suggestion."

Max asked Delilah, "Was there anything in the sessions that resembled, oh, a relaxation technique or—"

"Yes! That was quite a lot of what we did, in fact. He said it would help improve our focus."

"When did all this happen?" I asked.

"About two months ago. We started developing the new show after that—a show that included a disappearing act. In fact, we'd specifically wanted to improve enough to add it to our act. We'd practiced it before, but it had always been clumsy and unpredictable until we hired that coach."

"Garry?" Whoopsy said. "Are you all right? You look a little..."

I glanced at Goudini. He was staring at Delilah with an expression of such horror that I realized the truth. "You were lying! You *have* seen a coach!"

"Um…"

"*This* coach!"

He let out his breath in a rush. "Yeah. Okay, yeah. I have. I didn't intend to…" He shrugged. "It's a little embarrassing. Someone like me. Famous."

"Famous?" Khyber repeated doubtfully.

"Accomplished. Experienced. I didn't want anyone to…" He shook his head. "Look, I said *no* to him at first. I thought he was some nutty fan or fruity wannabe. But something about him was convincing. He had insights, he had confidence."

"But he wasn't brash," Delilah said. "His manner was kind of intellectual and humble."

"Nerdy," Goudini said.

"When did he approach you?" Max asked Goudini.

"About three months ago. Made me the same offer that he made to, er, Samson and Delilah. Just four sessions, reasonably priced—and the first one was free if I decided I didn't want to finish the course."

"How did he approach you?" I asked.

"I first bumped into him at my supplier's shop. A guy called Magic Magnus who—"

"Magnus?" I blurted.

"Zounds!" Max cried.

"You guys know Magnus?" Goudini asked.

"Is this coach a friend of his? A colleague? A confederate?"

Goudini blinked. "No. Magnus didn't like him, wouldn't let him post flyers in the shop, told him not to pester customers. Insisted he leave when he pestered *me*."

"I'll bet you that's how this guy met Joe," I said. "And Barclay. They're both customers of Magnus's, too. I'll bet *anything* that this guy was Joe's coach. And Barclay's committed to improving his act, has been working hard on it and could certainly afford a coach." It all fit. When we got hold of Barclay, he would undoubtedly confirm that he, too, had hired this guy within the past few months.

"But what about Duke?" Satsy asked. "He doesn't know Magnus."

"Duke's a wealthy magic aficionado who devotes time and money to his hobby and has many contacts among amateur magicians," I said. "He's been in New York for a couple of months, and he's flamboyant, someone that people notice—someone that other magicians probably talk about." We'd ask Duke, too, later tonight; but I knew in my bones that he'd confirm our theory.

"Yes," Lysander said. "He would have been an easy quarry for our villain to spot."

"And the sessions?" Max asked Goudini. "They were similar to what Delilah has described?"

"Yes. Also...well, like her, I didn't think about

them much once they were over, even though I felt my work improved as a result of them." He shuddered. "So that guy has been crawling around in my head? Using me as his conduit?"

"But how?" I murmured.

After questioning Goudini and Delilah for a while, Max determined that the conduit had been created by coaching them in the use of psychological "tools" to be employed before rehearsing or performing the act: mental phrases they used to clear their heads and mental exercises they did to focus their concentration.

"I have *always* been suspicious of this kind of New Age 'empowerment' shit," Whoopsy said.

"Oh, but it really worked, Whoopsy!" Delilah protested.

"Sweetie, it really worked," he pointed out, "because some demonic perpetrator of Evil was hexing you with supersonic mystical mojo."

"And then," Khyber added, "he used that opening to make Samson disappear."

"Which brings us back to the question of *why?*" I said.

"Ah. Yes." Lysander frowned. "Unfortunately, knowing *how* has not actually brought us any closer to knowing *why*."

"It's puzzling," Max admitted.

"Maybe if we knew who?" I said. "I mean, who is this guy?"

"He said his name was Philip Hohenheim," Delilah said.

Goudini snapped his fingers. "Yeah, that was the name!"

Max let out a wordless exclamation. Lysander said, "Of all the nerve!"

I asked them, "You know him?"

Lysander's expression suggested I was so ignorant that it pained him to speak to me. Max said, "Philippus Aureolus Theophrastus Bombast von Hohenheim is the real name of Paracelsus."

"Who's Paracelsus?" I asked. "And just how dangerous is he?"

"My God," Lysander said, "the condition of education in this country is appalling!"

"Paracelsus was perhaps the greatest alchemist of the sixteenth century," Max said.

"Ah. *Was.* Five centuries ago. So he's not our perpetrator," I guessed. "I gather our guy is enjoying a little joke by using that name?"

"And insulting the memory of a great mage," Lysander said with a scowl.

"Either way," I said to Delilah and Goudini, "we can assume Phil isn't his real name. But let's call him that for the sake of convenience."

Whoopsy frowned. "We're calling the villain Phil?"

"Yes."

"*Phil?*"

"I'm afraid so."

"It seems somehow anticlimactic."

"Maybe Magnus will have some clues about who he is," I mused, "if the guy was making a nuisance of himself at the shop."

"Yes, we should consult with Magnus," Max agreed.

"I'm sure he'll be delighted to hear from us again," Lysander said.

"So, shoot, girlfriends," Satsy said to Delilah and Goudini. "What did Phil look like?"

"Ah! Description." Khyber nodded. "Good idea."

"White male," said Delilah.

"Mid-thirties," Goudini said.

"No," Delilah said, "younger than that."

"Average height," Goudini said.

"A little shorter than that," Delilah said.

"Average weight."

"No, kind of thin," Delilah said.

"Black hair and a moustache."

"Dishwater-blond hair and a beard," said Delilah.

Lysander said, "Well, *this* is certainly a useful exercise."

Khyber wondered, "Are we dealing with *two* Phils?"

"No," I said, realizing the truth. "Phil wore disguises."

"Oh!" Khyber frowned. "So he'll be hard to recognize, to identify, won't he?"

"Actually, what he *looked* like isn't what I remember most about him, anyhow," Goudini said.

"Me, either," Delilah said.

"Ah," Lysander said. "You remember his power, his presence?"

"Did he have an aura?" Max asked. "Or tattoos that looked like ancient script? Or a strange odor, perhaps?"

"A strange odor?" I repeated.

"Sulfur, for example."

"Oh."

"No, nothing like that," Goudini said. "But he did have…" His eyes met Delilah's.

She nodded. "Yes, it was definitely the most noticeable thing about him."

"What?" Max asked her.

"Well, it seems a little snide to mention it. Samson and I were very careful to avoid noticing it during the training sessions."

"*What?*" I prodded.

Delilah said, "He had just about the most pronounced speech impediment I've ever heard."

CHAPTER

14

Of all the times for Lopez to be out investigating a homicide, I thought irritably. "No. *Hohenheim*," I said into my cell phone.

"We should not be involving the mundane police!" Lysander insisted, trying to get the phone away from me.

I shoved at the mage while I said to the cop at the other end of the line, "H-O-H..." Lysander shoved me back and reached for my phone again. "...E-N..."

"Please, no violence!" Max cried as the two of us continued wrestling.

"She's trying to involve this...this *Lopez* and his police force in the sacred duty of the Collegium!"

Since I had just been put on hold, I said to Lysander, "We don't know where Hieronymus is! We don't know what he plans to do next! We have no idea where to look for the disappearees—or, God forbid, their corpses!" I wanted to bite my tongue when Delilah gave an anguished gasp and sank clumsily into a chair with a dreadful expression on her face.

"Tactful as always," Lysander snapped at me.

"No, no," Delilah said in an awful voice. "We have to face this Evil thing. You mustn't pussyfoot on my account." A tear slipped from the corner of her eye.

Goudini extended a hand toward Delilah, hesitated, pulled it back, frowned, and then gave in and reached out to pat her back gently. When she sniffed, he pulled a handkerchief out of the air and handed it to her. That made her smile a little.

"Thanks, Garry."

I said, "We need help, Lysander! Someone who can stop or detain or inconvenience Hieronymus, in case we can't! Otherwise we may never find the victims— or find out what happened to them!"

"The police are not equipped to deal with mystical matters!"

"But they *are* equipped to prevent someone from getting on an airplane or renting a car!" I shot back.

"Do you think that will stop a true adept from fleeing?"

"Yes, I'm still here," I said into the phone. "No, Hohenheim is his alias. His real name is Hieronymus…" I glanced at Max to get the surname.

"Don't tell her!" Lysander said.

"I don't know his last name," Max said.

"*Max,*" I said.

"No, I really don't! The last time I even remember hearing it was when I was informed by the Collegium of his imminent arrival." He tugged at his beard. "What *was* it? Blogenviek? Burblenamen? No…"

"Delilah." I directed her attention to Lysander. "*He* knows. Get the name from him." Into the phone, I said, "Yes, sir, it's coming. Let me give you a description while I'm waiting for the surname."

Despite the shock, horror and confusion that followed our discovery of "Phil's" identity, Satsy, Khyber and Whoopsy had left for the Pony Expressive to get ready for their first show of the night. I'd insisted on this. The entire cabaret would have to be cancelled if they all went AWOL; and there was nothing they could do about our problem at the moment, if they remained here.

"Young woman… Er, Delilah," Lysander was saying as the beautiful drag queen wept against his chest and pleaded with him to cooperate with the authorities and find the evil wizard who was killing and torturing innocent disappearees. "Now see here. We *cannot* involve the police. For the love of Empedocles, we don't even know if the poor boy is guilty! I can't—"

"Wake up and smell the elixir, Lysander!" I put my hand over the receiver for a moment. "How many white male adepts are currently in the Greater New York area who have a pronounced speech impediment and the kind of power needed to pull off these disappearances?"

"Anyone or anything with that kind of power could have mimicked Hieronymus's unfortunate disability with the intention of creating precisely this sort of confusion and erroneous blame, foreseeing the possibility that we might get this close to the perpetrator's trail!" Lysander insisted, looking increasingly uncomfortable as Delilah clung to him.

"If Phil was imitating Hieronymus to create suspicion," Delilah said, raising her lovely, tear-streaked face to gaze into his eyes, "why did he wear multiple disguises? Why did he cast a spell to ensure we seldom even thought of him after our training was over?"

I said into the phone, "Yes, his distinguishing feature is a very noticeable speech impediment. He lisps, and he can't pronounce the letter *R.*"

Delilah continued. "I've never even seen Hieronymus. He hides in the cellar and speaks to almost no one. Why does he do that, if he's innocent?"

"Because he's shy."

Once again on hold, I said to Lysander, "Don't you get it? It's not a personality problem, like I thought—well, no, actually, I guess Hieronymus has a much more severe personality problem than I ever suspected. But why does he always skulk in the cellar when we're here? So he won't encounter anyone who might recognize him, that's why! He's been avoiding Delilah, Barclay and Duke."

"And me," Goudini said.

"You only arrived late this afternoon," Lysander said dismissively.

"And no one has seen Phil since," Goudini pointed out.

"We don't know that he *is* Phil," Lysander insisted.

I said, "Once we all started hanging around here, Hieronymus could scurry in and out of the shop occasionally without too great a risk of discovery, but only as long as he kept his head down and was surly and sulky—didn't talk. After all, most of us have never seen 'Phil,' and those who *have* seen him have only seen him in disguise. But he couldn't afford to open his mouth around any of the magicians!"

Goudini said, "We'd have noticed *that* resemblance to Phil right away."

"And the fewer people who heard him speaking at all, the better," I said. "Remember Satsy saying that Hieronymus would scarcely say a word when they met unexpectedly today? If Hieronymus's speech impediment was known to everyone, he'd soon be exposed as Phil. Yes, Officer," I said into the phone, "I'm still here. No, Detective Lopez is working this case. Uh-huh, classified as Missing Persons. No, Hieronymus what's-his-name isn't a victim, he's the kidnapper." I rolled my eyes. "Couldn't I *please* just have Detective Lopez's cell-phone number? I'm positive he'd want you to give it to me."

"If that's true—" Lysander began.

"Oh, it is," Delilah said. "Lopez has a thing for Esther, we've all noticed it. He'd want her to call him direct."

"No, I mean if it's true that Hieronymus's speech impediment means he must be Phil, then why did it take this long to make the connection?" Lysander said. "Perhaps we're simply grasping at straws in our desperation. Perhaps Esther's leap-of-faith assumption is wrong, and Duke, Barclay and Mr. Herlihy did *not* train with Phil. Perhaps Barclay and Duke didn't even *have* a coach. Perhaps we're jumping to exactly the same sort of wild, unfounded conclusions that led us to break into Magic Magnus's shop for no good reason last night!"

Delilah plucked at his collar. "That's a lot of perhapses, honey." She snuggled closer and whispered into his ear, "Please. Just tell us his last name."

"We almost never talk about it," Max said suddenly.

Blushing as Delilah ran her fingers over his cheek, Lysander croaked, "About what?"

I put my hand over the phone as my gaze met Max's. "That's right," I said, realizing. "We try not to mention it."

"What?" Lysander asked faintly as Delilah licked her lips.

"The poor boy's unfortunate problem," Max said.

"Exactly!" I said. "You always refer to it in that oblique way, if you even refer to it at all. After Dixie met Hieronymus, she commented that she could understand why he was so shy; but she never said anything more specific than that. Even you," I said to Lysander, "when talking to me about how Hieronymus's problem prevented him from saying certain incantations, never *named* his problem."

Delilah murmured to Lysander, "I had no idea Hieronymus had a speech impediment until tonight—after I told you all about *Phil's* speech impediment. I'd heard Hieronymus was rude, shy and sullen—but not that he lisped or couldn't say *R*. No one ever mentioned that."

"Being rude and sullen were his choice, so I figured they were fair game for comment," I said. "But he couldn't help his speech impediment."

"We try to be tactful about it," Max said.

"To be sensitive," Delilah added, nodding. "The same way that Samson and I always pretended not to notice Phil's speech impediment when he was coaching us. In fact, we never even really talked to each other about it."

"You felt it would be unkind to talk about it," Max said.

"Exactly."

"Even *I* tried to pretend I didn't notice Phil's problem," Goudini said, sounding surprised at his own consideration.

Remembering my first impressions of Hieronymus, I said to them, "And he made sure we didn't want to talk about it. He made sure we knew he was *sooo* sensitive about it. Huh? No, Officer, not you," I said into the phone. "It doesn't? You don't? Well, how long does a murder take?" Seeing the expressions on my companions' faces as they all looked at me, I covered the receiver and said, "I'm asking when Lopez will be back."

"Maybe we should just ask for another cop to take over our case," Goudini suggested.

I shook my head. "I really can't see myself explaining this case to another cop." Even bringing Lopez up to date was going to take considerable force of will, since I knew his opinion of our theories.

"If Hieronymus is innocent," Delilah asked, "where is he now?"

"Out investigating a lead," Lysander said. "And if he's not innocent, we'll deal with him when he gets back."

Delilah said, "What makes you think he's ever coming back?" When Lysander responded with a flinch of surprise, she pressed her advantage. "People who can identify him as Phil are coming here daily now. And sooner or later, someone's bound to stop being so tactful about his speech impediment, and then he'd be exposed. Unless he's a fool, he knew his time was running out. Whatever he's up to, he must have known for days now that he couldn't continue operating from here for much longer."

"That's right," Max said, his eyes widening.

"And now," Delilah said, "he's simply, er, disappeared. Left without saying a word to anyone. So, honey, what in the world makes you so sure he's going to come back here so you can deal with him?"

"No, Officer," I said into my phone, "we're thinking about it, but right now, we haven't the faintest idea where he might be. Or where he'll go... Well...if you don't mind, I'd rather just explain that to Detective Lopez when I talk to him. Yes, the name is Hieronymus... Just a minute." I looked over at Lysander again. "Well?"

"Please," Delilah said. "Samson's mother is so worried about him. So am I."

"And I'm worried about Alice," Goudini said. "By now, it's more than twenty-four hours since her last meal, and she's accustomed to a very consistent schedule."

I hoped Sarah Campbell wouldn't start looking appetizing to Alice, if they were both still alive somewhere.

Lysander sighed and gave in. "Blankenberg."

"Hieronymus Blankenberg!" I said into the phone. Then I got Lysander to spell it for me.

"So you're saying Hieronymus would have to keep track of when the performances were occurring," I said to Max and Lysander, "in order to work his mojo and cause the disappearances—but he wouldn't need to be physically present at the performances?"

"Not once he'd established the conduit, no," Max replied. "The coaching sessions would have secured his mystical connection to the magicians and their disappearing acts."

I said, "And we've established that Hieronymus was never *here* at the time of the disappearances."

"No, that's sheer speculation, young woman," Lysander said. "For instance, Max was interviewing Cowboy Duke at the Waldorf when he sensed Sexy Samson's disappearance, and we have no idea whether Hieronymus was here at that time."

"Allow me to rephrase," I said irritably. "We know there were disappearances that occurred when Hieronymus was *not* here."

"Agreed," Lysander said, "but that does not qualify as a pattern."

Delilah held up her phone. "No luck, Esther."

"Did you try with Garry's phone, too?" I asked.

"Yeah." Goudini waved his cell phone at me. "Same thing. No response at all."

Since I still wasn't able to reach Barclay or Dixie— or Duke, either, I'd discovered—we were trying with other phones. The bookstore phone got no response when calling their numbers, either.

"That's weird," I said. "Why would all three of their cell phones have stopped working?"

"Could they be stuck in a tunnel?" Lysander suggested.

Delilah said, "If they were, we should still be able to leave messages for them. But all we're getting when we dial their numbers is dead air."

"I don't understand this," I said, feeling uneasy. "I know those are the right numbers."

"Well, I'll see which company Dixie's service is with, and Duke's is probably the same one," Delilah said. "I'll find a customer service number, call and ask if the company knows what's going on."

"Good idea." I looked at Max. "Okay, what were we talking about?"

"Um."

"Oh, I know. Where was Hieronymus during the disappearances? If he didn't have to be at the performances, then why wouldn't he simply have been lurking here in the cellar at those times?"

"Hmm. Good question," Max said. "After he established the conduit, he would have needed to focus and concentrate to make the victims disappear. Creating the conduits gave him the tools to exercise his power through the magicians and their acts, but he still had to do the work when the moment was at hand. And causing a disappearance through a conduit would have been *work*." Max gasped. "No wonder he's been looking so tired lately!"

"Do you mean," I said, "that if Hieronymus had been asleep or distracted or busy doing his homework when Joe Herlihy performed the disappearing illusion that night, Golly wouldn't have vanished?"

"Correct," Max said. "Because Mr. Herlihy didn't have the power to make Miss Gee vanish. Only the person who had the power, namely Hieronymus—"

"Namely Phil," Lysander said tersely.

"Only he could cause the disappearance," Max said. "And only by exercising his power at the right time. When the magician reached that part of the act, the adept had to have completed his own rituals and be focused on his task, prepared to engage the conduit when he sensed the necessary convergence of energy and concentration."

"Hmm. That might explain why we skipped some days," I said.

"Pardon?" said Lysander.

"There hasn't been a disappearance *every* day since these events began. In eight days, we've had five disappearances. So maybe Hieronymus was busy, or distracted, or tired on the days when no one vanished."

"It's more likely," said Lysander, "that the frequency of the disappearances depended on the performance schedule of Phil's clients."

"Of course!" Max said. "Not everyone performing a disappearing act is a client of Phil's."

"And perhaps not every client of Phil's is performing this week," I said.

"Additionally," Lysander said, "there may be clients of Phil's who've performed recently but whose acts did not meet the requisite level of energy and concentration needed for Phil to engage the conduit and exercise his power."

I nodded. "That would explain why we gave several public performances of *Sorcerer!* before Golly vanished. Until that night, Joe was always so nervous and distracted, he probably made a lousy conduit."

"Precisely," Lysander said. "Because conduitism relies so heavily on another entity—and in this case it was relying on mundanes, which is always unwise—these disappearances must have been as unpredictable to enact as they were difficult to plan."

"So why the disappearing acts?" I asked. "Why was *that* part of each magician's performance targeted?"

"Simple," Lysander said. "Phil is using conduitism to exercise a form of sympathetic magic."

"What do you mean?"

Clearly pleased by the invitation to lecture me (again), Lysander said, "In sympathetic magic, a real-world object or action gives the practitioner a concrete focus for mystical energy in order to produce a desired result. An obvious example would be a poppet. If a practitioner of sympathetic magic wanted to inflict damage on you, he'd fashion a doll in your image and damage it. The more he could merge you and the doll into the same entity, the same life force, the more power would be vested in the poppet, and the more likely it would be that any damage he inflicted on the poppet would indeed be visited upon *you*. Therefore he might collect your hair—carelessly left in your brush, for example—to fashion into the poppet's hair, and steal an item of your clothing to make into the poppet's outfit."

"That's just creepy," I said.

"On the other hand, someone who wanted to *help* you might attempt to protect you by fashioning a poppet. As an inanimate object, it's far easier to protect than a busy modern woman is."

"So sympathetic magic can work either way? Benevolent or malevolent?"

"Yes. Like all things," Max said. "Even love."

"And the disappearing act provides a real-world focus for Phil?" I asked.

"No," Lysander said. "The disappearing act provides a focus for the mundane whom he is using as a conduit."

"Ah." Max nodded. "Yes, of course. The mental focus of the magician. The suspension of disbelief."

"Right!" Goudini chimed in. "During the decapitation act, I'm thinking about decapitation—so is the audience, so are the girls. Er, especially the girls. And during the disappearing act, I'm thinking about making Alice disappear."

"The incantations uttered during the act are also focused on the concept of disappearing," Max said.

"Right," I said. "The stage patter, the focus, the actions… In those few minutes, it's all about the vanishing illusion."

"In a way," Goudini said, "I even make *myself* believe I make her disappear."

Lysander said, "And that is quite probably the level of concentration, of sympathetic magic, that Phil needs in a mundane in order for the conduit to work."

"And then I really *did* make her disappear." Goudini looked sad. "Poor Alice!"

"It's really rather ingenious," Max said with professional admiration.

"But what's happening to the victims when they disappear?" I mused aloud.

"It depends on how he's accomplishing this," Max said. "By now, I believe translocation is far more likely than dissolution."

"Why?"

"Most forms of dissolution would cause instant death—or something remarkably similar to it. Why would Hieronymus do that? We know now that the magicians were his tools, not his enemies—he scarcely knew them. And the victims can't have been his enemies, either. In each case, he scarcely knew or never even met the disappearee." Max frowned, thinking it over. "So he must have needed to translocate a number of individuals for some reason, and conduitism was the method he chose."

"Why?" Lysander wondered. "It's so elaborate."

Max thought about that. "Perhaps it was the only way he could perform the translocations, for some reason?"

"Oh my God!" I slapped my forehead. It was becoming a habit. *"Incantations!"*

They both looked at me blankly.

"His speech impediment!" I said. "His results with incantations are unpredictable because of his speech impediment!"

"Incantations… Goodness, could *that* be why he's chosen such an unorthodox procedure?" Max said.

"Of course!"

They both suddenly started mumbling to themselves.

After a moment, I demanded, "What are you doing?"

Max paused in his muttering and explained, "There aren't that many incantations for a straightforward act of causing the involuntary translocation of an organic being. We're running through the ones we know."

"I know three," Lysander said, evidently finished with his muttering. "Esther's right. Hieronymus would have had considerable difficulty making any of them work. Far too many words with *S* or *R* in them."

"You know three incantations that would make me disappear against my will?" I asked uneasily.

"No, only one that would make *you* disappear. There's one that doesn't work on humans, and another that only works on Lithuanians."

"What *is* it with you people and Lithuanians?"

"Ah, interesting question," Lysander said. "Centuries ago—"

"Forget I asked. We don't have time." I frowned. "Exactly how essential is accurate pronunciation?"

"I am amazed that an *actress* can ask that," Lysander said.

"I know acting, not sorcery."

"One can fudge it in a number of incantations, but there are others where it's crucial," Max said. "In those cases, at best, saying an incantation incorrectly leads to disappointing or embarrassing results."

"And at worst?"

"Total disaster. Even tremendous danger."

"Really?"

"Oh, yes," Lysander said. "For one thing, errors in pronunciation can open a gateway to malignant forces. What begins as an attempt to protect a household can inadvertently summon a host of marrow-sucking demons."

"That would be bad," I said with certainty.

"Transmuting, translocating or levitating oneself call for fairly forgiving incantations. They're also quite brief. When Hieronymus left today, he may have taken the back way out, or he may have transmuted or translocated, if he was feeling energetic." I remembered what Max had said about the use of power being tiring. "He does have those skills. However, causing the involuntary translocation of another individual..." Max shook his head. "The incantations are much more demanding."

I took a breath. "So we think that, probably through trial and error, Hieronymus discovered he couldn't perform involuntary translocation of other people because he couldn't master the incantations. So—probably through still more trial and error—he figured out that he *could* achieve involuntary translocation through the use of conduits?" When they made affirmative noises, I asked, "The incantations involved in conduitism weren't an obstacle?"

"Conduitism is very abstract and esoteric," Max said. "Relatively little verbal skill is needed."

"It mostly requires mental mastery," Lysander said. "And, if I recall correctly, some strange ingredients in the laboratory work."

I said, "Do we have any idea where he translocates the victims *to?*"

"I don't think it's another dimension," Max said. "Now that we know Hieronymus is doing this—"

"Perhaps," Lysander said.

"—that seems unlikely. He evidently needs these people for something. And he is in this dimension."

"As is Phil," said Lysander. "It's difficult to imagine how the victims could be useful to him in another dimension."

"All right, good," I said, "we've narrowed it down to this dimension. How else can we narrow it down?"

Lysander frowned in thought. "He'd need...some sort of receiving location. Someplace very private. He wouldn't want to attract attention by performing his conduitism rituals where he might be seen or heard, or by the victims materializing in an unprotected place."

"Which explains why he's never here when the disappearances occur." I asked the most important question: "Are the victims still alive?"

"That depends on what he wants them for," Lysander said.

"Yes, *why* is he doing this?" Max wondered.

"You don't have any ideas, now that we know *who's* doing it?" I asked.

"Unfortunately," Max said, "I am as bewildered about that as I was before."

"There are still too many possibilities," Lysander said. "We need to know more about him than we do."

"We need to know," Max said, "what he *wants*."

"Yes. Then we may be able to ascertain his intentions."

"As his current mentor," Max said, "I feel a bit remiss."

"As well you should," Lysander said. "He obviously had far too much time on his hands!"

"Actually, he was neither prompt nor skilled at performing the tasks assigned to him," Max said, "so I've been decreasing my requirements—and my expectations—in recent months."

"And you see the result!"

"Back off, Lysander," I said. "It's not Max's fault that the Collegium sent a minion of Evil here to be his assistant. Though it's a relief to see you're finally admitting that's what's happened."

"I didn't say that," Lysander said quickly.

"Perhaps I should have been more concerned about his frequent and prolonged absences," Max admitted. "But young people are gadabouts, after all—"

"We're what?"

"—and it was easy to suppose that the city was a more stimulating and fascinating place for a healthy young man than my laboratory or this bookstore."

"Actually," Goudini piped up, "I find this a rather soothing place."

"However, that is not what I meant about feeling remiss," Max said. "To be quite candid, I was chiefly unconcerned about Hieronymus's absences because I did not find his company particularly appealing."

"That's understandable," I said.

"He was not prone to sharing his thoughts, and since I did not, I confess, take to the boy, I very soon gave up pressing him to share them. As a result..." Max sighed. "It's fair to say that despite having been his mentor for eight months, I know him only slightly. I have no idea what he wants, and therefore not the faintest idea why he's causing these disappearances or what he hopes to achieve. Indeed, I am forced to admit that I knew Hieronymus too little to feel either the sorrow or the sense of betrayal that a master in my situation might reasonably be expected to feel now."

"I didn't like him, either," I said. "Don't worry about it, Max."

"But now that we know he is a force of Evil—"

"We *postulate* that he *may* be," Lysander corrected.

"—it would be helpful in our current situation if I had troubled to understand the boy better."

"Water under the bridge," I said, unable to criticize anyone for not having been chums with Hieronymus.

"One thing is clear, though."

"What's that?" I asked.

Max said, "The lad has far more skill and power than he led me to believe."

"Ah."

"If he *is* translocating the victims," Max mused, "I wonder what method he's using for the transference?"

"Presumably," Lysander said, "he's translating their matter into the particles and waves I described earlier today, so that it can traverse shifting and semi-shifting holes or—"

"I think we can safely scrap that theory," I said. "As well as the theory that mundanes are behind these events. Those were both *his* theories, remember?"

"That doesn't mean there's no validity—"

"Yes, it does," I said. "You can't really think that he was foolish enough to tell you how he's been doing it? The less you know, the better for him. The confusing stuff he fed you today about waves and shifting holes leading to another dimension was just an attempt to get you off track. The way he got me off track by insisting mundanes were behind all this. His 'theory' about that helped convince me to break into Magnus's shop last night and go charging up those stairs."

"Oh." Lysander wouldn't say so, but I could tell he thought I might have a point.

"Misdirection," Goudini said. "Classic. The guy might have become a half-decent magician instead of an evil wizard, if he'd been raised right."

"I think we should leave his poor parents out of this," Max said sadly.

"Actually, Garry's brought up a good point," I said.

"I have?"

"I gather that the speech impediment is a mystical affliction, caused by a particularly vicious djinn cursing the pregnant Mrs. Blankenberg's womb?"

"Yes," Lysander said. "So if Hieronymus *is* Phil—which I do not yet concede—then obviously he is to be pitied rather than blamed."

"Guys, guys…" I shook my head. "Did it never occur to anyone in the Collegium that maybe a vicious djinn's idea of a really wicked curse involved a little more than just inflicting a lisp?"

"You mean…"

"I mean Hieronymus is evil," I said. "Since before he was born! Vicious-djinn evil! Cursed-by-an-evil-power evil! Something-wicked-this-way-comes evil! You know—*Evil.*"

"Oh dear," Max said. "She has a point."

Since Lysander didn't deny it, I assumed he agreed but would naturally rather die than admit it.

"And you folks," I said in exasperation, "taught him the secrets of the cosmos. Nice going, guys."

Lysander cleared his throat. "Whether or not he was born evil is a matter of conjecture, but that he was born with power is *not*. An individual with his inherent talent was going to learn the secrets of the cosmos whether he had teachers or not, Esther."

"True, true," said Max.

"The Collegium can neither grant power nor prevent the acquisition of skill. It can merely try to teach us to use power and skill wisely."

"Didn't work out so well with this lad, huh?" I said.

"Esther." Delilah bit her lip as she gazed at her cell phone. "Duke and Dixie do use the same company. Tech support has checked their service and agrees something's wrong. No response, just dead air. And no one knows why."

"What about Barclay?" I asked.

"No record of him, he must use a different provider. But tech support says that's even stranger. They've got no idea what could make three cell phones from two different providers simply…flatline like this."

I looked at Lysander and Max. "Could Phil do it?"

"I would think so," said Max. "Oh dear."

"Why would he want us to be out of touch? Why is he so determined to prevent us from talking to them?" I asked frantically.

The bells chimed, heralding a new arrival. We all jumped out of our chairs and ran for the door.

Duke gave a little start of surprise at the way we rushed him. Then he smiled. "Howdy, folks. I—"

"Duke!" I flung my arms around him.

"Er, uh, glad to see you, too, Esther."

"Are you all right?" I pulled away to examine him. "Is anything wrong?"

He frowned. "I'm just fine. How are *you?*"

"We were worried," Max said.

"Aw, I'm sorry," Duke said. "We tried to check in a while ago. Tried a few times, in fact. But, you know, it's the darnedest thing—"

"All three of your cell phones have stopped working."

He blinked. "Well, yeah. How'd you— Oh! You've been trying to reach us, of course."

"Where are Barclay and Dixie?"

The urgency of my tone made him blink again. "At the Magic Cabaret, of course. I helped them set up, watched them do a couple of run-throughs of the whole act."

"They're okay?"

"Oh, a little nervous. Performance jitters, that's all. You know how it is." He rubbed his hands together. "Anyhow, it's gonna be a great show! Come on, let's go watch the kids' professional debut!"

He seemed so normal and cheerful, I started to relax. I'd gotten worked up about bad cell-phone service. How ridiculous was *that?*

I shook my head. "We really wanted to, but now I don't think we can, Duke. We've got to—"

"Aw, come on," he said. "Max promised—"

"I did?" Max said.

"—and, of course, we've got to celebrate! By the way, where is my Dolly?"

"Your what?" Goudini said.

"I know she'll want to see little Dixie perform tonight," Duke said. "And I sure do want to see *her.*"

A terrible feeling crawled over my skin. "Duke, why do you think... think..."

"Oh, the phones weren't useless *all* day," he said. "Right before we lost service, we got Max's message."

"What message?" Max blurted.

Duke looked puzzled now. "Well...your message about solving the case."

"I didn't leave you a message," Max said in a hollow voice.

"But..." Duke looked from Max to me, then back to Max. "But Hieronymus phoned Dixie."

"Oh my God," I said.

Duke's expression was clouded now. He knew something was wrong. "He said you'd solved the case and rescued the disappearees. He said you'd meet us at the Magic Cabaret, that we should wait for you there. We'd all celebrate. But it got close to showtime, with no sign of you. And we realized y'all probably didn't know where the cabaret was and hadn't been able to reach us by phone. So I thought I'd just come back here and get you, and... Max, did something go wrong? What's happened?"

Max's mouth worked, but he didn't know how to

tell Duke we hadn't gotten Dolly back and still had no idea where she was. Still didn't even know if she was dead or alive.

Duke said, "Esther?"

"I'm sorry, Duke. Hieronymus was lying. We still haven't found Dolly. And he's the one who made her disappear."

Duke's expression changed into something awful. "But he...he told Dixie that Max said it was perfectly safe to go ahead and do the vanishing illusion now."

"What?"

"They spent two hours rehearsing it!" Duke's voice was flooded with panic. "They're gonna perform the disappearing act at the Magic Cabaret!"

CHAPTER

15

"The Magic Cabaret!" I shouted into my cell phone, trying to be heard above the engine of Barclay's van. "No, I'm asking if you have the address? Or the phone number?"

"Goddamn it! I thought for sure it was just off Broadway!" Duke said, anger and fear making his driving reckless and his language rough.

"I *know* you're not Directory Service," I said to the sarcastic cop on the phone. "Isn't Lopez back *yet*?"

"Where are we?" Max asked from the back seat, his voice laced with terror as the van sped through an intersection.

"Somewhere in Morningside Heights."

"Where's *that*?" Lysander, the out-of-towner, said from his seat directly behind me.

"Above the Upper West Side, below Harlem." Into

my phone, I snapped, "Well, *this* is important, too, goddamn it! Call Lopez! Tell him there's going to be another disappearance if we can't stop it! At the Magic Cabaret, somewhere around Columbia University! What? Yeah, *I* need a more specific location than that, too, Officer!"

"This doesn't look familiar!" Duke shouted. "I don't think I'm going the right way!"

"All right," Lysander said, "let's stay calm."

"Calm?" Duke shouted.

Lysander asked, "What do you remember seeing in the vicinity of the cabaret? Maybe that will help us find it."

Duke had left the Magic Cabaret in a calm, cheerful frame of mind, eager to see Dolly. He only realized now, as we tried to find the place in conditions of considerable stress, that he had not pinpointed its location as clearly as he might have before leaving it earlier.

"I don't remember!" Duke shouted. "All these doggone streets look the same in this gol-durned city!"

"Philip Hohenheim, whose real name we believe is Hieronymus Blankenberg, is about to make a girl disappear at the Magic Cabaret!" I shouted into my phone. "He's a bad man! He's got to be stopped!"

"Oh my God!" Duke cried. "My little Dixie!"

"Tell Lopez!" I said. "It's urgent!"

"What do you think the police are going to do?" Lysander said contemptuously.

"What?" I said.

Max, covered in a fine sheen of sweat as he gripped the sides of his seat and kept his eyes closed, said, "I'm afraid Lysander is right, Esther. No police officer can **st**op Hieronymus now. This is *our* duty. Please, hang up the phone. We shouldn't endanger mundanes."

"We *are* endangering mundanes," Lysander pointed out.

"These mundanes have chosen a sacred duty," Max replied. "Detective Lopez has only chosen police work."

"No, no!" I said into the phone. "*Don't* put me on…" I sighed and hung up. "He put me on hold."

"It doesn't matter," Max said.

He was right, I realized with a sinking feeling of acceptance. Lopez didn't believe in translocation or mystical conduitism. And even if he arrested Hieronymus, how could the cops hold an adept capable of transmuting through solid walls?

Worried by Max's ghastly appearance, I asked, "Are you all right?"

"I am mentally reciting incantations for our safety and survival."

"Hieronymus is that powerful?" I asked.

"I was referring to Duke's driving."

My phone rang. I answered it.

"Honey, this is Delilah. We've got confirmation. Phil was Joe Herlihy's coach, too."

"Good work!"

We had split up back at the bookshop. Goudini and Delilah had gone to see Joe while Max, Lysander, Duke and I were heading straight for the cabaret—if we could find it. "We've got confirmation, too. Phil coached Cowboy Duke. About six weeks ago. Duke didn't really think about it again after that."

"Joe, either," Delilah said.

"I'll *kill* the son of a bitch!" Duke said.

"We've got Joe in custody and are en route for the cabaret now," said Delilah.

"Well done!" I said. Max's plan was to get everyone who'd served as a conduit to gather in one place in the hope that he could figure out how to use their energy to reverse the effects of Hieronymus's translocations.

"Where *is* the cabaret?" Delilah asked.

"We're working on that right now," I said.

"There was a church!" Duke cried. "I remember now. A church! About two blocks away!"

Lysander said, "This city is full of churches."

"It was *big*. With towers. And there was scaffolding."

"St. John the Divine!" I said. "It's on Amsterdam, not Broadway!"

"Oh, thank the Lord! Which way is Amsterdam?"

"Turn here!" I said.

Lysander shouted, "Wait! No! That's a one-way street!"

Max started chanting loudly. The van rounded a

corner and sped recklessly down a side street, going the wrong way.

I told Delilah, "We're getting closer! I'll have an address for you any minute. Just keep driving north for now. Toward Morningside Heights."

I heard her give those instructions to their cab driver. Then she said to me, speaking so softly that I had trouble hearing her, "Joe is a little anxious, Esther, I'm not sure how useful he'll be."

"How'd you get him away from his wife?"

"I told Matilda we were on our way to recover Golly Gee, and if she didn't interfere, *Sorcerer!* could reopen by mid-week."

"So you're not just a pretty face," I said.

"*All* of my parts are pretty," she replied.

We turned onto Amsterdam while Max's chanting grew louder.

"Yes!" Duke cried. "This looks familiar! Yes! We came past here!"

"How far past here?"

"Why isn't this cabaret in the phone book?" Lysander wondered irritably.

"That street! This one right here!" Duke said.

Leaning over my shoulder, Lysander said, "But that's another one-way— *Agh!*"

"We're nearly there!" I shouted into the phone.

"I'll call the Pony Expressive's main line and have the girls meet us at the Magic Cabaret!" Delilah shouted back. "They'll want to help!"

"This is it! This is the building!" Duke cried, pulling to a stop. He jumped out of the van and ran up the stairs of an ordinary-looking, brick apartment building. "It's on the second floor!"

I gave Delilah the address and told her we were on our way upstairs. I hung up the phone and said to the sorcerers, "Come on!"

"Are we sure we want to get out of the car in this neighborhood?" Lysander asked.

I hopped out of the van while Duke pounded on the front door of the building and pressed every doorbell on the console. I opened the back door of the van and grabbed Max's arm. "Can you stand up?"

"Thank God we've stopped! Thank God we've stopped!" He briefly collapsed when I hauled him out of the van, then staggered toward the curb.

"Lysander, come on!"

As he descended, he asked, "Should we really leave the car unattended and sitting in the middle of the street?"

"Come on!" Duke shouted as the door to the building opened. "Hurry!"

We raced up the steps and into the building. It had probably been a nice place decades ago, but it was faded and worn now, with drab walls, eerily dim lighting and grime rubbed deep into the floor tiles.

"What kind of a cabaret is *this*?" Lysander demanded.

I saved my breath to follow Duke, who was charging up the steep stairs to the second floor. When we reached the landing, I saw that this floor had been remodeled at some point in its past. Instead of a hallway with apartments, we were confronted by a wall with one wide, curtain-covered entrance. Just to the side of the entrance was a little desk. A girl of about twenty, dressed in Goth style, sat at the desk. She smiled at us.

"Hi, Cowboy Duke! I saved you two tables at the front, just like you asked."

"No wonder we couldn't find a listing for this place," Lysander said fastidiously, sounding breathless as he reached the top of the stairs only moments behind me.

The girl beamed at us. "Are these your friends, Duke? That'll be ten dollars each— Hey! Wait! You can't go in without paying!"

I followed Duke as he plowed past the curtain covering the door, shouting, "Dixie! Barclay! *Stop!*"

We entered a small cabaret. Music was playing too loudly from strategically placed speakers for anyone but a few nearby patrons to hear Duke's shouts. The tables and chairs were an eclectic and shabby collection, as if someone had raided various church basements and suburban garages for the club's furnishings. The dreary surroundings were decorated—to use the word generously—with some stereotypical magic props. Instead of a bar, a folding table was set up in the corner; the beverages were presumably in the coolers I saw under the table. The audience was less than two dozen people; they were drinking out of disposable plastic cups.

This was Barclay's big break? I stopped feeling depressed about *my* career.

"No!" Duke cried.

Barclay was spinning a big, square, mirrored contraption around and around onstage while the music played. As Duke ran toward him, shouting in panic, Barclay suddenly gasped and staggered backward. There was an awful expression on his face.

"No!" Barclay cried.

"No!" Duke shouted.

"Oh, *no*," I said.

Lysander grunted and staggered sideways, bumping into me, affected by his proximity to such a powerful dimensional disturbance. I heard a terrible *crash! smash! clatter!* and some screaming right behind me. I whirled around. Even more affected than Lysander, it seemed, Max had crashed into one of the cabaret tables. Now he, the table, the candle, the drinks, two other people and their chairs lay in a messy, painful-looking heap on the floor.

I knelt down. "Max. Max!" He was unconscious.

"My God, she's *gone!*" Barclay screamed. "Dixie! Dixie! No, *no!*"

I looked at the stage and saw Barclay opening the vanishing box in search of the girl from Texas. Duke was helping, screaming Dixie's name, too.

"Max," Lysander said. "Rouse yourself, man!"

I left Lysander splashing a soda on Max's face and ran to the stage (such as it was). Duke was trying to crawl into the vanishing box.

"What are you *doing?*" Barclay cried.

"Send me after her!" Duke shouted. "Send me after Dixie! I'm gonna go get her!"

But he was a tall, broad, big-boned man who couldn't squeeze into a prop designed to be a snug fit for an average-sized woman. With the box all spread open from Barclay's search for Dixie, I could see how it worked—very similar to the crystal cage in which I'd rehearsed as Golly Gee's understudy. Duke couldn't fit into it; but I could.

I helped a frantic Barclay drag Duke away from the mirrored box. Then I returned to it and climbed inside.

"Esther? Stop!"

"Send me after her!"

"No! *No!*" Barclay said. "I won't! *Anything* could happen—"

I grabbed his collar. "I'm going to go get her! I'm going to go get them *all.* You do not for a *moment* suppose I'm afraid of that rat-faced pipsqueak Hieronymus, do you?"

"What?"

"If he's what's waiting at the other end of this journey, I'm going to wring his scrawny neck until his tongue turns blue and his eyes pop out of his head!" I shouted into Barclay's face. "Now *send me to him* so I can put a stop to his fun and games!"

"But—"

"Duke," I said, "help Barclay!"

"But—"

"Do it *now!*" I closed the door of the box.

I was immediately enveloped in pitch black. The suffocating closeness of the vanishing box pressed in on me from all sides. This thing was no more comfortable than the crystal cage. *God,* I hated magic acts.

I prayed this would work, prayed the conduit was still engaged. I was trying to follow Dixie's mystical route only moments behind her. Surely such powerful sorcery didn't turn on and off as quickly as a water tap? Surely I could catch the wave and go wherever it had taken that innocent girl? I doubted Barclay's concentration was in top form just now, but his energy level had probably never been higher. And the sympathetic magic of the disappearing act had probably never been as powerful as it was at this very moment. No magician involved in these bizarre events had ever believed in his ability to make someone disappear the way Barclay believed right now, with all his heart, in his ability to make *me* disappear.

I felt the box spinning, being moved around in a circle, the ritual Barclay performed as part of the act. He was trying, bless him. He was sick with terror—and probably with guilt—but he was trying to do as I'd asked.

"Come on, come on," I whispered. "Come and get

me, Phil. Pick on someone who knows your tricks, for a change. Come— *Argh!*"

The floor of the prop box disappeared. So did gravity. I plunged down *and* up at the exact same moment—or so it seemed. Sucked in both directions, yet in neither direction. I gasped so hard I choked on my own breath, whirling in a powerful blackness that smothered me as I moved at a speed so fast, I felt like my skin and my stomach were being left several thousand miles behind me. Caught upside down in a backward momentum of blood-draining force, I was too terrified and disoriented to react, let alone think.

When it stopped, I did the one thing in the world I most wanted to do: I screamed.

Since I was out of breath and also trying not to choke on my own bile, it wasn't as loud or as long a scream as I'd intended. I was drawing breath for another effort when I realized people were talking excitedly all around me.

I was lying down, stretched out on my back, on something hard and bumpy, cool and rather slimy. It seemed to be whirling…until I realized that was just my head, still trying to recover from whatever had happened to me.

I heard a strange, low rumble. Was that the subway? Then more talking. Then a snarl. No…not the subway. More words. But I was thinking about that rumbling. It sounded almost like…

I felt hot breath on my face. Not exactly like a bad date. More like a blow-dryer on low setting.

"If you can hear me," a woman said, while the breath fanned my face, "don't move. She's really very friendly to people she knows, but strangers make her nervous. Plus, she's quite hungry by now."

"*Alice?*" I blurted, remaining as immobile as possible while I lay on what I realized was a slimy, uneven stone floor.

"How do you know her name?" The woman's voice was startled.

"Sarah Campbell?" I asked, keeping very still and not opening my eyes. I didn't want to see Alice from this position. I felt a muscular leg the size of a young tree trunk pressing against my shoulder as the tiger breathed on me.

"Yes, I'm Sarah!" the woman replied. "How do you know my... My God, someone is looking for us!"

"*Esther?* Esther Diamond?" That was unmistakably Golly's voice.

"You know her?" a man asked.

"Samson?" I croaked.

"She's my understudy," Golly gasped. "They're doing the show *without* me?"

"Hi, Golly," I said.

"That fucking asshole Herlihy's made you disappear, too! And they're doing the show without *me!*"

Still feeling that hot breath on my tender throat— the breath of a large, carnivorous species known to prey on mankind—I said, "Can someone do something about this tiger?"

"Alice!" Sarah Campbell said brightly. "Here, Alice! Alice! Let's roll over! Come on, Alice! Let's roll over!"

"She tired of that game hours ago," a new voice said. It sounded aristocratic.

"Clarisse Staunton?" I guessed.

The girl gasped. "Does Barclay know I'm here? Does he know what's happened?"

"Can someone do something about this tiger?" I repeated.

Several of them started shouting her name, trying to distract her.

Alice growled irritably and kept sniffing me. Apparently I didn't smell *quite* like dinner to her—at least, not yet. After breathing hotly on me for another few moments, she allowed herself to be lured away.

"You can sit up now," Samson said.

I opened my eyes. I was a little startled, since I occasionally imagined the first glimpse of single-woman's heaven might be like this. An absolutely gorgeous man was kneeling at my side. He was smooth and faintly tanned all over, beautifully toned and wonderfully built. He wore nothing but a little gold lamé G-string. He had a chiseled jaw, soft brown eyes and even softer-looking wavy gold hair.

"Delilah and your mom are worried," I said to Samson.

He looked deeply moved for a moment. Then he helped me sit up. "It's awful when you first come through that...that...whatever it is. Gateway. Experience." He put a reassuring hand on my back. "Give yourself a minute."

"I puked when I got here," Golly said.

"Yes. You did," Clarisse said coldly. "And when I arrived, I found myself lying facedown on the *exact* spot where you'd puked."

They glared at each other. I sensed that shared hardship had not necessarily forged a bond of sisterhood.

There was another woman here, too. Middle-aged, a little plump, dressed in a cowgirl costume studded with sequins and rhinestones. She was lying on the floor, too, and seemed to be out cold. Clarisse was holding her hand.

"Is Dolly all right?" I asked.

"She just hit her head when she fell. But I don't think it's too serious," the society girl said. "She'll come round."

Poor Dolly. I continued scanning the chamber.

"Alice," I said weakly, coming eye to eye with the tiger. In other circumstances—a zoo, a magic show, the Discovery Channel—I'd probably find her quite beautiful. Up close and with nothing between us, though, she just looked terrifying. Especially when she sneered at me.

"We need to get out of here," Sarah said pointedly. She was a pretty woman, about my age, wearing a lovely evening gown.

"Yes," I agreed, eyeing the hungry white tiger. "That much is clear."

Golly, still dressed as Virtue, looked unkempt, dirty and haggard. Clarisse Staunton was a pretty blonde in her early twenties; she wore a skintight, black leather outfit, which wasn't how I had pictured Barclay's stage partner dressing. Dolly looked pale and unconscious. Samson looked chilly.

We were in some kind of large underground chamber. No windows, of course. The walls were made of stone. Very old. They were damp and cracked, covered in mold with a scattering of fungus. There was an archway leading into what was presumably another chamber like this one. Strange writing—or symbols? glyphs?—was scrawled above and around the arch.

It looked like water often came through the high ceiling above us, perhaps during heavy rains. At the moment, though, the flow was restricted to a fairly generous trickle coursing down one wall to land in a huge puddle.

"That's how we've survived," Samson said, nodding to the water.

"God only knows what kind of parasites I've picked up, drinking that," Clarisse said.

Samson added, "And he brings us food sometimes."

"Thai," Clarisse said. "Chinese."

"Our leftovers!" I said, realizing.

"Esther, tell me seriously," Golly said. "Do I look like I've lost weight?"

"What is this place?" I asked. "Where *are* we?"

"We're somewhere beneath Castle Clinton," Samson replied.

"Ah! In Battery Park. Okay." That helped me orient myself. Originally an armed harbor fort protecting the city, Castle Clinton was a tourist spot now; people bought tickets and boarded ferries there to see Ellis Island and the Statue of Liberty. "There probably aren't people around this time of night," I said, "but we could try screaming, even so."

"It's nighttime?" Samson asked. "We've had trouble keeping track."

"And we've tried screaming," Golly said. "Lots. He told us it was pointless, and he was right."

"We're *way* beneath Castle Clinton," Samson explained. "Or thereabouts."

"What was this place?" I wondered, looking around. "An arsenal? A crypt?"

"Maybe," Samson said. "Or something to do with the harbor. Or the water system. Or sewage."

"Eeeuuw!" Golly said.

Alice growled.

I smelled something that seemed to confirm the sewage theory, then realized it was undoubtedly the natural result of several people and a tiger inhabiting an enclosed space with no plumbing. Shared hardship might be an understatement, I realized.

Samson added, "You go down a couple of levels, and you find weird stuff all over this city. Forgotten tunnels, old caverns, abandoned switching stations..." He shrugged and smiled bashfully. "I was working on a degree in urban planning before I became a performance artiste."

"How do we get out of here?" I asked.

"We can't. These chambers were sealed off a long time ago. Probably before the Civil War. There's no way in, and no way out."

I gasped. "*That's* why he needed the conduits!"

"What?"

"He researched what lay beneath the city until he found a private, forgotten place that suited his needs. He could transmute through layers of soil, rock and crumbling stone walls to get here. Through layers of time. But then..." I nodded. "Then he discovered he couldn't bring his victims here. He couldn't utter the incantations correctly. So he developed the conduits to get you here!"

"*That's* why he ruined my performance?" Golly said. "Because of his lisp? He needed Joe? For fuck's sake! He couldn't have waited until the show was over?"

"But why?" I wondered. "*Why?*"

Sarah gasped. "You don't know?" She looked at the others. "She doesn't know!"

"No, that's what we haven't been able to..." I looked around at their faces. "*You* know?"

Samson and Sarah exchanged a glance. Then Samson said to me, "I don't mean this the way it sounds, but, er…you're not a virgin, are you?"

Somewhere else in these underground chambers, a woman started screaming.

CHAPTER

16

Dolly awoke. "Dixie? *Dixie!*"

"Dixie!" I jumped to my feet—then froze when Alice growled and crouched like she intended to spring for me. "Is that Dixie?"

As the screaming continued, Clarisse helped Dolly try to rise. Sarah shuddered and tears filled her eyes. Alice gazed at me, her tail swishing back and forth in a way that made me long for a rifle. I like animals, but not as much as I like staying alive and unmaimed.

"Dixie?" Samson repeated. "Yes, that's the name Dolly started screaming when the new girl appeared here. Just a few minutes before you arrived."

"*God,* I hope that girl's had sex," Golly said.

I blinked. "What?"

Clarisse said, "Dolly tried to protect the girl from

him. He knocked Dolly down, and that's when she hit her head and passed out."

Dixie screamed again. Dolly moaned, trying to pull herself together and go to the girl, but was obviously disoriented. I tried to move toward the chamber where the screams were coming from—but I stopped when Alice flinched reflexively in my direction, as if about to pounce on me.

"Control your tiger!" I ordered Sarah.

"I can't! Goudini and her trainer are the only ones who have authority over her!"

"*Take* some authority, damn it!"

"Have you ever tried to take authority over a cat?"

"Oh good God!" I said.

"It's no use, er... I didn't get your name," Samson said.

"Esther." I took off my shoe.

"It's no use, Esther."

"What choice do we have? I'm not going to be hampered in this battle by one of the *hostages,* for God's sake!"

"No, I mean—"

"Don't anyone move." Holding Alice's gaze, I assumed the role of a lion tamer in no mood for pranks and walked toward her, staring her down. Alice's tail twitched harder and she growled at me. She looked about five feet long, if you didn't count the tail, and I estimated she weighed about three hundred pounds. "Alice," I said firmly, "go to your corner and stay there."

"She doesn't have a corner," Golly said.

"Alice," I repeated, "go to your corner. Now."

The tiger glared at me. Praying I would live through this, I whacked her sharply on the nose with my shoe. Alice flinched and ran to a corner, where she crouched and growled, tail still twitching, now doing her best not to look at me.

"I'll be damned," Golly said.

"All right," I said loudly, shaking like a leaf, "let's go get Dixie from that scheming twerp!"

"But, Esther—"

I crossed the floor and walked through the archway to enter the chamber whence the screams came. Or I tried. When I got to the arch, I bounced so hard off an unseen obstacle that I fell to the floor. Alice's growls mingled with Dixie's screams as Samson helped me off the floor.

"I tried to tell you," he said. "We can't go into that chamber. I think these symbols he's written all over the doorway give him power over who can enter and who he can keep out."

"Dixie!" I shouted through the archway. "Hang on! I'm here! Hang on! And kick that little creep in the balls!"

"Esther?" she cried. "Esther, is that you?"

"Yes! Are you all right? Dixie? Dixie, answer me! Who's frightening you? Is that Hiero— Oh, my God, it *is* you!" I exclaimed as Max's skinny, sullen, young assistant suddenly appeared before me—in the normal sense: he walked round the corner that hid most of the other chamber from view. Dragging Dixie with him, he stopped when he reached the archway, just on the other side of the invisible barrier. She was struggling against his white-knuckled grip on her arm. He gave her a hard shake to make her hold still.

Glaring at me as if *I* were somehow to blame for all his problems, Hieronymus snarled, "She'th not one, eitheh!"

"Sheathe *what?*" I said.

"She's not one, either," Samson translated.

"Not one what?" I asked in confusion.

"A virgin," Samson said.

"She's not?" Dolly cried. "Oh, darlin', thank *God!*"

Dixie's face was tear-streaked. She looked disheveled and terrified. "Dolly! Are you okay?"

I glanced at Dolly as she staggered toward us, gradually regaining full control of her limbs. "Oh, honey! I was so scared! I'm so glad! Thank *God* you're not a… Er…" She frowned. "Oh my goodness! I thought *sure* you still were!"

"You won't tell Daddy, will you?"

"No, of course not, sugar. Women gotta keep each other's secrets. But, honey, just reassure me. You weren't, you know… I mean, no nasty young man forced—"

"Oh, no, no! He's a very *nice* young man, Dolly! Very sweet! You'll like him! Daddy likes him. But, of course, Daddy doesn't know about…"

"And he won't ever find out," Dolly promised her. Then her face fell when she realized just how true that statement seemed likely to be.

"Shut up!" Hieronymus shouted. "Shut *up,* shut up, *shut up!* I'm tho thick of you! Tho thick of *all* of you!" He glared at me. "Ethpecially *you!*"

"Gosh, and I just got here," I said.

"I won't even botheh with you. I think we can thafely thay *you* awen't a vi'gin." His face screwed up with distaste as he added, "An *actweth.*"

"Excuse me, I didn't catch that final word?" When his face darkened with rage, I added, "Hiewony-muth."

"Maybe I can't thacwifithe you to Avolapek," he said furiously, "but I *can* kill you."

"So you *are* sacrificing the victims!" I paused, confused for a moment, and then it hit me. "Oh good grief! You're sacrificing *virgins?*"

"Twying to," he said sulkily.

"You can't be serious!" I said.

Glowering, he replied, "Do you have *any* idea how hawd it ith to find a vi'gin in thith thity? Juth *one?* One little vi'gin! That'th all I want! That'th all I need! One vi'gin! One! But *noooo!*"

"You had sex with Barclay?" I blurted, looking at Dixie.

"You won't tell Daddy?"

"When did you and Barclay have *time* to— Oh! Of course. The night you went out for a nightcap. Barclay took you back to your hotel after Duke was already asleep in his own room?"

Dixie nodded, blushing.

"And none of us is a virgin, of course," Samson said to me.

Golly Gee snorted. "Not for a *long* time."

"And Alice has had cubs!" I said, remembering.

"Even the goddamn *tigeh* ith not a vi'gin!" Hieronymus shrieked, little flecks of spittle flying out of his mouth.

"So you're trying to sacrifice a virgin? Oh, Phil, Phil, *Phil*." I shook my head while Hieronymus gasped at my use of his alias. "Oh, of all the pathetic, misogynistic, cliché-ridden, phallocentric, stereotypical, B-movie bullshit!" He sulked as I continued, "Hieronymus, don't you see how *sad* this is? How absurd? How bourgeois?"

"It ith *not* bouwgeois! I'm going to wule Manhattan! Wule New Yo'k! Become mo'e powe'ful than Twump, biggeh than Bloombe'g!"

"You? Who are you kidding?" I shot back. "In one of the biggest population centers on the planet, *you* can't even find a virgin!"

"I am thtwanded in Thodom and Gomowah!"

"What?"

"He's stranded in Sodom and Gomorrah," Samson said. "We've heard this rant before."

"Dare I ask what you need a virgin *for*?" I said.

Samson said, "To summon Avolapek."

"Who's Avolapek?"

"Some demon that he thinks will make him bigger than Trump, more powerful than Bloomberg," said Clarisse.

"And once you summon this demon and become all-powerful throughout the five boroughs," I said to Hieronymus, "do you think you'll suddenly gain the ability to translocate these people back *out* of this hole in the ground? That's why they're all trapped down here, isn't it? You developed conduits to bring a virgin sacrifice here, and instead you got stuck with hostage after hostage who isn't a virgin and can't call forth Apolamak!"

"Avolapek!" Hieronymus snapped. "He will only come in anthweh to one who ith clean."

"Oh, that old 'sex is dirty' pathology? Please! Grow *up*," I snapped. "Now that you've brought half a dozen people and a tiger down here, you can't figure out how to get rid of them! Some threat to Trump and Bloomberg *you* are!"

"Avolapek will get wid of them!"

"Oh, really?" I said with a sneer. "How?"

"He will eat them."

I flinched. "What?"

Clarisse said to me, "You just *had* to ask, didn't you?"

Hieronymus said, "He will claim hith vi'gin pwize—"

"Gross," Golly said.

"—and then he will be hungwy and need food. For him, that meanth people."

"He eats people?" I blurted.

"*Many* people," Hieronymus said. "Big appetite."

"*How* many?" There were seven of us…

"A few hundwed a day."

"Whoa! Let me get this straight," I said. "You want to rule New York, so you're trying to summon a demon that will rape a virgin and then eat hundreds of people a day?"

He shrugged. "No pain, no gain."

"Are you *insane?*" Dolly cried.

"He's evil," I said.

"I'm twying to get ahead in a *vewy* competitive town," Hieronymus said.

I said, "Well, it's not going to work, you slimy punk. Max is on to you!"

"That pathetic old man?" he said with a sneer. "He ith a fool. I am not afwaid of him."

I wanted to hit the skinny creep. I wanted to hit him *so* much. Instead I tried to think of a way to distract him. "Forget it, Phil. After half a dozen disappearances, you still haven't got a virgin. Face facts, you'll never find one. This is New York, kid!"

"I will engage anotheh conduit! And anotheh, and anotheh! I *will* find a vi'gin." He looked at Dixie with disgust. "But not tonight."

Using the leverage of his grip on her arm, he flung her through the archway. She cried out in surprise and flew straight into me, Samson and Dolly. All four of us fell to the ground together. I got up as fast as I could untangle myself and tried to get through the archway so I could strangle Hieronymus. But I bounced off the invisible barrier again. Samson was right. I could only pass through that thing if Hieronymus willed it. And I could tell by the look on his face that he knew exactly why I wanted to join him in his separate chamber, and he had no intention of letting it happen.

Suddenly his whole body stiffened and he inhaled sharply. "Anotheh…"

"What?" The floor trembled. "Is that the subway?"

"No." Samson looked distressed. "That happens when…"

The walls started trembling, too.

"Anotheh ith coming!"

Hieronymus closed his eyes and raised his arms. He shouted a few hoarse, guttural words, but otherwise just stood there with his eyes closed, apparently welcoming the new arrival.

The floor and walls were shaking hard now. I felt sick. The air started glowing, and I prayed for unconsciousness as something eerie passed through the air, through me, through my blood. This wasn't as bad as being translocated, but it was pretty nauseating, even so.

"I *hate* this!" Golly said.

Dixie clung to Dolly as the older woman said, "It'll be over in a minute, honey, don't you fret."

The glowing air started to descend and resolve into a distinct shape on the ground between me and

Hieronymus. Its nearness burned my foot. I fell back a few steps. As it became more solid, Hieronymus made a sharp summoning gesture with his hands—and the glowing shape slid closer to him.

"No!" I ran forward, realizing what he was doing. But I couldn't touch the shape, it was too hot. I tried again anyhow—and this time, I bounced off the invisible barrier. Whoever was being translocated was on the other side of that thing now. Alone in the other chamber with Hieronymus.

When the glow faded, I recognized the new arrival. "Lysander!" He didn't stir.

He must have entered the mirrored vanishing-box after me, trying to rescue me and Dixie. A terrible coldness flooded me. Where was Max? Still unconscious? Or about to follow Lysander's path and wind up in the same predicament?

Lysander gasped, choked a little, and then started breathing hard but evenly. His eyelids fluttered and his fingers moved, but he wasn't in control of his senses yet.

Hieronymus smiled at me. A ghoulishly smug grin. "I've found one."

"No!" I cried.

He kicked Lysander in the head, hard enough to ensure a few minutes of unconsciousness, then bent down, grabbed him under the arms and dragged him away, hauling him around the corner.

"No! Lysander! Hieronymus! *Stop!*"

"What are we going to do?" Dixie asked me.

"Why's he taking him back there, where we can't see?" I asked.

"That's where his altar is," Samson said. "The one he built to make a virginal offering and summon Avolapek." After a moment, he added, "The altar's kind of cool, actually. Very ritualistic. Something like that might be a neat backdrop to design for our show, the next time that Delilah and I start working on a new…oh." It apparently dawned on him that there might not be a next time.

We heard chanting. It didn't sound like Latin to me. Greek, perhaps? I didn't know.

Golly said, "Maybe he can't do the spell right?"

I said, "We can hope. But I have a feeling that if you've got a virgin staked out on your sacrificial altar, a man-eating demon probably overlooks your pronunciation errors."

Behind me, Alice growled. I glanced over my shoulder to see her pacing nervously. When I looked back into the other chamber, I saw shadows dancing on the walls now. Hieronymus was lighting candles, creating a substantial glow. A pool of light spread gradually across the floor, and the shadows we could see on the wall became more pronounced, more discernible. I could identify Hieronymus moving around while he chanted.

"You're off-key!" I shouted. "This demon will eat you first, if he comes."

"I don't think demons eat their summoners," Samson murmured, "do they?"

"How would I know what demons do?" I replied. "But I wouldn't want to bet on Avolapek's behavior in a new setting any more than I'd want to bet on Alice's."

"I think she's being very good," Sarah said, "given the circumstances."

I could see an enormous shape on the shadow-painted wall. Something moved on top of it: Lysander on the altar. Then Hieronymus cold-cocked him again.

"You coward!" I shouted at Hieronymus. "An unconscious, older man? Why don't you come hit a *girl*?"

"He did hit me," said Dixie.

"You bastard!" I shouted. "Why don't you come try to hit *me,* you oily, smelly, effeminate, ineffectual little creep?" It didn't work; he continued his chanting without missing a beat. "We need to break his concentration," I said to the others. "If only we could get through this barrier!"

"I don't know if it'll do much good, sugar," said Dolly, "but I can scream at a pitch that turns men's bowels to water."

"Maybe if we all do that together," Clarisse suggested, "it would throw him off a little?"

"Give it a try!" I said.

Dolly wasn't kidding about the pitch of her

screams. I thought my eardrums would bleed. Golly Gee and the other women did well, too, but Samson was the real surprise; I never knew *any* man could hit notes that high. Alice made noises like she'd kill someone soon. I just hoped it wouldn't be one of us.

Apart from a brief flinch, though, Hieronymus's shadow showed no signs of distraction. In fact, he was so absorbed in his chanting and his summoning that he didn't even seem to notice when the body on the altar started moving again. Lysander's head was shifting restlessly, as if our screams were bothering *him*, at any rate.

Then—suddenly—fog, steam and spirals of smoke with tiny sparks of fast-dying fire billowed into being, filling the air with multiple explosions of noise and roiling fury.

"My God!" Dolly cried.

"I think the demon is coming!" Samson shouted. He started coughing as shafts of churning smoke, unimpeded by the barrier that restricted us, started pouring through the archway in thick, fast-moving columns.

My eyes stung and I started coughing. I waved a hand in front of my face, straining to see the shadows on the wall, but it was useless now. The air was too thick and murky with mingled smoke and fog. The smoke was hot, dry and smelled vaguely of sulfur. The fog was damp and soft, and it stank like a swamp.

"Avolapek! Avolapek!" Hieronymus cried. Then he resumed chanting, his voice loud and triumphant.

Lysander gave a terrible scream. Then another.

Was Avolapek arriving? If so, maybe that was enough to distract Hieronymus. Hoping his attention was elsewhere and his grasp on this portion of his power was weakening at the moment, I flung myself at the invisible barrier again—and this time flew straight through the archway. I landed in a heap somewhere on the rough stone floor of the other chamber.

I couldn't see the other hostages through the fog and smoke, so I assumed they couldn't see me. I hoped they'd try the same maneuver, but I didn't want to shout out to them; it might alert Hieronymus, and he'd resurrect the barrier. I needed to disable him. Hoping that what worked on a Bengal tiger would work on a demented adept, I took off my shoe again, and crept through the smoke toward the sounds of Hieronymus's voice and Lysander's coughing. I got close enough to see Hieronymus, and I stalked up behind him. His back was turned to me. I hit him at the base of the skull with my shoe, as hard as I could.

"Argh!" He staggered away and whirled toward me. *"No!"*

I dropped my shoe and picked up one of the tall, cast-iron candlesticks that he'd conveniently positioned nearby, then swung it at him like a bat. It caught him on the shoulder. He screamed and stumbled backward.

I shouted to the others, "The barrier's down! Come get Lysander!" Then I hit Hieronymus with my cast-iron weapon again. He flew into a wall, then slid down to the floor. He appeared to be out cold. I hit him again, just to be sure.

Other people's screams joined the sound of Lysander's. I turned around and squinted through the mingled fog and smoke. I staggered toward the noise, trying to find them. "Lysander! Lysander! Where are you?"

Alice growled again, and I flinched at how close she was—until I realized... "That wasn't Alice, was it?" No one answered me. They were too busy screaming. "Oh, *no.*"

The thick veil of white mist, that noxious supernatural fog, cleared and melted away as I approached the altar. I found Samson and Dolly trying to remove shackles from Lysander's hands and feet.

I couldn't see Sarah, but I could hear her somewhere nearby, shouting, "Alice! Come, Alice! Alice, come! Eat the demon! Aren't you hungry, sweetheart? Come *on,* Alice!"

Dixie and Clarisse stood their ground near the altar, each armed with another candlestick. Dixie was screaming. Clarisse was shaking and shiny with sweat. I looked at the thing *they* were looking at. Candlesticks wouldn't stop it, not even cast-iron ones. Nor, I suspected, would a hungry tiger.

My heart stopped beating and my lungs stopped working as the thing that Hieronymus had summoned finished shaping itself out of smoke and fog and fire. It rose to its full height—eight feet, I guessed, vaguely surprised I could still think—and grinned at us. Dixie, Clarisse and I all fell back a step with a collective gasp. Its rows of fangs dripped with saliva. Its lumpy, mottled red flesh glowed with inner fire. Its long arms ended in massive claws. When it breathed on us, I smelled death and decay.

"Don't look at it," I said to Dolly and Samson.

"Alice! Come eat the demon! Come on!" Sarah urged.

Avolapek growled at us, a deep, menacing rumble that echoed around the chamber. Then the demon saw Lysander. It seemed to swell with delight, and it reached for him.

Without thinking, I brought the candlestick down with all my might on its massive, hideous arm.

This seemed to annoy it.

"Hit it again!" Lysander shouted. "Hit it again!"

"Celibacy was a bad idea," I told Lysander. "Do you hear me? A *bad* idea!"

Dixie helped me hit the beast again. With one flick of its arm, it sent us flying across the room. But things could have been worse. It might have eaten us.

"Celibacy!" I said again, picking myself up. "Of course!"

"Huh?" Dixie said.

I tried to get my bearings. The room was still so foggy it was hard to make out shapes. Especially inert lumps on the floor. But I found the one I was looking for while Clarisse boldly swatted the eight-foot-tall, flesh-eating demon.

"Grab his other arm!" I instructed Dixie. We hauled Hieronymus's unconscious form off the floor and dragged him over to the altar. "Hey! Avolapek! Look! Uh, *vide!*" I was fairly sure that was Latin for something like *see*. Not that I had any reason to suppose Avolapek spoke Latin. "A virgin!"

If Lysander and Max kept themselves "pure," I'd bet my bottom dollar that a power-obsessed nutbag like Hieronymus did, too. *"Virgin,"* I repeated. "Nice, clean, pure, virginal, evil lunatic! Right here! Come on, fetch! Just your type. And much younger than the guy staked out on the altar. Yum!"

"Got it!" Dolly cried, finally managing to get one of Lysander's shackles loose.

"Me, too!" Samson cried, freeing another limb.

Lysander leaped off the altar—and crashed to the floor. He was still shackled to the altar by one foot. "Argh! Get it off! Get it off!"

"A little *help* here?" I said to him. "I'm trying to keep a demon from raping you!"

"Oh!" He looked at Hieronymus, who was starting to stir in my grasp, made a few gestures with his hands and shouted some stuff in Latin.

Hieronymus's body flew out of my grip and straight into the demon's arms.

"Excellent!" I said.

"That doesn't solve our problems!" Samson said, trying to help Dolly with Lysander's final shackle.

"He's right!" Clarisse shouted, still waving her candlestick at the beast. "As soon as he's done raping a virgin, he'll want to eat a few hundred people. And we're stuck down here with him, with no way out!"

"Goddamn it! It's always *something.*" I bit my lip, wondering what to do next.

Dolly got Lysander's foot free. "Yes!"

"Come on!" I shouted. "Retreat! Retreat!"

Moving en masse, we fell back, rounded the corner, and retreated into the other chamber. I was wearing only one shoe now, and my steps were uneven as I fled. Once we were all in the original chamber, I pointed out to Lysander the writing that covered the top and sides of the archway. "We think he was using those inscriptions to control who can and can't pass through this doorway. Can you do the same thing?"

"I'm not sure!" He frowned. "I don't recognize all the symbols. I'm not sure."

In the next chamber, around the corner and beyond our range of vision, Hieronymus screamed horribly.

"Try!" I insisted. "We've got to get something between us and that thing!"

Lysander's lips were moving silently as he tried to interpret the symbols while Hieronymus continued screaming in the next room.

"I thought a demon wouldn't attack its summoner?" Samson said.

"Demons are notoriously unpredictable," Lysander said. "Particularly, the power-granting, flesh-eating ones."

"Don't distract Lysander," I said to Samson.

From the next chamber, the beast made a long, loud noise that was horrible beyond belief. It sounded suspiciously like demonic sexual satisfaction.

"Come on, come on, come on," I chanted under my breath. There were no more noises from Hieronymus, who had evidently passed out again—or was perhaps dead. I sensed we had only moments left before we became Avolapek's midnight snack.

Lysander raised his arms to touch the sides of the archway, closed his eyes and murmured an incantation. After a moment, he said, "I think I've got it! I think it's done!"

I stepped forward—and bounced off an invisible barrier. "Good work, Lysander!"

We all screamed and fell back a few steps as the demon rounded the corner and came into view. It looked even redder now, as if flushed with post-orgasmic well-being. I wanted to throw up. *This* was the thing that Hieronymus had intended to turn loose on a virginal victim. No fate was too horrible for that twisted little creep.

I murmured to Dixie, "Thank God you slept with Barclay."

"Yeah," she said faintly.

"Thank God we got this barrier up in time," Clarisse said.

"Indeed," said Lysander.

Then Avolapek, looking rather hungry, walked right through the barrier and grabbed me.

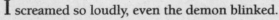

CHAPTER

17

I screamed so loudly, even the demon blinked.

"Hah!" Dixie and Clarisse charged him with their candlesticks. He swatted them aside.

Unnerved by the aggressive invasion of a total stranger into the chamber, Alice confronted the demon, her tail twitching and her fangs bared in a snarl. Avolapek paused to look at her. This gave Lysander a chance to distract him by bringing some rubble from the ceiling crashing down on the demon's head. The beast dropped me. I rolled across the floor, jumped to my feet and scurried out of reach.

"What happened to the barrier?" I shouted.

"Apparently it doesn't work on the demon!" Lysander said.

"But now *we're* locked in here? Oh, nice going!"

"Is this really the time for recriminations?" he shot back.

I never got a chance to retort. Something big and heavy fell straight down on top of me and I hit the ground. I lay there winded and stunned for a moment, seeing spots and unable to breathe. I brushed away the white hair that was covering my face and getting into my mouth...then realized what had hit me.

"Max? Max!" I'd never been so glad to see anyone in my life. "Max!"

"Sorry," he wheezed. "I'd hoped that wouldn't happen. But one never knows."

"How'd you get here?"

"Translocation, of course. But I miscalculated a trifle."

Samson, Dolly and Dixie helped us off the floor. The commotion had frightened Alice, who was back in her corner. The demon was stalking toward us, obviously ready for dinner.

I said, "That's—"

"Indeed," Max said. "Fortunately, I anticipated this and am prepared."

He began chanting in an unfamiliar language. Avolapek kept coming closer to us. Lysander prudently stepped behind Max.

"Max," I said.

"Hush!" said Lysander.

Max kept chanting. The demon was almost within arm's reach of us.

"Dr. Zadok!" Dixie cried.

Max pulled a small glass vial out of his pocket and held it up, still reciting his incantation. Avolapek reached for him.

"Max!"

He dashed the vial on the floor. The glass broke and a pink mist arose from it to twine around the demon's feet. Avolapek paused in the act of reaching for Max's throat. His ghastly jaws parted, and a noticeable quantity of demon drool dripped down to the floor.

"Gross!" said Golly, from the corner where she was huddled. It was the first time I'd noticed her since the demon's arrival, so I supposed she'd been there ever since then.

A strange gurgling noise rose up through the demon's massive body. It looked heavenward, stretched out its arms and went stiff as a board. And then it just stood there. Immobile. But that weird gurgling noise kept coming from somewhere deep inside.

It was moments before I remembered to breathe. Then, without ever taking my gaze off the demon, I asked, "Is he dead?"

"No. And he won't be neutralized for very long, either," said Max. "So we must act."

"Act? Act how?"

"Too late!" cried a familiar voice—one that I loathed with every fiber of my being.

Hieronymus stood framed by the archway. He was bruised, bloody, very disheveled and walking in a hunched-over way that suggested the loss of his so-called purity had been extremely painful.

"Your barrier can't keep *him* out, either?" I said to Lysander.

"I wonder what went wrong?" he mused.

"Too late," Hieronymus repeated. "I will take you all with me! You cannot ethcape me now."

"Where do you *get* that corny dialogue?" I said.

"Let us end this like decent men," Max said quietly. "You know what must happen now. Why harm others? It's over, son."

"It ith not oveh! Not until *I* finish it." Hieronymus's bloodied lips parted in a hideous grin. "What ith youh weak element? Oh, yeah, now I wecall..."

He spread his arms and the enclosed chamber burst into flames. Alice howled and jumped toward me. Her weight shoved me against Avolapek, who fell over, still gurgling loudly without moving at all. Dolly shrieked and quickly moved to smother flames that were crawling up the train of Sarah's gown. Golly Gee was screaming, trapped in her corner by the flames.

Max raised his arms, shouted something in Latin— and water came pouring through every crevice and crack in the ceiling. With another gesture, he took command of the water that was trickling down the far wall, the flow that had served as the hostages' water supply. Chanting and gesturing, he used his power to direct it like a fire hose, dousing the flames. Golly Gee screamed even louder when the urgent spray of water drenched her. Alice ran all over the room, frantically trying to avoid water as well as flames. Sarah was calling to her, trying to calm her down. Dolly, Dixie and Clarisse clung to each other, just trying not to get killed.

When Hieronymus howled and raised his arms as if to counter Max's tactic, Lysander shouted, "No!" He raised his arm, finger pointed, and Hieronymus flew backward, as if punched by a heavyweight prizefighter.

"Wow," I said.

Max trotted forward through the water that covered almost everything and the steam that was rising from the floor to hover throughout the chamber. He stood over Hieronymus's prone, gasping body and said, "It was a good try. Fire is indeed, as you know, my weakest element. Luckily, water often works well against it."

"Don't gloat," Hieronymus said bitterly. "Do it."

"I'll help," Lysander said, crossing the floor to join Max.

"What are they going to do?" Dixie asked.

"I don't know," I said.

The two mages bowed their heads and spoke an incantation together in almost perfect unison. Hieronymus's eyes glazed over and he started breathing harder. As their voices rose, he gritted his teeth and made some strange noises. His body seemed to start moving involuntarily, as if it was becoming wavy and insubstantial. At the last moment, he shouted, "No! *Noooo…*" It was a pathetic sound, a sad and despairing cry. A plea for mercy that he was much, much too late in seeking.

And then he was gone. Just gone.

There was a strange hissing sound near me. I looked down and saw Avolapek the demon disappear, too. Only a faint pink mist remained where he had lain.

"Ah!" Lysander said. "Very nice. I must say, Max, yes, that was very nicely done."

"What did you do?" I asked, looking down at the pink mist as Max ambled over to stand near me.

"To Avolapek?" He, too, gazed down at the dispersing mist. "It was an alchemical neutralizing formula. As soon as I realized we might be dealing with a case of ritual sacrifice, I prepared it. In most instances, it can immobilize the mystical effect of a sacrifice, a summoning, or a raising for a brief period. Its potency is quite limited, but it has the virtue of being effective on a broad array of phenomena."

"It seems to have worked potently on Avolapek," I said.

"No, we had very little time, in fact, and I'm sure Hieronymus knew that. Avolapek was merely stunned, in a sense, and would soon recover. But since we were able to dispatch his summoner before he did recover, he has been returned to the primordial essence whence he came."

"The demon's not dead?" Samson asked in disappointment.

"Alas, no. Under the circumstances, I wasn't able to summon the necessary resources to slay a demon."

"Oh, but you did real well, Dr. Zadok," Dixie said.

"You sure did," said Dolly. "Whoever you are. Why, we'd be demon dinner right now, if it wasn't for you!"

"I'm here to help," Max said, beaming at them.

"Wait," I said. "How did you, er, dispatch the demon's summoner? I mean…where'd Hieronymus go?"

Lysander, perhaps feeling that our gratitude had shone exclusively on Max for long enough, responded, "That was dissolution."

"*That* was dissolution?" My eyes met Max's. "Something 'remarkably similar' to death?"

"My evil young assistant is at one with the cosmos now," Max said.

"And permanently neutralized," Lysander said.

"Well, thank God for that," Golly said. "That guy was a prick!"

Alice, crouching in a corner and watching warily for more disturbing events, growled.

"We need to get out of here," Sarah said.

"Of course!" Max said.

"But how?" Dolly wondered.

"Lysander, if you will assist me?"

Following their instructions, we all stood in a circle and held hands. Since Alice had to be at the center of our circle in order to be included in our escape, this was a rather nerve-racking process. We closed our eyes and concentrated all our will on returning to the world above—specifically, to the Magic Cabaret, where our reappearance was anxiously awaited, while Max and Lysander sang an incantation chock full of the letters *R* and *S*.

The return trip was nearly as nauseating as the one here had been—but at least this time we knew we were going home.

"Yes," Goudini said into his cell phone, "I've got her locked in the ladies' dressing room here, and we've thrown about five pounds of sirloin in with her to tide her over. So we'll be fine until you can get here with a dose of tranquilizers and her cage. What? Yes, okay. Good. I'll be waiting. And—oh, yeah—so will Sarah."

The only thing better than knowing Alice was safely isolated behind a locked door was knowing that Hieronymus was dissolved into the cosmos, forever neutralized, and that the nightmare of the disappearances was finally over.

I raised my plastic beer-filled cup and proposed a toast: "To our rescuer, Dr. Maximillian Zadok!"

"Hear, hear! To Max!"

"To Dr. Zadok!"

"To my hero!"

"Oh, no, no, really." Max beamed. "Just doing my duty."

"I was there, too," Lysander reminded us. "Fighting Evil. As is *my* duty, too."

Our sudden reappearance at the Magic Cabaret had been greeted by a standing ovation from the audience, who thought we were enacting the greatest, if strangest, disappearing-and-reappearing act they'd ever seen; and by cheers, hugs and tears from our friends, who had all arrived at the cabaret by the time we returned there. The translocation had left us sprawled messily all over the stage (such as it was), and Alice's nerves were so frazzled that it had taken Goudini considerable effort to get her under control and into a dressing room.

"One thing I don't understand," I said to Max as we sat chatting at one of the little cabaret tables. "Why was your translocation to the underground chamber so different from Lysander's? And mine?"

"Ah!" Max nodded, took a sip of his beer and said, "Lysander arrived there via the conduit, which was gradually weakening, but still engaged enough for one of us to follow you. We knew it was our only hope of finding you and Dixie. We also knew that it could well become a trap, so we mustn't *both* go that way."

Lysander, sitting in the other chair at our table, said, "After your precipitate pursuit of Dixie, Esther, which I can't say I think was the wisest course of action—"

"You're going back to Altoona in the morning, right?" I said.

His brows lifted. "Yes."

"Just making sure."

Lysander continued. "After you disappeared, I felt it would be best if *I*, rather than Max, followed you."

"That was very brave of you," I said, trying to be nice, "knowing that you might well wind up in Phil's trap."

"Well, I *am* younger and fitter than Max," Lysander said, "and I do have considerable experience of danger."

Deciding that Lysander had talked enough, I said, "But, Max, how did *you* find us?"

"Before he left," Max said, "Lysander and I engaged a spell that would enable me to follow and find him. Anywhere."

"Sort of a mystical tracking device?"

"You might say that," Max said.

"If you wanted to oversimplify it," Lysander said.

Max said to me, "So Lysander followed you to the chamber. And I tracked his trail."

"But you cut it rather close," Lysander said. "What took you so long?"

"I hadn't realized I'd have to transmute about

eighty feet or so straight down after I translocated across the city."

"Ah! Of course."

"And I want you to know," Max said kindly to him, "I don't hold you in any way responsible."

Lysander frowned. "For what?"

"For sending me an assistant who wanted to take over New York with the help of a virgin-raping, mundane-eating demon."

Lysander stiffened. "I am *not* 'in any way responsible' for that!"

"You did authorize the assignment," I reminded him.

"Well, I— I—" Lysander cleared his throat. "The decision was made at headquarters. All I did was sign the standard paperwork."

"And I'll keep that in mind," Max said sweetly, "when I file my formal complaint about the assistant whom I received in response to my request for, er, *help* here."

Lysander scowled and, for once, seemed to have nothing to say. After a moment, he muttered something about wanting to get a refill on his drink, and he fled our table.

"I shouldn't have teased him like that," Max said, looking a little guilty. "He's really quite a good fellow, you know."

"In his way, I suppose," I admitted. "But he could use a little teasing, Max."

He nodded, and we clinked our plastic cups together in agreement.

"Max! Maximillian, come over here and let me pour you another!" Duke cried.

He waved a beer bottle at us. We rose from our table and joined him. Thrilled to have his daughter and his dear Dolly back safe and sound, a tearful Cowboy Duke had decided to buy drinks for the whole house. Several times in a row. People were getting a trifle tipsy.

Clarisse Staunton, looking a little the worse for wear by now, had had a happy reunion with Barclay—who was having an even happier one with Dixie. They made a cute couple, holding hands and beaming with delight whenever their eyes met.

"But that Hieronymus seemed so nice when I talked with him yesterday in the cellar at the bookshop!" Dixie said, shaking her head. "Who knew he'd turn out to be an evil creep trying to summon a demon? I mean, when we talked, he seemed like such a good listener. He really encouraged me to…" Her eyes flew wide open and she gasped.

"To do what, honey?" Duke asked, his arm firmly around Dolly.

"To do the act with Barclay tonight!"

Barclay said, "Oh, so *that* was how he knew about tonight's performance."

"And that was when he formulated his plan," I said. "Delilah was right, Hieronymus must have known his time was running out. He was getting desperate. And he thought he had a second shot at getting his victim via Barclay—through tonight's performance! He obviously thought Dixie was a vir... Um. Go on, Dixie, you tell the story."

She nodded. "I told Hieronymus about our plans when we were talking. And I said we naturally wouldn't do the disappearing act. He agreed that was wise, and he said lots of nice things about how good it was of me to help a friend and how he wished we could solve the case before the show so that Barclay and I could do the *whole* act. And I said, gosh, I sure wished for that, too, because Barclay felt so bad about Clarisse, and Daddy missed Dolly so much."

"So when Hieronymus called you today," I said, "and told you the case was solved and it was safe to do the disappearing act..."

"It never occurred to me I couldn't trust him! He was Dr. Zadok's assistant, after all! And he'd been so nice to me!"

"And then he hexed our cell phones," Duke said, "to make sure no one else could get in touch with us."

"Even with Max giving us the green light—as we thought—we were nervous the first time we rehearsed the disappearing act," Barclay said. "But it went smooth as silk, so we had no worries after that."

"The conduit was never engaged in rehearsal," I said. "Only in performance. Only when energy, concentration and focus were at their peak."

A little while later, I found Max blushing under Delilah's grateful hugs and kisses as she thanked him profusely (again) for returning her dear Samson to her. Samson apparently hadn't been as chilly as I'd supposed, since he was still wearing nothing but his gold lamé G-string. Since the "girls" had left the Pony Expressive in the middle of the performance to come here and help if needed, they were all dressed for work. Whoopsy was as scantily clad as Samson, Khyber looked like a harem boy, and Satsy was in glorious purple drag.

Joe Herlihy had been so relieved to see Golly Gee alive, he'd embraced her. After that, though, it took only a few minutes for them to remember how much they disliked each other, and they were soon sitting at separate tables.

I sat down with Joe now and said, "Hey, we can get the show up and running again!"

"Once the crystal cage is ready."

"I'll talk to Magnus," I said, "and he'll have it ready soon."

"*You* believed the cage might be dangerous, too, didn't you?"

"The thought crossed my mind," I said.

He hesitated. "Esther, did you and your friend Max... Um, wait no. Never mind. I don't want to know."

I watched Golly flirting with Goudini and sighed. "I guess I'm back in the chorus."

"It's a shame." When I looked at him in surprise, Joe said, "Don't get me wrong. I'm very, very glad I didn't inadvertently kill Golly, which is what I was terrified might have happened. But you're a lot better as Virtue, Esther. I wish you had the role." He sighed and shook his head. "But Matilda wanted a young pop star for the leading lady."

"Life upon the wicked stage," I said. "Oh, well. My turn will come."

"Yes, it will."

To my surprise, I found I kind of liked Joe. When the pressure was off, he was just a nice, ordinary fellow, instead of a basket-case magician.

Suddenly Whoopsy rose to his feet, looking anxious. "Fuzz!"

My heart skipped a beat as my eyes were drawn to the entrance of the cabaret. Lopez flashed his shield at the Goth girl trying to block his entrance. He was in his working clothes: a gray suit, white shirt and dark blue tie. As he put his badge away, his suitcoat flapped open for a moment and I saw his holster and gun.

He scanned the room. He frowned when he saw Max, and his brows lifted as he studied the interestingly clothed (and unclothed) performers in our festive group. Then he saw me. He went still as our gazes locked.

He looked tired, puzzled, a little worried...and

God, he looked good to me. If Avolapek had escaped, he might have eaten Lopez, I suddenly realized. I was so glad that hadn't happened.

Lopez's gaze traveled over me as he approached the table where I sat with Joe. I realized for the first time what I must look like after fighting with a demented adept, being manhandled by a demon, nearly getting immolated, being drenched with water of highly questionable origin and translocating twice in one night. We stared at each other.

Then he said, with obvious concern, "Are you okay?"

"I am now." I smiled at him. "How'd you find this place?"

"It was a little harder than I expected—how do their customers find them, I wonder?" He shrugged. "But I'm a cop, I'm good at finding things."

"I'm glad you came."

As Khyber walked behind Lopez, probably in search of more beverages, he gave me a thumbs-up sign and mouthed, *He's hot.*

"When I got here, there was a nice van, abandoned in the middle of the street, being towed away," Lopez said to me. "I don't suppose you'd know anything about that?"

"Oops." I'd have to tell Barclay. Meanwhile, I should change the subject. "Are you off duty yet?"

He looked around with a skeptical expression. "I'm not sure." He froze. "Is that Golly Gee?"

"Huh? Oh, yes. And over there—that's Clarisse Staunton."

He gave me a sharp glance. "They're back?"

"Yes."

"Where were they?"

"You can ask them," I said. "But you won't understand the answers."

"Where's Hieronymus?"

"Hieron…" I frowned. "Um…"

"When I got back to the house a little while ago, I found two messages from you. Both kind of garbled. Apparently you wanted me to come here and…" Lopez spread his hands and shrugged again. "And stop a really bad disappearing act that was about to be performed by someone named Hieronymus? Whose stage name is Phil Hohenheim?"

I looked down at my drink. "Oh, he never showed up."

"Where is he?"

I shrugged. "Who knows?"

He sighed. "I was told you sounded frantic when you left those messages. There was also something about a kidnapping, and—"

"Oh, ignore all that. I'd had *way* too much coffee," I said.

"You're not going to tell me what's going on?"

"Everything's back to normal now," I assured him.

"I am *so* afraid to ask you what that means." He

glanced around the room. "That woman over there. Is that Dorothy Mertz?"

"Who?"

"Uh, Dolly the Dancing Cowgirl."

"Yes." So he had continued looking into the case today. A man of his word, I thought, liking the way he looked even when he was tired and a little exasperated with me. I added, "And Sexy Samson has come home, too." I touched Lopez's sleeve. "Everything really is back to normal. You can drop the case."

He eyed Joe. "What about you?"

Joe appeared nervous again. Well, cops had that effect on some people. From several tables away, Whoopsy was still watching Lopez the way a monkey would watch a snake. "Me?" Joe bleated.

"Mrs. Herlihy accused Miss Diamond of vandalizing the crystal cage," Lopez reminded him. "She also complained about Dr. Zadok harassing you."

"Oh, that? Those were just a couple of silly misunderstandings, Detective. It's all water under the bridge now."

"You're not going to press charges?"

"No," Joe said firmly. "We're not. Definitely not."

Lopez met my eyes again. I said, "We're hoping to get the show up and running again in a few days. You wanted to come see it?"

Joe said, "Hey, I'll get you a couple of complimentary tickets, Detective! No problem!"

Still holding my gaze, Lopez said, "Thanks, Mr. Herlihy. But I'll only need one ticket. I'm not bringing a date."

"Detective Lopez!" Max joined us, smiling broadly. "What a pleasant surprise!"

"You seem to be celebrating something," Lopez commented, as I rose from my seat and used a napkin to wipe some of Delilah's lipstick off Max's cheek.

"Yes! We have tracked Evil to its lair," Max burbled, "confronted it there and triumphed! Would you like a cocktail?"

"No, thank you."

"A sober young man," Max said to me, beaming with approval. "And polite."

Lopez asked, "Why do half of you look as if you've just come through a siege?"

"Ah! *There* you are!" Goudini shouted, seeing his tiger's trainer at the door. "Come on! I'll show you where we've locked up Alice!"

Lopez stiffened. "Now you've locked someone up? Esther—"

"Oh, it's just the tiger," said Max.

"You've got a *tiger* with you?"

"The poor thing was so frantic," Max said. "First the hunger, then the demon, then the fire, then the water, then the translocation… Well! You can imagine what an ordeal it all was for her."

"Strangely," Lopez said, "I almost can." He looked at me, waiting for an explanation.

"*I* want a cocktail," I said.

"Esther was the heroine of the evening," Max continued, and I realized from the reckless glitter in his eyes that he'd been imbibing rather freely. "I am told she even broke through the invisible barrier to beat the stuffing out of Hieronymus, with scarcely a thought for her own safety."

"Hieronymus?" Lopez repeated. "Indeed?"

"I suddenly need some air," I said. "Detective, would you escort me outside?"

"Not just now." He said to Max, "Tell me more about Esther's brave confrontation."

Obviously intent on doing a little matchmaking, Max said enthusiastically, "Well, Lysander, who saw some of the episode from his position on the sacrificial altar—"

"*Where* was this Lysander?" Lopez asked, blinking.

"He says that Esther walloped Hieronymus with a cast-iron candelabra!"

"It was just a candlestick." When Lopez gave me a dark glance, I wished I'd kept my mouth shut.

"She saved lives!" Max said.

"So this man—Lysander—was a witness?"

"If you pull out your notebook," I said to Lopez, "you can forget about a free ticket to the show."

"Oh, you're going to see *Sorcerer!*" Max said. "Me, too! Perhaps we can go together! What night would be good for you?"

"Uh…" Lopez looked to me for help.

"Will you take me outside *now?*" I said to him.

"Perhaps we could have dinner together before the show," Max said to Lopez. "Oh, unless you're Lithuanian? I have nothing against Lithuanians, mind you, it's just that trying to share a meal with one can be a little complicated for me."

"Okay," Lopez said to me. "Outside."

"Or, no, here's an even better idea!" Max said. "We'll take Esther for a late supper after the show! Won't that be nice?"

Lopez's hand in the small of my back urged me to speed up as we crossed the floor and headed for the exit. I kept stumbling.

"Why are you only wearing one shoe?" he asked.

"I lost the other. It upsets me to talk about it."

We passed through the curtain covering the doorway and let it drop behind us. Then he let out his breath.

"Okay, remember how I said I'd rather you stayed away from Max?" he said.

"Yes…"

"Right now, I'll settle for you just keeping him away from *me*. Deal?"

"Deal." I stepped a little closer and toyed with his tie. "So…are you off duty yet?"

"Officially. But…" He shook his head. "I caught a homicide tonight."

"You make it sound like catching a cold."

"So I still have to go back to the house and do all the paperwork I left lying around—"

"Heigh-ho, the glamorous life."

"—when I found messages from you on my desk. One of which asked me to come here right away."

"Oh." I leaned a little closer to him. "You dropped everything for me?"

His coal-black lashes veiled his eyes. "I did."

"That's nice," I said. "Even though I am a tax-paying citizen entitled to the dedicated protection of the police force."

"What happened tonight?" he murmured, leaning a little closer to me, too.

"It doesn't matter now. It's over."

His lips looked full and firm, and I really wanted to know what he tasted like.

He whispered, "You're not going to tell me, are you?"

I whispered back, "Are you *ever* going to kiss me?"

He smiled a little and I felt his breath on my cheek just before our lips met. His mouth was warm, and he tasted sweet and unfamiliar, lush, tempting—and a little bit like coffee. His lips were pillowy, even richer than I'd expected, and, oh my, he knew how to use them.

"Mmm," I said. "*Mmm.*"

I sank bonelessly against him and slid my arms

around his neck. Deepening his kiss, he backed me up against the wall and tightened his hold on me, pressing his body all along mine. After a long, dark, spinning moment, he pulled away just enough that we could both breathe. My heart was thundering, and I felt light-headed and weak—in that *good* way. I clung to him as he nuzzled my hair.

Then he murmured, "Uh, Esther?"

"Hmm?"

"Why do you smell like sulfur?"

"Just kiss me again," I whispered.

He did.

And for a little while, the whole world disappeared.

* * * * *